PRUDENCE

A Tempestuous Night of Pervasive Desires

LES ZIG

First published in 2023 by ECG Press
This edition published in 2024 by ECG Press
www.ecgpress.com

ISBN
Paperback: 978-1-7636892-0-6
Ebook: 978-0-6454853-5-6

Please send all permission queries to info@ecgpress.com

A Cataloging-in-Publication entry for this book is available from the National Library of Australia.

*To those thoughts, fears, and desires,
that fester in the darkest recesses of our mind.*

Preamble

Everywhere I look, there are stories.

I see them in the magic of this beautiful city, in the cold of this bitter night, and, most tellingly, in the faces of the people arrayed at the entrance.

For the most part, they are eager twenty-somethings and thirty-somethings dressed in their finest, a mixture of wide-eyed tourists and knowing locals, every one of them nurturing the same desperate hope that tonight, they will be deemed worthy.

Tonight, they will be allowed entry.

But the truth is some *will* be turned away for any number of reasons. They won't look right. Or they won't be dressed right. Or they won't *feel* right. Sometimes, it might seem security are deciding on a whim. It's unfair and discriminatory but such is the way of the world, no matter how much people try to change it.

Those granted entrance will mill in the lobby as they pay their fee, have their palm stamped, and ponder where to go first. If they have been here before, often they are cocksure and haughty, as if they are already privy to secrets newcomers are not. Newcomers gape in a combination of excitement and wariness. They see the red brick still evident behind the stucco, the buttressed ceilings and ornate cornices, and marvel at the stories of an ancient cathedral transformed into a prestigious club. Some delight in the possibility, as if there is further gratification in misbehavior when there's some underlying defilement.

Now that they're inside, I can study them better, although I already know what I'll see in each of their faces, as well as their hearts. Rarely am I surprised. They come for a night out. They come for fun. They come to let go. That might not seem any different to any other club, but there's a volatility to indulgence here, a capriciousness that can be incendiary.

Out in the world, many of these people would lead virtuous lives and exalt themselves for doing so, never understanding the arrogance of their own pride, and the missteps sometimes taken to maintain it. Others flitter around the boundaries of temptation, trespassing occasionally, wittingly or not, and gradually become inured to possibilities they only ever previously nurtured in their most secret fantasies. And some commit themselves wholly to excess, exploring beyond the reaches of their desires as they court oblivion.

The truth, though?

Everybody's malleable, whatever their engagement.

And every engagement invites danger.

Of course, that's not something they are thinking about as they bustle into the juncture, an antechamber with a high, basilica ceiling that projects a myriad of colors upon their eager faces. Hung above the entrance is a big, round bronze plaque depicting a beautiful woman in a scanty toga. She has two faces: the face to the right looks at a mirror held high in one hand, as if she is regarding what she sees; and the face to the left looks at a serpent held in her other hand.

In Roman mythology, there are four cardinal virtues: prudence, justice, fortitude, and temperance. This plaque depicts Prudentia, the emblem of "prudence" – the ability to govern oneself with reason, although reason is something that can progressively grow in short supply here.

Curled under her, embossed on the plaque, are these words:

Veritas Vos Liberabit

The phrase is Latin, and most will leave it at that. They won't seek its meaning, or question if the words have a purpose, instead deeming they're little more than an affectation.

If only they knew.

In each wall, archways funnel into every offering we have. There are many floors, many rooms, and a variety of entertainments and attractions, although for the purpose of tonight, I will focus only on a few.

Some relax in the Cardinal, Verdant, or Brimstone Lounges, which are intimate piano bars; others retreat to the Restaurant, with its dulcet tones, candelabras, and five-star menu, although most order something trivial and woefully unbecoming, like nachos, to share amongst a group.

In each room, the respective centerpiece is an octagonal pillar with mirrored walls rising from the floor to the ceiling and ten feet in radius. People stare at them as if trying to divine the purpose of their existence, or marvel at their own reflection, as if they're seeing themselves for the very first time.

Others waft into the gaming rooms to explore the tales they've heard about the Icons, to engage them in pool and other contests, or to play the various arcade machines – some state of the art, and others that are classics. A few pursue the private rooms to confirm their existence, or possibly even hunt for the fabled basement, where it's rumored unspeakably decadent things occur.

Most, though, will head into the Gallery, where the dance floor is like a meteorite hit it, leaving a crystallized crater. Another octagon sits in the middle, this one larger. People circle it, as if its sheer size commands their orbit. Lights flash, music roars, and the air shimmers with passion, creating a synergy that infuses every patron.

At opposing ends of the dance floor are the North and South Bars, long and arched, made of glass, with white light shining up from their bases. They are the lighthouses in the Gallery, a way to orient oneself when the night may have impaired judgment and choices go awry.

Suspended adjacent to the bars, high, high, *high* above, is Constance's office. Also octagonal, it is tiled in tiny mirrors. The lights that refract off it make it sparkle like some ethereal heart beating in mid-air. The stairwell that zigzags from its doorway is lost in shadow.

Nobody strays onto the stairwell.

Nobody.

It's not just out of respect for Constance, nor because of the behemoth security clad in black slacks and polos who patrol, but because trespassers on that stairwell are immediately ejected.

It might seem petty in a place where *anything* could happen.

But even in chaos there are rules.

I

Every dream is inherent with opportunity, a choice to turn left or to turn right. More than that, every choice is inherent with its own requirements. Some are accepted unthinkingly. Others are considered. And a few leave the chooser in a quandary.

That's the thing with dreams: you never know where they're going to take you.

Or what they'll demand.

At a table on the second-floor patio overlooking the dance floor sit three twenty-something women sipping cocktails. Each is one half of a couple. They met one month ago at a restaurant in Barcelona, and have been inseparable since, backpacking across Europe together, until the path led them here – a whimsy they felt was warranted.

Holly is an Australian, an archetypal blonde, stunning and seemingly unattainable, although there is a girlishness about her – an impishness that underlies the measured way she portrays herself. As a teen, she pursued acting, and elocution lessons mitigated much of her accent, taming her husky voice into something very deliberate. Her legs are crossed, extending from her leather miniskirt, and her cleavage shimmers in her skimpy blue blouse.

As she sips from her Tequila Sunrise, she surveys the figures below grinding against one another on the dance floor. The memory that flashes through her mind is so incendiary and recent that she can feel the heat in her skin and smell the sweat.

"Can I tell you something?" she says, although she is not asking for permission – at least not from anybody but herself.

She has wrestled with whether she would disclose this story – especially to such new friends. But they are already close and enjoy a strong bond that she believes will sustain their friendship even when they each go home.

Holly sets her drink down on their small table. "I was in a bar yesterday afternoon waiting for Marcus," she says. "I was wearing my red dress."

"The little one?"

This is from Amber, the demurest of the trio. There is a shyness about her that almost suggests innocence, and the Louisiana twang of her accent communicates a courtesy that is provincial. Outside of the trip to Europe, the most daring thing she has done – and she had to be convinced – was to highlight her hair copper. She is uncomfortable in her frilly green dress and would much rather be in jeans. Her Vodka & Orange is untouched. She just wants to be done with the night.

"Marcus texted me to tell me he'd be late," Holly says, "so I ordered myself another drink. I'd already had a couple, and I was starting to feel mellow."

The third member of the trio, Flavia, arches a single brow. She is an Argentinian who is the embodiment of smoldering sensuality if it could be packed into a vacuous nature. She is all the clichés – tanned and dark haired with captivating gray eyes, a sultry beauty who moves through the world obliviously, unaware of the effect she has on others. She wears a small body-hugging black dress, and a little wrist-purse – where she keeps her phone – strapped to her left wrist.

"Marcus is never late," she says. "Is he?"

Her smile suggests something sly – that is how her mind works, never accepting anything as it's presented.

"He was this time," Holly says. "The bartender brought me my drink – a Tequila Sunrise. I'd just taken a sip from it when a handsome, well-dressed man came up to where I was sitting at the bar and laid five hundred Euro down by my glass."

Flavia's eyes widen. Amber covers her mouth

"He thought you were a hooker?" Flavia asks.

Holly nods. "He and his friend wanted me for their lunch hour."

"*Friend?*" Amber says.

"Sitting in the corner was another business executive, this one more handsome than the one who was propositioning me."

Holly takes another sip, not for fortitude, but needing something to do while she awaits the inevitable questions. Although she's known these two for only a month, she thinks she can predict how each will react, so it surprises her that both – especially Flavia – are quiet. Flavia is struggling to process such temerity.

"So, what did you do?" Amber asks, almost meekly.

"The first man laid down another five hundred Euro while his friend came over and put his hand on my hip."

"I hope you set them straight," Amber says.

Holly finishes her drink.

"I hope you set them straight," Amber says again, but now emphasizing each word.

Holly tosses her head back to cast her hair from her eyes.

"*Holly?*" Amber says.

"I quivered."

"You quivered?" Flavia asks.

"The first man laid down another one thousand Euro," Holly says. "The other man ran a hand up my back, leaned in close to me, and whispered in my ear how much he wanted to fuck me."

"This seriously didn't happen," Amber says, but more so like she's trying to convince herself. *"Did it?"*

"Their scent was in my nostrils. Their lust. Their *hunger*. Their desperation. I could smell how much they wanted me."

"Because they thought you were a hooker, Holly!" Amber says.

"I envisioned how they wanted to possess and dominate me, how only I could satisfy their cravings. They felt they had ownership over me but, in that moment, they were slaves to *me*."

"They were paying!"

"Yet I held all the power."

"I don't think they were slaves to you."

"What happened?" Flavia asks.

Her tone is even, but her breath short. The prospect tantalizes her. Flavia wants to be risqué, but her love life has been remarkably mundane. She has confided that her partner, Dante, has proposed watching her make love to another man, although that might just be Dante testing her commitment to monogamy – and him. At any rate, Holly thinks that Flavia never would accept Dante's suggestion. Flavia is talk. Well, mostly. Dante definitely is.

"I picked up the money, folded it, put it in my purse, and followed them to a nearby hotel."

Holly waits for an indignant exclamation. Or even acceptance. Amber's big brown eyes are wide and round with disbelief, her mocha complexion paling under the fluorescent lighting until she is almost faint. Flavia has that incredulity, but also the smallest smile. Something so daring and illicit and forbidden excites her. This is the world she always dances around.

"The air conditioning was out," Holly says. "The room was a furnace. And it was cheap – the walls shook, the closet rattled, and we could hear the people in the next room. I'm sure they heard us. That just made it even more amazing."

"It sounds nasty rather than amazing," Flavia says, although not with disapproval.

Amber nods.

"Where do you go in sex when there are no boundaries?" Holly says. "I don't mean *physically*. Or *just* physically. But emotionally. Spiritually. When nothing exists but *wanting* to fuck."

"Are you mad?" Amber says. "You don't know what might've happened! And I'm not talking about what they *wanted* to happen. They might've been psychos or … I don't know."

Holly does not want to concede this possibility – once they'd gotten in the room, she had felt a sudden and overwhelming uncertainty. As they had caressed her, as they had groped her and torn off her clothes, she had worried they could overpower her and abuse her. Her lust had contended with her wariness, and by the end of it all she knew was she would never, could *never*, do something like this again. But she cannot confess this, cannot validate Amber's reservations.

"I knew they wanted only one thing," Holly says.

"I still can't believe you did this," Flavia says, but Holly can hear the envy in her tone.

"I've never behaved as I did with them," Holly says. "Not with Marcus, not with anybody. It was like losing myself. Maybe the money made it wanton. Or dangerous. But to be devoured, where it's inescapable – anywhere you turn, it's passion. Arousal. Lust. Submission … "

She picks up her glass, only realizing now it's empty.

"How did this end?" Amber says.

"They got dressed and left. I showered, got dressed, and met Marcus for lunch. I apologized for being late. He was fine with it, though. He'd gotten caught up talking to Quinn about something."

Quinn is Amber's fiancé. He can be every bit as naïve as Amber, if not more so. He is nervousness packed into an extraordinary frame, a man who should stride through the world with confidence, but instead believes that anything that can go wrong *will* go wrong.

"Later," Holly says, "I saw a wedding dress. I went in, bought it with the money I'd made, and arranged for it to be shipped home."

Amber shakes her head, as if she's taken Holly's behavior as a personal affront. She and Quinn have been the least adventurous of their group, often retiring early, and not wanting to try new things. When the two marry, they will probably spend most of their nights at home in front of the television, only realizing in middle age they've never done anything with their lives.

"How could you, Holly?" Amber says.

"I've never done anything like that before and I'll never do it again." Holly pauses contemplatively. "Just the other day, I started wondering is this who I'm meant to be? Is this *all* I am? It was like this terrifying crippling doubt. So I don't know what you'd call this: maybe it was casting inhibition to the wind before settling down to a life of monogamy with Marcus – one last fling. Men do it all the time. The other thing is that, sometimes, just between us, he's not the most adventurous or satisfying sexually."

"Thanks for that, too," Flavia says. "Now I can never look at him the same again, either."

Holly laughs. "The longer our relationship's gone, the less attentive he's become to, well, *lasting*."

"So maybe that's your motivation: Marcus being lousy in bed?"

"Marcus isn't lousy all the time. He's just not always considerate of my needs. But that's something we can work on. The craziness is out of my system. And that's what it was: a temporary insanity."

"A temporary insanity?" Amber says. "You're rationalizing!"

"Amber, you're not handling this well."

"What if he finds out?" Amber asks.

"How? Neither of you are going to tell him, are you?"

Flavia shakes her head, but Amber begins fidgeting – not that she would ever surrender a confidence, but one day very soon, Amber and Quinn will marry, and Holly knows Amber might just be the sort of wife who shares *everything*, which is a concern given Quinn's and Marcus's friendship. At least Flavia can be trusted with Dante.

"You *won't* say anything, will you, Amber?"

"Of course she won't," Flavia says. "Neither of us will. It's just so … unbelievable."

"But … poor Marcus," Amber says.

"It was a one-off thing," Holly says, the first bit of defensiveness entering her tone.

"What if you were to see them again? I mean, what if you were to bump into them?"

"I'll think about that *if* it happens, not before. You worry too much, Amber."

"And you worry too little. I'm just concerned. For *you*."

Holly puts a hand on Amber's wrist and gives her an assuring squeeze. "I'm fine."

Amber's eyes go pointedly to the engagement ring on Holly's finger – eighteen-karat gold, a melee of brilliant, small diamonds surrounding a diamond shaped like a teardrop. Or perhaps ostensibly it is meant to be a heart.

"I just don't want you to lose what you have with Marcus," Amber says.

"We're fine. I know it wouldn't seem it given this but, really, we are. Who knows? You and Quinn will get married one day – one day soon. He's already got a new car, a down-payment on his own house; you've picked out all his furniture. Surely a ring can't be far."

"You're just saying that."

"You know it's true."

Amber smiles bashfully. She is traditional. This is something she wants more than anything.

"Maybe on your hens—"

"*Never.*" Amber snatches her hand away from Holly and glowers at her.

"I was teasing."

Amber's eyes brim. She picks up her Vodka & Orange and gulps half of it.

"I'm sorry, Amber."

"It's okay."

Amber stares into her drink. Holly shrugs at Flavia, as if to suggest she didn't mean to overstep. Flavia rolls her eyes. However pedestrian her sex life is, she is not judgmental, and – like Holly – knows Amber tends to overreact.

Flavia's biggest concern now is how uncomfortable it's become and thinks of ways to move the conversation forward. She looks around with the intention of finding *anything* to use as fodder, then peers over the balcony.

"I wonder where the guys are … Oh my God!"

She shoots to her feet and leans dangerously over the balustrade. A horde of people are lined up at the South Bar, while others have taken up occupation on the barstools. The bartenders – dressed in black leather pants and vests with shiny buckles – move with crisp efficiency to serve them. It's impossible to pick who's hooked Flavia's attention.

"What?" Holly says.

"That's Edan LeBeau at the bar."

"Edan Le who?" Amber asks.

"You don't know Edan LeBeau?"

Flavia tells them that Edan LeBeau is a media powerbroker, and an executive with Hermes-LeBeau Enterprises. He has created and produced a string of news specials, exposés, and series for various networks and streamers. For anybody wanting to get into media journalism, he is the man to meet.

Holly and Amber flank Flavia and follow her line of vision until they see him: in another life, he might've been lost in a crowd of men who might be considered good looking but unspectacular. He wears the struggles of a hard life – one that has weathered his face, and that he carries in his thickset frame, as if he's expecting to fend off an attack. Wealth has tempered that desperation, but only with moderate success. Circumstance has not just cultivated him to be a fighter, but a predator.

"If I could meet him," Flavia says, "who knows where it could lead? Television, maybe."

"Flavia," Amber says, "you're a dreamer."

Flavia scowls. "Anything *but.*"

"Is this really the time and place?" Holly asks.

"It's the perfect time and place," Flavia says. "You can't get through his handlers or his receptionists." She smiles. "Opportunity, right? We never know when it might be there." She pushes off from the balustrade. "I'll be back."

"Wait!"

Flavia slips into the crowd.

"Flavia!" Amber calls after her. "We can't let her go on her own!"

Holly is bemused more than anything – Amber is the sort on a night out who would fraternize only with people she knows. She would not talk with strangers, and certainly wouldn't try to turn a random encounter into an opportunity. There is only danger.

But Holly feels something she doesn't understand, something similar to what she initially felt in that hotel room – a sliver of unease that threatens to grow into something more. She cannot explain it but decides that perhaps some wariness is merited now. Flavia is so starry-eyed it could affect her judgment.

"Come on," Holly says. "Let's make sure she's okay."

○　○　○　○

There are many lounges, each with their own motif.

The Verdant Lounge is furnished in shades of green, ranging from the rippled juniper curtains to the mint tablecloths, from the pine chairs to the chartreuse booths, from the basil stools to the emerald marble bar. Even the glasses are tinted green. There is an artistry to the complementation that seduces the eye and immediately impresses an idyllic, if not meditative nature.

The candelabras hanging from the ceiling and ensconced in the pear-colored walls bathe the Verdant Lounge in a soft pixilated glow that poets and songwriters who have visited try to reverently capture in words, although they can never truly explain its appeal.

But Quinn discerns none of this as he strides in, his right knee aching the way it does whenever he overextends himself. He does not know – nor appreciate – that the décor is antique Hepplewhite that's intended to communicate a sense of stateliness.

Couples are scattered around; some stare lovingly at one another, some hold hands, while some fix their attention on the pianist in the furthest corner, his fingers a blur across the keyboard of his shamrock-green grand piano as he plays a melancholy sonata. Quinn knows little about classical, but thinks it might be Beethoven, although he is only guessing.

At the rear of the Lounge is the mirrored octagon. Quinn sees himself tall and lean, his dreadlocks – an attempt to shake up the torpor of his life and be rebellious – ill-fitting. The reflection makes him feel as if he himself is trapped within one of the octagon's faces. He leans across to the right, his reflection stretching disjointedly across to the next face. He pulls back sharply, fearing he is about to be torn in two.

Quinn – as so many do – marvels at the octagon's existence. It creates the illusion that the Lounge is bigger than it is, extending into an inescapable prism, although the reflections are fractured given the angles of the octagon's walls.

Now, behind his own reflection, he spots the man he came here to see, turns, and approaches warily.

Mr. Hermes is seated in a booth in the deepest, shadowy corner of the Lounge. He is so tall and bent and thin that many marvel that he is even alive – a bundle of broomstick limbs and knobby joints, his jaundiced skin taut over the curves of his skull. His wispy hair doesn't seem to have thinned from age, but as a result of some illness. His charcoal suit is too big and cut sharp at the shoulders.

"Please," Mr. Hermes holds his hand out, "sit."

The booth is a perfect three-quarter circle. A candelabra extends from the wall above it. The bulbs pulse and flicker, the way bulbs do before they blow. The wiring must be bad. Quinn has seen it often enough at work. He is sure it's a fire hazard. But that is not his concern right now.

He eases himself into the booth – his right knee is reluctant to fold, and his thighs brush the underside of the table.

Now, in the light from the candelabra, Quinn sees that Mr. Hermes's face is remarkably smooth, although crow's feet extend from mismatched eyes – one gray, and the other blue. His brows are thin and inscribed on his face.

"I …" Quinn begins, but he can't hold Mr. Hermes's gaze, can't form the words to take this where it needs to go.

"You don't know whether you should be here," Mr. Hermes says. His voice is soft – so soft that Quinn must lean across the table to hear him – but coarse, like it's been exhausted from overuse. His teeth are perfectly even and white, although the rims of the gums are raw. "You're not the first to think that. But like those before you, you're eager for an opportunity. Everybody desires opportunity, Quinn. The question is how far you're prepared to go."

"I—"

"No false bravado, Quinn. Not yet at any rate. A moment, though. Do you have a phone?"

"A phone—"

"Yes. Most people carry them nowadays. Do you have one?"

"Yes …" Absently, Quinn takes his phone out of his pocket. He doesn't know why he does it.

"Turn it off."

"What—?"

"If you wish to have an audience with me, then you have an audience with me. Exclusively. You will not be disturbed. Another will not take your focus from what I have to say. These are the rules, Quinn. Now decide."

Quinn unlocks the phone and switches it off. Then he puts it back in his pocket as a waitress arrives. The first thing Quinn sees are her legs, lithe and taut. The tightness of her leather shorts shapes her crotch. Quinn continues looking up. She is small breasted, with long, coppery hair and full lips.

"Can I get you something?" she asks.

"My usual, Prelude," Mr. Hermes says, "and a Corona for the young man."

"Of course."

The waitress leaves. Quinn tries to be inconspicuous about looking at her as she goes. The swell of her buttocks peek out above the waistline of her shorts.

"So, I guess that's meant to impress me?" Quinn asks, returning his attention to Mr. Hermes. "That you know I drink Coronas?"

"I'm not here to impress you, Quinn. Why would I bother? I don't care who you are. I don't care what you do. I don't care what you think. If there should be any respect in this relationship, it should be your respect for me. You know who I am, of course."

"You own this club. You own Prudence."

Mr. Hermes chuckles. "The relationship is a little more complicated than that – I'm part of a Camarilla, a consortium if you will, who co-own and oversee various heritages around the world. But Prudence is something more, no? You'll learn that." He lifts a bony finger to his thin lips. "Before we continue, you need to understand – as you should've been told already – that by sitting opposite me, you are entering an unspoken contract. You may decline whatever opportunity I present you, but by sitting here and listening to me, you are then obligated to introduce somebody else."

"Like a chain letter."

"Exactly like a chain letter."

"And if I don't? Or if I said I would, but didn't?"

Mr. Hermes's thin lips draw into a wry smile. "Now why would you do that, Quinn?" He leans across the table. "There are many forms of power in this world, Quinn. I may appear old and frail; indeed, the body is weak. Flesh is weak. *Temporary.* But some things, such as obligation, are eternal."

"Are you trying to scare me?"

"Quinn, if you are not at least unnerved yet, then you are either a very stupid young man or a very arrogant one. Which will it be?"

Quinn knows this *is* wrong. But the possible pay-off could set him up for life – could set him and Amber up. And he feels he is owed. A basketball star in college, a knee injury ruined his prospects. Now he is an electrician, but already discontented. It is a trade he fell into – necessity demanded he do something to support himself. This meeting with Mr. Hermes could solve all his problems. Then he could buy that ring he put a small deposit on. He could do it tomorrow. Propose to Amber tomorrow night. A fancy dinner – maybe go to that charming little place down the road, the Café Acheron. Just the two of them. Kneel before Amber. Be traditional. They could put a date on their wedding. Plan the names of their children. Live the future he has always dreamed about.

That promise overrides all the stories about Mr. Hermes: at the very least, he is a media mogul who owns a film company, a popular streaming platform, a television network, and various print and digital vehicles – a self-made, semi-retired billionaire who lets his nephew run his empire while he amuses himself. Edging into a darker realm are stories of his connections to organized crime; that various mobs help him enjoy success in exchange for favors, ranging from investments in dummy corporations to the laundering of money, and the use of his transport network for drug smuggling, and sex slavery. And then there are the outlandish stories – that he is otherworldly, some satanic manifestation who exploits vulnerabilities, dines on perversion, and feasts on souls.

But for Quinn all of it is unimportant.

All he knows is that Mr. Hermes has money.

"I'm here, aren't I?" Quinn asks, almost brazenly. "I'm listen—"

"Behold our waitress."

The waitress, Prelude, leans idly against the bar, her shorts tight, her legs long, smooth, and toned. Other men in the restaurant try to be as every bit as inconspicuous as Quinn was earlier in studying her, just as the women are in their regard for the waiters.

"Beautiful, isn't she?" Mr. Hermes asks.

Quinn folds his hands on the table in front of him. "Yeah."

"Could you see yourself with somebody like that, Quinn?"

"I have a partner."

"Serious?"

"Yeah."

"And your feelings for her are true?"

"What sort of question is that?"

"It doesn't stop you thinking, does it?"

Quinn says nothing.

"It's fine to think, Quinn. We all do. And it's part of what I want to preface with you. Are you ready to communicate, Quinn? You still have a chance to leave."

Quinn considers it. Then, finally: "Go on."

"You must understand that the everyday world is constructed of layers. It's like having your girlfriend at your residence for the first time; you might perform an impromptu clean-up so as not to make a bad impression. It comes down to what we can be, what we are, and what *is*. Often, the latter is lost, or infrequently revealed. Look at our waitress, Quinn."

Prelude chats to the bartender as he places their drinks onto a tray – a Corona with a slice of lime in it and a small glass with a clear liquid that holds a lemon and three blocks of ice.

"Gorgeous," Mr. Hermes goes on. "And we objectify her. How many men – and women, for that matter – see her tonight and their first thought is imagining how they would fuck her?"

Prelude lifts the tray with their drinks and comes toward them.

"But who is she behind this image? What are her hopes? Her dreams? Perhaps she's studying to become a lawyer or a doctor.

Or possibly she has a drug habit. Or perhaps both. Is this really her? We accept it is. We don't question. But if you stop to think, it's unlikely it is. So, who is she really?"

Prelude arrives at their table and puts their drinks in front of them.

"Thank you, darling," Mr. Hermes says.

"You're welcome." Prelude smiles, picks up her tray, pivots on her heel, and leaves.

"A beautiful smile, isn't it? A man could fall in love with a smile like that, don't you think, Quinn? Is that what did it for you when you met your partner?"

Amber's smile *did* entrance Quinn – so pretty, so guileless. She'd been sitting in the second row. He was having the sort of game that was drawing the attention of scouts. People had been screaming for him, caught in the fervor of his brilliance. But she'd been genuine – and the only person to stay with him when he injured his knee just three months later, and the offers evaporated.

"Those lips are beautiful. But, if you paused to think, to contemplate, where have they been? How many men has she fellated? None? One? Five? Fifty? Five hundred? How about women? Would you think about that when you kiss her? What kind of women is she in the confines of her bedroom? What has she done with partners? What has she allowed partners to do to her? In this layer that we see, she is young and happy and healthy. But perhaps behind closed doors she is something else entirely."

"Do you have a point?"

"We exist, Quinn, both in the mainstream and undercurrent of society. We market ourselves in the mainstream. In the undercurrent, we are who we really are. We might deny it for a while, or be recalcitrant to show it when entering relationships, but you cannot deny your true being."

"I still don't see your point."

"What're you looking for, Quinn? Product? Or reality?"

"I don't see the difference."

"You will when it's done."

Mr. Hermes lifts his glass and swirls it under his nose. He puts the glass down, plucks out the lemon, and bites the pulp. His face doesn't register its taste. He swallows it, downs his drink in one gulp, and plops the lemon rind into the empty glass.

"I sit here, and I offer temptation, Quinn. People – young fools such as yourself – sit opposite me hoping I will pay them one million dollars if they fulfill the Temptation I set them. But you know this. That's why you're seated opposite me. And you, like so many, see it as a possible doorway to a ready-made future."

Quinn nods.

"Three young men, three very, very macho and egotistical young men, once sat opposite me and I set them the Temptation that if they formed a sodomy-chain and engaged in the act to fruition in one of the private rooms, I would pay them one million dollars. *Each.*"

Quinn is just lifting his Corona to his mouth. He stops. "Did they …?"

"Two of them were willing. One declined. The two – with help from considerable alcohol – talked the other into it. In the lead-up to the act, though, one of those two reneged. The original protester followed. That left one disappointed young man, although he did exhibit obvious relief. You see, Quinn, they could deal with the product, but not the reality. Many young men and woman have sat opposite me, but very rarely, extremely rarely, have I had to pay – and when I have, there have been … *consequences* for the payee, in dealing with what they've done. Product and reality rarely reconcile."

"Why? Why do you do this?"

"Isn't it obvious?"

"I don't understand. I didn't believe it when I heard about it. But I saw the … I just … Before you go ahead, I just want to understand."

"We have a symbiotic relationship, you and me. You have a need. I offer the potential to fill it. If there were no needs, I would cease to exist. That is as close to an answer as I will give you. Otherwise, the reasons are my own. The question now, though, is whether you are still interested?"

Quinn plants his hands into the face of the table and begins to slide himself out of the booth. He stops, his right knee creaking in this position. One million dollars. He and Amber would never look back. But then he visualizes three men in a sodomy chain. He slides out of the booth.

"You could just propose anything," he says.

"I don't propose outrageous acts for even in such random anarchy, there are fools who would acquiesce in their greed for money. I read you. And I choose my Temptations accordingly. I don't force them upon anybody. You must be a willing participant."

"And if I decline?"

"You walk away."

"And if I fail?"

"Then you may learn something about yourself."

"Nothing else?"

"Nothing other than what I stated initially: you must introduce another to me."

Quinn slumps back into the booth.

"Excellent, Quinn. Now it is time to learn about you. Tell me about yourself. Omit embellishment. Change nothing. I will know if you do."

Quinn nods and finishes his beer for courage.

○   ○   ○   ○

I can break down the people who come here into two groups: Transients and Staples.

The Transients are the tourists, or the locals who come once or twice, and – either through design or circumstance – that will be it for them. When they chat to friends or colleagues, they will casually slip in, "Oh, I went to Prudence", as if it's an offhand revelation. When they are pressed, they will talk about the exclusivity, and the wonder of their night, even if they did little more than drink, dance, and chat – things they could do at any bar or club. But something would've touched them – something they are incapable of understanding, and engaging with, and which they only glimpsed.

The Staples are often here, attuning to the energy and feeling something beneath it – a seductiveness to open up and explore and give more of themselves, until they leave behind their inhibitions and see where their desires will take them. Some become addicted to that journey of self-discovery until they lose themselves.

Then there are Bodie and Ox, who are *always* here – or so it seems. The first time they appeared, they were callow and cocky, and sometimes over-awed. But time has little meaning here, and while I could say they have been here at least two decades, they now exude their own timelessness – if quizzed, people might assume they are as young as twenty-five, or as old as sixty.

Perhaps that's why they have become a pastiche of the decades in how they present themselves, with the only constant being that they prefer black, and wear ankle-length overcoats. Ox also wears Ray Ban sunglasses, although it's questionable how he sees anything in them in here, and a jaunty Mariner's cap. Bodie's lone idiosyncrasy is his boots, which are leather with silver buckles.

For as formidable as Bodie and Ox might appear, they are good natured and handsome – Bodie with his spiky hair that makes him almost adolescent, like a miscreant schoolboy, while Ox proudly boasts an overgrown mullet tied back, and a thick, thick beard.

In another life, they might've worked odd jobs to get by while they sat on a beach, sunning and surfing, and always searching for the next wave to conquer. Or they might've been poets in some beatnik bar, offering whimsical insights on how they see the world. Or … well, anything where they could roll with the Earth's orbit, and find those minor truths so many are oblivious to, but which they delight in.

They sit on stools at the end of the South Bar – well, Bodie sits on a single stool, while Ox's girth means his buttocks require two stools. Each drink a Gallia Lager. Just nudging past Ox is Edan LeBeau, moving like a man who expects others to step aside for him.

The bartender who greets him is one of our more experienced bartenders. He wears the black slacks, white shirt, and black vest that is uniform here, although his vest has gold buckles – a measure of rank. His name-tag identifies him as "Prince". His smile is disarming. He is whatever the customer needs – mentor, confidante, or servant.

"There you go, Mr. LeBeau," Prince says, sliding a Tom Collins across the bar.

LeBeau thrusts forward a fifty. "Thank you, Prince," he says.

Prince takes the fifty but doesn't bother making change – this is a transaction that has become rote.

LeBeau picks up his Tom Collins, sips at it, and surveys the crowd. "Something in the air tonight," he says.

"Magic?" Prince asks.

LeBeau snorts. "I'll catch you later."

As LeBeau moves to leave, he bumps into a lithe redhead approaching the bar. He jerks back his drink. Drops of it splash on Ox's sleeve.

"Watch it, man!" Ox says.

Bodie and Ox have seen LeBeau here often, although they have never interacted with him. They classify him as one of the social elite, rich and aristocratic. Some earn wealth and use it for altruism. But not here – both Bodie and Ox recognize that. It has cultivated LeBeau to be disdainful, if not cruel, a man who no longer wants for anything material, and seeks pleasure from the power he can wield over others.

He does not offer them an apology. At best, LeBeau affords them a dismissive glance, steps around the lithe redhead, and moves on.

"What a dick!" Bodie says.

Ox takes a crimson handkerchief from his pocket. "Maximum dickage." He wipes his sleeve dry, then thrusts his handkerchief back into his pocket.

They finish their beers and plant the bottles back on the bar, side by side.

Ox slaps the bar. "Two more!"

Prince – serving a couple of blondes – holds up his hand to acknowledge that he's heard their order. Bodie and Ox swivel back to survey the crowd – or at least Ox does. Bodie gauges the aesthetic of each individual patron.

"A lotta action here tonight," Bodie says, finishing his beer.

Prince appears behind them with two more Gallia Lagers. He holds them out. Bodie and Ox reach over their respective shoulders to take them. No money is involved here. The goodwill extended to Bodie and Ox is endless – something that Prince has never understood and has never delved into. It is a directive from Constance.

"Sometimes," Prince says, "you can have too much action."

"You're only saying that because you work here every night," Bodie says.

"And I serve you two every night!"

"Now that's a good point," Ox says.

"It is, isn't it?" Bodie says.

"The man's a point-maker," Ox says.

"Why don't you get moving?" Prince asks. "Circulate. There are lots of beautiful women. How about those two?" He points at a pair of women on the second floor who stand up from their table – none other than Holly and Amber, just after Flavia has left them. "They're alone."

"Blonde does nothing for me," Bodie says.

"She's gorgeous," Ox says.

"But not in a lustful way. She's the sort you'd romance. Who you'd take to romantic dinners and cuddle on the couch with. The type you'd propose to on one knee, and who'd have your children."

"I concede your argument," Ox says.

"That's not what you want?" Prince says.

"I like her friend," Ox says, as Amber disappears from the balcony. "She's meek, but I can imagine her cutting loose. There's something sly about her. I could let her do indecent things to me. I can imagine crossing boundaries with her. Oh yeah. She's somebody I could objectify. More than that, she's somebody who'd want me to objectify her. And she'd like to objectify me."

"Do you really believe all that?" Prince asks.

"God no."

"Is that what you're looking for in a relationship?" Prince asks.

"Who's looking?"

"You have a tendency to over-analyze."

"The man's got another point," Ox says.

"To points," Bodie says.

He holds up his beer. Ox toasts it. Both drink.

A woman emerges from the crowd, angelic but sultry, her long, dark, wavy hair bouncing on naked shoulders. A leather satchel hangs on her right hip. The strap arcs over her right shoulder and cuts across her cleavage, pronouncing her breasts in her leather vest. Her black leather pants are so tight they show not a single crease. The heels of her stiletto boots are ludicrously high – a fine gold chain around her right ankle – but she moves as if she is wearing skates.

Because Bodie and Ox are such fixtures here, they have seen countless beautiful women. But this one – her name is Joy; she wears it like a marquee – is something more than that, somebody willful who moves through the world as if she expects the world to reshape around her.

They each see her as she would appeal most to them individually, and for a moment are breathless. This is not just beauty, but something celestial that robs them of their banter and demands from them mute worship.

She smiles at them as she passes.

"Amazing," Bodie finally manages to breathe out.

Joy pushes through the crowd and heads into the juncture.

o   o   o   o

They say Constance's office is the higher brain function here. Perhaps that's because it overlooks much of the club and has surveillance screens accessing cameras in every room. The truth is that it's just an office: stylishly furnished with ergonomic chairs, a sectional couch, a marble desk, and a mini bar. A small compartment (the entrance camouflaged in one of the walls) contains a bathroom.

If there's a brain here, I've always thought it's a collective consciousness – like a hive mind, with every Transient and Staple contributing. But that's nothing unusual, and certainly not preternatural. Clubs and bars all around the world develop their own identities, and those identities govern their evolution and how they're perceived.

Perception becomes reality.

Such is the reality of Constance's unparalleled splendor. At fifty, she is just beginning to age – belatedly, some have conceded begrudgingly. Others will snipe that she has not aged enough, and query if she has gone under a plastic surgeon's knife – well, maybe long, long ago, although I can only speculate.

She is statuesque, encased in a pink latex dress that is cut garishly low at the front and lower at the back to the swell of her buttocks. Her blonde hair is bouffant, an homage to another generation in which she was revered globally; her eyes blue, deep, and haughty; her features classical, her thin, pointed nose making her almost imperious.

Sitting at her desk, she peruses her laptop, implacable and untouched by the demands of the night. There is not one speck of smudged make-up, nor the tiniest droplet of sweat, or any sign of tiredness. She is preserved, frozen in time as best as she can manage to exist only in this very moment.

Behind her is her chief of security, Teo. He is a man whose past is lost in war and bloodshed and violence – a history that has weathered his face and cost him his right eye; now he wears a leather patch, although the jagged points of a scar extend above and below it. You could only guess at his heritage, although it would be with no certainty – European or Middle Eastern might be the best suggestions. Some say he was captured and tormented for months, and from the pain everything cosmetic and superficial was stripped away to leave this. While the sharpness of his face and body might've been sculpted with ludicrously painstaking detail, it's that unswerving determination that simmers beneath the surface that demands everybody hold him in awe. Rumors abound that he punched a hole into the chest of a man who once tried to assault Constance just after she left one night. Of course, I'm not sure what happens once people leave, as memories fade, or grow confused – well, usually.

Seated in one of the chairs opposite Constance is Nico, a handsome young man who, despite his experience and lineage, is meek, if not diffident. The fringe of his hair loops down in a way that would encourage a girlfriend – or a mother – to brush it clear. His shadowy growth is not a result of a lack of time to shave, but careful cultivation with a trimmer. Like many young people, he is the construction of pretense. This is what is popular and attractive now. Typically, in trying to stand out, he is a slave to trends, although he is boyishly handsome in a way that he beams with appeal. That gives him something – not a lot, but *enough* to make him *almost* distinctive.

"Nico, do you know what goes on within these walls?" Constance asks.

Nico nods.

Constance consults her laptop. "Your bartending experience is impressive. You haven't padded this résumé, have you?"

"No, ma'am. You can call every place I've listed. And there are references at the back."

Constance's eyes widen momentarily. "And your surname – have you been put up to this?"

"No, ma'am."

"This isn't some game?"

"No."

"Or powerplay?"

"I want to make it on my own. That why I've been busting my balls – excuse me – as you can see from my résumé."

"You want to be a career bartender?"

"I wanted to be a writer!"

Nico chuckles, but neither Constance nor Teo buy into his self-depreciation.

"I was convinced that was a foolish dream," Nico says.

"All dreams are foolish, or they wouldn't be dreams," Constance says. "But we nurture them because we need to believe in the impossible, otherwise what is there but the mundane?"

Emboldened, Nico nods and grins. "I've been working hard at *this* – I want to own my own place. Eventually, of course."

"Stand up."

Nico jumps to his feet, while Constance unwinds to her full height. She comes around the table and stops before Nico.

"What do you think, Teo?" she asks.

Teo shrugs noncommittally. He is rarely impressed – the people who come to stand before Constance are just about always a manifestation of indulgences. When he thinks too much about them, his mind grows murky – he begins to imagine how they would function in the landscapes he has frequented, but then he forces a veil across those ruminations.

Constance leans against her desk and folds her arms across her chest. "Do you know where you are, Nico?"

"Of course I do."

"Do you really know?"

"Yes."

"We're not like other clubs. We're not like other bars."

"I understand."

"No, I don't think you do – you can't. I have been here so long and don't fully understand it. It's the intangible. It's what makes Prudence unique. It's why a Camarilla of the world's richest people each own a stake. There are no other places like this one."

"That's why I want to work here."

"We don't just hand out jobs, Nico. There's a hierarchy. Opportunities must be earned. But once they're earned, the sky – as the cliché goes – is the limit. I was little more than a used-up model when I first came here, a single breath from the streets, if not worse. But I became the face of Prudence and, inevitably, her hostess."

"I'll do anything."

"Anything?"

Nico nods once. "Anything."

"Undress."

"What?"

"If you need to ask, I guess you wouldn't do anything."

Nico understands that hesitation will only hold him back, so he eagerly snaps off his t-shirt, and throws it aside. He kicks off his shoes next. His jeans come down a little slower, although they *do* come down. He bundles them around his feet, steps out of them, and kicks them behind him.

"All the way, Nico."

Nico pulls down his briefs, steps out of them, and crosses his hands in front of his crotch.

Constance pushes off from the desk and circles Nico. She admires the tautness of his buttocks, the V of his back, the roundness of his shoulders. He has a body built in the gym – Constance doubts he's ever genuinely known a hard day's work in his life. This is a man who has been pampered, and whose good name has helped pad his résumé.

"Remove your hands."

Nico turns to her.

"Now, please."

Nico uncrosses his hands. His cock extends from his trimmed pubic hair. Constance imagines what it would be like hard – it's length, its girth. She takes the shaft, runs her fingers down to its head. Nico's cock stiffens in her hand. He looks away meekly. She arches one brow.

"Don't be embarrassed," she says.

Nico's eyes fleetingly lift to her. Constance releases him.

"What do you think, Teo?" she asks.

Again, Teo shrugs.

Constance smiles fondly. She nervously gave Teo a similar examination when she first hired him over twenty-four years ago. It ended with him taking her on the desk in a variety of positions – the only man who had dared confront her temerity, and the only man she ever felt open to engage. She had met his passion and they had battered one another to mutual oblivion, albeit an oblivion saturated with satisfaction. Now, Constance sinks into her recliner and leans back.

"Do you trust in me, Nico?"

"Yes, ma'am."

"Then that's your first mistake. Trust isn't something I would surrender freely here. It must be earned. Or bought. However, I do think we can find a position for you – if you could start immediately."

"I can!" Nico nods.

Constance swivels in her recliner. "Where do you think, Teo?"

Teo scowls. "He has Icon written all over him," he says.

"Perfect," Constance says.

O O O O

Despite how many people I see, and despite how infrequently I may see them, I am good with faces. I could tell you how often they come, the nights they do, the drinks they have, and where their interests lie.

I can read them and see into their lives, see *who* they are.

There's truly little I *couldn't* tell you.

Even the motives of the newer faces are identifiable. I've been watching a long time, so it's easy to pick up patterns, those tell-tale behaviors that foreshadow their interests. It's also easy to tell *who* will be a Transient and *who* will become a Staple.

I can tell you just about anything.

Which is what makes Joy so perplexing.

This is her first night here, but she walks with the surety of a long-time Staple. Even somebody as arrogant and cocksure as Edan LeBeau had to disguise his nervousness and excitement the first few times he came here. That is usually the norm. As with anything, familiarity breeds equanimity. Not with Joy, though. There is a stillness about her, but also a whimsy, as if she finds a condescending amusement in what she sees.

Upon entry, she heads straight into the Gallery and struts across the dance floor. The eyes of every man follow her. Women glower. Her body, her outfit, even her sultriness, are all tangible things that earn attention, but there's also something else about her, something that smolders just beneath the surface that alerts everybody she passes. They feel her heat; the impulsive, the foolish, and even the idealistic, are drawn to her, while the insecure, the wary, and the envious, retreat.

One man in a leather jacket with a big, flared collar accosts her, asking her to dance. She declines and continues on. Another man offers to buy her a drink. She refuses and tells him perhaps later. Another simply asks her to fuck. She tells him she will if he can come up with a better line than that. He doesn't.

She tours the upper floor next, as if gauging its size and its vantages of the events below. For a while, she stands in the very same position that Flavia did, surveying all below as if cataloging what she sees. Then she returns downstairs and enters the Cardinal Lounge.

Whereas most candelabras here have globes, in the Cardinal Lounge the candelabras have maroon candles, their flames dancing and flickering as if in a frenzied ritualistic appreciation of desires unseen. The décor, the tables, and the chairs, are furnished in various shades of deep, blossoming red, as if the room itself is the forge of every desire people have ever known. The bar is made of Rojo Bilbao marble – red like a raw and bloody steak, with streaks of silver, black, and gold that hint at a whirlpool ready to spin and suck everybody here through its epicenter and into some forbidden destination.

For a minute, Joy stands in the center of the Lounge, eyes closed, head lifted to a candelabra, her face bathed in its light, her image reflected in several faces of the octagon. A waiter approaches and asks if she's okay. Her eyes shoot open. She is in no way frightening or austere – at least not in appearance – but the waiter murmurs his apologies and excuses himself.

Next, she heads for the bar, and orders herself an iced water. Her foot taps in accompaniment to the pianist. She recognizes it as Beethoven's "Moonlight Sonata". She scans the room, again cataloging people, and breaking them down just as I do, just without the same ambivalence.

A stiff man in his early forties, wearing a charcoal suit and a lavender tie, approaches her. His face is somber, with already deepening lines – evidence of one who cares too deeply and too often. This is Rupe. His manner is quaint, a holdover to a time long forgotten, when men held doors open for women, picked up the tab, and offered them only a chaste kiss after bringing them home.

"May I buy you a drink?" he asks.

"I already have one," Joy says.

"But you're almost done."

"Then I'll order myself another."

"When I've already offered?"

Joy downs her water. She puts the empty glass on the bar. Rupe holds up two fingers to the barmaid, a purple-haired Amazon named Providence. Rupe then points at the empty glass. Providence nods and pours two more iced waters.

"What's your name?" Joy asks.

"Rupert."

"Rupert?"

"You're amused?"

"Rupert is the name of a much, much older man. A distinguished, learned man – English, maybe. Yes, English, I think … although I detect an accent."

"I moved here, some years ago. From South Africa."

"You look more like a Rupe."

"My friends *do* call me Rupe for short."

Providence slides the iced waters across the bar. Rupe thrusts a twenty-dollar bill at her but Providence waves it off. Joy picks up her drink and walks the length of the bar. Rupe is quick to follow her.

"And you?" he asks. "What's your name?"

"Joy."

Rupe's eyes narrow. They run the course of her body.

"Do I look like a Joy?"

"I don't know. I've never met a Joy before."

"Don't you have stereotypes?"

"I try to accept everybody as they are."

"That could be a mistake, Rupert."

"Oh, really?"

Joy sits at a table furthest from the pianist, swinging her satchel around so that it rests on her lap. The strap goes loose around her body. Rupe pulls out the chair opposite her but stops himself before he sits. He indicates the chair with an incline of his head. Joy nods. Rupe sinks into the chair.

"Do you know what I think?" Joy asks.

"What do you think?"

"Everybody has their boundaries. Those boundaries define them. That's who we accept them to be. But once those boundaries are pushed or broken, neither them nor your acceptance of them is ever the same again."

"That's what you think?"

"That's what I think."

"Have you ever exceeded your boundaries?"

Joy absently flicks open the top button of her vest. Whether she has done so because the Cardinal Lounge is hot or to tease poor Rupe is unclear.

"What do you think?" she asks.

"I'm not sure."

"Why aren't you sure?"

"Because I don't know what the boundaries are. Yet."

"Some things shouldn't be known, Rupert." Joy downs her water in one gulp. She gets up, uncoiling from the chair the way a cobra might from a basket.

Rupe sips from his water – frowns at it, as if just realizing what he's ordered – and leans back in his chair. "You've intrigued me."

"And where will that take you?"

"It depends."

"On?"

"How far your boundaries allow."

"Some boundaries come with a warning to keep out. Others are dangerous, perhaps barbed, or electrified. And some are plain unassailable. Which do you think surround me?"

"Does it matter?" Rupe again sips from his glass.

"I would hope it does."

"Regardless, boundaries – like rules – are there to be broken."

Joy's smile is mischievous. "So, you break rules?"

"Sometimes. And you?"

"Nothing's inflexible."

Joy leans over the table so that her face is inches from Rupe's. Her breasts hang low in her vest. He does not look – a gentleman who would not dare intrude – although his initial glimpse tells him she's not wearing a bra. He shifts uncomfortably, but not out of lust. This is awkward; he doesn't like to be in a position where he could take advantage of her, even if that advantage is just to be seeing what he shouldn't.

"But then again," Joy continues, "there are no certainties in life, are there?"

She caresses his cheek, then rises – swiveling her satchel around so that it rests back on her right hip – and slips away.

○　○　○　○

The leather pants pinch Nico's crotch and chafe the inside of his thighs. He tries to pick them clear, but it's only seconds of comfort before they seize him again. The vest sticks to his naked back and scratches his chest. It smells also of mothballs.

"This is uncomfortable" he says.

Teo leans on the jamb of the doorway of the change rooms. "You won't be wearing it long."

"What?"

"Come on."

The gaming rooms are interconnected through a series of winding hallways. Nico tries to map their course in his head, but it's not long before he's disoriented. The twists are many and he's sure there is a gradual descent. The architecture goes from Napoleonic to Early Modern – not that Nico is an expert in such things. The music from the Gallery continues to be piped in. It's the one constant that unifies the different activities: in several rooms there is karaoke to instrumental renditions of the Gallery's music; arcade games that span the decades in others; virtual reality games; card games that involve stripping competitors; dancing competitions; and more. It's such an eclectic and jarring mix that Nico has trouble reconciling any single activity, let alone all of them.

They arrive in a domed room with a pool table, this the demesne of one of our top Icons, Patricia. A buxom brunette, Patricia wears lingerie, a leather miniskirt, and fishnets. Her breasts bulge in her corset with a firmness that convinces Nico they're implants. When she bends over the table to have her shot, her miniskirt hikes up. She wears a G-string, the swell of her cunt framed between her buttocks. Around her, a crowd of guys cheer as she misses her shot. They believe they are privy to forbidden delights, but every move Patricia makes is artful.

She steps back, sees Teo, and rolls her eyes.

A young guy approaches the table, his face serious, his jaw set. He could be playing for his life. He isn't. But his concentration is unfailing.

He leans over the table and pots the fifteen, an easy shot in the middle pocket. His next shot – the thirteen – misses the corner pocket but ricochets off the banks and enters the opposite corner. The other guys in the room cheer.

"Good shot, Chester!" Patricia gushes.

Chester lines up the black in the corner pocket. A bead of sweat runs down from his temple. He shoots. The black goes in. The chorus of cheers overwhelms the music piped in from the Gallery. Chester throws his arms up triumphantly.

Patricia approaches him and lifts one leg, cordoning him off and balancing her heel on the edge of the table.

"One stocking," she says.

Chester's hands tremble as he reaches for the garter holding the stocking. The other guys start a slow hand clap with such gusto they might actually believe they have invented it. Chester fumbles with the task. Patricia negligently flicks the garter clear. Chester grabs the hem of the stocking. The hand-clapping quickens. Chester pulls the stocking clear to reveal Patricia's taut leg. The other guys roar.

Nico wanders across to an archway into an adjacent room. There's another game going on, although this room is filled with screaming women. The player is one of our most prized commodities – Savage, a bald, bronzed, muscular young man, a long topknot of hair held in a gold ring flowing behind him. He's dressed like Nico is. Intimidated, Nico pivots, and watches as Patricia strides to the corner of the room. An upended hat sits on a table. She reaches into the hat and pulls out a raffle ticket.

"Blue fourteen," she says.

Another young man jumps forward from the crowd. "That's me!"

"Set them up."

Patricia approaches Teo. Teo beckons Nico to return. He does so, and while he reflects that Patricia is gorgeous, an exotic doll manufactured to appeal and intoxicate, he senses an underlying belligerence that just needs ignition, and a haziness about her eyes that suggests she indulges.

"Who's this?" she asks.

Nico picks she is American. Up close, she is breathtaking, her lips small and set in a permanent pout, her forehead glistening with a smattering of sweat. The long, curled lashes flutter demurely. Around her neck, she wears a tarnished gold-shaped locket – it is big and clunky and sits there like an anchor.

But now simmering at the heart of the belligerence he picks a deep and brooding melancholy. Nico knows nothing of how she aspired to become a top international model; how she was told she was too short, that she didn't have that intangible quality, and her look was suited to something lowlier; and how she went from lingerie catalogs to softcore magazines and websites, her standards deteriorating, until she found herself here, and developed a habit to cope. But he feels the lament – she is somebody whose life hasn't gone to plan, and he is determined not to follow her.

"Nico. Patricia," Teo introduces them.

"Pleasure to meet—" Nico begins.

"Nico's going to become an Icon," Teo says.

"Half your luck," Patricia says.

"Thanks," Nico says.

"Your bad luck," Patricia says.

"Easy, Patricia," Teo says. "I need you to show him the routine."

"What routine? Play to lose, let them strip you off one piece of clothing at a time. It's not neurosurgery."

"They're set up!" the young man calls from the pool table.

"I've got to go."

Patricia heads back to the table. Nico turns to Teo.

"I'm a bartender," he says.

"We don't hand out bartending jobs to just anybody," Teo says. "You've got to earn it."

"But isn't this …?"

Nico watches the game unfold. The young man is average at best, but Patricia is hopeless. With her first shot, she miscues, and the cue ball rolls harmlessly off to one side. Surely she cannot be so bad. But of course she's not, because this isn't about winning for her. She is a sacrifice to the collective lust and desire in this room, no more than a prop who might be discarded when she's done – or at least that's what Nico concludes.

The game itself doesn't just feel wrong. It *is* wrong. How is this happening here? It's a tawdry exchange suited to some seedy bar, or a cheap strip club; a transaction where inhibition has been shredded and self-decency mocked. Even the men who vie for Patricia's virtue seem ill-fitting, dressed-up goblins masquerading as humans in a place they never should've been allowed into.

"Isn't this what?" Teo asks.

"Cheap," Nico says.

"Things go on here, Nico. I'm sure you've heard stories. Everybody circulates them. Some of them are even true. This may be cheap, it may be the extreme end of the petty scale, but it's games like this that let us know where people stand. Get it?"

"No."

"And nor do you have to. So, what do you say?"

"I don't have much choice, do I?"

Teo grins. "Watch and learn. Then we'll get you your own room."

○　○　○　○

Dante stands in the corner, a small man in an oversized and tacky suede blazer who shifts nervously from one foot to the other, then back again. His whole life he has been considered a runt and was nicknamed the "Weasel" at school, a result of his aquiline nose and sharp cheekbones, his pointed, clefted chin, and eyes that too intently fix upon whatever he looks at. But there is a symmetry to his face's construction that is oddly compelling. His dark hair is thick and flowing, the sort that bounces with every step, and swirls dramatically when he twirls – just one of the many affectations he has cultivated to compensate for his insecurity. Even his time in the gym has not helped him; the muscles makes him appear squat – or at least he thinks so. The one thing he takes pride in is his English, learned from echoing dialogue from a variety of American movies.

He watches Patricia bend over the table as she prepares to break. There's something sublime about her that stirs in him feelings greater than simple lust. She's the girl he wished he could've ended up with out of high school, the girl who would've made him the envy of anybody who would've seen him – not that he has any complaints with Flavia. But confidence and aspiration lift her into a stratum where he feels he doesn't belong, and he must cling onto her toes so that she doesn't soar out of reach. She would shudder at what Patricia is doing here, whoring cheap thrills for money, but he feels this is what makes Patricia's relatable. She does not occupy rarified air. They are breathing the same oxygen.

Marcus claps him so hard on the shoulder that Dante's arm jolts, and his Bourbon & Coke splashes from the glass. He licks it clean from his hand, takes a drink, then pulls his phone from his pocket.

"I told ya!" Marcus says, his words quick, that Australian pitch sometimes cutting off a syllable before it's finished. "It gets better than this!"

Like Flavia, Marcus beams self-confidence, but it is twisted here – Dante still can't work it out, although he often fears when Marcus and Flavia have interacted; they are two of the kind: striking, purposeful, and oblivious, as if the world is a playground that has been designed for their indulgence, and others are just toys to be used, exploited, and discarded.

And then there are Marcus's aquamarine eyes, that pale blue like cellophane that has been pasted on a diamond. They are beautiful – Dante has never appreciated another man this way, but he can with Marcus because that's how he looks. If there is an Australian stereotype of rugged and windswept, Marcus has exceeded it. His only flaw is his neat, pointed goatee – a common thing that is out of place, like a disguise he wears to make him seem as ordinary as everybody else.

"What would the girls say if they saw us?" Dante asks.

"They're having their own fun."

Dante checks his phone. Nothing from Flavia. Not that he is expecting anything.

"Put the phone away, Dante," Marcus says.

"This is madness."

Marcus plants a hand on Dante's back, right below his neck. "You're on holiday. Let go. Have fun. Be free."

"I might try to find Flavia—"

Marcus's hand tightens behind Dante's neck.

"Geez, Dante, you're not chained up yet and even if you were, the leash shouldn't be that short. Even dogs get retractable leads."

"What's wrong with spending time with the woman I love?"

"You'll be doing it the rest of your life. One day, you'll regret the time you didn't make use of."

"To do what? This is like cheating!"

"You think if the situations were reversed, Flavia wouldn't have some fun?"

"Flavia wouldn't be doing something like this."

"It's amazing what people do when they think nobody's looking."

Dante is unsure if Marcus is hinting at something – but that is Marcus. It's not his words. Often, they are straightforward. And it's not even his tone. It's familiar and affable. But it's a cast of the eyes – a sly twinkle, as if he is trying to find something to manipulate. He is one for risks, like when he took Dante and Quinn to that underground casino.

"Five minutes!" Marcus says. "Just five more minutes – okay?"

Dante types a text to Flavia, asking her to meet him for a drink.

"*Okay?*"

"Okay, okay." Dante sends the message and lowers his phone.

"Put it away."

"What?"

"Put it away."

Dante slides his phone into his pants pocket. He feels the ring box there. Flavia had idly pointed it out a month ago when they'd passed a jeweler's store. He has been building the courage to ask her and thought he might even do it tonight – possibly in the restaurant. Now, it's a remote possibility.

"Where's Quinn?" he asks.

"Quinn?" Marcus says. "Seriously, that's the pussy you want to look at now?"

"Just asking."

"Dante, enjoy the night. We're just getting started."

II

Flavia hurries from the upper floor and down to the bar. Edan LeBeau is just leaving. She pursues him, silently rehearsing how she'll introduce herself. In her mind, she sounds glib and confident. She would be with anybody else. But with Edan LeBeau, Flavia knows rehearsal won't necessarily reconcile with execution.

LeBeau doesn't so much weave his way through the crowd, but projects himself so that people bustle out of his path. Flavia trails him, and at one point almost gets close enough that she reaches out to tap him on the shoulder. But he is accosted by a blonde in a tight fluorescent lime dress that barely contains her huge breasts. Flavia rolls her eyes. Silicone blondes. They are their own species. Marcus calls them *silicunts*.

The blonde gushes over LeBeau and tells him how much she loves him. LeBeau listens stonily, brows arching into sharp angles. Flavia can't hear precisely what the blonde is saying over the music but can tell that she is faltering. Her words come less freely, she fidgets, and sways. Then, just as she is in mid-sentence, LeBeau leaves her.

Flavia follows him to a reserved private booth in the corner. He slides into his seat, lifts an arm onto the backrest, and stares out at the dance floor. Flavia stops, letting the crowd lap around her. Their rhythm becomes meditative. She is the single heartbeat in this uncaring mass. Everything dims. It's just her and LeBeau. The music grows muted.

He takes a gold case from his pocket, opens it, and extracts something – from this distance Flavia cannot see what it is. He pops it into his mouth, snaps closed the case, and slides it back into his pocket. Perhaps it is a breath mint. But she suspects it's something illicit.

Flavia takes a step forward. Now is the time – before he gets stoned or whatever the case might be. But she still has no idea what to say. She cycles through possibilities and tells herself over and over she can't afford to gush – not like the big breasted-blonde. Nor can she be obsequious. She must be measured.

Hello, Mr. LeBeau, I'm Flavia Rojas.

That's as far as she gets. She doesn't know what comes next. LeBeau transfixes her: his eyes are cold; his lips full, pursed, as if in disapproval; his bronzed skin surely the product of hours lying on a yacht (or at least that's what she pictures a man like him would do); his shoulders broad, rounded, feeding into the muscles that ripple around his neck. He is not human. He is somebody masquerading as a man, some satyr who can only offer an approximation.

Flavia knows right now she should re-join Holly and Amber. Better yet, she should find Dante.

Almost as if in concord with her thought, a vibration runs up her left arm. It's her phone, kept in the small purse strapped to her left wrist. She fishes out the phone and finds a message from Dante.

Where u? Lets get drnk.

It's an invitation she shouldn't decline. She and Dante could have a drink in one of the Lounges and share a table, hand in hand. They could laugh about her futile pursuit. They used to laugh at the misfires in her career aspirations, although that was when such dreams seemed improbable.

Better yet, they could just go – *should* just go – and maybe grab a quiet bite somewhere. She is sure now, as sure as she has ever been about anything in her life, that it's wrong to be here and no good will come of it.

She turns off the phone. Puts it away, unanswered.

And stays where she is.

Unmoving.

○ ○ ○ ○

Holly and Amber weave their way through countless bodies generating a heady effluvium of perfumes, colognes, sweat, and alcohol. A young but weedy lothario leers at Holly.

"Dance, baby?" he asks and swivels his hips.

"Maybe later," Holly tells him.

"How much later?"

"Never."

Holly grabs Amber's hand and forages on. The crowd clusters around the balustrade that perimeters the dance floor. There are lots more people than when they first arrived. Holly and Amber detour and seek respite in a small pocket of emptiness.

"Can you see her?" Amber says.

People crowd around them and trap them. Holly is reminded of the hotel room with the execs from the bar, their bodies sandwiching hers, the cologne the first one wore musky and intoxicating in her nostrils. But she hadn't noticed it then. It had been him thrusting inside her. His hands had been clumsy on her breasts the way Ian Heller's had been in high school; just sixteen, they'd been making out during the lunch break, secluded on the slope of the creek by the soccer field, Ian clutching at her like he was trying to divine some unexpected delight – and he did. He'd cum in his pants.

"This is hopeless!" Amber says.

Holly and Amber don't realize they are within arm's reach of Flavia, separated only by a string of couples, laughing and swaying to the music. Two of the couples part briefly, offering an unobstructed view of Flavia staring at LeBeau, but Amber's distracted by the color in Holly's cheeks and the sweat covering her face.

"Holly? Holly? Are you all right?"

Holly wipes her brow. It's too hot and she's struggling to breathe. Amber reaches for her. Holly tries to grab her wrist and start away abruptly, but she misses Amber entirely. Without tether, Holly stumbles, and falls to her knees. Two guys in front of her turn. Their crotches point at her. It had been like this in the hotel room initially. How easily it had unraveled – she'd unraveled – and now the story begins to lose the allure it held when she recounted it to Flavia and Amber.

The guys help Holly up and ask her if she's okay. Holly smiles her gratitude. This time, she makes sure she has Amber's arm, and drags her aimlessly through the crowd. The bar lights up in front of them – but it's the North Bar. Somehow, they've ended up on the opposite side of the dance floor.

They retreat from the Gallery, picking their way through the crowd until, finally, they find themselves in the juncture, standing by the entrance under the big bronze plaque. Fresh air greets them, washing away the heat and disorientation. It's sweet relief on Holly's skin.

"Holly?"

"It's so hot in there."

"It *is* hot." Amber wipes her brow, almost as if in support, but she also feels something else is at work here. "You okay?"

Holly leans against the wall. The other man had been a terror on the bed. His stubble had scratched the inside of her thighs. She'd propelled her hips toward him. He'd hoisted her legs over his shoulders, the tip of his tongue running across her clit while his finger slipped into her. The first man had kissed her gaping mouth, had suckled the nipples he'd fondle only shortly later, then had risen before her and stroked his erection across her lips until she'd taken him in.

"Holly?"

Holly folds her arms across her chest, hiding her stiffening nipples. She has no idea why these memories have become resurgent. Maybe it is the clash of bodies in the Gallery. But she doesn't like it. Doesn't like that the excitement is interlaced with edginess, and that edginess is disorienting her.

"I'm okay," she tells Amber. "I might find a bathroom and splash some water on my face."

"You want me to come?"

"I'll meet you back where we were. At the table."

"And Flavia?"

"Try texting her."

"And if that doesn't work?"

Holly sighs. "I guess she'll have to find us."

Amber is reluctant to leave her, but Amber is reluctant about a lot of things this night. Anxiety is a tremor in her chest and highlights the potential for everything that can go wrong. She clamps down on it, and tells herself she is overreacting, but can't deny the fear.

"Okay," she says. "I might also see what the guys are doing."

"What they're doing or check on them?"

"Same thing."

There's still concern in Amber's expression. She's unsure about leaving. She really is too sweet. Holly takes Amber's hands in her own, gives them a shake.

"I'll see you soon," Holly says.

"Okay."

They separate, moving down opposite hallways in the juncture.

o o o o

Teo leaves the gaming room and performs a patrol, which he does every forty-five minutes, unless he's otherwise occupied with Constance. It's rare that there's trouble, but he feels the potential simmers here greater than anywhere else he's worked. It's in the gaming rooms, the way people compete, and the way talent like Nico and Patricia are offered as meat; it's on the dance floor, where the energy is combative; it's on the patio, where people retreat to gawk and gossip and – sometimes, when the risk takes them – to fornicate.

For right now, though, everybody is in sync. The collective is a single pulsating lifeform. Teo nods to himself as he circles the dance floor. People give him a wide berth. Despite how long he's worked here, despite being Constance's confidante, he is the interloper on patrol – the saber that cuts through the emotion. He has never had trouble getting through a crowd. But here, nobody obstructs him.

At the South Bar, he sees Bodie and Ox. Teo throws out a hand. Bodie and Ox shake it in turn, chorusing, "Teo!"

"You two jokers!" Teo grins at them. The grimness and threat do not fall away. His smile awkwardly masks them, an ill-fitting garment that everybody is too afraid to comment on. "You're in here every night, you sit at this very spot, and you do … *nothing*. Why don't you get out there? What do you think Prudence is about?"

"Prudence is about sitting here, drinking our beer, and looking damn cool doing it," Ox says, holding up his Gallia Lager.

"Oh yeah!" Bodie says. He toasts Ox. "And Constance loves us right here. We're her ornaments. Speaking of Constance …"

Constance sweeps by, performing her own patrol. She's also given a wide berth, but for different reasons – awe, respect, admiration, lust, and even fear. Often when people see her, they will not know how to respond, or what to feel, until she is gone. Then most will react as if they have seen a celebrity, although here Constance's marquee borders on divinity. Her security trail her like a presidential guard. She leads them toward the juncture.

"Busy night for her," Teo says. "Now, getting back to you two, why don'tcha get on out there and meet somebody?"

"We admire from afar, Teo."

"You two wouldn't know what to do if a pretty girl fell into your laps."

Amber flits past, trying to penetrate a gap in the crowd. A behemoth turns and unwittingly bumps her. Amber is knocked into Bodie and Ox. Their reflexes are immediate – you would not think they could move so quickly given how much they drink, and how indolent they appear. They catch her, and steady her, careful not to touch her inappropriately.

"You okay?" Bodie asks.

"Sorry," Amber says. "Thanks!"

"You're welcome," Ox says.

Amber moves on, disappearing through the crowd.

Teo waves in her direction. "Point made!" he says.

"Come on, Teo," Bodie says. "We don't see women the way everybody else sees them."

"Nobody sees *anything* the way you two see it."

Prince approaches them from behind the bar. He hands Gallia Lagers to Bodie and Ox, and a shot of Pisco – a Peruvian grape brandy with a pale yellow hue that sits in a small glass – to Teo.

"Thanks, Prince," Teo says.

"These two bending your ear?" Prince asks.

"Hey, no bending about it," Bodie says, sipping from his Gallia. "There are women you lust after, there are women you chase after, there are women you dream about, and there are women you fall in love with."

"And in all this," Teo sweeps his arm expansively, "what sort of woman are you looking for?"

Bodie and Ox stare at each other wordlessly.

"You two are hopeless," Teo says.

"You know we're not here for the women," Bodie says.

"You can take a moment to relax."

"When we're so busy?" Ox says, lifting his beer.

Teo bellows uproariously with laughter. "Never change. The world needs people like you. Later."

He downs his Pisco in one gulp, hands the empty glass to Prince, then resumes his patrol.

○ ○ ○ ○

Constance strides through the Gallery, incandescent amongst a crowd that is largely dark and conformist. That's exactly what they must become to be in here – they must become what we want. They might think themselves individuals, might think themselves original, but few people are. Somewhere, somebody is doing the same thing you are and commending themselves for their originality.

A young man tentatively pats Constance on the butt as she passes the DJ station – it could be inadvertent contact, but the young man's leer confesses a different motivation.

One of Constance's gargantuan security grabs the young man by the scruff of the neck. Another twists his arm behind his back. The young man dangles between them. Security might literally tear him apart – or at least that's what the surrounding crowd fear.

"Wait!" Constance says.

They're so close to the speakers now that her voice is indistinguishable from the music. It vibrates in their bodies and in the walls. Glasses left unattended on tables shake and rattle.

Constance steps up to the young man. He can't be more than twenty-one, with a crew-cut and heavy-lidded eyes that make him appear dull-witted. He doesn't care about what he's done. This is a story he'll be able to tell forever, how he grabbed Constance's butt – already he is embellishing the story in his mind.

"You want to have some fun?" Constance asks.

"Why don't you blow me?" the young man says.

Constance caresses the young man's cheek, then traces her fingers down his neck. He shudders within the vice of security. Constance steps closer to him until her breasts press against his chest. His gaze descends. Constance's hand continues to move, although now it's obscured by her proximity to the young man. It is clear, however, it moves in the direction of the young man's crotch.

His breath stutters.

His head tilts back.

His face reddens.

Constance steps away as a damp stain spreads across the young man's crotch. A woman in a blue dress is the first to spot it and points it out to her friend. Her friend doesn't so much laugh, but *cackles*. Others catch on. Now everybody points and guffaws at the young man. He flails. Security releases him. The young man flops onto the dance floor.

He scrambles to his feet and tries to bust through the crowd. They circle around him and push him this way and that. He ricochets between laughter and scorn and condemnation. It's a combination that crushes him. The laughter grows louder. He grows tearful. Now some pity him – although not too much. Mob mentalities are common, and often cruel. A gap opens in the perimeter. He crashes through and disappears.

Constance continues onwards. These interactions are not new to her, although they have grown infrequent as she has aged. One day, this attention will stop. It is an inevitability. She *knows* it. Sometimes, when the mood strikes her, she allows herself to wallow in a mixture of self-pity and sadness until she can recompose herself.

Now, she bypasses the bar and enters the juncture. At no point does she pause or slow. The various funnels that lead to the gaming rooms and restaurant are of no interest to her. Now this is *who* Constance is – focused and purposeful. She is magnificent. There is but one thing on her mind.

Entering the Verdant Lounge, she plots a course for Mr. Hermes and slides into the booth alongside Quinn. He's conscious of getting too close to Mr. Hermes, so holds his position as best as he can, but now he has Constance's body pressed against him. She's hot. Burning. He's not sure where to look, so he stares down at the table. The security hold back respectfully and do not spare him a moment of scrutiny. Despite his size, he is no threat.

"Can I help you, Constance?" Mr. Hermes asks.

"What're we going to do with you?" Constance says.

"Careful, Constance, you mustn't overstep."

"You are here at an indulgence."

"Not yours, but," Mr. Hermes waves his hand vaguely, "others."

"Regardless, heed the gentle reminder."

"A gentle reminder given too often becomes a bore."

"It's important you remember the boundaries."

"A reproach that applies to you also."

Constance places a hand on Quinn's. He blushes.

"Is the money he's offering worth the Temptation he's set you?" she asks.

She is overwhelming. Quinn can neither consider her question nor conjure the rationale to work through it. Neither does he see Amber duck her head into the entrance to look for him, nor does she see him as Constance obstructs her view. Such is the way here, where whim can change the entire outcome of a night. And a life. Amber moves on.

"He'll reach into your soul, read your heart, hold aloft what you love most and strip it bare to see if you can handle it," Constance says. "He'll enjoy how that shocks you and how you recoil and shudder and how it makes you everything you *do not* want to be." She offers the smallest smile, just a single corner of her lips turning up. "Is money that important?"

"I ... I ..." Quinn wants to tell her he can walk away, but that is no certainty yet.

"He has planted a seed," Constance says, "and, if you are not careful, it's one that'll blossom through your life and corrupt everything and everybody you know, encourage perversion and deceit—"

"Come, come, Constance," Mr. Hermes says. "I don't recall you ever being so prudish. You've become too soft. When you first came here, you were hard and desperate."

"Desperate perhaps, and not for those reasons."

"Do you remember Sarah?"

"My predecessor."

"She was once hard. Sharp. Unforgiving. She could've cut through diamond. But time softened her. She became everybody's friend – a cautionary tale. Your position *isn't* about being *everybody*'s friend."

"Recently, I've begun to wonder what it *is* about."

"Certainly not about needlessly scaring a poor young man either."

"I don't think what I'm doing is much different to what you do."

"I don't frighten, Constance. I liberate."

"You are a treacherous old fool with a black heart."

Mr. Hermes throws his head back and laughs.

"Some people sit opposite him for greed," Constance tells Quinn. "Some people sit opposite him because they have debts they need to pay. And some people sit opposite him just for the challenge, as if they think they can outsmart the devil himself. Regardless of the motive, when the night's come and gone, will you be able to live with yourself?"

"You *are* getting too soft, Constance."

Whereas before, Mr. Hermes chided her, now an edge enters his tone. His eyes blaze. But Constance is unaffected. She smirks – somebody who has grown largely indifferent to the dangers of life, and now navigates the day with a wry amusement.

She slides out from the booth. "Choose well," she tells Quinn.

"Excuse me, ma'am!" Quinn calls after her.

Constance pivots on her heel.

"Why do you let him do this?"

"Consider him yang to my ying. All life is about balance."

"Indeed, it is," Mr. Hermes says.

He pats Quinn's hand. Whereas Constance's touch was warm, Mr. Hermes' is cold.

"Well, Quinn?" Mr. Hermes asks.

"I'll leave you to it," Constance says.

She sweeps from the Lounge, security trailing behind her.

Amber stands under the bronze plaque in the juncture, unsure where to go. There are so many archways funneling off to so many different places – it seems many more than when she first came in. She believes it is folly to assume that she will stumble upon Quinn by accident, although she does not understand how serendipity can work here. Marcus said they were going to have a game of pool, but where are there pool tables here? *Why* are there pool tables? Like so many others, she struggles to reconcile the pastiche of options.

She takes out her phone and sends a text to Quinn, asking where he is. People pass her. Guys gauge her appreciatively. Several flirt with her. Unnerved, she retreats to the lobby, where at least it's quiet enough that she can ring Quinn.

The call goes through unanswered.

The automated message tells her that his phone is somewhere out of range or that it's been turned off. She cannot fathom a reason Quinn would turn his phone off. Perhaps it's just the reception.

She wanders back into the juncture and ducks her head into the restaurant, then each Lounge, then re-enters the juncture and takes another course, thinking it must lead her through to the gaming rooms. Instead, she re-emerges into the Gallery, but from the other side.

The crowd is tightly knit, the way people huddle around accidents. Amber knows she should continue her search, but curiosity gets the best of her. She tries to push through, and when she can't, tries to detour and, when that fails, retreats, ending up at the South Bar. But here she can see the object of the crowd's attention.

Joy.

She's dancing with a man, thrusting her crotch upon his, the satchel slung around her shoulders bouncing on her right buttock. The crowd cheers. Her dance challenges and invigorates and shocks them all at once as she gyrates to her knees as if she were going to fellate her partner. She undulates back to her full height. The man runs his hands down her side and onto her butt. Joy swings her arms outward, sending the man's arms windmilling, then pivots, grinding her buttocks into the man's crotch.

Amber knows they are dressed, and that dancing like this is simply dancing, but she feels caught in something perverse. Just as Holly's story shook her, she is surprised anybody could exhibit such abandon. She still struggles to make love to Quinn with the lights on.

"Are you all right?" a gentle-faced older man asks her – Rupe. The concern in his eyes is genuine. It grounds Amber. He sips from his martini.

"Just trying to find somebody," she says.

"I'm sorry I cannot help," he says. "My attention has been riveted."

"I'm not surprised."

"She is the love of my heart."

"She might be the lust of everybody else's."

"A conceit."

"Why don't you cut in?"

"It's part of the game."

"The game?"

"We stalk one other, neither knowing who'll lunge first."

"Why do men always play games?"

"We all play games," Rupe says. "Even as she dances, don't you think she's aware I'm talking to you, considering whether to intervene or not?"

Joy's back is pressed to her partner, one arm tossed over her head, her hand running through his hair. The man's arms are folded around her, his hands crossed over her belly. Their hips sway in tandem.

"I don't think she's aware you exist," Amber says.

"Ah, it would seem so," Rupe says. "But it's all part of the game."

Now Amber grows frustrated. "Good luck with that."

She hurries back into the juncture, this time making sure she's choosing funnels she hadn't taken before. The gaming rooms are like each link in a spider's web. As just about everybody does, she's sure she's drifted from the club into a completely different establishment. But while others let the marvel take them away, or proceed curiously, she grows agitated. It reminds her of snorkeling with Quinn, and once diving so deep she was worried she would lose all sense of which direction was up.

In some rooms, people play interactive arcade games, shooting at targets on screen, or dance frenetically to a rhythm; in others they play air hockey, and other table-based sports; then it's games Amber's never encountered before, but which must be cutting edge technology, as the players wear virtual reality helmets and wave glowing wands; and then it's simply plain old pool.

At first, Amber doesn't notice anything odd about the latter. It's two people at a table – a man and a woman – and a crowd watching them. She marches on. But the atmosphere is wrong. In each room, the celebrations are too shrill and intense. Why would anybody be this rambunctious about pool?

She stops in one of the rooms. The crowd is all women. Some look older than those in the Gallery – in their thirties, if not forties. Amber sees the faces of housewives and mothers. They are tired but made up to look their best, some of the hair-styles products of bygone generations, like they have wandered in from different eras to be exhibited here. Their faces are bright, their manner – the way they tilt their heads back and laugh or lean into a friend to joke exuberantly – unburdened.

Amber sees her own future. This is what it'll be like in twenty – or even ten – years for herself. She and Quinn will be married.

They'll have children. Every now and again, she'll have a night out with the girls. Away from home, from responsibilities, she'll be able to relax – however briefly – and long for a time that was unencumbered, although only now does she realize such a time does not exist. Fear and worry have always restricted her.

The woman playing pool pots the black ball. She throws her arms up triumphantly. Her opponent is Nico. He approaches her tentatively, as if afraid he'll be devoured. The woman peels off his vest, teasing it down his biceps, shaking it from his wrists, then twirling it the way a matador would unfurl a red cape before a charging bull. The other women cheer. Amber watches but feels she shouldn't.

She darts from the room and into the next. Patricia balances her foot on the bank of the table. None other than Dante peels her fishnet stocking down her leg, the smallest tremor in his hands. The other leg is already bare. Guys cheer and clap. Amber sees Marcus loitering in the corner and confronts him.

"What the hell are you doing?" she asks.

"Having fun," Marcus says.

"What if Holly saw this?" Amber says.

"She'd understand."

It *feels* wrong, like cheating. Worse, Marcus is doing it oblivious to Holly's feelings. Then Holly's confession rings in Amber's mind. Who knows the people Marcus and Holly are behind closed doors? They are still new friends. Holly is sweet, but Marcus has an edge that threatens to cut at any time. Amber has talked to Quinn about whether they'll remain friends after the holiday – with Holly, it's a yes; with Marcus, she's not so sure. She does not want to be his friend; nor does she want Quinn to be. She has never understood that trepidation and feels that this is validation.

"You hope!" Amber says. "And what if Flavia saw Dante stripping this bimbo?"

"It's a show," Marcus says. "Lighten up!"

"Where's Quinn?"

Marcus shrugs. "We split before we even got in here."

That offers Amber relief – at least he is not a party to this.

"What the hell's going on with him?" she asks.

"What do you mean?"

"He's been … I don't know. *Jittery*, I guess."

Marcus holds up his hands, as if to say he can't help her.

Amber strides from the room, and bumps into one of the buff waiters, his only attire – a set of leather briefs – barely containing him. His body is hard and muscular and has been sprayed with oil to glisten. Amber doesn't know where to look. This is not how the wait-staff are attired in the Gallery. She's sure now she's not only in a new establishment, but also a new world.

"Whoa!" he says. "You okay?"

"Yeah. Sorry. Thanks."

"Raffle ticket?"

"Sorry?"

The waiter holds up a book of raffle tickets. "Five dollars a ticket or five tickets for twenty dollars."

"Sure," Amber says, pulling a twenty from her pocket.

She does it because back home she is always buying raffle tickets, albeit for worthy causes – helping her niece when she sells tickets for the raffle at school or buying them from telemarketers to raise money for research into an illness or something like that. Her actions come unthinkingly. It's only after the waiter's taken her money that she realizes a cause is unlikely to be the case here.

"And your name?" he asks.

"Amber."

The waiter scribbles her name down on the tickets, then gives them to her. "Have fun!"

Once he leaves, the room opens to Amber – another one filled with women. A bronzed man, his head shaved, except for a flowing topknot of hair bound in a gold ring, twirls his hips as a middle-aged woman pulls off his vest to reveal his chiseled physique. This is Savage – one of our longest-serving Icons.

Once, he'd been studying to be a nurse, and had taken work here to pay his way through school – an old cliché, but one that holds truth for many. But then he found he could make a good living just doing this. It exhilarated him – the adulation, as well as the power he held over an audience. He declined offers to move from Icon to bartender, which would be the normal progression. But all that was years ago. Now he pulses in the malaise of his choices and is unsure where he goes not just from here, but in his life. The chorus of piercing cries do not affect him in any way. He finds a sadness in that, although he does not let it show. His performance is exuberant and captivating.

"All right, ladies!" he says. "I'm determined not to make it easy for you!"

Amber makes her way to the door. A buxom thirty-something woman grabs her by the arm. Her tight black curls have been teased out and highlighted copper, and her deep brown eyes are soulful. There's something familiar about her which Amber's sure she should know.

"Hey, where're you going?"

"What?" Amber says.

"Where're you going?"

"I …" Amber falters.

The buxom woman thrusts out a hand. "Gabriella!" she says.

Amber shakes her hand. "Amber."

"Don't go yet, Amber. You just bought tickets."

"Tickets?" Amber blinks at them in her hand. "Tickets for what?"

Gabriella gestures at Savage, who's plucked a ticket out of a hat. "Red twelve!" he calls.

A short-haired blonde woman leaps up exultantly, waving her winning ticket.

Amber sinks into a chair, dumbfounded.

A waiter passes with a tray of beverages. Gabriella snatches two tall glasses of beer from the tray and hands one to Amber. Amber takes it without thinking, just as she meets Gabriella's toast without thinking. Then Amber takes a long drink, gulping down half the glass. A foam mustache forms on her upper lip. She brushes it off. Holly was right. It *is* too hot in here.

"That's the spirit!" Gabriella says. "You'll love it!"

Amber, unsure how she has found herself here, says nothing and takes another drink.

o o o o

Rupe downs his martini and plants it dramatically on the bar, as if he is trying to emulate a scene in a movie as a means of finding courage. He pushes his way onto the dance floor, swaggering comically – not that he knows it's comic; he is sure it is suave and confident and focused. Joy writhes her hips while her dance partner runs his face down her chest.

"May I cut in?" Rupe asks.

Joy's dance partner towers over Rupe. He is a hulk – not just physically, but in the menace of his presence. This is a bully who is accustomed to getting everything he wants. I suspect in the world outside, he is a violent criminal lieutenant, or a ruthless corporate demagogue – they amount to one and the same.

Tinkling with laughter, Joy puts her hands on Rupe's shoulders.

"Hey!" her dance partner says.

Joy casts a dismissive look over her shoulder. "Go."

Rupe is certain he won't. This man feels Joy is indebted to him. He's made an investment in her, and there is a commitment in their dance to something more. Simply, he wants to fuck her. Rupe can see it in the wildness of his eyes, the hopefulness of his expression, and even in the tell-tale bulge of his crotch, so it's inexplicable when he lowers his head, and dodders away like a scolded child. The reaction so surprises Rupe he does not hear Joy's question, nor the change in music to something slow and brooding. Joy steps up to him. He is unsure where to put his hands. He rests them just above her hips.

"I am sorry," he says.

Joy reaches out to Rupe, like she plans to wrap her arms around his neck the way one does when dancing closely with a partner. He is reminded of how he danced with his late wife, of the love they shared, and those final dances in their lounge room, her frame skeletal in his hands.

The memory evaporates as Joy spins and walks from the dance floor.

Rupe is flabbergasted. He chases after her, pushing through people and occasionally jumping so that he can peer over heads to make sure he's not losing her. He sees her entering the juncture and pursues. She heads into the Verdant Lounge.

He tails after her and is panting when he finally catches her at the bar. She gives no acknowledgment of his presence, instead surveying the room. An old man sits in a booth in one corner – he is dignified and proper in his charcoal suit, his bearing stiff, his face imbued with a mild disdain. His eyes catch Rupe. They remind Rupe of the day his wife passed: that bleak hopelessness as he seriously contemplated taking his own life so he could be with his wife – or, at the least, stop being without her.

Rupe pushes the memory out and shudders.

"Perhaps we can get a drink elsewhere," he says.

"When you have just caught me?" Joy asks.

"Have I?"

"Perhaps not," Joy says.

"So, you're still teasing me," he asks.

"Do you think I am?"

"I think this is all a show for my benefit."

"You think highly of yourself."

"I think highly of you."

"Would you chase me if I stopped?"

"If you stopped," Rupe says, "would I have caught you?"

"You're too good for this place … and for this time." Joy takes his hand and leads him to the bar. "Two Slammers!" she calls to the bartender, a well-muscled man who wears a name tag that identifies him as Promise; the buckles of his vest are bronze. "And an iced water for me."

"Slammers?" Rupe asks. He's never heard of such things, and curses that he's shown his ignorance.

"Have you never had a Tequila Slammer?"

"No."

"It's good to try something new."

"There are many things I would like to try."

Joy loosens his tie and undoes the top button of his shirt. "What else would you like to try?"

Rupe opens his mouth, certain he'll have something glib to offer, something charming, but there's nothing.

Joy laughs. "How long are you preparing to chase me?"

"Until you answer me definitively."

"Nothing is definite in life, Rupe. Surely you are a man who would understand that."

"But some things can be made certain."

Promise slides out the iced water first, then lays two shot glasses filled with tequila on the bar. Next, he hands each of them a slice of lemon. Rupe stares at his quizzically. Joy holds her hand out to Promise; he sprinkles a line of salt from the base of her thumb to the knuckle of her index finger.

"Hold out your hand," Joy says.

Rupe does so; Promise sprinkles a line of salt across the top.

"Now watch," Joy says.

Joy bites into the lemon, licks the salt off her hand, and downs the shot in one quick swill. She finishes by slamming her glass down with a flourish.

"Now you," she says.

Rupe is already grimacing in anticipation when he bites into the lemon. The salt defuses the sourness in his mouth while the tequila chases it into his stomach. He goes to slam his glass down on the bar but misses, over-extends, and has to pull himself up abruptly so he doesn't fall headfirst into the floor. Joy takes his wrist to steady his hand, guiding the glass to the bar.

"That wasn't so hard, was it?" she says, sipping from her iced water.

"A strange ritual."

"And you followed blindly."

"I followed you."

"And what if I misled you?"

"Would you?"

Joy's smile is enigmatic. If I was to indulge and play matchmaker, I would never pair these two. But I know it's not her beauty that enchants and entrances him, but her manner. All I can read from her is she is charmed by his innocence. His goal is neither to bed her nor conquer her, but to win her favor, as if she was some prestigious woman from an Elizabethan age who need first be courted with exquisite respect.

"What do you think?" she asks.

"Misleading me would hardly serve a purpose."

"Perhaps it would show me how true you are."

Rupe blinks as he tries to digest that. "Would it?"

"Everything may happen for a reason, but we don't always need a reason."

"Is that a warning?"

"A glimmer of wisdom." Joy gestures to Promise. "Set us up again." She looks at Rupe. "Then I think I might shoot some pool."

○   ○   ○   ○

A waitress brings LeBeau a drink. He beckons to her with one finger. She leans over the table so he can whisper in her ear. Flavia wonders what he's saying. Is he trying some pick-up line? Would a waitress satisfy LeBeau? They're hit on relentlessly through the course of a night, and despite how stunning they are, they're common – or at least Flavia deems them to be.

The waitress nods to LeBeau, and strides directly for Flavia. Flavia fears she has not only been caught, but that this is a violation of his privacy. Perhaps security will be summoned to escort her away, or even to throw her out. These are all irrational concerns, but Flavia has heard stories about LeBeau.

Just as she's about to retreat, the waitress reaches her.

"He wants to see you!" the waitress shouts above the music.

"Me?"

The waitress nods. "You know what you're doing?"

"No."

"Then he'll like you." The waitress smiles. "I'd walk away. But the choice is yours."

Her advice infuriates Flavia. Who is she to preach? She is *just* a waitress. Flavia knows she's being unkind – her aspirations not only buoy her, but they inflate her sense of purpose until everybody else is tiny beneath her.

She pushes past the waitress and approaches the booth.

LeBeau gestures that she should sit beside him.

Flavia's heart thumps. She slides into the booth but keeps her distance.

"So … do you …?"

Flavia misses half of LeBeau's question. The music's too loud. He gestures. Flavia remains where she is. LeBeau beckons once more. Flavia leans in, rather than moving closer.

LeBeau cups one hand around her ear. "I'm not going to spend the whole night talking like this," he says. "Move or go."

Flavia curses herself for moving too quickly. She does not disapprove of how she might appear eager to LeBeau, but of how willingly she gives herself. Dante pops up in her mind. Would he understand? No, not at all, because Dante is often jealous, and his jealousy is usually petty. He is as insecure as a man could be, and his attempts to master that see him become jittery, a scalded dog who is unsure how to please. Sometimes, Flavia worries that his smallness will restrict her, as if the limited way he sees the world will limit her, too.

LeBeau lifts one arm behind her, along the backrest of the booth. It's not an advance. Flavia tells herself that over and over. He's making himself more comfortable to address her.

"So, what do you want?" he asks, taking a sip of his drink. It's in a short glass, with a clear fluid and contains a slice of lime.

"My name's Flavia Rojas."

"What?"

"Flavia Rojas—"

"What do I care what your name is?"

"I …" Flavia doesn't know where to go with this.

"You've been watching me. Is this the best you got? Are you attracted to me, or do you recognize me?"

"I want to audition for you." Flavia blurts it out before she can lose the courage.

LeBeau snorts.

"As a host," Flavia hurries on. "For one of your shows."

"We're always on the lookout for good presenters."

Flavia smiles.

"What do you do?"

"What?"

"What's your background?"

"I'm a journalist."

"Locally?"

"Um …"

"Speak up."

Flavia braces the word in her mouth.

"Well? Locally?"

Flavia's lips draw thin.

LeBeau laughs. "Remotely, yes?"

Flavia nods.

"Do you present? Or write?"

Flavia opens her mouth but is unsure what to say, unsure what answer will serve her best.

LeBeau laughs again. "Let me guess," he says. "You cover minor local news. Weddings. Births. Deaths."

Flavia feels her face aflame. "I want something in front of the camera."

"Who wouldn't?"

Flavia nods vigorously, as if her enthusiasm is all the reference LeBeau needs.

"Have you got experience?"

"I also work in event management and have hosted—"

"That wasn't what I meant."

"No?"

LeBeau's hand lands on her thigh. It's huge and feels like it could almost close all the way around her leg. One finger slips under her dress. Flavia clamps her legs shut. LeBeau leans in closer. Flavia squirms. She can smell his hunger. It's not naïve or hopeful or even desperate, like other men who hit on her. This is something darker. Whether he has her or not is ultimately irrelevant to him. She is just another to be conquered. Then pillaged.

"This isn't something for nothing," he says.

Flavia starts to push back, but LeBeau's fingers hook into her leg.

"Forget the audition," he says, "I could *give* you a job."

Flavia freezes.

"You're pretty. I like your voice."

Flavia can't help smiling.

"But I'm sure you can guess the cost."

Flavia's smile fades. "The world doesn't work like this anymore," she says.

"The world will always work like this. A few martyrs only sweeten the rewards."

His hand relaxes. Flavia could slip away.

"Go," he tells her. "Run. Tell everybody what I said. Where do you think it'll get you?"

Flavia hates the powerlessness she experiences. But she *is* a nobody. This is Edan LeBeau. He must face a torrent of these accusations. And yet he is still Edan LeBeau. She will be dismissed as an opportunist.

"I've got a boyfriend," she says.

"Is he auditioning too?"

Flavia pushes free so she can flee the booth. LeBeau catches her wrist. She spins to face him.

"The thing with breaks is you don't know if you'll ever get another," he says.

He releases her wrist.

Flavia stays there a moment longer than she knows she should. But then she slides out from the booth and plunges into the crowd.

Holly sits on the closed toilet in a bathroom cubicle, her legs splayed, her hand slipping into her panties.

She is soaked.

Her breath splutters from her clenched lips; she grinds her teeth to stop the whine escaping her throat. She should find Marcus now. That would be the best option. Maybe he could smuggle her into the men's. Or perhaps they could go into the side alley outside. Or even grab a private room – well, if the private rooms exist. *Anywhere.* It would be a first. Something daring in a sex life that has become tempered.

But thinking of Marcus is reflex, the way a partner must – by rights of the relationship – think of their significant other in such a situation of arousal. The obligation lacks conviction. It's the dingy hotel room that occupies her thoughts, of being bent over the foot of the bed, her execs alternating in quick, ferocious sessions, the collision of their hips on her buttocks savage applause that exhilarated her.

Holly hisses as her body tenses, then trembles. Her chest heaves and she goes limp. Her heels squeal against the floor as her legs convulse. Her breath comes raggedly. She doesn't know how long it is before she regains her senses. Seconds, she'd like to think, but likelier a minute. She sits there, unbelieving not only of what she's done, but how she's responded.

Her panties are too wet and uncomfortable to continue wearing. She pulls them from her legs, uses them – then some toilet paper – to pat herself dry, and deposits her panties in her bag. For the rest of the night, she'll have to be careful to be going panty-less in such a small skirt. But there's also a thrill about it that makes her shiver. She does not know from where this sudden temerity has emerged. Or *why.* Perhaps it speaks of some unease – the typical glimmer of doubt everybody in a serious relationship encounters but dismisses in the name of love. But this feels darker.

She presses her palms to each side of the cubicle and hauls herself up to her feet. Her legs are shaky. She pulls down her skirt and flattens out the creases, takes a deep breath, and reaches for the cubicle door. She stops, flushes the toilet, then leaves the cubicle.

There are other women in the bathroom, fixing their make-up in the mirror and chatting gaily, as if they were talking over an afternoon coffee. Their faces are bright, sweat shining on their temples. Not one of them regard her with any curiosity.

"Hot in here," a lithe redhead notes to Holly as she takes a position at the mirror.

Holly nods, not trusting herself to speak, and washes up. She wants to be out of the bathroom. It's a crime scene now. Best she flees. But first she adjusts her make-up. The last thing she needs is for the others to notice how flustered she is – particularly Amber. It feels increasingly as if it might've been a mistake to disclose to her. Amber's perception of her may have been irrevocably damaged and, with it, her trust.

Leaving the bathroom, Holly wanders aimlessly until she finds herself in the juncture, right by the entrance and under the bronze plaque. The air is cool and refreshing here. She could stay here all night. People hurry past her. Everybody wants to be somewhere. They are all drawn to something, even when they don't understand it.

Holly leans against the wall and tilts her head up.

"Holly!"

It's Quinn, emerging from the restaurant. He always looks as if somebody has given him a fright, but now he is particularly stricken.

Holly's self-conscious of her appearance, although she knows it was fine when she checked it in the bathroom. She is also self-conscious of her skirt. She presses her hands flat against it, like a gust of wind might blow it up, even if it clings to her like a wrap. But Quinn's eyes flit back and forth. He is too distracted to notice anything.

"Can I talk to you?" Quinn asks.

"What's wrong?"

"Please?"

Quinn leads her to the Verdant Lounge, where they grab the table behind the Octagon. Holly orders Kronenbourg beers, gives Quinn space to talk, but when he doesn't fill it, begins to prod him. He says nothing until the drinks are delivered. Then he takes a gulp, finishing half the beer. Holly watches him, wide-eyed. Quinn is Amber's counterpart: *meek*. But there is something desperate about him now – desperate but simple. This is *all* he is now.

"About two weeks ago," he says finally, "Marcus, Dante and I went to a gambling house."

"A casino?" Holly frowns.

Quinn shakes his head.

"Was this an illegal place?"

Quinn nods. "It was …"

Holly can guess what he is about to say. "It was Marcus's idea, right?" she says.

"It doesn't matter," Quinn says. "We came off okay and it was just a stupid night out. You know Marcus? He likes to try everything once—"

"Cut to the short of it, Quinn," Holly says.

Quinn takes another swig of beer. "I won, so I went back. I won again, so I went back again. Then I lost. So, I went back to try and recoup—"

"How much?"

Quinn stares into his beer, his hands clamped around the bottle.

"Quinn, how much?"

"I lost everything, Holly. The down-payment on my house, the lease on my car, the deposit I was going to put on a ring – all of it! It's gone. Gone …"

"Go on."

"I convinced them to let me run a tab. Holly, I'm into them for nearly half a million dollars."

"What?" Holly is louder than she intends. People turn to her. She pulls her chair into the table, then leans across the table-top toward Quinn. "How do you lose so much money so quickly?"

Quinn snorts ruefully. "Trust me, there are ways."

"Amber's about to explode waiting for you to pop the question."

"I know. I know. That's when … that's when I heard about the guy."

Holly frowns as she takes her first sip of beer.

"This old guy …"

Quinn's eyes dart to the corner of the Lounge. Holly glances over her shoulder, and sees Mr. Hermes seated there, drinking from what looks to be a glass of water. He is nothing unusual in appearance – a small man that the years have bent, and one who probably spends his days on a park bench, feeding bread crumbs to pigeons. The smallest smile plays about his lips, and it alights in his mismatched eyes, one a mercury gray, and the other fiery blue.

Those different colored eyes may be nothing more than a curiosity for most, but for Holly they speak of a division. She shudders and sees now not a man who sits on park benches feeding birds, but one who surveys children playing on swings. This is not a real man. A shadow masks his true form. Holly has never experienced prescience before. But she knows that this man feels *wrong*.

"He sets people … *Temptations*, he calls them," Quinn says, his voice dropping. He finishes his beer, then stares down at the foam in the bottom of the bottle. "If they carry them out, he pays them a full million."

"That's an urban legend, isn't it?"

"It's for real. He's a billionaire."

"Quinn, who would seriously do something like—?"

"Mr. Hermes."

Holly frowns. The name is familiar.

"He's one of the co-founders of Hermes-LeBeau Inc."

It clicks now. Of course. It's the company Flavia mentioned earlier.

"Not that he's really in business anymore – well, as far as I know," Quinn says. "His nephew runs almost everything now. He's become like a silent partner or consultant or something. Except for this. He does this. I don't know why."

Holly can't guess but knows it's unimportant – she thinks of the hotel room and the two executives.

"I thought he was going to set me something to do," Quinn says. "I didn't care what it was. I was gonna do it. But it's not about me …" He casts his face down into his hand. "Holly, I've got guys gunning for me. If I don't pay them back …"

"What's the actual Temptation, Quinn?"

"It involves Amber."

Holly's eyes widen. "Why've you come to me?"

"Who else is there? Marcus will tell me to go for it. I'm sorry, but he will!"

Holly doesn't dispute that.

"Dante will panic. Flavia's off in her own little world. You're always … always … so in control."

Holly almost snorts with laughter.

"You're the only person I can talk to."

"Quinn, I don't know what I can do. Where's Amber?"

"I can't face her. I thought this guy was gonna be my solution. But now that it's turned out like this, I can't look her in the eye. I can't. I can't!" Quinn picks up his beer, but it's empty. He plants it on the table and clamps his hands around it.

Holly pats Quinn's wrist. "All right, Quinn. Let's try to work this out. Tell me what this guy wants you to make Amber do."

○ ○ ○ ○

Flavia stands in the juncture where Holly stood only a few minutes earlier, shivering, although Flavia's cheeks are flushed and sweat dries on her brow. She doesn't know why she's surprised. Of course this is the way the business may still work. Yet she expected that LeBeau would be so enamored with her, he'd give her a shot for no explicable or deserved reason. Men have always fallen over her. LeBeau didn't – at least not in the way she hoped. Amber is right. She's a dreamer.

Flavia heads through the nearest entry and is surrounded by red – it's the Cardinal Lounge, filled with people, their attention fixed on the pianist. He sways on his stool, face lifted to the ceiling, the top half of him dressed in a tux, his bottom half in jeans and pristine white loafers. His fingers ripple across his keys. Flavia doesn't recognize the melody, although she thinks it could be Mozart, but anything that sounds classical she automatically classifies as Mozart.

The bar beckons. Flavia takes a stool. The barmaid, Providence, is immediately opposite her. The buckles on Providence's vest reflect a dazzling prism of light – Flavia dismisses them as crystal, although they're actually diamonds.

"What can I get you?"

"Vodka & Orange," Flavia says. She takes a twenty out of her purse and slaps it on the bar.

"Vodka & Orange coming up."

Providence upends a shot of Absolut Vodka into a squat glass, while Flavia cups her hands on the bar. She had been convinced it was a sign to see LeBeau here. If it hadn't been, then what was it? A tease? The illusion of the future that she can never have?

"If you don't mind me saying," Providence says, pouring orange juice into the glass, "you have the look of a woman who doesn't know whether she wants to be alone or with friends."

"You can tell that?"

Providence slides the drink across the bar. "You can read people after a while."

Flavia downs her drink in one gulp and grimaces. She takes a chunk of ice into her mouth and sucks on it. Its coolness runs down her throat. She should find Dante and they should go. She keeps telling herself that. But maybe there is a reason: *that* is her future. Love, marriage, a family, and the pedestrian daily duties of working and running a household, always longing for something more – something greater. She is thankful when Providence pours ice into a new glass.

"Want to double up on the vodka?" Flavia says.

"Anything I can help you with?" Providence pours another shot into the glass.

"Bartenders really listen to problems? Isn't that cliché?"

Providence fills the glass with orange juice, slides it across the bar, but holds onto it as Flavia reaches for it.

"To be honest, I want to gauge how far I'm going to let you take this. People come here, they get lost easily. Then they go from bar to bar, like it's a pub crawl. You seem together enough. But – no offense, honey – there's a bad vibe about you right now."

"A bad vibe?" Flavia tries to snatch the glass free, but Providence holds onto it. "You a spiritualist or something?"

"I'm a bartender." Providence releases the glass.

Flavia takes a sip. "You married? Engaged? Attached?"

"I'm attached."

"So am I. We've been going out for nearly five years. We'll probably be engaged soon. He used to be …"

Flavia trails off, lost in her reflection in the mirror that forms the wall behind the bar. She is unsure how this has become about Dante, but a small part of her mind screams danger. They met at a club. They danced. They drank. They went back to his place and had drunken sex. It had seemed so free. But maybe it wasn't as free as it was simply drunken. That night had prejudiced how she viewed the relationship, and she fears that to examine it too closely now will exploit the cracks – and what they expose.

"What?" Providence asks with some cynicism. "Caring? Loving? Considerate?"

"Yeah. Now everything's so familiar." Flavia tries to gulp her drink, but it's too strong. She sips at it instead.

"It happens."

"I used to like this thing he'd do on my birthday – or the birthday night, to be more exact. He'd ask me what I wanted."

"He indulged you."

"Totally. Wholly. So, I started doing the same for him. On his last birthday, do you know what he wanted?"

Providence shakes her head.

"Nothing."

"Nothing?"

"Nothing."

Flavia scowls and now she does gulp her drink, then slams down the glass so hard what's left inside splashes across the bar. Providence casually grabs a sponge from a sink, wipes down the bar and the underside of the glass, and then puts the glass back down.

"He said he was tired," Flavia went on. "Then, in bed, we talked about sex, about where sex could go. He suggested watching me make love – no, *fucking* – another man. He tried to joke it off when he saw how shocked I was ..." She shakes her head and stares at Providence. "Do you know you're the first person I've ever told that story to?"

"Has he done something tonight to stir up these memories?"

"I've barely seen him. But I wonder sometimes about a man who'd throw out a suggestion like that."

"What about yourself"

"What about me?"

"Do you want to fuck another man?"

Flavia blushes. "N–n–no! Of course not!" she says, but the rebuttal is more reflex than conviction.

"Don't you have fantasies?"

"Do I?"

"You had that conversation with him. Surely you had something in mind."

"Of course." Flavia holds her breath. "I wanted to do it in a public place." She sighs. "Not *in* public, of course. But somewhere there was a risk of getting discovered."

"That turns you on?"

"There's something about it. And it's something you share together – the risk, the embarrassment, the excitement. But he wants to give me away. Do you think it's possible to fall out of ... well, not to fall out of love, but to fall out of *being sure* that you're in love? Or doubting the love you're feeling is *real?*"

"I wouldn't know. What I do recognize is a woman arguing a decision with herself and what it'll cost her."

"How far would you go for a job?"

"Getting a job here wasn't easy. Working my way up to the bar was more trying than I enjoyed. Sometimes, though, you have to let Prudence take you to where you want."

"Are you advising me?" Flavia finishes what remains of her drink, although it's barely a mouthful.

"I wouldn't do that. You find your own course."

"And if you don't? If you *can't?*"

"Trust your instincts," Providence says.

Flavia purses her lips and stares into the mirror.

III

The more that I watch her, the more unusual Joy becomes to me.

There is an endless stream of beautiful women who come here. If you could survey one hundred people and ask them to describe their fantasy partner, you would find them here – and then some. It is a menagerie and part of what makes being here so enticing, if not seductive – it's not just the elitism, but that pursuit of avarice and decadence. Most try to deny it. But some, they give in a little. Others give in wholly.

Joy is different. Yes, she is beautiful. Yes, she is sexual. And, yes, she is confident. But now that I have watched her, I can feel that she exalts herself above the others here – or perhaps she doesn't, and just *is* above the others here. The truth, I think, is that those who have no desire to come here are those who shall be exalted. Perhaps that's what I feel from Joy: that *dismissiveness*.

Striding from the Verdant Lounge, she enters the Gallery, her chin held high as she takes in the sights of couples dancing, drinking at either bar, or making out in darkened corners. Sometimes, she smirks, as if she understands their passions. Other times, she gives a little shake of her head.

Rupe keeps trailing her, like a puppy wanting a treat. He comes here trying to fill a void he has long nursed, but he's never deemed anybody worthy. It's not that he's decided Joy will be the one – he does not even understand her – but he *does* sense that she is set apart from every other woman he has encountered here, which speaks to something unique that he lost, and which he now covets, even if it's only in facsimile.

I'm not sure where Joy plans to head next, which is unusual, because after all this time I'm generally a good judge. Joy glances at Constance's office, and for an instant I think she might charge right through security and take the stairs. But then she saunters through the gaming rooms, finally entering Patricia's pool room.

Patricia, in only her corset and a tight little skirt, draws a raffle ticket from a hat. There's not a man in the room who can take his eyes from her. Some shift uncomfortably, their fantasies exuding from them like a fog that clouds their memories of partners, families, and homes. Their judgment is so easily distorted – embarrassingly so, but this is men, or at least most of the ones I've known.

"Green twelve," Patricia reads the ticket she's pulled out.

"That's me!" Marcus says, waving his ticket above his head.

The mood in this room has emboldened Dante. He claps Marcus on the shoulder. Dante is enjoying being part of a throng, even if they have no conscious awareness of his existence. But he is mindlessly accepted, and that's enough for him.

Marcus struts forward. He is charismatic and has become a leader in the room. Other men envy his easy charm, his cavalier manner, and his sun-bleached good looks. They wish they could be him, or like him, but for now are content to live vicariously through him.

Their cheers bounce off the walls, and they pat one another on the back, like they have been responsible for some great accomplishment.

Just like that, that hive mentality announces itself: a seemingly companionable mongrel that would sit docilely at your feet. But ticking away in some unexplored corner is the imminence of threat. This crowd exist in that niche, and while that might not be fine, it's *manageable* as long as they can be kept there.

"I'll play you," Joy says.

All eyes turn to her. Irritation flickers across Patricia's face.

"Have you got the right room?" Patricia says.

"You discriminating?"

"Just checking."

"Are you sure?" Marcus says.

Like me, he has sensed something, albeit on a much shallower level. Yet he has sensed it all the same, and it threatens him. He does not like that Joy is brazen and confident. It does not fit his ideals of what a woman should be – at least in this room, which, for Marcus, is how he sees the world.

"I'm where I need to be," Joy says.

She is a vortex that draws in each man and captures them. The cheers trail away. The silence becomes thick. Security are attuned to unusual shifts in this mood, and this *is* unusual – not the same-sex challenge. That goes on all the time. But the *weight* of the challenge. It is confrontational. Security charge into the archways to check that everything is okay.

"How about if I play her?" Joy proposes grandiosely to the room. "Strip for strip. Wouldn't you like to see that?"

The men murmur excitedly, some grinning stupidly at each other, as if they cannot believe what they might see, or as if they have engineered this themselves. Now they are not just adolescent, but simple – *stupid*. It easy to captivate such men. But that simplicity is also provocation because they understand so little else and see everything through an arbitrary filter that has no reason.

"Go for it," Marcus says, almost challengingly.

His endorsement breaks the stupor. The men roar.

"I shouldn't be doing this," Patricia says.

Joy pulls the balls from the pockets and fills them into the rack. "You have their undivided attention."

Patricia joins Joy at the table. "What's happening for these guys is a show," she says quietly. "I'm really good. You don't want to lose."

"I won't."

She doesn't.

Patricia sinks two balls from the break, then another two, before *just* missing her next shot – an attempted bank into the middle pocket. From there, she doesn't get another shot. Joy clears the table, then strips a stunned Patricia of her corset. Underneath, she wears a sheer, semi-transparent bra. In the next game, Joy breaks, then clears the table. She removes Patricia's skirt to the catcalls of those who watch, transfixed. The third game unfolds identically, leaving Joy to slowly unclasp Patricia's bra. The men shriek and clap but Joy leans in over Patricia's shoulder and whispers in her ear.

"This is demeaning," Joy says.

"You don't know what's at stake," Patricia says.

"I know everything," Joy says, and in that instant, I believe her – she knows every secret there is here, as well as every reason for *why* things happen. The chorus of appreciation loudens, but it is like white noise to Patricia as Joy continues. "What've you got to lose?" she asks, tapping the heart locket that Patricia wears. "That is if you haven't lost it already."

Joy undoes the remaining clasp on Patricia's bra and pulls it clear. Men jump and whoop, insubordinate and juvenile. All reason is gone now. A spotlight has hit that niche. The companionable mongrel rumbles. This is when they are at their most reckless.

And dangerous.

Joy heads for the door, holding Patricia's gaze while letting her bra fall to the floor.

"I think that's about it for me," she says. "You fellas can do the rest." She looks sidelong at Rupe. "Still interested in the chase?"

"More than ever," Rupe says, following her out.

$$\circ \quad \circ \quad \circ \quad \circ$$

Quinn and Holly sit shoulder to shoulder: Quinn is like a dog that has been brought to the vet, tense and eager to be gone; Holly has drawn herself upright, wanting to look down upon and command the situation. Quinn marvels at how she can be unafraid given he thinks what they're trying is crazy.

But he says nothing.

And tries to give away nothing.

Holly puts a hand on his. He flinches briefly, but then curls his arm around her back. She nestles into him with familiarity that comes with surprising ease, but which embarrasses him. He could never be like this with anybody but Amber. Just doing this feels like cheating.

Mr. Hermes is inscrutable as he surveys them each in turn, although he holds Quinn's gaze much longer than he holds Holly's. It's cliché when somebody is described as looking *inside* another person, but that's what Quinn experiences.

His memories flash through his head, a chronology of his life, meeting Amber, the first tentative kiss, the first time they had sex (shy, fumbling, and in the dark, Amber had to coax him to erection because he was so self-conscious), falling in love, and the dreams they had of forging a life together.

But now, something infects the warmth and purity of those memories – the world most don't consider, where dreams are shattered and the ugliness of life creeps in: the misery of missteps and misdeeds; the randomness of injury, illness, and ill fortune; and the obliteration of the best of intentions.

Quinn forces himself to stare back unblinkingly. To look away would be an admission of guilt. But Mr. Hermes has him now – has all of him. It was stupid to come to him, and worse to draw Holly in. Holly won't recognize the danger. Like Marcus, she will welcome it, confront it, and try to brave through it.

But there is no braving through some things.

A small smile plays at Mr. Hermes's lips.

"So, we were wondering," Holly says, "whether you could come up with a different Temptation."

The waitress, Prelude, brings them drinks – the lemon with three blocks of ice in the clear liquid for Mr. Hermes (Quinn is now beginning to suspect that the clear liquid is nothing but water), the Corona with the lime for Quinn, and a Tequila Sunrise for Holly.

Quinn's concern grows. They hadn't ordered.

"How about if I came to you instead and that way, you lay the Temptation on Quinn and pay me out?" Holly asks once Prelude leaves.

Mr. Hermes picks up his glass and swirls it so that the blocks of ice clink. "Amber, is it?" he asks.

Holly nods. She stirs her Tequila Sunrise with the straw so that it becomes a muddy pink.

"The Temptations are there to take or leave," Mr. Hermes says. "They are not a negotiation. Secondly," he turns sharply to Quinn, "I warned you not to lie to me."

Quinn wants to confess to salvage the situation, but the humiliation engulfs him. He stamps down on the fear and tries to feign indignation. Nothing but a croak comes out.

"Lie?" he asks finally.

"I fell in love with your description of your fiancée," Mr. Hermes says. "I fell in love with her sweetness and innocence

– oh, I know, that is such a cliché, and it makes me seem such a dirty and corrupt old man. But there is not enough innocence in this world, and particularly in here." He takes a drink. "This is not your fiancée." He uses his glass to gesture at Holly. "Although there *is* something enchanting about you. Something brazen. Those wide, open eyes; that husky voice; your full, pouting lips. What have you been doing with that voice, those lips?"

For an instant – but an instant is long enough – Holly is taken aback. Her hands tighten around Quinn's. He's sure she's going to bluster her way through this, although it wouldn't do them much good. But her pause allows Mr. Hermes to sweep on.

"Perhaps you'd care to make some money yourself," he says, "and give Quinn what he needs."

Holly wrests her hands from Quinn's and takes her Tequila Sunrise. Her instinct is to fight this out, but Mr. Hermes is not meant to be fought. Not like this. This fight is fixed.

"Well?" he prompts. "Or would you like to continue with the façade?"

Holly drinks from her Tequila Sunrise.

Mr. Hermes's smile is all gloat – Quinn used to see that smile on the basketball court when the opposition had an unassailable lead. The rest of the game was just a means to an end.

"Fine," Holly says. "Let's hear it."

Now Quinn finds not only his bravado, but an iota of selflessness. He has damned himself, but he can save Holly – not only *can* he, but he *must.*

"Don't do this," he says.

"No, it's okay," Holly says.

"Please—"

"I'm in charge of the situation." Holly has not deviated her attention from Mr. Hermes. "Like he said, it's mine to take or leave."

"Yes, it is," Mr. Hermes says. "Leave us, Quinn."

"No—"

"It's okay." Holly pats his hand.

"Are you sure?"

Holly nods.

Quinn plants his hands on the tabletop – his fingers claw into the surface. This is a mistake. This has all been a mistake. But it has the irresistible beauty of a tragedy – the roadside accident that commuters slow to watch, which they'll pity briefly, but make small talk about later.

"It's okay," Holly says again.

Quinn slides out of the booth

"Quinn!" Mr. Hermes says.

Quinn turns nervously.

"Your Temptation remains open – it's yours to take or leave. That's *your* decision to make. That's the reason for Prudence. Haven't you learned that by now?"

Quinn feels bound to the spot, netted by his own stupidity. He would flee now if it weren't for Amber. He must make it right for her. He must make *all* this right. But still, he doesn't know *how*.

"Now go," Mr. Hermes says.

As Quinn leaves, the last thing he hears Mr. Hermes say is, "Now tell me about yourself … Holly."

Prince slides two Gallia Lagers across the bar.

Bodie and Ox are synchronized as they take them, swivel around, and drink. They could be a pair of street mimes who have rehearsed the routine, although as comical as it is to see, as light-hearted as they can be, there remains that underlying sense of … well, what is it exactly about them? I'm unsure, although I have known them and watched them since they first appeared.

The crowd parts slowly to reveal Constance, beautiful and breathtaking. She pauses before them, security keeping a tight perimeter around her. Bodie and Ox lift their Gallia Lagers in salute. Ox slides across to the next stool; Constance sits on the stool he's just vacated. Very few people can show such familiarity with Constance. Bodie and Ox come across like mischievous little brothers whom Constance indulges.

"You know," Bodie says, "I'm not sure if our stock goes up or down when you sit with us."

"You've got a point there, Bodie," Ox says. "Women pass, they look at us – you know, it's not like we're ugly or anything. But then they see you."

Constance listens patiently.

"Then when they see you," Bodie continues, "they must think if she's stopping to sit with these two guys, what hope have they got?"

"Or maybe they think you have a claim on us," Ox says.

Prince appears behind the bar and offers Constance a Manhattan. She takes it without turning.

"Thank you, Prince," she says.

"These two spieling?" he asks.

"As always. But there's a sense to their inanity if you know how to listen."

The eyes of those around them linger on Constance. It's not just her beauty that appeals, preserved as she is, but her stature. Many do mistake her for an Icon, just a face with some minor marquee that is meant to impress on some superficial level. But closer, you can feel her authority, sense the gravitas behind her, and appreciate her presence. She is elevated in a way that many defer to her, and those who don't, or who are outright impudent, learn the error of their ways.

One tall man at the bar has a vantage point directly into her cleavage. Bodie waves the man away. The tall man scowls and it seems he might take issue. Bodie glowers at him and the man stops. He takes in Bodie, then the ubiquitous security, and murmurs a hurried apology to Bodie. Bodie points at Constance. The tall man is momentarily confused, but then it dawns on him: he apologizes to her. She nods her head, accepting his contrition. He returns his attention to ordering his drink.

"You'd prefer I didn't stop by and have a drink with you then?" Constance asks.

"No! No!" Bodie says

He lifts his Gallia. Ox toasts it, holding his own Gallia there. Constance toasts them with her Manhattan.

"You're welcome any time," Bodie says. "Just like you welcome us every time."

"Whenever you want," Ox says.

Constance laughs. "You are my favorites – always have been," she says. "There's no pretense about you. You are who you are. That's why I love you so much. In another time, another place, I could learn to fall in love with either of you."

"Again?" Ox says, and it is unclear to me if he is joking or not.

Constance tinkles with laughter, her fingers dancing on his chest.

"You still could," Bodie says.

"Prudence won't allow it and I have so little life of my own," Constance says. "An unfortunate reality."

"When you first started getting us in here …" Ox says, but then he trails off and nods at Bodie. "When was that?"

"Seventeen … eighteen years ago?" Bodie says. "Maybe more."

"I think it was more."

"Time loses meaning in here."

"I think it was twenty."

"Or more."

"Well, whenever!" Ox says. "I remember you had a couple of relationships. It's only now that I think about it, that you stopped."

"That was before I became every bit the institution that Prudence is," Constance says. "When I still thought I could have a relationship in my life. Now, without intending to be immodest, I'm wanted because of my celebrity. Do you know how people want to come to Prudence just to be able to say they were here? That's why I'm desired."

"Nonsense," Ox says. "You're desired because you're just so damned magnificent."

"That's kind of you to say, Ox." Constance pats him on the thigh. "But do we ever know another's true intentions? Or do we just accept what they tell us at face value? I've been here a long time. I've learned to read people. I've been hurt. Some have tried to use me. I've grown smarter. That's part of the reason I have you here."

"So, when's the last time you had a proper relationship—?"

"Twenty-five years ago."

"That was quick," Bodie says.

"I was in a long-term relationship the night Prudence was offered to me. We'd come to party – young, foolish, drunk, and stoned. The previous hostess had been given her notice. The Camarilla who owns the establishment recognized me. They thought I was an ideal replacement, given my celebrity, and offered me the position – if I could clean myself up and consented to training. I accepted. That was the end of my relationship. When I first began to work, there just wasn't time."

Teo strides through the crowd. "Constance," he says, "we've got a problem that needs your attention."

Constance finishes her Manhattan, puts it on the bar, and slides from the stool. She holds out her arms expansively. "My life partner," she says. Then she kisses them each on the cheek. "Be good."

"Are we ever anything but?" Ox says.

Constance laughs, pats each fondly on the knee, then allows Teo to lead her back into the sea of people. No sooner is she gone than Joy emerges from the crowd – Rupe still trailing behind her – and seizes Ox's hand.

"Dance with me," Joy says, tugging Ox from his stool.

"Me?"

"You."

Joy drags Ox from the stool – Ox hurriedly handing his Gallia to Bodie – and leads him to the dance floor, leaving Rupe to stare after her forlornly.

"You look like a man in love," Bodie says.

"I'm in something," Rupe says. "Mind if I take this stool?"

"Go for it," Bodie says.

Rupe sits on the stool, swivels, and finds Joy on the dance floor.

○　○　○　○

Constance's intake of breath is a sharp hiss.

She and Teo stand before the array of screens in her office, their attention fixed on the screen displaying Gaming Room 7: Patricia – in nothing but her tiny G-string – sinks ball after ball. The guys in the room groan. Patricia pockets the black ball. There is no fuss about her victory. Some of the guys quit the room – there's only half as many as were in there when Joy played Patricia. Unceremoniously, Patricia draws another ticket from her hat and calls out the number. No response. Whoever owned the raffle ticket is long gone. As is the bearer of the next ticket. Third time lucky, she draws somebody.

"She keeps winning," Teo says. "And she's good enough not to lose to any of the buffoons in there with her."

"They're meant to win a few when they get to the end," Constance says.

"Savage's doing it in his room and making a show of it. Patricia's bullying these guys. Humiliating them."

"As much fun as that sounds, it's not what she should be doing. She's always been a model employee. What triggered this behavior?"

"I don't know."

"Rewind the recording," Constance says. "Let's see if one of these fools somehow sparked this indignation."

"She's been trained to play the game – they all have."

"Everybody has a breaking point. We know that well enough."

Teo takes the chair at Constance's desk, activating her laptop out of standby. He accesses the surveillance logs.

"Out of curiosity," Constance says, "how's Nico doing?"

Teo looks up from the laptop. "He won't last the night," he says.

"I didn't think so," Constance says. "But perhaps that's a good thing."

Teo frowns.

"What?" Constance asks.

"Temperance? From *you*?"

Constance frowns, the observation as much a surprise to her as it was to Teo.

"We all change as we get older," she says. "Don't we?"

Ox has never been a dancer. *Never.* In all the time he and Bodie have come here, they've adhered to an uncompromising routine: they're the first ones in, they sit at the bar, they chat, they ogle, they drink, they're the last to leave. They have been propositioned

– after all, they're two good-looking guys. But nobody, no matter how stunning the individual, has ever tempted them.

But now Ox is in the center of the dance floor – this behemoth who towers over the other dancers by a head, whose girth dwarfs everybody around him. His dancing is clumsy and leaden. The only thing that shows life is his overcoat, which swirls around him. His sunglasses almost fall from his face.

Joy dances nimbly around him, like she is teasing him – baiting him – to action. She grinds her crotch against his hip. Ox falls back a step; he has no idea what he's doing, or how to handle Joy's explosiveness. Joy thrusts her hips at him. Ox falls into synchronicity with her energy. He has not her grace – not even an iota of it – but he does his best to match her enthusiasm. She seems amused, if not dismissive, of his efforts.

When the song has ended Joy bounces back toward the bar and grabs Bodie by the wrists. Ox follows behind her. Rivulets of sweat stream into his thick, unruly beard. His chest heaves.

"Your turn, handsome," Joy tells Bodie.

"I can't dance," Bodie says.

"It didn't stop your friend."

She tugs Bodie from his stool. Ox takes their Gallia Lagers from Bodie, then Bodie is gone, swallowed into the hive which is the dance floor.

Ox sinks onto two stools, as is his wont. He drinks, then holds the bottle to his neck as he glances at Rupe. Rupe watches Joy, transfixed, as she dances with Bodie. Bodie rocks from his toes to heels. It's as close to rhythm on the dance floor as he can manage.

"She's out of control," Ox says.

"She's a force unto herself," Rupe says.

"Ain't you jealous?"

"Insanely!"

Prince arrives with another Gallia just as Ox finishes his bottle. He swaps with Prince, empty Gallia for a full one.

"Thanks, Prince," Ox says. Then, back to Rupe, "How can you just sit there? She's gorgeous, she's hot, she's happening. Make a move."

Prince grins wryly. "Careful. This is the blind leading you."

"Come on, Prince! I've been around. I'm not that bad."

"You're probably worse." Prince moves off to serve another patron.

"How about it?" Ox asks.

"When the time's right," Rupe says, "I'll make my move."

"And when will that be?"

"A woman like Joy you can't just solicit, as if she was just some unthinking floozy," Rupe says. "She is classy. Sophisticated."

Ox frowns.

"She must be courted, honored, and then, and only then, must she be approached – when I have done everything to deem myself worthy in her eyes."

"You're crazy."

"Perhaps. But love is crazy."

"You're in love already? Like, at first sight?"

"At first glance – sometimes, a glance is all it takes."

"I think maybe you need to rethink this," Ox says. "Won't be me or my friend, but she just may pick a dance with the wrong guy and then, well, you'll see if the time's right."

O   O   O   O

LeBeau gets up from his booth and ambles across to the dance floor. The crowd has tightened around Joy and claps in tempo with the music. Her dancing is primal. Some people in the world lead. Others inspire. Some do both. That is Joy. Everybody has fallen in rhythm with her, as if this was some complicated dance number choreographed for a pop diva. Bodie is almost abashed, continuing to rock on his feet. It's not that he hasn't a clue what to do on the dance floor. He hasn't a clue what to do with her. Or himself.

But LeBeau has ideas. He always has ideas. He would've liked to take some time with Flavia. He'd smelled her vulnerability. It aroused him to the point that he now needs a release. He could have just about anybody here – just as he has done so repeatedly in the past. But that's too easy. He needs a challenge. This brunette is as elevated as she is sultry and commanding, a woman needing to be broken. He would like to break her and bend her to his whim.

LeBeau walks out onto the dance floor. People melt from his path. The overcoated fool she's dancing with doesn't flinch as LeBeau glowers at him. LeBeau has seen him and his friend here regularly, and always believed them to be stoners, if not artists – the sort of lowbrow riffraff Constance would think would add some romanticism.

But now, with Bodie holding his gaze, LeBeau realizes he might've overstepped. This guy isn't a typical fop. LeBeau can see it in the set of his shoulders, in the way he holds his arms, in the way he measures LeBeau. This man is a hunter. LeBeau has retained people like this for odd jobs. The wise thing would be to withdraw, but wisdom isn't something LeBeau always practices – especially when the possibility of sex is involved.

"Mind if I cut in?" he says.

He would've told anybody else he was cutting in – non-negotiable. But now, he presents an offer, as small as it is, an opportunity for this goof who can't dance, who looks like he's not enjoying himself out here, to escape with his dignity intact. Well, that's the way LeBeau reads it. And he can see Bodie knows LeBeau wants him to read it that way. But Bodie snorts. It infuriates LeBeau. There's no moral superiority here. When

Bodie steps back, it's as if he does so with the intent that LeBeau fail.

"Be my guest," Bodie says, and heads back for the bar.

LeBeau doesn't care, though. Or he tries not to, instead searching for his equilibrium as he loses himself in his desires. Joy is magnificent. She throws her arms around his neck and sways in front of him. She gyrates down to his knees, so that LeBeau looks down on the top of her head and thinks this is exactly the angle he wants to see her in. Then she uncoils to her full height.

"That was rude," Joy says.

LeBeau falls into beat with her tempo. He's majestic on the dance floor. One thing he learned when he was young is there's no better pick-up than good dancing. His hands move down Joy's sides – his left hand sliding under Joy's satchel – and cups her buttocks. She doesn't tense, as some women do, unsure how to handle such a sudden solicitation. It tells him she's accustomed to this – well, that's how he interprets it.

"He didn't deserve you," he says.

"You do?"

"Know about the private rooms here?"

"You got something in mind?"

"IIow simple do you want mc to put it?"

"Real simple for a real simple girl."

"Let's fuck."

Joy grins and runs a finger down LeBeau's sweaty chest. He usually doesn't perspire – at least not severely. But he's soaking now. She's pristine, and he has an urge to sully that. He wants to see Joy bracing a headboard as he bangs her from behind, her butt fitted in his hands just like he's holding it now. His hands fumble like a teenager having an awkward grope. He meant to impose his will upon her, but something is happening; he feels like he's whirlpooling down around her until he's losing himself to insecurity and uncertainty that he hasn't felt since he was an overweight teen.

"So, what do you say?" he asks, a desperate, wheedling quality entering his tone.

Joy presses up against him and stands on her toes until they're face to face. She's hot. Literally. LeBeau's never felt a woman physically as hot. She must have a fever or be on Ecstasy or X'cess or one of those designer drugs that comes with weird physical side-effects. Not that it matters – all the better.

LeBeau leans in, the way a lover does to suggest a kiss. She's unmoving. He thought earlier she was accustomed to such solicitations, but now a new possibility opens up to LeBeau: she's fearless.

"I'm not that simple," Joy says.

"Want to start?"

"You know, sex is going to get you into trouble."

"Hasn't yet …"

LeBeau frowns, as if he's now truly seeing Joy – seeing something to which I'm not privy.

"I know you, don't I?"

Joy tinkles with laughter. "Well, that's original."

One of the reasons LeBeau has succeeded in business is his eidetic memory. He remembers everything vividly – that includes the women and men he has seduced, and how he took them. Joy is not in that catalogue, but she beams with a similar familiarity – a sexual conquest, only she is not the conquest. He feels in this situation he would be.

"I don't think you're on my level quite yet," Joy says.

He opens his mouth because any other time he'd have a rejoinder, but nothing emerges. He doesn't like this powerlessness. It feels like when the Camarilla questioned him exhaustively, prodding him incisively at times, toying with him at others as they measured whether he was worthy to succeed his father. He'd passed – *just*, he feels, as the Camarilla did not offer him a seat at their table. He has never before or since felt so impotent.

Well, until now.

Joy lays a single finger across his lips. She leans closer toward him. LeBeau latches one hand into the arch of her back, his other moving up to her face. This is something he knows, and he tries for one last desperate gambit.

He moves to kiss her.

She pirouettes on her heel and breaks through the crowd.

"Hey!" LeBeau says, stumbling forward now that's she's no longer there to brace him.

Joy keeps walking.

"Hey!"

She disappears into the crowd.

○ ○ ○ ○

Bodie leans on the bar and wipes the sweat from his brow with the cuff of his sleeve.

"Was that the best you could do?" Ox says.

"You know that saying 'I'm a lover not a fighter'?" Bodie asks.

"Yeah."

"I'm a sitter – well, most of the time, anyway."

Prince appears and hands Bodie a Gallia. Bodie takes a gulp and turns just in time to see Joy leave a flabbergasted LeBeau in the middle of the dance floor. LeBeau frowns – he is a man struggling to process something he's never had to deal with: *rebuke.* Bodie can't help smiling. Couldn't happen to anybody better. Maybe it'll teach LeBeau some humility, although Bodie doubts it.

"I was telling you sooner or later she'd meet the wrong guy," Ox says to Rupe. "I thought it'd be him."

"She's better than that," Rupe says, jumping up from the stool. "Excuse me."

He flees across the dance floor, allowing Bodie to resume his vacant stool.

"What's his story?" Bodie asks.

Ox shrugs and takes a drink from his Gallia.

○   ○   ○   ○

Flavia stumbles from the Cardinal Lounge, pinballing between people. She murmurs her apologies the first few times, but then shoves her way through. It's gotten busy but the people are faceless to her. She feels like one of them: part of a mass with no distinguishing features. *Ordinary.* She has never felt ordinary in her life, but now that possibility frightens her.

She enters the juncture, coming to stand under the bronze plaque. The cool breeze wafts through the entrance and, for a moment, she allows it to reinvigorate her, to rouse her from her melancholy. Then she presses on, breaks through two guys, and bumps into Quinn. His eyes widen at the sight of her. She's startled at his surprise. Then just at seeing him. But the familiar face grounds her. Maybe she is looking for success in the wrong places. As much as the world refuses to believe it now, life can be purely about personal betterment, rather than material achievement. Flavia grasps the potential of that as a concept and finds it repugnant.

"Quinn!" she says, but that's as far as she gets.

There's another rush of people. But they're not hurrying to go anywhere – they're moving for security, led by Teo, who takes long, urgent strides. They head into the Brimstone Lounge. The crowd thins again.

"Flavia!" Quinn says. "Where's Amber?"

"I don't know. Where's Dante?"

Quinn isn't sure how to answer. After they'd split from the girls, Marcus had brought them to one of the gaming rooms where a brunette was playing strip pool. Quinn quickly excused himself to see Mr. Hermes. It's likely Marcus and Dante are still in that gaming room, but should he really be bringing Flavia to see that? To see them ogling a stripper? Amber would be aghast. Flavia's much more liberal but …

"Quinn?" Flavia says.

"I … well, I left them a while ago … and … and …"

Flavia sees through his pretense. "You know where they are," she says. "Take me there."

There is something imperious about her. Quinn can see why she always gets her way with Dante.

"*Now.*"

Quinn nods. "Follow me."

O   O   O   O

Most agree that the décor in the Brimstone Lounge is hideous, comprising an array of ghastly mustard finishes that're unsettling on the eye. It's the least visited of the piano bars, and those who come do so just to say that they've been in it, and that they can't believe it's the color it is.

As with the other Lounges, candelabras supply what dim light there is. Shadows flicker across the Lounge and threaten to darken into something black and sepulchral, although the truth may be that even shadows do not want to abide here.

The pianist plays exquisitely – one of Beethoven's sonatas – and the small audience is transfixed. For Rupe, who follows Joy in, the people appear mesmerized, but Joy is indifferent as she takes a position at the bar and orders herself an iced water.

She plucks a cube out of the glass and suckles it between her lips as she closes her eyes. Rupe watches her, uncertain why he's holding his breath. Then he realizes: it's because she is. She purses her lips, extracts the cube, and deposits it back in her glass.

"You should stop following me," Joy says, rattling her glass and staring down at the sparkling ice cubes.

"I will if that's what you want."

"I would've imagined that my behavior would've discouraged you."

"Perhaps that is why you are behaving this way."

There is sadness in Joy's face as she caresses Rupe's cheek. "You have an innocence about you," she says. "But you are in lust with an illusion."

"Anything but."

"Then you don't think I'm an illusion?"

"I'm not in lust," Rupe says.

Teo and his security team enter. Nobody else regards their entrance, instead staying fixed on the pianist. His head rocks and his body sways as his fingers race across the keys.

"Constance would like the pleasure of your company in her office," he says.

"About?" Joy asks.

"You may discuss that with her."

Joy finishes her water, sets the glass down, and pushes off from the bar. Rupe moves to follow. Teo holds out one hand. The security team hulk threateningly, a posse just waiting for their opportunity. In an instant, Rupe projects an unfortunate chain of events – beaten by security, dragged from the Lounge, and tossed into the street.

"*Only* the lady," Teo says.

"Goodbye, sweet Rupe," Joy says, touching his cheek once more. She follows Teo from the Lounge. Security close around her.

Rupe sits back on a stool.

O   O   O   O

Despite the momentary diversion, Bodie and Ox now sit as they always have – butts on stools, backs against the bar, elbows cocked onto on the bar top.

The music changes. Bodie's unsure what it is – and always has been. For as long as he's been here, the music has been white noise to him, one song blending tunelessly into the next. The only thing he recognizes are changes in tempo, and what's come on now is something slow and moody – something that would be played for lovers. Ox is little better, his knowledge of music encapsulating the 1980s and only that decade. Everything else is irrelevant. But he tilts his head at the new melody – a ballad. He thinks it's awful and decides that if any couples think it's worthy of dancing to then they're not in love but stupid about each other, although it might amount to the same thing.

"I'll tell you one thing," Bodie says.

"What's that?"

"Every night has its epoch."

"Indeed it does."

Prince shows up behind them with two Gallia Lagers. "How is it you two don't get drunk?" he asks.

Bodie takes the Gallia. "We're beer nymphs."

"Deities of beer and drinking," Ox says, grabbing his Gallia.

"We drink among you mortals as an entertainment."

"A pleasure."

Their manner is grandiose. They have always been so, but there are times Prince is sure he catches a glimpse of something else, something *serious* that they work hard to mask with their constant banter and irreverence. Prince is sure they have a greater purpose in life than to be barflies, and what he's seeing here is just a conceit.

Bodie and Ox toast the necks of their bottle.

"To beer goddery," Bodie says.

"Is that even a word?" Ox says.

"It is now."

They drink and return to surveying the crowd.

It's always dangerous when events shape the mood of a crowd. Earlier – and as has been the case almost every night Patricia has been an Icon – the general mood was lustful but good-natured. There are some nights it can get ugly, when the wrong element instigates a mindset that is dangerous. Tonight, though – thanks solely to Patricia – the crowd is desperate and humiliated.

Patricia sinks the black. It's her twelfth straight win. She pumps her fist theatrically. Her opponent, Dante, glowers at Marcus. It's one thing to be beaten by an opponent who'd earlier been considered inferior, but it's another to be beaten by somebody who is *meant* to lose.

Dante, whose self-esteem has always been shaky, if not fragile, feels an all-too-familiar humiliation that is temporarily incapacitating, before erupting into indignation. This is a fix that's gone wrong. That's all there is to it. Patricia has beaten others, so it's not just about him. He clings to the image of Flavia – a beautiful, talented woman, and she's with him. She wouldn't be with a loser.

"Guys," Patricia says, "I'm taking a fifteen-minute breather."

She wants to slip away so she can take an X'Cess pill. It's a casual but necessary addiction she has developed, or at least that's what she tells herself. X'Cess breathes life into her and allows her to *feel* – a necessity when everything else has become so mundane and rote. The only problem is that the effects are short lived.

"You can't do this!" Dante says.

Timing is vital in life. Most never find that synchronicity where events coincide with opportunity. It's usually blind fluke when it occurs. Just as it is now when Quinn and Flavia appear in the archway.

Flavia gasps when she sees Dante take hold of Patricia by the wrist.

"You're … you're unbeatable!" he says. "You …"

Patricia has endured her share of violent and controlling men. This one is bluster. He wants to intimidate her, but he is faltering. She has seen this before, too: he is enamored with her. His eyes soften and his grip on her loosens. She almost feels sorry for how pathetic he is.

"I'm sorry—" he begins.

As novel as an apology is, Patricia doesn't need it. She spin, breaks free, and starts for the opposing archway. A group of men block her path. She puts her hands on her hips, as if challenging them. It's a brave move. And foolish. Sometimes, all it takes to beat a bully is to stand up to them, but a pack? That's a different matter. Fortunately, on this occasion it works. They have been exposed as cowards and part to let her through.

But Marcus waits behind them. He is not a coward, and unlike Dante, he doesn't need to feel part of a pack. He has always been a leader. The pack follow him, and if they do not understand what needs to be done, he will show them.

"Now where do you think you're going?" he asks.

"Get out of my way."

"Why don't you make me?"

Patricia tries to sidestep to the right; Marcus blocks her. She tries to sidestep to the left; Marcus blocks her. He enjoys the power, and, unlike the others, he genuinely has a streak of cruelty that comes from his upbringing – his father was a drunk, abusive, adulterer. Marcus often tells himself he is not his father, but on occasions like this behaves just like him.

"Out of my way," Patricia tells him.

Marcus takes a step up to her, leering at her bulbous breasts almost touching his chest.

"Come on, babe," Marcus says. He runs a finger up her arm, over her shoulder, and caresses her cheek. "Let's play nice, huh?"

"Marcus, come on," Dante says, recognizing this is going somewhere he's not prepared to follow. "Enough's enough."

"I'll tell you when enough's enough," Marcus says.

"Let her go."

"Stop being such a girl, Dante."

Flavia stomps into the room and grabs Dante by his sleeve. He spins and, briefly, he pulls his fist back, preparing to fight. Truth be told, he's anticipated security will accost him, and he's stayed his counterattack not because he's seen it's Flavia, but because it'd be foolish to tackle security.

"Dante!" she says.

Her cry distracts Marcus long enough that Patricia breaks past him. He pirouettes to catch her, but too late. "Fuck!" he says, although he feels the smallest relief worm its way into his head. In the aftermath of such encounters, he recognizes he is his father's son, and the shame washes over him. But another part of his mind – where the dissonance pulses and threatens to blossom and consume him – dismisses the pangs of conscience and encourages him to embrace that feeling of power such behavior grants him.

Flavia's attention, though, is focused only on Dante. "What the hell do you think you're doing?" she asks.

"Having fun," Dante says. "Lighten up." He grabs her by the waist, pulls her close to him, and runs his hands down to her butt. "How about we have some fun?"

He would never usually be so bold, but he's been drinking, and the events of the night have fueled him not so much with bravado, but stupidity. On a good day, Dante is not an overly intelligent or emotionally aware man, so such episodes push him into a territory where he can become hurtful and inconsiderate.

Flavia shoves him in the chest, twirls, and tries to get out of there. Dante snatches her back by the wrist so hard that Flavia yelps.

"Dante!"

"Take it easy, bud!"

It's a young guy with a crew-cut and the bearing of somebody fresh from the military. He's just stepped into the room and assessed the situation – the disorder – immediately. His shoulders are huge, and his calm is disconcerting. This man has seen action. He is a man who should be heeded. But Dante feels he has no business here.

"This is *my* girl, *bud*," Dante tells him.

"She don't belong to you."

Dante shoves him in the chest; Crew-cut stumbles back a step. He cocks his arm to prepare for a punch. Then Marcus is there. He catches the punch mid-swing, spins Crew-cut around, and throws a punch of his own. Crew-cut staggers back – but only for an instant. He has been trained to absorb punishment, process pain, and respond instinctively. He grabs Marcus by the collar. Dante releases Flavia and jumps on Crew-cut's back.

Flavia decides it's time to leave the men to their idiocy.

O   O   O   O

Flavia angrily storms past Quinn.

Quinn is torn with indecision. He should make sure Flavia is okay, but now a scuffle has broken out and his friends are involved. Marcus fights with that abandon and grace he brings to all things, while Dante is a scrapper – he gets hit but bounces back and is tussling with anybody he can grab hold of. Crew-cut is a beast now, enraged, and righteous, some of his own friends trying to restrain him before he unwittingly kills somebody.

The melee swells in front of Quinn and pushes him toward the archway. He decides to hell with it and ducks out, catching a glimpse of Flavia just before she disappears into the crowd. He pursues, although he doesn't know what he'll say to mollify her. In the little time he has known Flavia, he has found she is headstrong and tempestuous.

He passes through several gaming rooms, and stops, confused. The gaming rooms have multiple archways. Who knows which Flavia has chosen? Now he has assorted options and has to explore each tentatively, then backtrack. He overthinks it and becomes lost – or, at the very least, loses Flavia.

Her course has been simple: *straight.* She has ploughed through gaming room after gaming room, oblivious to cheers and celebrations and all the theatre. Every step increases her anger until she is so enraged, so self-absorbed, she does not notice passing Amber at the pool table.

Amber is lining up the thirteen ball – the last of her balls. The crowd of women behind her collectively hold their breaths. One could imagine if they were to release it simultaneously, the ceiling would blow off. Flavia is nothing but a shooting star to them. Their focus is on Amber.

"Come on, Amber!" her new friend, Gabriella, calls. "You can do it!"

Amber knows the game is a fix, that the Icons are instructed to lose, but that does nothing to lessen the tension or the excitement. It's not about beating her opponent but being the one to do it and becoming the envy of the crowd. She does not know why she wants this but can only imagine it's the need for approval that she has rarely gotten from anywhere else in life. It's wrong to think this way, but she's had several cocktails, and the alcohol has softened her wariness.

Her opponent, Savage, paces around the table until he poses behind the pocket Amber's aiming at. He wears nothing but a sheer black, leather G-string tied with a bow at the left hip. The bulge in his crotch shapes his penis – as long as her hand from wrist to the tip of her middle finger. His skin is a healthy bronze – the complexion of somebody who is often outdoors, rather than lying in a solarium. Each muscle has been carved into his body, the product of hours of weights, aerobics, and yoga designed to produce this physique. The topknot ponytail makes him look exotic. He's not. But it makes him look it.

"You can do it, Amber," he says.

Amber strikes. Her shot is sure – she played lots with her brothers when she was a kid, and has the odd game with Quinn, sometimes even letting him win so that his ego isn't deflated. But there's more at stake here than Quinn's ego. She can't believe she just thought that, and almost barks nervously with laughter.

The cue ball races across the table, pounds the thirteen into the corner pocket, then rebounds off the bank and rolls to the middle of the table, right opposite the black. The women in the room scream.

"That's it, Amber!" Gabriella says.

Savage walks around to the middle pocket. His buttocks are taut and well-rounded. Unbidden and spontaneous, Amber visualizes having her hands clasping them as he thrusts into her. Of course, that's wrong. She is with Quinn. But it doesn't hurt to *think*, and that's all it is – a fantasy. It scares her, though, how thin the line between fantasizing and actualization is.

"This is it, ladies," Savage says as Amber lines up the black. "Sink the black and it *all* goes!"

"Go for it, Amber!" Gabriella says.

Amber bends over the table and lines up the black. It's an easy shot – easier than the previous shot. But there's a tremor in her hand. She takes a deep breath, closes her eyes, and exhales slowly. Somebody will beat Savage; that's inevitable. That's his function.

But she understands she needs this now, this flirtation with something tawdry and risky. She thinks about the story of Holly's impromptu threesome and tries to squelch it, but now gains the tiniest sliver of appreciation for how such a thing might just happen.

Opening her eyes, Amber strikes – too hard, it seems. The black hits the middle pocket, bounces off the cup, then rolls around the rim. Gasps ripple through the room. Every person in here now lives vicariously through Amber. She feels them pulsing in her chest. The black sinks into the pocket. The women roar.

Amber pumps one fist into the air – the same celebration of victory that Quinn employed when he was playing basketball.

Savage takes her cue and lays it on the table along with his own, then models himself, pacing back and forth so that everybody can admire, if not revere, him from every angle. He stops in front of Amber, then holds up his hands like he's surrendering for arrest.

The other women shout encouragement and advice, telling Amber to do it quick, to do it slow, to tear it off with her teeth, and all sorts of things Amber would normally never consider, but which she is now finding far too easy to imagine.

She has barely looked at his face this whole time – his brows have been groomed into fine angles; his gray eyes narrow, the pupils two lasers of black light that lock her to him; two gold earrings dangle from his left ear and one from the right; his chin clefted but pointed, almost lost in designer stubble; and his thin lips curling into a challenging smile.

Her hand trembles as she reaches out. It's embarrassing. She seizes the drawstring from the bow and pulls. The women roar. The bow unties and the drawstrings fall to his leg, but the G-string itself remains unmoved, supported by his cock and the band going around the other hip.

Savage folds his hands behind his head and shakes his hips, like that will dislodge the G-string, but to no avail. It's not happenstance. He has done this so often he knows how to prolong and build the excitement. The women hoot. Amber turns back to them, as if for advice. What she hears is predictable, but the endorsement makes her feel good anyway.

She kneels before Savage, grabs the band, and pulls his G-string clear from his crotch and slides the remaining loop down his other leg. His cock unfurls in front of her face, the way one would thrust a hand forward to engage a handshake. It's large and circumcised, surrounded in a neat thatch of pubic hair. Like the rest of Savage, it's bronzed.

Amber kisses its head lightly, as if in greeting. Then there's nothing but screams from the other women. Amber's sure there must be a fire or an assault. But it's a cheer, building, building, building, until the screams melt into one continuous shriek filling the room.

Savage grabs her by the hand and hoists her to her feet. Amber springs from the floor and into the air. Savage catches her, his large hands clutching her buttocks. And, as providence works here – or perhaps it's not providence, but a conniving of everything that is primal – this is when Quinn, trying to find Flavia, appears in the archway.

His mouth drops open as he watches Amber hook her legs around Savage's hips. Then Gabriella, jumping and waving her arms in the air, obstructs Quinn's view. He tries to see around her but becomes wary of what he *will* see. No. He has seen enough. He retreats, leaving Amber to whoop to the ceiling as she feels the length of Savage's cock parked against the crotch of her panties.

He spins her around and around and kisses her. Amber's tongue tries to part his lips, but he keeps them closed. Then, as they spin, his hands loosen around her buttocks. Amber unwraps her legs and her feet touch the floor. His cock draws a line from her crotch up to her belly. Savage stops spinning. He hugs her, although it's the sort of hug friends share – despite how Amber feels, despite how the other women feel, this is his job, and he has divorced himself from the physicality of it, regardless of how well he plays the enchanter.

"Well, ladies, that's me for the night!" he says. "Congratulations to all the winners and I hope the losers had a good show!" He scoops up his G-string and heads for the archway but stops just as he reaches it. "Oh, Amber?"

Amber's eyes widen.

"The prize!" Savage tosses his G-string to her.

Amber catches it. Savage disappears through the archway. Gabriella rushes over to Amber, grabs her by the shoulders, and shakes her excitedly.

"What I wouldn't have given to have been in your position when you pulled that G-string down!" she says.

Amber blushes. She feels hot. And moist. She looks at the G-string in her hand and scrunches it up.

"I can't believe you did what you did!" Gabriella goes on.

"Neither can I."

"Come on!" Gabriella says. "Let's get a drink!"

Patricia doesn't fully understand what's taken hold of her, but the rage that courses through her body is exhilarating. She's never experienced this, instead surrendering to people who either took advantage of her – as occurred increasingly the more decadent her modeling career became – or who ordered her around because she was afraid to stand up for herself.

Usually, Icons leave the gaming rooms in the accompaniment of security. Now, Patricia's alone and despite the state of her undress, she is ablaze with pride and indignation and – most of all – potential. She feels that, right now, she could do anything.

Men ogle her but none accost her, bowed by some unseen force that is irresistible and undeniable but, in truth, simply amounts to confidence. Women stare at her with envy. She scowls at the lot of them, ready to blast the first one to get in her face. None do. Her brazen defiance even infiltrates the minds of a few, inspiring them, although they do not understand why. She almost wants some guy to make a smart remark. That would be better. She's ready to fight. But there's nothing.

She arrives in Nico's room. Of course she does. This is where she was always heading.

A crowd of women, most of them thirty-something and overly done up, gaggle inanely, imagining they're having a good time because it's how simply they conceptualize fun. Patricia loathes them. They're entitled to let go, to get away from their everyday troubles and responsibilities, but this is pathetic now, and if they're pathetic, Patricia loathes herself for being the object of a similar group's fervor.

Her arrival startles them, and they chatter to one another behind their hands, commenting because they need to comment, but also afraid that Patricia might hear them. Patricia feels there's something drastically wrong here. It takes her a moment to pinpoint it: it's the room's mood. Usually, an Icon would stir the room into a frenzy. But this is sedate. Like a Tupperware party.

Nico's in the corner. He's topless from the waist up and he cowers from his audience, embarrassed to be seen in such a state. It speaks to his state of mind: he is not indecent, and still wears more than he would wear at an outing to the beach, for example, but it's not the bare skin that troubles him.

It's the vulnerability.

Patricia grabs him by the arm and swivels him around.

"What …?" he begins.

"Get out of here!" Patricia tells him. "You don't want this. Go!"

"I don't—"

"I got into this because I needed money, but I've been stuck here ever since, dying a slow death. You forget what it is you do. They strip away your dignity and feed from your humiliation. Walk out!"

Nico's eyes go wide. Patricia thinks surely she couldn't have alarmed him that much. But he's not looking at her but over her shoulder.

Patricia knows what she'll find before she turns: Teo, flanked by security.

"Patricia, Nico," he says, "come with me."

"What's happening?" Patricia says.

"Constance would like to see you both," Teo says.

Patricia considers resuming her rampage, but this is security now. They'll seize her and drag her to see Constance or throw her onto the street just as she is. There's a story that one Icon was thrown naked onto the curb and had to find his way home just like that. Patricia doesn't know if that's true. Stories not only abound here but propagate and become legends.

"Now," Teo says.

But here is one truth: Teo, Constance's lieutenant and confidante, is a man who imposes himself on the unruly, who beats chaos into order and frightens belligerence into resignation. While urban legends speak of him – just as they do about Constance – there is enough practical evidence to substantiate he is not a man with whom anybody should trifle.

Ever.

Patricia and Nico nod.

"I apologize, ladies," Teo says, "but we'll have another Icon in here promptly."

○ ○ ○ ○

Mr. Hermes smiles, exuding malice and condescension and something else, something vile and irreconcilable, something that Holly cannot understand, that she doubts any sane or rational person could comprehend.

She had entertained the belief that perhaps his Temptations might be altruistic, that he might be some eccentric billionaire interested in helping those trying to find a start in life. But, of course, that's a silly, romantic notion. She now understands Mr. Hermes's only motivation is subjugation. He wants only to bend her to his whim so he can feed off the humiliation.

"I feel you have not told me everything about yourself, Holly."

Holly tries to hold his searching gaze, but she is stripped bare, sitting naked, not just physically, but all her thoughts; her memories; her fears, joys, and shames. They tumble to the front of her mind, stark and confronting and wholly unnerving.

"I can't control what you feel," she says.

Mr. Hermes drinks from his glass of clear liquid. "Not to worry. I've read more in your words than you might think you'd said. Let us reflect: you work in PR, although it is a job for you, and not a career; you are engaged to be married; and you lead a relatively sedentary life, socializing with friends, and enjoying only the occasional night out. At home, you enjoy ordinary pleasures, such as restaurants, movies, and a game of pool. This trip is one last fling before domesticity, isn't it? And then it's life in the suburbs, children, football, and school concerts, until one day you wake up, find you're forty, and regret the things you didn't do and the experiences you didn't have."

The heat flushes in Holly's cheeks. It's not an unusual life course, but as Mr. Hermes talks about it, it becomes empty and unsatisfying. She has always been happy to let life take her where it will, but that now proves to be falling hideously short of expectations. But why? It's not a question she can answer.

"I'm sure you would probably expect something vulgar and predictable from myself in terms of a Temptation," Mr. Hermes says. "Something shocking. Perhaps the suggestion of something … well, where do we go here?"

He pauses, but Holly expects he already knows what he's going to propose. She won't play his game. Won't hang on his bated breath. She's already given him too much power. He is a master manipulator. She downs what remains of her muddy-pink Tequila Sunrise. It's gone warm and she gags on it, so she gestures to the waitress for another, then turns back to Mr. Hermes, like she's forgotten he was in the middle of a sentence.

"You were saying?" she asks.

"Do you expect something—?"

"Decadent?" Holly finishes, determined to seize control of the conversation. "You're so predictable. What a shock that it's come down to sex. You're just a dirty old fucker."

"Perhaps. We all have our dark sides, don't we? I offer Temptations, but they're around us every day in life. We try to resist them. Sometimes, we don't. Sometimes, they blind us and disorient us, until we lose ourselves in them and can only reflect in shame once the excitement, the glamour, has faded."

Whatever little control Holly has wrested away evaporates. She knows exactly what he's going to say next – as if he's reading a cue from her own experiences.

"You surely would not be affronted by the suggestion of something like a ménage a trois, would you?"

Holly fights to contain herself, but the guilt pulses from her skin. She takes a deep breath and tries to roll with the conversation. She will not win control of what's happening, but neither does that mean she has to surrender it entirely.

"Why would you think suggesting a threesome would shock me? Do you think I wouldn't do it for a million dollars?"

"Maybe you would."

"Maybe," Holly admits with aplomb.

"Maybe you already *have*."

Holly takes a breath, trying to use the silence to break Mr. Hermes's momentum while she tries to process what's going on.

He *knows*.

He knows, he knows, he knows.

"Has your fiancé made any large deposits or expensive purchases recently?" he asks.

"You don't know who he is." The words are hollow. Holly speaks them out of reflex.

"No, I would know little about one Marcus Handley – or so it would seem. Tell me, Holly, and be honest, has anything unprecedented occurred in your life recently? Anything unforeseen?"

The pieces form a picture. The old man stipulated earlier that by taking an audience with him, she was obligated to introduce him to somebody new – just as Quinn introduced her. And who could've introduced Quinn? Yes, it would be Marcus – Marcus, who is always looking for an opportunity, always chasing a thrill, always shattering boundaries.

She shoots up from the booth and bumps into the waitress who's brought her drink. The Tequila Sunrise flips in mid-air and sprays Holly's skirt. The waitress apologizes and runs to the bar to get a towel. Holly pats herself down. She's wet and sticky. It reminds her of the hotel room, of the end, lying under the two business execs.

"Now don't forget, Holly," Mr. Hermes says, "I still have a Temptation to set you."

The waitress arrives with a hand towel. Holly shoves her aside and runs out, missing Quinn by moments as he charges into the piano bar and up to the booth.

"Get the money ready, you old fuck!" Quinn says. "Because I'm about to collect."

Mr. Hermes smirks.

"What're you laughing at?"

"Remember what I told you, Quinn."

"What? *What?*"

"Flesh is weak. Temporary. Remember I told you that."

Quinn leans toward Mr. Hermes, planting his fists into the tabletop. "What the fuck does that have to do with anything?"

"Because here's another lesson for you, Quinn, one you would be wise to remember: the only things eternal in this life are those feelings that are most primal to us – rage, lust, survival. What do you feel now, Quinn? What do you feel now—?"

"Fuck you!"

Mr. Hermes tinkles with laughter – a gentle lilting sound full of condescension. Quinn has never been violent, never been in a fight his entire life, but right now his face mottles, veins bulge from his neck, and his clenched fists tremble. Mr. Hermes' laughter grows loud and damning. Quinn thumps the table with his left hand so hard that Mr. Hermes's glass jumps and is upended; Quinn will learn much later that he's broken a knuckle. For now, though, he feels nothing but oblivion.

He turns and charges out, Mr. Hermes's laughter ringing in his ears.

LeBeau sits back in his booth, surveying the women who pass him. He gauges buttocks first, then cleavage, hips (and, where attire allows, crotches), then faces. One of the reasons he enjoys coming here is the smorgasbord of gorgeous women – and that's how he sees them, as a buffet from which he can choose.

He follows the progress of a lithe redhead as she walks to the bar, then a short blonde waif and her busty raven-haired companion, then a voluptuous brunette with her bearded suitor. LeBeau catalogs everybody in his immediate vicinity. Once, simple beauty appealed to him. Then his tastes grew to vary. But now, nobody appeals beyond the most superficial level.

Now he needs more.

He sips from his double Tom Collins. One of the waitresses – a lean blonde – walks to the bar, carrying a tray filled with empty glasses. LeBeau studies her butt. Perhaps the service is something he can try, although employees are strictly off-limits – at least while they're at work. It's a stupid policy. He should talk to the Camarilla, or to Hermes, about changing it.

A figure blocks his sight. He doesn't have to look up to know it's Flavia. It's not her body he identifies, but her desperate neediness. He snorts dismissively, then sips from his Tom Collins.

"Oh, you again," he says, then leans over so he can peer at the waitress, but she takes a tray of drinks and disappears into the crowd. LeBeau looks up at Flavia. Her jaw is hard, and her shoulders squared. She's angry. He likes that.

"I want to audition," she asks.

"Funny," he says.

"What?"

"You're full of it."

"No." Flavia slides into the booth and puts her hand on LeBeau's thigh.

"Is that meant to impress me?"

"It's meant to be a start."

"You talk the talk," he says.

"I walk the walk."

"I just need somebody who'll fuck."

She steels herself, absorbing the comment as if it was a physical blow.

LeBeau chuckles, reaches into his jacket pocket, and pulls out his gold case. He opens it to reveal an array of small, triangle lime pills contained in foam niches. He takes a pill, pops it into his mouth, and washes it down with a drink from his Tom Collins.

He begins closing his case, but then it occurs to him, almost as if little more than an afterthought – if men such as LeBeau have afterthoughts, and everything isn't premeditated through some grand design – to reopen it and thrust it in Flavia's direction. She stares uncertainly at the little lime pills.

"What are they?" she asks. "Ecstasy?"

"A derivation. Designer brand. X'cess. Much better."

Like many adults, Flavia has experimented, but only scantily – although she gives Dante the impression it's more extensive to impress upon him her worldliness. But on each of those occasions she knew what she was taking, and it was in a controlled situation, or at least with friends who could take care of her if anything went awry.

She worries what will become of her if she takes this pill. What will she do? Will it lower her inhibitions? Will she lose control? There are so many questions that she cannot answer, and that frightens her. She shouldn't be here as it is, and that indignation that gave birth to her bravado wavers.

LeBeau grins broadly. "Yep. Just the talk."

He starts to withdraw the case, but Flavia catches him by the wrist. She snatches a pill before any doubt can halt her, pops it into her mouth, then takes LeBeau's Tom Collins and sips from it.

The gin is bitter – it's never a drink she's adopted – but she tries not to let it show as she sets the glass down.

LeBeau snaps his case closed. "Well, well, well," he says.

IV

Constance leans against the edge of her desk, arms folded across her chest. She has been hostess a long time and remembers many eventful nights. Indeed, she remembers *every* night in vivid detail, once recalling them with surprise and uncertainty, then with condescension and judgment, then with amusement, and now with a wry disassociation.

There have been attacks against Icons, fights on the dance floor, journalists sneaking in attempting to find the famed basement or searching for an exposé of licentious practices, numerous acts of copulation in dark corners, and even an attempted robbery.

But tonight has been different because it's involved an uprising. The only time Constance has experienced anything similar was the night she was offered the position of hostess and her predecessor, Sarah, tried a last, desperate grab at power, although that attempt amounted to little more than her offering herself to Mr. Hermes and the Camarilla to do with her as they would – as if they hadn't exercised that practice numerous times already. Constance has always sworn the she would never be so pathetic.

Lined up before her are Dante, Marcus; Patricia, wrapped in a towel; Nico, face downcast, and dressed again; and Joy. Constance surveys them closely. Except for Joy, they are meek. *Afraid.*

It's Joy who Constance lingers on longest. The others are young fools. Constance can read them as if their histories were printed on their faces. Joy is a similar age, but inscrutable. Constance senses in her an unnerving implacability. It feels *wrong.* Everybody who comes here has an agenda, one not only driven by the most base instincts, but also slave to them, the way they might be slave to a narcotic even when they know it's killing them.

"Busy night," Constance says.

Teo is unimpressed. "We've had busier."

While Teo sees more than he lets on, he doesn't always understand it. He is happy to accept that regardless how hard they try to contain what goes on here, sometimes it explodes, and they're left to deal with the clean-up. But Constance can discern two things: that explosions can wreak irreparable damage, as well as hurt bystanders, and that this isn't the explosion – this is the timer counting down now.

She pushes off from her desk and approaches Nico. He is wringing his hands and staring down at his feet.

"From the onset, you've been diffident, Nico," she says. "You haven't had the heart to let go. It's not something you learn. It's something you can do, or you can't. You are not what you think."

"What?" Nico says. "What aren't I? Tell me. I don't understand."

"Then that's the problem, Nico. You don't get it. You don't get Prudence. If you need to think about it, you don't fit. You just need to *be.*"

"That's just … just silly."

"Perhaps. But it is what it is. It's surprising given your family."

"I'm not my uncle. I'm not my brother."

"That might not be such a bad thing."

"Then what do you want from me? All of you, what do you expect?"

"I can only speak for myself, Nico: I expect nothing. You're dismissed."

"I can go?"

"We're done, Nico."

"I'm sorry I disappointed you."

"Nico, I don't understand why you're here. Perhaps you should honestly examine your motivations."

Teo grabs him by the elbow and ushers him toward the door. At one point, Nico tries to ask a question, but Teo continues urging him, a large hand in the small of Nico's back. Teo's been in this position many times – ex-employees wanting explanations as to what they've done wrong, or what service they haven't filled, or what they can do to be better. It's best to see them out instead of engaging in conversations that can become circular and unfulfilling.

Constance waits until Nico's gone and the door's closed before she turns her attention to Marcus and Dante. She considers Dante amiable but diffident, while Marcus isn't just handsome, but *beautiful* – something not often associated with a man's appearance. Out in the world, Constance is sure young women would linger on him, first impressions concluding that he would be a fine catch. But she senses an underlying mean-spiritedness. Worse than that, it's petty.

"Fighting is a serious offense," Constance says.

"We didn't start it," Marcus says evenly. "It was that other guy. Why didn't you drag him in here?"

"Marcus, is it?"

"Yeah."

"We have surveillance." Constance idly waves at the array of screens. "We saw what happened. You confronted this Icon. Your friend manhandled a young woman—"

"My girlfriend!" Dante says.

"That is absolutely no excuse to manhandle her."

She glowers at Dante, ablaze in her fury. He shrinks before her – a child trapped in a man's body. She is tempted to have him tossed but doubts that would teach him anything. He needs to learn, and she sees that this is the night that will be his educator, whether he likes it or not.

"This other man attempted to intercede – diplomatically," Constance says. "You provoked what occurred next."

"This wouldn't have happened if it weren't for her!" Marcus thrusts a finger at Patricia. "She fucked up the whole room!"

Constance directs her attention upon him, but he is unflinching. She can read his mind: he is thinking of her sexually; he thinks he would like to teach her a lesson through sex, as if he could fuck her into obedience and subjugation. He is the sort of man who looks at his cock as a weapon, as laughable as that is. He is dangerous – not irredeemable, not yet. But he *is* reckless, and that could go anywhere.

"We saw you also," she says. "We saw the way you treated our Icon."

"All I told her was that she should play nice."

"So, your motives were altruistic?"

"Yeah."

Constance laughs. "You're a brazen one. Here are *your* options – you can be banned permanently from Prudence, or you can serve a penance."

"A penance?"

"You will be an Icon tonight."

Marcus's grin is immediate. "What?" he says. "Play pool, lose, and strip for women? Like that's a punishment. Where do I sign up?" His face turns somber. "Wait, no tricks, right?"

"No tricks," Constance says.

"How is this going to punish me? What do you think this is going to do?"

"It will teach you what it's like to be on the other side."

"You think that's gonna bother me?"

No, Constance thinks. It won't bother him. But tossing him would do no good. That would become a spur for him – a reason to justify his attitude toward women. He might enjoy playing the Icon, but she hopes that, somehow, a sliver of understanding will sink in and germinate. The world needs less men like this one.

"That remains to be seen," she says. "As for you," Constance turns to Dante, "you're free to go."

"Just like that?" Dante asks.

He's astonished; Marcus is equally flabbergasted. Good. These two, so recently joined at the hip. She sees their mutual history now, Dante following Marcus blindly. Now their paths have been split. It will sow the seed of discontent between them, perhaps force Dante to think for himself.

"Just like that."

"Why're you giving me a penance and not him?" Marcus says.

"Given your reaction," Constance says, "I didn't think what I'd handed you was a penance."

"I'm just wondering."

"You tell me this woman you manhandled is your girlfriend?" Constance asks Dante.

Dante nods.

"Then you are in enough trouble." Constance folds her arms back across her chest. "You can go. You – Marcus. Wait outside until I can have somebody set you up."

Teo guides them to the door. Dante's happy enough to be out of there and keeps his eyes straight ahead. But Marcus pivots, backtracks, and shrugs off Teo's guiding hand.

"After the performance I put on," he says, "you're gonna give me a job."

"We'll see," Constance says.

Teo ushers them out and closes the door.

O   O   O   O

Now that Dante has cooled and escaped punishment, he has space for the contrition to leak in. He thinks about how he can make things right with Flavia. He's screwed up in the past but never like this. He blames the room, and the pack mentality, and excuses himself of any culpability.

Marcus is scornful. He understands the reasoning behind Constance's treatment of him but dismisses it. He's sure Constance has both misread him and underestimated him. By the time the night's done, she'll be embarrassed that she believed such a stupid penance could humiliate or educate him.

"We're lucky," Dante says.

"Why's that?"

"I heard she tore the balls off a man who messed up one of the rooms. He went crazy on ecstasy and assaulted an Icon. Security stripped him and held him while Constance tied fishing line around his testicles and pulled until he screamed for mercy."

Marcus laughs – it's the typical embellishment that's used to build mystique. He sees it often in Holly's work, although never with such grandeur. Why would anybody misbehave here when such urban legends are floating about? It powers his determination to create his own legend.

"That's bullshit," he says.

"Maybe."

"She let you off. She made me an Icon for a night. You really think those are the actions of somebody who castrated a man?"

Dante shrugs, unconvinced.

"What're you gonna do while I'm entertaining?"

Dante knows he should be honest with Marcus, tell him he's going to seek Flavia's forgiveness, even if it means getting on his knees and begging her. But Marcus will mock him for being soft. Marcus, after all, is never soft with Holly – well, not in the time that Dante has known them. Dante doesn't understand how Holly deals with it.

"I'm gonna find Flavia," he says, sliding his hand into his pocket and feeling the ring box in there. This is a sign. Yes, that's it. That's exactly what it is. Just as his and Marcus's paths converged, now they will diverge. The prospect excites Dante. His hand tightens around the box. He'll find Flavia, plead for her forgiveness, suggest they grab a bite, and propose in the restaurant. Or outside. No, that'll be too cold. The Café Acheron on the corner where they had dinner before coming here – yes, that's it; the Café Acheron, with its tan stone walls, dim alcoves, and candlelit tables. He'll suggest they have a coffee, grab a table, then get down on a knee before her. She will lift her hands to her mouth to clamp down on her excited shriek. He grins foolishly, sure that reality will follow his imagination.

"You okay or you had an aneurysm?" Marcus asks.

"I'm good," Dante says.

Now he's not abashed, but indignant at how Marcus might scorn him. But it doesn't matter because Marcus doesn't matter. He's been a temporary influence. Dante thought that was something he could enjoy, or learn from, but he was wrong not only to think it, but to believe that it was something he both wanted and needed. The benefit is it's clarified not only what he wants, but how he'll achieve it.

"I'm gonna find Flavia and do some entertaining of my own," he says, because it's the type of answer that'd satisfy Marcus.

Marcus cackles and holds his fist up. Naturally, he thinks of sex. He sees it in his head – Flavia bent over a table, her cries a mixture of pleasure and submission. It's how he likes to see Holly – sometimes he can get her there. Sometimes. And other times … He grins.

Dante releases the ring box, pulls his hand out of his pocket, and half-heartedly knocks Marcus's wrist.

"I'll see you," Dante says.

"Later," Marcus says.

Dante heads down the stairwell from Constance's office.

○ ○ ○ ○

Constance paces back and forth, pausing only to stare at the array of screens and survey what's going on while her attention is squandered here.

It's rare for any long-serving employee to betray the trust invested in them. Transgressions usually occur in the first three months, when either the novelty and infamy, or demands and scrutiny, of working here are likeliest to overwhelm any newcomer.

Constance stops in front of Patricia. Patricia's eyes are big and dark, her face bereft of all guile. Although she has had a hard life, although many have taken advantage of her, her petulance is that of a child who has misbehaved and fears the imminent punishment.

But there is something else also – a haziness about her that Constance pinpoints as a telltale sign of some addiction. This woman is surviving through self-medicating. This act of rebellion was a grasp at feeling alive – something she has not experienced naturally for many years.

"If Nico had any hope of finding it in himself to be an Icon," Constance says, "to be who Prudence required him to be, your little outburst discouraged him. You've been a faithful employee for five years. *Why?*"

"I'm sick of being leered at," Patricia says, "of being degraded and objectified, of being propositioned—"

"You hold the power, Patricia."

"That's a rationalization."

"Maybe in the world outside these walls, but here it's a truth."

Joy is sitting calmly in a chair by the door, hands folded in her lap, her satchel resting against her hip. She could be waiting for her car to be serviced. Funnily, Constance does not remember her sitting down; Teo led in the troublemakers and lined them up before her desk. When did Joy slip away? And why hadn't Teo stopped her?

Constance is renowned for her composure, for being unflappable regardless of the situation. She has always been haughty but measured. It creates an aura around her that intimidates others. But now, some uncertainty slips through – a tiny amount, but more than she has experienced in many years – and it unnerves her.

"You inspired this sudden rebellion," Constance says to Joy. "What are you? A radical?"

"Hardly."

"Then?"

Joy leans back in her chair but says nothing.

"We've examined your depredations on our surveillance." Constance waves her hand at the array of screens as evidence. "You've gone from one room to the next, wreaking a trail of havoc. You remind me of myself when I was younger."

"A compliment?"

"An observation."

"You've lost yourself then."

"Because I'm no longer young and stupid?"

"You're a tired queen who holds court over her frivolous subjects," Joy says. "But you've lost touch with them, with Prudence, and with the Camarilla."

Anger flashes across Constance's face. She has heard everything over the years – insults, demands, and propositions. It has never flustered her. But she sees something in this woman she struggles to identify; I see it, too, finally. It's not just that she is like a young Constance, but that she is filled with ambition that overrides any equanimity.

Joy folds one leg over the other, clasps her hands across her knee, and rocks back in her chair.

"Prudence is carnal," she says. "That's what attracts everybody. That's what they feed one another, feed these walls. That's what the Camarilla wants. But now it's parlor tricks. This," she scowls at Patricia, "petty little fool proves how out of touch your current employees are with the foundation on which Prudence was built. What will you do with her? Dock her?" She chuckles. "Suspend her? Or, God forbid, dismiss her?"

"And what should I do with her? Here is a boon to you: how would you handle her?"

Joy rises and directs her attention at Patricia. "Come."

Patricia's eyes flit to Constance, seeking approval. Constance is about to nod, but Joy is upon Patricia, crossing the distance between them in a shadowy blur. Joy's hand knots into Patricia's hair and yanks her closer. Patricia shrieks. The towel falls from her body. Joy holds her aloft so that Patricia rises onto her toe-tips. Patricia's hands close around Joy's wrists, but if she's trying to free herself, she fails. Teo moves to intercede, but Constance holds up a hand to halt him.

"Perform one last duty and you'll be free from being an Icon forever," Joy tells her.

"Please!" Patricia says. "You're hurting me!"

"What do you say?"

"Yes! Yes!"

Joy shoves her down until Patricia collapses to her knees, tearful. Constance only now reconciles that Joy is neither a Transient nor a Staple, but something else entirely; something spat out from the collective heart of where the deepest, darkest desires of every Transient and Staple who has ever set foot in here lurks. It is a birthing Constance knows only too well – it is the course she took herself.

"Who are you?" she asks, approaching Joy slowly, and finally taking her in – studying every curve, every shadow, every blemish. "Some model excommunicated by the industry?"

Joy is stoic.

"A failed actress, perhaps?"

Still, Joy does not move.

"Maybe even something pettier like … a porn actress, possibly?"

The tiniest flicker of irritation crosses Joy's face, although whether it's because Constance has guessed correctly, or because Constance's guess is so insulting, is unclear.

I can't tell.

"The Camarilla like those who have aimed high and fallen short, or fallen foul, consumed by wanton excess," Constance goes on, as she stops before Joy. "Those who have become open to the very decadences born out of hopelessness and desperation."

"There are things happening of which you're aware, but over which you have no control," Joy says. "However, first," she looks at Patricia, "let's deal with her."

Rupe doesn't know what to do after Joy is taken. He sits in the Brimstone Lounge, wondering what she might've done to be seized by security. Of course, Rupe recognizes she is a free spirit – he knew that the moment he saw her. But there are many free spirits here – or at least they are free while they *are* here. There was something else about Joy, though. It was freedom with purpose.

Leaving the Brimstone Lounge, Rupe wanders aimlessly – onto the second floor, to the North Bar and South Bar, back into the Cardinal Lounge, and finally to the Verdant Lounge. He goes to the bar and orders a Gin & Tonic, although he contemplates going home. The night is empty, like all the others have been. Maybe this is his lot and there is no escaping it, and excursions like this are nothing more than exercises in foolish naivety.

If he were younger, he'd entertain thoughts of rescuing Joy. He'd storm up into Constance's office, if such a thing were possible through all the security. He'd argue persuasively and win Joy's freedom, and she would be forever indebted to him. Of course, he is not younger and such notions are juvenile.

He takes his Gin & Tonic and sits in one of the booths. Mr. Hermes is in the next booth, a man who the years are trying to claim. His face is nothing but lines, and the skin sags over his eyes and jowls. The lobes of his ears are so large, and his nose so pointed, they may be props that are melting from his skull. Only his mismatched eyes, one as gray as storm clouds and the other an oceanic blue, are bright – too bright, as if somewhere behind those pupils an unquenchable fire burns to power him even as his body wanes.

Rupe thinks about the stories he's heard of this man and would like to believe them apocryphal. The stories add to the mystique here and are exaggerated upon retelling until they bear no resemblance to the truth – if there is indeed a truth. It's likelier that Constance has retained an actor to play the role of Mr. Hermes since the real man is said to be a reclusive billionaire, often spoken of, but rarely seen publicly the last twenty-five years.

"You would be wrong, though."

It's Mr. Hermes who speaks. Rupe hears an accent, although he cannot identify it. Likely it's something that has been mongrelized over the years, if not decades, to the extent it has evolved and become unique.

Mr. Hermes sips from a glass of clear liquid. "I have seen you here before," he says. "Many times. And yet we've never crossed paths."

"I have never needed you," Rupe says.

"And why would anybody need me?"

"I hear you sell dreams. For a price."

Mr. Hermes chuckles. "Such an interesting turn of phrase. And what of yourself? Have you no dreams? Romance? Love? Happy ever after?"

"You've read me well."

Mr. Hermes might be seeing right into Rupe's heart, although Rupe knows that's both silly and cliché. But he does recognize in Mr. Hermes a man who can gauge character – a skill he has no doubt developed over the years he built his empire.

"You've experienced loss. Not recent."

"My …" Rupe cannot name her. *My wife.* The words reverberate in his mind. But he cannot speak them. "An inoperable brain tumor."

Mr. Hermes laughs, but not unkindly. He appreciates Rupe's mourning – that a man can express such devotion, even beyond death. What's more, although Rupe himself doesn't know this, this is the closest Mr. Hermes has come to exhibiting compassion not only this night, but for many years.

"It stays with you – the pain," he says. "It is the wound that never heals. We learn to exist with it."

"If you can call this *existing*," Rupe says.

"Then why come here? The companionship found here is fleeting."

"That's a generalization."

"That is a rule."

"There are exceptions."

Mr. Hermes pauses in the act of bringing his glass to his mouth. "You know what I do."

"I think I know."

"As you said, I sell dreams. But at a price. Some say the price is the cost of morality, or virtue. I say it is just a test. As the years have gone on – and I have been doing this a long, long, time, Rupe, not just here but in other establishments, on street corners, in darkened alleys, and in the corners of people's most disturbing, unspoken thoughts – I have found the parameters have changed. It used to be so much simpler to outrage. To *test*. There was a time when proposing adultery was unthinkable. But today ..." Mr. Hermes shakes his head sadly, and finally takes a drink from his glass. He sets it down and shakes the glass so the ice rattles melodically. "Declining standards, Rupert. Declining standards. Deteriorating morality. I should enjoy the disintegration of our scruples, but the truth is that it'll be the end of us all."

"Then why do it—"

"Because it is a necessity. For the lack of a better term, people want to believe in magic."

"Magic?" Rupe arches one brow.

"Perhaps it is best called *opportunity*. There is magic in opportunity, in the boundless potential of what could be. But this is an art. I could propose the outrageous – such as bestiality, just for example. But there would be some degenerate who'd be more than happy to comply when the reward is a million dollars."

Rupe splutters into his drink. "A million dollars? This isn't for real, is it?"

"Here, our fantasies *are* real. That's why Prudence exists. Why the Camarilla wants Prudence. Why I'm here. But this position becomes more demanding. It takes a studious eye to determine what lies at the heart of one's fears, what cripples them … or at the very least repulses them. In the end, you could consider me a liberator of fears, inhibitions, and conformity."

"And what lies on the other side of that?"

"Ecstasy."

"Really?"

"Or perhaps chaos." Mr. Hermes purses his lips, his face narrowing until it is particularly skeletal. "Perhaps you should abide here. Lust is a marvelous salve. And there is freedom like you have never known – not liberty, which imposes upon us laws and rules, but genuine freedom to do as we will."

Nico enters the Lounge and strides right over to Mr. Hermes's booth, sliding in with familiarity.

"I was fired," he says.

"My misguided nephew," Mr. Hermes explains, almost apologetically, to Rupe, before turning to Nico. "Then I guess your dreams of avarice will just have to come through hard work."

"The hard way's not fair. I should have my father's—"

"Your father left his position – and your inheritance – in trust with me until I deemed you ready to handle it."

"Still—"

"*Just* as it was for your older brother. But he quickly proved his worth. Of course, your brother was not the reckless and irresponsible teenager you were, Nico. "

"But—"

"This is *not* a negotiation, Nico."

"But—"

"Silence!"

Nico lowers his head, his jaw bulging as he clenches his teeth.

"See?" Mr. Hermes says to Rupe. "The youth of today – greed and entitlement. They expect luxury to be handed to them. And I set the boy such an easy Temptation. Could he prostitute himself? Many would find it simple. Enjoyable. Not Nico. He is rare. Reserved. Shy." He squints at Nico, as if trying to decipher his form. "If you found that distasteful, you'll find your father's and my business far more unpalatable."

"I nearly managed it."

"One thing you must learn in life, Nico, is that you either accomplish or fail. There is no *nearly*. So, tell me: are you ready to go again?"

○　○　○　○

Bodie and Ox no longer drink with the abandon of earlier. Their eyes flit nervously among passers-by and their conversation is hardly as glib, although if somebody were to overhear them they would think it as meaningless as ever.

"That brunette's panty-less," Bodie says

He points with the neck of his Gallia at two women who walk past. The brunette is in a tight pink dress that shapes the curves of her buttocks. Her friend is a tall woman wearing a mini skirt.

"The other one's wearing a ... a ..." Bodie's eyes narrow speculatively.

"Am guessing she's also going commando," Ox says.

"Gotta look out for her on the dance floor."

A fair man with a wealth of curly hair and a designer beard passes, shedding a wake of rank cologne.

Ox waves a hand in front of his face. "Is that meant to pass for cool?"

"Hopefully it's just meant to pass," Bodie says.

"If there's one thing about places like this, it brings out the tryhards."

"You'd think there'd be some authenticity here."

"Can't get authenticity from people who don't know who they are."

Bodie toasts Ox in agreement.

Prince appears behind them, leaning over the bar. "Guys," he says, "what's this proving?"

"What *isn't* this proving?" Bodie asks.

"It *isn't* proving that you're *not* a pair of primordial dickwads," Prince says.

"Prince, that cuts," Ox says. "That really does."

A short but statuesque blond dressed in hot pants and an equally tight vest walks by.

"She just had sex," Ox says.

"Yep." Bodie nods. "She's got fuck-me bruises."

"Fuck-me bruises?" Prince asks.

"On her hamstrings," Bodie says.

"Comes from her ankles up on her guy's shoulders, the guy's hands clawing into her legs," Ox says, mimicking the action.

"You can always tell a woman who's had sex that way."

"You guys are kidding me," Prince says.

"Nope."

"How do you tell the guys who've just had sex?"

"Most of the time?" Bodie says. "By the stupid grins. Well, *stupider* grins."

"Guys are about simple pleasures."

"Sex is a great pleasure."

"So they get overloaded."

"Hence the stupid grins."

"See all the small and insignificant things we notice, Prince?" Ox says.

"But that's all they are," Prince says. "Small and insignificant, unless you work out a way to put them to some use, and I can't see that such a way exists. Trying to impress me with them isn't going to cut it. You're coming across as nothing but a pair of throwbacks."

Bodie laughs – a hearty, good-natured laugh at his own expense, but there's a seriousness about his face. Here is what others have glimpsed, and which I see truly now – that their flippancy is a cover for something greater, something they work hard not only to conceal, but distract others from, just as they've distracted Prince these many years.

"Prince, we're not trying to impress you," Bodie says. "This is what we do."

"This is who we are," Ox says.

"We're just trying to demonstrate that we notice things."

Prince leans forward on the bar, sensing what I've picked up. He looks from one, to the other, and back again, then withdraws, unnerved. These two have never given him cause for concern – they've never given *anybody* cause for concern, sitting there drinking as they do each night. In the early months when Prince first met them, he would marvel at their inactivity. But, after a while, he acclimated to them, and accepted them as part of the furnishings.

In the world outside these walls, Prince's life is hectic and full, and he's always been certain of not only his own place, but the places of the people around him. Now he's not so sure. Now he fears that these two men who he has served beers for so long, with whom he has had meaningless exchange after meaningless exchange, with whom he has developed something of a friendship, are not the people he thinks. They are something darker wearing masks of flippancy to fool everybody around them – well, everybody but Constance and Teo. They would know.

Prince's curiosity gets the better of him, and despite the reservations where he *tells* himself he shouldn't, he decides to probe.

"Do you ever notice anything with perhaps a bit of meaning?" he asks.

"Of course we do."

Prince braces himself, almost regretful he has pursued this conversation. He knows it can't go anywhere he would like. Still, he forces the next word from his mouth: "Like?"

"You ever notice how hot it gets in here?" Bodie asks.

"Yeah. Of course."

"Every club's hot. You get an enclosed area full of people, it gets stuffy. Have always thought here's worse. Don't know what it is. I tell a lie. I think I do but … maybe I don't know."

"It's damn hot in here," Ox says.

Bodie nods just the once. "You'd think you'd get used to it, us coming here as long as we have, the way we have. But you don't. Of course, you never do with heat. It's like summer when there's a heatwave. You'd think when you get a string of hot days that at some point, you'd acclimate. You don't, though. You just wait for the heat to break. Sometimes, when it goes long enough and you get desperate enough, you pray for it to break."

Bodie lifts his Gallia to his lips but has second thoughts about taking a drink. He presses the bottle to the side of his neck.

"'Course, you get out there in the juncture, right by the entrance to the lobby, right under that plaque, and you feel that cool breeze waft in from outside. Just funnels right down the hall there. Sweet relief. Sometimes, at the end of the night when we're going, I just stand there, close my eyes, and revel in it, revel in it like I know the heat's at an end and the change is coming. So, you know what else I notice, Prince?"

Bodie's soliloquy has overwhelmed Prince. Never in all the time Bodie's come here has he spoken uninterrupted and as earnestly for such length. Prince becomes conscious of the beads of sweat on his temple that break and race down his cheeks, and the way Ox sits up straight, hulking, until he dwarfs everybody around him. Patrons coming to the bar give him a wide berth, like he is a tethered vicious dog who might snap at them if they get too close.

"There's a change coming," Bodie says. "But it's not getting cooler."

○ ○ ○ ○

As Flavia follows LeBeau, her legs tremble and her heart thumps so hard she is sure each beat will be the last. She wants to dismiss that it's guilt and tells herself that instead it's the bass from the music or, likelier, the drug she took. The sweat beads on her forehead. Her dress is scratchy against her skin.

Now every small thing she notices is pronounced and overwhelming – from the way the straps of her shoes cut into her heels, to the tightness of her dress, to the bounce of her hair on her neck, to the air that wafts across her face, to the shadows that play about LeBeau's figure.

This is madness to give herself to LeBeau. And for what? A career? Revenge? Neither motive is right. It's not too late to decline LeBeau and call it a night, but part of herself that she wants to deny is excited both about how illicit this tryst is, and just what it's meant to yield.

As LeBeau leads them through the array of gaming rooms, Flavia's only reservation is that they might bump into Dante. Such a possibility should horrify her. What would she say? *Hey, Dante, this is Edan LeBeau. He wants to fuck me.* But the possibility doesn't horrify her. There's no revulsion. In fact, there's almost a perverse glee. Yes, Dante should see her, just as she saw him with that stripper, or whatever she was. See how he likes it.

Although, of course, she's sure that Dante didn't take it further. He wouldn't have. Somebody like Marcus might. Marcus is sociopathic that way. Flavia has known men like him who treat women as a conquest. She sees it in his relationship with Holly; he treats her as a trophy he has won and brandishes. But Dante is all bluster. He would've flirted, felt good about himself, and then possibly even sought her out so he could engage in some vicarious fantasy, using some tawdry lines that would most likely appall her. That's Dante's way. If the stripper would've reciprocated, it would've frightened him.

LeBeau is like neither. Marcus is arrogant. He expects things because he is good looking and charismatic and doesn't understand when something doesn't fall his way. He carries with him a sense of entitlement. Dante is diffident. He meekly plots his course through the world, surprised when something beneficial happens. He is a beaten dog begging for scraps. But LeBeau is confident to the point he is prescient. He has had interactions like this so many times he has learned to read people, to predict their responses, and to subtly manipulate them to the outcome he wishes.

It's why now he moves with purpose. They have passed through the gaming rooms. Flavia doesn't know where they are. The music has faded so that she can only imagine hearing it. The light dims. There's no sign of people. The walls aren't the same red bricks either, but big tan stones, like they saw in the Café Acheron earlier. There are big brown doors in them. The private rooms, perhaps? It's foolish, but Flavia's sure they're somewhere else altogether now, that they've absconded through some secret passageway into some other establishment.

They reach the end of the hallway. At first, Flavia doesn't discern the man who lurks in the shadows. He's dressed in a stylish black suit and wears black sunglasses. Then his head swivels toward them; his sudden smile is two big rows of white teeth that might open up and snap them in half. LeBeau expects his movement, but Flavia jumps.

"Prometheus," LeBeau says.

"Mr. LeBeau," Prometheus says, inclining his head.

He opens the doors. A stairwell plummets into a small antechamber, dim light seeping in from an adjacent hallway.

Flavia has heard the stories of what goes on in the basement – sex games; an underground realm; a secret society where sex is currency, reward, and punishment all at once. Of course, they *are* stories. Nobody she knows has ever been in the basement. Stories are always relayed via a friend of a friend of a friend, and such retellings always come with aggrandizement. Well, that is what Flavia tells herself, and tries to hold onto as a new certainty punctures her numbed mind: those stories are in no way big or wild enough to genuinely reflect the truth.

LeBeau takes her hand.

Flavia holds her ground.

LeBeau grins wryly at her. "Well?"

Flavia checks back over her shoulder. She can't see more than ten feet, and strains to hear music, to hear people. There's only silence now, other than for her heartbeat echoing in her ears. Dante is somewhere back there. The perverse glee evaporates. Dante, so meek, so loving, and usually so devoted.

The guilt is resurgent.

Flavia closes her eyes and tells herself that if it's meant to be with Dante, he'll contact her in the next ten seconds. Her phone will ring. Or vibrate. It'll be Dante suggesting they get together for a drink. It'll mean they're meant to be and, with that being the case, she'll turn and head right back out of here.

Time stops. LeBeau awaits her. As does Prometheus. But neither says anything. There's only stillness, and a dull roar in her ears as she counts – counts so slow that her ten amounts to twenty-five seconds. She wills Dante to contact her, and when nothing's forthcoming she forces the interpretation that it's a rebuke. That's how simple it is. He is rebuking her because he is inconsiderate! It does not enter her recollection at all that she turned her phone off earlier. She would prefer to feel spited rather than reasonable.

Flavia tells herself that this inexplicable need for Dante's intervention is mere superstition, a desire to validate the merits of their relationship, to show that their love is built on proven tangibles, like the way Dante occasionally surprises her with breakfast in bed, or the way he has held her when she's come back from unsuccessful interviews, or the way he'll whisper he loves her after they have had sex and he has orgasmed, although often she is unsatisfied.

But logic is overridden. The sign here is simple: perhaps it's just not meant to be, and that her career is more important – a rationalization, no doubt, and one that Flavia knows may come back to haunt her, but her thoughts are scrambled, and in this moment it is just her, LeBeau, and whatever future she can wrangle from this tryst.

LeBeau's grip tightens.

She opens her eyes.

LeBeau tugs her hand.

They go down the stairs.

Prometheus closes the doors behind them.

The restaurant is small and cozy, the décor dull earth tones – the walls brown, the carpet tan, the tablecloths beige. Antique crystal candelabras hang from the ceiling, casting shadows that ebb across the floor like an incoming tide. The mood is subdued, the music from the Lounges muffled, as the restaurant is mostly soundproofed.

There are not many here presently – there rarely are. Although the restaurant is (or can be) first class with both the menu and the service, the few people who come here want something fast and quick. It's a pitstop before launching back into the Lounges, the Gallery, or any of the other indulgences.

The exceptions are couples holding hands and staring lovingly into one another's eyes as they invest in the dream of love, union, and happy-ever-afters. Occasionally, there have been proposals. I wonder how those marriages are going now. I wish I knew. In my limited understanding of the world outside, I can only imagine relationships bonded here would go nowhere out there.

Amber and Gabriella sit at a table for two in the corner, each enjoying a Long Island Iced Tea. There's a bowl of nachos between them. They both pluck out a nacho, turn it over for a perfunctory examination, then put it in their mouths. Realizing they've mirrored one another, they laugh.

"I've played hundreds of games of pool here," Gabriella says. "I mean, I come here just to play. Especially with him. With Savage. There's something about him. But I've never gotten the privilege you got tonight."

"Privilege?" Amber stops in the act of eating a chip.

"Come on! You didn't enjoy it?"

Amber pops the chip into her mouth and smiles guiltily.

A waiter, Primo, approaches – a typical waiter here with model features, the bronzed complexion, his lean figure sculpted through hours in the gym. He is a dancer who auditions daily, albeit with no luck so far. His hair has been shaved on the sides, the top elongating into a short ponytail.

"Is everything to your satisfaction, ladies?" he asks with an inclination of his head. "Can I get you anything else?"

Gabriella holds up her Long Island Iced Tea.

"Two more of these, please," she says.

"I shouldn't," Amber says.

Primo, who was about to go, stops.

"Another's one not going to hurt," Gabriella says.

Amber picks up her existing drink. She's never had one before. There's no real taste of alcohol, although Gabriella has told her it contains every white spirit. But it tastes more like a strong apple juice. She gulps down what's left.

"Sure," she says.

Primo nods and leaves.

"So," Gabriella says, and then in a rush, *"what did it feel like?"*

"What?"

"The kiss!"

Amber's face is afire. She finishes her drink to try and cool herself down, but now that she is caught in the memory she is burning.

"It was just a little kiss," she says, trying to downplay it not for Gabriella's benefit, but her own.

"They would've had to pull me off that thing, let me tell you!" Gabriella says. "I would've been attached to it like it was life support."

Amber laughs. "Are you married? Do you have a boyfriend?"

"Been married ten years."

"Ten years?"

"Yep."

"Kids?"

"Two."

"Then how could you say that?" Amber asks. "What about your family?"

"I'm sure, in the world, there are great families. Love, warmth, closeness."

"Yours isn't …? Sorry, this is personal."

Gabriella reaches across the table and pats her hand. "It's okay. My marriage isn't horrible. He doesn't mistreat me. Doesn't abuse me. We don't argue any more than most couples. But do you know what I've worked out?"

Primo returns with two Long Island Iced Teas on a tray. Amber wonders how they were mixed so quickly. She does not know how well the bar-staff read the clientele, how they anticipate their desires. It's part of their training.

"There you are, ladies," Primo says, putting a glass down in front of each of them.

"Thank you," Amber says.

She picks up her empty glass and goes to put it on the tray but misjudges, striking the edge of the tray with the bottom of the glass. Primo catches the tray in time.

"I'm sorry!"

"No harm done," Primo says, taking the glass from her. He puts it on the tray. Gabriella finishes hers and hands it to him. He puts it on the tray also. "Enjoy," he says, leaving them.

"You know," Gabriella says, growing somber, "when you're young, you fall in love, but you don't really know what love is. You fall into that cycle that a lot of young people do – meet somebody you get involved with; you think you've fallen in love because you don't know any better; because you think you're in love, you get engaged. Then you get married. Buy a house. Get a mortgage. Have some kids. Maybe take out an investment. But as this goes on, do you know what you discover?"

Amber shakes her head.

"If you were given a couple of years with your partner in circumstances that simulate a marriage, you'd discover that while you might have a very deep affection for them, it's probably not love – not the sort that means you're passionate about your partner, that you're still devoted to them even when you see them at their most unattractive day after day, and definitely not the sort that should be forever."

"You want a fairy-tale love."

"That's what we all want, isn't it? The fairy tale? Nobody wants the reality – a partner who won't take the bins out, drinks too much, farts in bed, gets pudgy, needs to be hassled to do homework with the kids, stays too involved with his sports and friends and, well, that list goes on. I'm sure he has his own list of problems with me. Does anybody want that? Do you want that?"

"I guess not."

"It's like a job you tolerate." Gabriella smirks. "It's *good enough*. But that's about it."

Amber thinks about Quinn and wants to believe they're more than *good enough*, but she sees cracks in her relationship. They've always been there. But now she truly sees them. Quinn is needy. He's had little ambition since the knee injury ended his basketball prospects. Because basketball had occupied everything he'd done until he was twenty-one, he's inexperienced in the world and life – not that she's much better. Is that what attracted them to one another? A likeness? A need to support one another because of feelings of inadequacy?

They're not like Holly or Marcus, who are so forward and sure of themselves, taking on the world with a gusto that borders into foolhardiness; or Flavia, whose ambition can override everything else in her life; or even Dante, who might be insecure, but is still trying to get somewhere.

"I've got friends who can't wait to get out of the house," Gabriella goes on, "who do nothing but complain about their partners. I think they're always just that one drink, or even just a single sweet word away from cheating. I shouldn't moralize because, well, you know, security would've had to drag me off

Savage. I think I would've just let go. Sometimes you just have to. Right?"

"And how would you have faced your husband in the morning?"

Gabriella purses her lips. "With a smile and me telling myself everything is okay."

"Even if it isn't?"

"That's marriage," Gabriella says.

○ ○ ○ ○

Quinn doesn't know what his plan is. His outburst at Mr. Hermes was impulsiveness. It felt good at the time, but now that the anger has seeped out of him, the pain in his knuckle throbs into his palm. Perhaps that's all that *is* to remain – the pain. He stumbles from the Verdant Lounge, and into the juncture, coming to stand by the entrance under the plaque. He has no idea how he can collect on Mr. Hermes's Temptation, or whether he should.

He sees himself lurching out into the night, and never turning back. What would Amber think? Would she miss him? Would she *truly* miss him? Or would she find some relief in his departure? Quinn knows he's being melodramatic and self-pitying. He has to work out a plan – something *real*.

Emerging into the juncture is Savage, dressed now in jeans and a t-shirt, his topknot of hair bouncing behind him. It could be coincidence or fate. Quinn opts for the latter. They are all actors following cues. Mr. Hermes offered him the Temptation. Now here is Savage. It all fits, and maybe because it all fits this is the way it's meant to be.

Quinn envies Savage and hates him. Savage is everything Quinn believes he is not: composed, well-built, striking – and not just handsome, but striking in a way that demands attention. Quinn is sure Savage would kill with the ladies. Of course, he would. It would all come so easily to him. That's just how some people are built.

And how others aren't.

Now the inferiority bubbles into something hot and raw that scathes Quinn. He follows Savage into the Brimstone Lounge. The mustard décor is an affront to Quinn's eyes. He is unsure why they would use this color. He can only think of bile. Perhaps that's why they keep it so dim in here – to dull the garishness.

Savage sits on a stool at the bar and orders a drink – a rich brown beer in a tall glass. Quinn sits next to him. The bartender, a buxom woman with her dreadlocks drawn back into a tail, turns to him. Quinn sees that her name tag identifies her as "Prosper". The buckles on her vest are something blue and sparkly.

"Just a Corona, thanks," Quinn says. "With a lime."

"Corona with a lime coming up," Prosper says.

"No. Make it a lemon."

"A lemon?"

Quinn nods.

"Ooh," she says. "Living dangerously."

Quinn is irked he's being mocked. It's a little thing, but that's this night: a highlight of what he sees as a bundle of shortcomings that sum up his life. If he hadn't injured his knee, things might've been different: a professional career in basketball, money, opportunities, fans, adulation – not that he would've needed the latter. Amber is more than enough. And he would've been worthy of her. There'd be none of this questioning. He wouldn't be sitting here contemplating what he's about to do.

As if reading his unease, Prosper offers him a smile so big and assuring, it flusters him. He spins away from her and sees Savage sipping his beer. Quinn doesn't know how to open. Savage is just as likely to punch him in the nose. Quinn wouldn't blame him if he did. In fact, Quinn makes a vow to himself: if hostility is Savage's response, Quinn will take that as a sign, walk out of here, and deal with the consequences.

"Saw your show," Quinn says.

"Sorry?" Savage says.

Prosper places a Corona in front of Quinn. He slides a twenty across to her. "Keep the change," he tells her.

"Thank you." Prosper leaves them.

"Your show," Quinn says. "Just before. I saw it."

"Hope you enjoyed it," Savage says.

"I saw you with my girlfriend."

Savage rises from his stool. His shoulders shoot up, his muscular arms coiled not just to defend himself, but to attack first. Quinn almost laughs. Like Savage should find him threatening. But this is probably a reaction he's had to deal with a time or two – the jealous partner.

"She was the one at the end," Quinn says, forcing himself to stare into his Corona, trying to be as measured as possible. "It's okay. I'm not angry."

"You're not?" Savage says.

"Not at all."

Savage frowns unsurely; he assumes that Quinn saw everything – right down to Amber's kiss. Other women have asserted themselves similarly. Savage has always remained in control, always found a way to subdue, then disarm that sort of behavior. What he's never faced is somebody who's witnessed their partner in such an act.

"Sit down," Quinn says. "I've got a proposition for you."

Savage doesn't move. Quinn can see he's considering whether to leave or not. Right then, Quinn just wants to smash his Corona over Savage's head. Savage owes him after the way he handled Amber. The least he could offer is a bit of his time.

"Sit. *Please.*"

Savage surveys Quinn, as if figuring out what sort of threat he might be, and if he does become a threat, how he could be handled. Quinn feels ill-equipped under the scrutiny. He has height. His basketballer's physique has melted into an everyday physique. He still has his core strength, but Savage moves with the purposefulness of somebody who has either studied some fighting discipline or has fought so much he knows how to handle himself.

"You know, girls come to my show," he says, sitting back on his stool. "I don't ask them. They come. And I try to give them a good show – the best show in Prudence. It's nothing personal. It's work for me – money to pay bills and live my life."

"I want you to make it personal."

"What?"

"I want you to fuck my girlfriend."

Quinn expects incredulity. He doesn't get it. Surprisingly to Quinn, but unsurprisingly to myself, Savage has heard this proposition often: men wanting to watch him fuck their partners, or interested in a threesome or foursome, or women wanting to share him, or men hoping he might be bi – there have been numerous propositions. Savage used to indulge, but has grown desensitized to such solicitations.

Again, he sizes Quinn up. Quinn is not like others. He's *wholesome*, a boy in a man's body uncomfortable with moving around in a hectic and sometimes perverse world. And he's *nervous*. This *is* new to Savage. Quinn's nervousness doesn't come from a lack of bravado, as it might from others; it comes from some quiet, desperate place swirling with fear. Lust does not motivate him. It's something else.

"You don't seem the type," Savage says.

"You'd be wrong." Quinn gulps from his Corona. "And I'm sure she'd like it."

He doesn't know why he says this. He thinks possibly he's baiting Savage, as if expecting Savage will say, *No! I'm sure she loves you!* That'll put everything in context then. It'll make everything all right. And it'll render meaningless what he saw earlier when Amber had her legs wrapped around Savage.

"Oh, of that there's no doubt," Savage says.

Quinn's hands tighten around his Corona. "You do this, and you do it tonight, I'll give you five thousand dollars."

The offer of money isn't new either. What's unusual for Savage is that judging by Quinn's blazer and his ill-fitting pants, he doesn't have that money to spend. But he *is* earnest. That comes across. Whatever's going on here, Quinn will follow through. Savage had thought Quinn was full of fear. It's not. It's *terror*. Quinn is terrified of what comes next.

"But it must be done," he says. "All the way. What do you say?"

Savage gets up from his stool, leans against the bar, and finishes his beer. "Where is she?"

"I don't know."

"That doesn't help."

"It's a big place. We got separated."

"Women usually get a drink or two after my show, then go back to see the next Icon. It's addictive for some. Don't worry. I'll find her."

"Where're you going to do it?" Quinn holds up his hand. "No, wait, don't tell me. I don't want to know anything."

"Nothing? Don't you want proof?"

"Proof?"

"How about I bring you her panties?"

"Her panties?"

"You'd recognize them, wouldn't you?"

Savage is sure the talk of proof will shake Quinn's convictions. He'll understand the reality of the transaction. The thought of bringing his partner's panties to him would truly make this *real* for him.

And Savage can see that in Quinn's wild eyes that it has but, no, it hasn't dissuaded him at all. For whatever reason, he wants this. *Needs* this.

He remains unmoved, a lumbering oaf that a fitful breath could topple.

"I just want to know that it's … done," he says.

Savage grins. "Don't worry," he says. "She will be."

o   o   o   o

Dante drifts into the Cardinal Lounge, his phone pressed to his ear. His call to Flavia doesn't connect. He checks his phone. It has three bars of reception, so that's not the problem – at least not on his side. But given all the brick, there must be areas where reception is dubious, which begs the question of where Flavia is. Dante puts his phone away. He'll try again in five minutes, although he's already tried three times.

He takes a seat at the bar and orders a Bourbon & Coke. The bartender, Providence, mixes it deftly. Dante stares at her rounded hips, at the size of her breasts. She is intimidatingly statuesque. He's never had a woman like that and doesn't understand his sudden captivation. Like many men, he appreciates beautiful women, but this appreciation has something else about it, something that doesn't entirely sit comfortably, and which he tries to wrestle with.

"Problem?" Providence asks.

"Just …"

"What?"

Dante is about to tell her he's lost contact with his girlfriend. His hand goes into his pocket and feels the ring box there. Providence smiles at him. It's a great smile. Dante would like to see her face contorted into a variety of other expressions. Of course, he knows that's not going to happen. And he justifies now that his objectification is nothing more than harmless fantasizing, just like he fantasized in the gaming room about the Icon Patricia. But Patricia had a sweetness about her – well, until she grew rebellious and confrontational. Providence already has that manner. Dante can not only see it but is in awe of it.

"I've gotten separated from my friends," Dante says.

"That happens. Prudence is like a city unto itself."

She pushes his Bourbon & Coke across the bar. He hands her a twenty.

"Keep it," he says.

"Thank you." Providence sticks the money in the register but doesn't pocket any change.

Dante leans one elbow against the bar, trying to be as casual as possible as he surveys the people in the Cardinal Lounge. There's only a few, and the bulk of them are men, handsome with square jaws and gym-junky builds. They could be models retained to create a profile of flawless clientele – striking, silent men who are frozen in this snapshot of perfection. They highlight to Dante just how imperfect he is. He should be airbrushed out of this shot.

"Searching for somebody in particular?" Providence asks.

"Where are all the women?"

"The place is filled with them."

"Not in here."

"It fluctuates. What're you looking for?"

"I don't know."

"You don't know?"

"No."

"Maybe you'll never know."

Dante grins at her, although he's worried he's coming across as oafish. Marcus is the master of façades: he could be an actor with a library of responses to call upon depending on whoever he's talking to. Quinn always has that babyface naivety, although that's appealing in its way. No doubt, that's what entranced Amber. Dante doesn't think he has anything as flattering. He's always worried he comes across as a clod.

"How about you?" he asks.

"I'm on duty."

"When do you get off?"

Dante appreciates how cliché this sounds, and knows he is horribly ill-equipped to use such a line. She should laugh at him now. Or roll her eyes. Or walk away. Or, worse, throw his drink in his face. Or even summon security to toss him. Dante sees each scenario play out in his mind. But Providence does none of these things. She leans over the bar so her face is inches from Dante.

"Do you really think you could handle me?" she asks.

Dante has a moment of indecision – he should back off. But he feels reckless after the events of the night. As wrong as it is, he decides to double down. There's still no harm being done.

"I could try," he says.

"What if I said let's go for it right now?"

Providence unbuttons the top button of her vest, teasing a glimpse of cleavage. Dante can see the swell of her left breast. The sight shouldn't fluster him as it does, but it's not the sight itself, but Providence's confidence. These things aren't meant to happen – least of all not to him.

"What if I said I could take you somewhere private just sixty seconds away and you could have your way with me?" she asks. "Do you think you could handle me?"

"Would you?" Dante's eyes flit around the Lounge. "Really say that, I mean?"

There's nowhere he can see that offers immediate privacy, although the back corner, behind the mirrored octagon, is secluded. He swallows nervously from his drink. He cannot believe what he's said. He should've been like Marcus. Marcus would've been equally as aggressive, but also eloquent. Would've artfully counter-attacked. Dante's unsure why he's back to trying to emulate Marcus – perhaps because Dante himself feels so out of his depth he needs to be anybody but himself.

Providence reaches across the bar and puts a hand on his arm. Her cleavage is more apparent. He should lean in and kiss her; that's exactly what he should do. Instead, he jumps when she touches him. Sweat trickles down the sides of his face. She pulls back.

"I don't think you could handle me," she says.

Dante laughs. She is right. And he accepts that there's no shame in that. This is his lot. She could take him in her hands, scrunch him up, and dump him into a wastebasket. That in itself is about as big an honor as he deserves.

"I think not." He finishes his Bourbon & Coke, swallows some of the ice into his mouth, and slides the empty glass across the bar. "Do you do that with all your customers?"

"Just the ones I want to prey on." Providence puts the empty glass into the sink, grabs another, and shovels some ice into it.

"Why? Why would you want to do that?"

"Most men are like lions born and bred in captivity. Sure, they're fearsome in that habitat. But take them out of their zoos, put them back in the wild, and they just don't know how to survive."

Providence slides the Bourbon & Coke across the bar. Dante reaches for some money. Providence holds up a hand.

"On me," she says.

"Thanks." Dante takes a sip. She's made it strong. "So, what was the purpose of this little interplay?"

Providence buttons up her vest. "Just wanted you to know you're in the jungle now," she says.

"What's that mean?"

"Just watch out who you try to bite."

○   ○   ○   ○

Marcus doesn't know how the Icons wear these outfits. The crotch pinches, the Velcro seams chafe, the armpits scratch, and the leathers are too hot. He just wants to be out of it. Of course – and now he can't help grinning as two members of security escort him to his assigned gaming room – that'll happen soon enough.

He thinks he should be nervous. There should be a shortness of breath, or his heart should thump. But there's just excitement. He can't believe it, but he really wants to do this – is looking forward to it more than he's looked forward to anything recently.

When he steps into the gaming room, the first thing that greets him are the cheers and wolf whistles. He holds a hand up. Faces confront him – too many to take in at once. Most seem older than him, though – in their thirties. He guesses they're bored housewives out for a night on the town. At the back is a small twenty-something group of deliriously excited women, one with a sash declaring her the bride – a hens party. In the opposite corner are several older women, possibly in their forties. More power to them.

Marcus throws his arms up and pivots on his heel as he makes his way to the table. "Ladies, the show is back on!" he says. "And I am the prize!" He folds his hands behind his head, gyrates his hips and feels corny doing it, but is gratified when the women roar. "All righty! Let's get down to it!" He takes a book of raffle tickets out of his pocket and waves them in the air. "Who wants a ticket?"

The women surge forward not just enthusiastically but aggressively. Marcus backs into the table, fearing he'll be crushed. Even though he sees them as *only* women, the sight of so many of them convinces him there's a delicate balance to be maintained. He is at their mercy, but they can't ever work that out for themselves. They *mustn't.* He must control them, just as they should be controlled.

"Whoa! Whoa! Whoa! Ladies!" Marcus thrusts his hands at them, like a traffic cop gesturing for cars to stop. "Let's take it easy!"

He pushes his hands back again and the women pause, then take a step back. They survey him hungrily. Their eyes consume him. Marcus unbuttons the top button of his vest. Some of the women are still, but others cheer or laugh, and a few even shout out lewd compliments. This is so easy, and empowering, to control them at a whim, but he has always been good at seduction, although never on such a large scale. The cheap titillation empowers him. He is the focus of adulation here and loves it.

"Okay," he says. "Who wants a ticket?"

"I'll take them all."

The voice cuts through the din so that it falls flat, then silent; Marcus is sure who it is. The heads of the women turn. The group parts. Holly stands there, money crumpled in her fist. She strides down the aisle the women have formed and right up to Marcus.

"You can't do that!" one of the women says. She'd be in her forties, maybe even fifty, a diminutive woman, her brown hair cut in a bob. There's a sadness in her eyes and her face is too heavily made-up. Marcus assumes she is married to some loser, and this is an escape for her. Holly imagines she's married to somebody overbearing, and her struggle to make it work leaves her disconsolate.

"This guy's my fiancé," Holly says.

Her eyes don't leave Marcus's. He's seen her angry – plenty of times. Usually, she screams and rants and gesticulates. She's never like this, as if the rage has overloaded her programmed responses and rerouted her anger into this tight focus. Only one thing could make her like this, although he doesn't know how she would've found out. He decides it's best to be oblivious.

"Too bad," the diminutive brunette says. "You can't protect him by hoarding all the tickets. He's open slather."

"Who said anything about protecting him?" Holly asks. "We've got issues to deal with."

"Take it to a marriage counsel—"

Holly's head cocks back. She glowers at the woman. The woman shuts up.

"You know, I'd love to entertain you, Holly," Marcus says, "but you couldn't afford this whole book of tickets." He waggles them in front of her face.

"Fine."

Holly puts her money away. Marcus is sure he's dissuaded her. But instead, she grabs a cue from the rack on the wall.

"Let's play tit for tat," she says, chalking the tip of her cue. "You win, I strip. I win, you strip."

Marcus likes the idea – a contest; moreover, it's a contest he's sure he'll win. She's good at pool, but not as good as him. He'd like to strip her, item by item, in front of a crowd, and show her – and everybody else in here – just who's in charge. It's a lesson in love, relationships, and roles.

"You're just gonna make a fool of yourself," he says, knowing that no warning will stop her now. This is Holly: she is indignant. She will pursue this regardless of the circumstances.

"Wouldn't be the first time," she says.

"Okay." Marcus darts around the table, fishing the balls out of the pockets. "I'm gonna send you out of here with your tail between your legs, then I'm gonna give these ladies the show they deserve."

As he grabs the rack and sets up the balls, the diminutive brunette goes up to Holly and puts a reassuring hand on her shoulder. "No offense, honey," she says, "but I'm getting the feeling you're engaged to a prick."

The comment's indiscreet. Marcus is *meant* to overhear it. Just like that, the mood in the room has changed. There's no heady anticipation. When Marcus surveys the women, he sees recrimination. Typically, they've banded behind Holly. He should excuse himself, say he has to piss maybe, then just not come back. That will get him in trouble with Constance, but so what? The only thing which stops him is he refuses to let a group of women – even a mob – intimidate him. Anyway, security remain in the doorway.

He takes the rack from the table. "You want to break?" he asks Holly. "Or should I?"

○　○　○　○

Teo opens the door to Constance's office. Patricia, wrapped again in her towel, exits, not looking back. She knows it wouldn't be wise and Teo can't blame her. The tension has clogged his lungs. The sound of the door closing is a starting pistol that rouses him that this is a contest. Constance stands up straight. She is always imperious, and there is always the hint of underlying menace, the stringency of her authority, but now she is terrible also. Any of her employees would bow their heads, afraid to face her. Not Joy, though. Hands on hips, butt cocked jauntily, satchel resting on her belly, she glares at Constance.

"I asked it before," Constance says, "and I'll ask it again: who are you?"

"Do you remember when you first came here, Constance?" Joy asks. "You were an arrogant, spoilt girl. However, you were also methodical. Calculating – at least once you got straight." She walks to Constance's bar and traces a finger across the various bottles. "Age has brought you wisdom and maturity. You've grown up. Maybe, worse than that, you've outgrown Prudence."

"This isn't the Camarilla." Constance laughs. "Or not *only*. Did that old fool send you?"

"He *is* a fool," Joy says, "but he's merely a face, isn't he?" She approaches Constance. "Prudence is greater than one man, greater than the Camarilla, even if they don't realize it themselves. She is a world unto herself."

"The way you handled Patricia—"

"Is the way you would've handled her, once upon a time. You've grown complacent. You've grown," Joy reaches out and, as if for emphasis, pokes Constance in the left side of her chest, "soft."

"Teo, get this woman out—"

Joy fires a hand at Teo, one finger pointing to condemn him. "Stay!"

Teo had been in the process of kicking off to cross the distance as quickly as possible, but now he is frozen. He recognizes the command in Joy's voice. He hears it in Constance's every night. This is the voice of irrefutable authority.

But there is something different about Joy – that lack of familiarity he hears with Constance. Joy's tone is cold but flawless. *Single*-minded. It is the only thing Teo hears, and it incapacitates him.

"Even calling for your footpad," Joy says, "is such a sign of weakness."

"So be it," Constance says. She tries to maintain her nonchalance, but her voice is far away, and a roar fills her ears. "Just between us, then."

"But not for much longer," Joy says.

V

Amber is unsure where her Long Island Iced Tea has gone. She holds the glass in her hand, but there's only a sip left in it. The room sways around her. She should've stopped when she felt tipsy one drink ago. That was the sign she usually would've observed. But she is enjoying the freedom, if not the recklessness, of drinking. She has never been senselessly drunk before, so has no frame of reference for how this will unfold, or how she'll regret it in the morning. Opposite her, Gabriella prattles on, just as she has since they first arrived. Amber doesn't mind. Gabriella's familiarity is comforting.

The waiter, Primo, arrives with a tray bearing another two Long Island Iced Teas. His starchy professionalism while being semi-naked is surreal as he rests a glass in front of each of them. Both Amber and Gabriella tilt their heads at him.

"We didn't order these," Gabriella says.

"Compliments of the gentleman." Primo points toward the rear of the bar.

Seated there, in jeans, leather boots, and a semi-transparent white shirt, is Savage. He lifts his own drink – a bottle of Asahi

– to toast them. Amber takes several moments to identify him in civilian clothing, and several more to absorb him, but Gabriella covers her mouth in astonishment.

"Oh my God!" she says.

Savage rises from his barstool and comes across to their table, almost gliding across the floor.

"Mind if I join you, ladies?" he asks.

"Be our guest!" Gabriella says.

Savage grabs a chair from a nearby table, puts it between them, and sits down. Amber can't help looking at his crotch. She doesn't mean to, but there's a bulge there, and she can imagine the way his cock would nestle against his lap under his jeans. She wonders if he wears underwear. He wouldn't.

Usually, such ruminations might embarrass her, but the Long Island Ice Teas have loosened her inhibitions, and she enjoys the fantasy. It's safe because it *is* just a fantasy, regardless of what happened earlier. Her rationalizations are confused and hollow. She dismisses them as unimportant.

"I've seen you here before," Savage says to Gabriella, and – for an instant – Gabriella forgets her husband, forgets her kids, and contemplates the likelihood of fucking Savage until she is sore and dehydrated and breathless. "But, you," he turns to Amber, "this is your first time?"

Amber nods. Gabriella, who's already abandoned hopes of Savage wanting her, who'll go home tonight and wake her husband and ride him as if she were breaking in a stallion while thinking of Savage, gives Amber a surreptitious thumbs up.

"So, what do you do?" Savage directs the question at Amber, but then reclines on his chair, and alternates his attention from Amber, to Gabriella, and back to Amber again.

"Hairdresser."

The answer comes from both simultaneously. They gape at each other and laugh.

"You sisters?" Savage asks.

"We just met tonight," Gabriella says. "Loved your show."

"I aim to please."

Savage puts a hand on Amber's thigh. Now she does grow mortified. This has just graduated from fantasy to something very real. But she also likes the way his hand feels – so big, so warm, so secure. She likes that she is the object of his desire. She likes that she is wanted by somebody confident and assured. It's such a different feeling to Quinn. She has been hit on before, but the advances have always been sleazy or needy or desperate. Savage is something else.

"That probably sounds cliché, doesn't it?" he asks.

"Not at all," Amber says.

"When you're in that room with me, I want you to forget everything except being in that room. Forget your problems, forget your family," Savage's voice drops, "forget your partners. I know it becomes a crowded room, but I want every woman in there to think it's just her and me. Not from an egotistical point of view, of course. It's just the atmosphere I want to create, because when I'm performing, I feel like I'm soaring. I want to take you on that ride."

"You don't fail," Gabriella says.

"You?" Savage leans in toward Amber. "Did you feel something?"

"I felt something."

Amber's unsure if she spoke or just mouthed the words. Then she laughs nervously. She *did* feel something. Her cheeks grow hot with embarrassment. But now she embraces what she did. She has never let go in life. This is what Holly must've felt. There is power in it.

"Excuse me," Gabriella says. "I need to visit the bathroom. Then ..."

"Then?" Amber asks.

"Maybe I'll catch another show."

Amber knows what Gabriella's doing – absconding so she doesn't get in the way. If Amber were sober, she'd protest that Gabriella's departure is unnecessary. But given how much Amber has drunk, given how her thoughts are leaning, she welcomes being alone with Savage.

Gabriella circles her forefinger and thumb and thrusts them toward Amber, encouraging her to go for it. Then she turns and leaves the Lounge.

"Well," Savage says, "I guess it's just the two of us."

○ ○ ○ ○

Holly lines up the number six in the corner pocket. Marcus, his hands folded around his cue, grins infuriatingly at her. Holly strikes the cue ball harder than she has to. It races across the lush felt and hits the six, which thuds into the cup of the pocket, pinballs there, but does not go in. Some of the women in the back of the room gasp, the way a crowd might during a tennis match when a shot clips the net after a long rally. Holly straightens and chalks her cue while Marcus walks up to the table.

"How many times have you been here before tonight?" she asks.

"A handful."

"A handful?"

"We've only been here the week."

Marcus leans over the table and hits the thirteen into the middle pocket. He lines up his next shot – the eleven into the opposite corner – but feels Holly's eyes on him. Her face is icy. It makes him want to laugh. She's too wholesomely pretty to carry any sternness. It has all the ferocity of a growling puppy.

"So I've been here," he says. "Who doesn't want to come here?"

Marcus hits the eleven in, then the nine, before missing banking the fourteen. Bank shots trouble him, although he's obsessed with making them work.

Holly's always seemed indifferent when she's played pool, but has shown enough talent to be threatening. Marcus knows he can't take her lightly. He wants to beat her. More than that, he wants to break her, and teach her a lesson for challenging him. The thought excites him.

"What's it matter?" he asks.

Holly pots the four, then chalks her cue. "Ever run into the old guy in the Verdant Lounge?"

Marcus tells himself not to react and he's sure he doesn't move, but Holly must see something in him – Marcus doesn't know what.

"So, you have?" she asks, missing the one.

"Well?" Marcus pockets the ten, then lines up the fifteen.

"What Temptation did he set you?"

Marcus shanks his shot, lifting the cue before he's struck the cue ball. The cue ball skews into the side of the table, rebounds, and fortunately hits another of his balls – the twelve.

"How did you know …?" Marcus asks, rising from the table.

"I didn't. I do now."

Marcus chuckles appreciatively. She has always been much more observant and insightful than he's ever given her credit for. He's unsure why he keeps losing his grasp on that. The first time they'd met, she'd been part-time modeling for a class he'd taken on sketching with charcoal. He'd aspired to be an artist – well, until his father kept condemning it as an unmanly pursuit. But Marcus had been serious about it. And good. No, better than that. *Great.* He'd kept drawing – *sketching* – secretly, hiding it from not just his father, but his three brothers and mother.

Later, he'd solicited Holly to model for him. They went out one night for a meal, then a movie, then had sex in an alley. Usually, that would've been enough. But he kept coming back to her. They had a casual physical agreement for years, fucking in-between (and sometimes *during*) Holly's various doomed relationships. She had a proclivity for picking selfish men. Marcus has to admit there was something more about her that attracted him, but it never usurped his physical understanding of her. Eventually, almost by default, they became a couple.

"Well?" Holly says.

"Play your shot."

Holly studies the table. She's only hit in the four. Marcus has the twelve, fourteen, and fifteen remaining. He can see the resolve in her face. She knows she must remain competitive. More than that, she must win. Her interrogation will go nowhere if he beats her – and beats her easily. She needs time. And lots of it.

She pockets the seven in the furthest corner, then the five in the middle. The crowd of women cheer. She's developed a fan club. A bank shot off the one cannons into the six, which thunders in, leaving the one taking its place. Her fan club gasp. The three's next in the middle, then the one. She lines up the two for a simple shot into the corner.

"Nervous?" she asks.

Marcus scowls at her. Her eyes shoot to the way his erection bulges against the crotch of his leather pants. She's a whirlwind when she lets herself go. That's when he wholeheartedly enjoys the competitiveness between them. The thought of having her at his mercy excites him. This is something he *does* understand: fucking is a battlefield, a war of bodies and technique and desire. His wins have been few. And, given how long they've been together, he's sure he's lost ground. He figures that must be why this victory so appeals to him.

She hits the two in, then lines up the black. It sits just outside the corner pocket – not a difficult shot by any means. But as Holly aims – as her fan club shout encouragement – Marcus sees that she freezes. She's conscious of the stakes and what it would mean to miss. She plays the shot softly – much softer than she should've. The cue ball strikes the black too finely. It trickles toward the pocket, hits the corner, and stays there. A collective sigh of disappointment fills the room.

"Tell me," Holly says.

"What do you know?" Marcus says, sending the fourteen into the middle pocket. He moves quickly now, knowing he must seize his chance. The room's turned against him. This isn't the way it was meant to be. He knocks the twelve in, then lines up the fifteen. "Well?"

"You tell me."

"I don't know how much you know."

"Then there's something *to* know."

Marcus pockets the fifteen, then lines up the black. It's the easiest of shots. He could hit it in with his eyes closed. But he lines it up, holds the cue over the course the cue ball must take, then kneels by the corner to examine the shot. Holly rolls her eyes. The women in the room jeer him.

Marcus doesn't care. He'll show the lot of them.

He smashes the eight in much harder than he has to. It's a stupid thing to do. He watches the cue ball rebound around the table, unsure where it'll end up. It could easily finish in a pocket – and it does get close to a middle pocket. Some of the women encourage it in, but it falls short, albeit precariously.

Marcus grins at them, then turns to Holly. "Tit for tat, remember?" he says.

Holly reaches for her mini skirt, then stops. Marcus purses his lips. She's got a great little butt, which will be distracting.

He thinks she knows it, too. But when she unbuttons her skirt, letting it fall around her ankles, she reveals herself to be naked underneath. Marcus gapes at her. Her self-consciousness flares briefly, as her hands go to her crotch, but then she spins, as if she were modeling herself at the end of a catwalk. Her temerity inflames her fan club. They cheer her – cheer Holly for defying the expectation this should be embarrassing or shameful.

Only Marcus thinks this way – he starts toward her, intending to cover her. Her face softens. He stops himself. No. Whatever game she's playing, she's going to see it through. He pulls the leathers from the crotch of his pants. His erection feels so hard and painful he's sure it'll explode.

"No panties?" he asks.

"I know how you've always liked my butt," she says.

"You think it'll put me off?"

"You tell me."

"It won't," Marcus says, trying to convince himself.

"Then set them up," Holly tells him. "We ain't done. Not by a long shot."

○ ○ ○ ○

Quinn sits on a toilet in a cubicle, his knees jutting up at absurd angles. The toilet, so small in proportion to his frame, could be a children's toilet under him

The bathroom reeks of disinfectant. They must pump it in for it to remain this strong at this time of night. Perhaps it's a way to keep people from congregating in the bathroom for too long, or perhaps it's just a constant antiseptic safeguard.

For Quinn, it's irrelevant. He digs his fists into his eyes to stem the tears. He's not moving.

The bathroom door swings open.

Laughter.

Then footsteps, heading across to the urinals.

"You see that blonde?" one voice says. It's deep but coarse, the sound of somebody who's been smoking too heavily for too long, although Quinn pictures the man as young with bronzed skin, a cleft in his chin, and black hair. He has a Cockney accent, which makes him sound jocular. Next comes the sound of somebody urinating. Then it's echoed.

"In the red dress?" another voice asks. This is smoother, oily almost, the accent French. Quinn bets the man is dark and athletic and has never had a woman decline him. "Or the one with the little top?"

"Little top."

"Yeah."

"What do you think my chances are?"

"That shit she was doing with you on the dance floor was indecent."

Husky Voice laughs.

Quinn knows nothing about these men, and he knows they're not talking about Amber, but he recognizes they're predatory. Like Marcus. They see something they want, they hunt it. Women aren't women. They're conquests. And yet what's he done? Taken the one thing he had and given it to somebody to pillage.

Planting his elbows into his thighs, Quinn drops his head into his hands. He can't believe he's done this. He should leave now — collect his money from Mr. Hermes, pay off his debts, take a little for himself, and leave the rest to Amber as an apology. Maybe he could start over somewhere, although he knows that wherever he goes, he'll always carry the shame of what he's done.

Of course, he can't collect from Mr. Hermes until Savage consummates the deed. That he *will* consummate it is a certainty, although Quinn doesn't know why. Amber's always been faithful, has always been chaste, but perhaps that's what makes it a certainty – she's a lamb to Savage. The thought twists Quinn up so tight he's sure it'll tear him apart and leave him shredded on the floor. He sobs, a guffaw that explodes from his throat, and clunks a hand against the wall of the cubicle to steady himself.

"Hey, man, you okay in there?" This comes from Husky Voice.

Quinn looks up through bleary eyes, then dries them with a fist.

"Hey?"

"I'm fine!"

"Okay, man. Just asking."

As Quinn leans back on the toilet, he hears the footsteps move to the sinks, then running water. Flashing through his mind is the image of Amber, her legs wrapped around Savage's hips as he spins her around. Then it transforms into them naked, Amber shrieking uncontrollably as Savage drives himself into her again and again.

Quinn collapses shapelessly onto the floor, leans against the toilet bowl, and dry retches as the sound of hand driers fills the bathroom. The blue toilet water reeks of disinfectant. Quinn's eyes water and the smell fills his mouth. The hand driers cease. Footsteps head out.

Quinn bows his head.

He's alone.

Rupe knows it's foolish to remain any longer. As he takes a seat at the North Bar and orders a Vermouth, he concludes he's foolish to be coming here at all. Around him, there are young faces, people vibrant with energy and their whole lives ahead of them. He is a relic best left in the past.

He takes out his wallet. In one of the plastic pockets is a picture of his wife, smiling in front of a tree. Despite her pain, despite the way she wasted away and grew skeletal, she held onto her grace. Her smile is mischievous – *A smile for all time*, she told him. There is a similarity to Joy – at least vaguely.

Rupe took the picture in the park, just an hour before his wife died. She'd convinced him to take her out, and she *had* been more energetic. But then she'd collapsed as they shared waffles at a little outdoor cafe. The picture forever exemplifies the sadness that followed. He has never eaten waffles again. It's a simple thing, perhaps insignificant, but it is the emblem of his grief.

He strokes her face with his thumb, imagining the warmth and softness of her skin. He is stupid to come here, to chat up women ten years younger than him, if not half his age. There is nowhere any relationship can go. People don't come here to settle down. They come here to let go.

As for Joy … what was he thinking? There hasn't been a single man tonight who *wasn't* attracted to her, who *didn't* lust after her. How can he compete? But he was sure there was something there, although it was likelier a middle-aged man's foolish whimsy, a clumsy grasp at validation that he is still relevant.

Rupe closes his wallet and shoves it into his pocket. The flirting is done. The game is over. He will make one final play for Joy. It will be futile – he is sure of that. But it will put the exclamation mark on his endeavors. Then he will go home, take the gun he keeps for home security from the desk drawer in his study, put it to his temple, and that will be that.

He swallows his Vermouth, slams the glass on the bar, pushes his way through the crowd and heads out into the juncture, until he's lurking by the entrance under the plaque. People stream past him, as if riding the slipstream of the breeze coming from the lobby. Its coolness dries the sweat on his brow and tickles a chill down his shirt.

Ahead of him looms the stairwell leading up to Constance's office, guarded by two behemoths. Rupe wavers. Naturally, there would be security. He was stupid – or idealistic, although perhaps it amounts to the same thing – to forget them.

Rupe wonders if he could charge them – run right through them while they're unprepared and race up the stairs. He doesn't fancy his chances. He has been to clubs and bars and has never seen security so militant, so prepared. It would be easier breaking out of hell than causing trouble here.

He leans against the wall, lifts his head up to the ceiling, and revels in the breeze. He's never realized it before, but this really is the best place to be. There is nowhere cooler, the crowd is thinnest, and the music is muffled. It almost gives one room to think.

Rupe closes his eyes. He can wait. That's the plan. Sooner or later Joy will emerge. Then he will pick up the game they've been playing.

And, one way or another, finish it.

○　○　○　○

Nico and Mr. Hermes stare at one another, almost as if each is daring the other to break the silence. But it is no contest. Nico has no idea what to say. He has failed. There is not much place to go from here. They both know it. The best choice would be to leave.

When Mr. Hermes smiles, Nico notices two things for the very first time: that he has never remembered Mr. Hermes as being anything other than this old; and that his face is thin, with high cheekbones that seem almost sculpted to sharp points, and a grin of manic, if not senseless glee. He's a wasted corpse animated into the caricature of life whereas previously, Nico always thought of him as a plain man, plain and solid, but with an underlying sternness that was never seen fully but hinted at something terrible.

"Shall we begin?" Mr. Hermes asks.

"Why do you do this?" Nico asks.

"That is not the way the game is played, Nico."

"I don't care how the game's played."

"Do you question why the sun comes up? Why there's crime in the world? Why injustice runs rampant? When you hear of random shootings, do you question whether you should go out and live your life? Or do you hide? Cower? That was your father, Nico. Life is a game with ever-changing rules."

Nico glowers at Mr. Hermes, an angry rebuke dying as a waitress brings Mr. Hermes another iced water, and Nico a scotch rocks. Mr. Hermes lifts his iced water and swirls it, like it was a fine wine whose bouquet he wanted to enjoy.

"Is everything all right here?" the waitress, Prelude, asks. "Can I get you anything else?"

"We are fine, dear," Mr. Hermes says.

Prelude leaves.

"Your father and I built our fortunes from nothing but, as the cliché states, blood, sweat, and tears. But your father, he couldn't enjoy it. He feared losing it. Every day presented a new danger. Inevitably, he locked himself in his house. Locked the world out. Withered away. Became a gibbering old fool with too much power and too little sense. Surely you remember, Nico. Your parents might've divorced, you might've seen your father little, but surely you remember the man he became."

Nico drops his gaze from Mr. Hermes.

"Of course you do. I may have my faults, but I've lived this life. And then some. I took a kingdom and built it into an unassailable empire."

"By cutting my father out—"

"I did what was necessary, Nico. It had nothing to do with your father. He was my best friend. He married my stepsister, your mother. But he had become a ship whose hull had been compromised. Like the *Titanic*. Do you think they stayed aboard trying to keep the ship afloat? No, they understood the need to cut their losses, just as I did, even though it meant the sacrifice of life. Your father was a brilliant business mind, *once upon a time*. When he was no longer serviceable, when he was no longer committed to the very ambition we pledged to pursue when we were young, then I had to do what was necessary. What about you, Nico? Can you do what's necessary?"

Nico picks up his scotch rocks and takes a sip. He wants to appear debonair, but is sure that Mr. Hermes can hear his heartbeat, can see how rapidly his chest heaves to accommodate his breathing, can smell that his sweat is not from the humidity but from fear.

"Of course—" he begins.

"You couldn't even fulfill a simple Temptation – the simplest Temptation. Who wouldn't want to prostitute themselves for women? *You.* You are your father's son. You have his dreaming spirit, but not his endeavor – well, his initial endeavor. You are the embodiment of what he became: *fear.*"

Nico downs his scotch and, immediately, the waitress is putting another one in front of him and taking his empty glass away. Has Mr. Hermes planned this, to ply him with alcohol and make him malleable? Nico doesn't care. Before he becomes malleable, he'll grow ornery – at least for a little bit. Hopefully it's for long enough.

"You asked me if I was ready to go again," he says.

"How would you like all this?" Mr. Hermes waves his hand idly. "Indeed, how would you like your father's fortune?"

"How?"

Mr. Hermes reaches into his jacket and produces a gun – an old silver automatic, the words "Chiefs Special" inscribed across the slide, the Smith & Wesson logo imprinted on the black rubber wraparound grip.

He places it gently on the table.

Nico knows this gun. He's seen it before.

"Is that—?"

"The gun your father used to kill himself. Of course, you know that. You found him, this gun in his hand. He asked me for it."

Nico's mouth drops open – he's never known this detail.

"Did I know why he wanted it?" Mr. Hermes shrugs indifferently. "With this gun, he consolidated my fortune." He slides the gun across the table to Nico. "With it, you can consolidate yours. The question is, will you?"

Nico gulps his scotch, sets the glass down, and picks up the gun. The waitress is by his side, replacing his empty glass with another full one. Nico tries to drag the gun under the table but hits the edge of the table instead. There's a clatter that draws the attention of people close by. Then he has it hidden. The waitress is oblivious. She takes his empty glass and leaves.

"Well, Nico?"

"You expect me to shoot somebody?"

"I expect you to do what's necessary."

"I'll go to prison."

"The poor, the middle-class, the unprepared, they go to prison, Nico. But the Camarilla can protect you. Well," Mr. Hermes's smile is almost shy, "*I* can. Death can be liberating – just as your father's death liberated me, liberated everything we'd built, from his entanglement."

Nico doesn't know what to say. Many rumors have surrounded his father, his brother, Mr. Hermes, and the Camarilla –

preposterous stories involving murder, conspiracies, influencing global economics, and profiting from gross misfortune, if not engineering misfortune to profit from it. But now these stories gain credibility. Now, they seem possible.

"Well, Nico," Mr. Hermes say, "what are you prepared to do?"

○ ○ ○ ○

LeBeau's hands are on Flavia as soon as the doors shut and the blackness swallows them. His lips are on her neck, and his right hand clenches at her butt while his left hand cups her right breast. Flavia wants to protest, but he pulls her to him. His erection is huge through his pants and grinds into her crotch. His lips close on hers. His tongue finds hers. He tastes like a mixture of gin and peppermint, but what fills Flavia's nostrils is his lust; it's desperate and consuming.

"Wait," Flavia says.

LeBeau spins her; Flavia plants her hands into the wall to steady herself. He hikes her skirt up. One hand runs down over her panties. Flavia's moistness greets him. She hisses, embarrassed that she is so willing. His stubbled chin brushes her neck.

"Well?" he says.

He's not asking her. It's a challenge. And an *out.* She can decline him. She has that choice. But she doesn't entertain notions of escape. Only one thing is now on her mind: she not only wants to accept the challenge, but smash it, and teach LeBeau a little something about her. Who knows how many people he's done this to? She's going to teach him that she's *different.*

"Let's go," she tells him.

He grabs her wrist and drags her after him. Flavia almost stumbles. The ground disappears under her foot. LeBeau catches her and effortlessly hoists her into a fireman's carry. Flavia's breath explodes from her lungs as each step LeBeau takes jolts his shoulder into her stomach. They're heading down a long, tapered stairwell.

When they reach the bottom LeBeau lets Flavia slide from his shoulder. A hallway unfolds in front of her, defined only by dim orange lights from small, round portals at regular intervals on either wall. They continue endlessly on the most gradual decline.

LeBeau's hand tightens around her wrist. Flavia must canter to keep up to him. Her skirt stays bundled around her hips. She can see her panties are askew, exposing her small tuft of pubic hair and glistening inner thighs. She tries to adjust the hem of her dress but it's too difficult at this pace. Their footsteps echo and Flavia sees the marble floor gleam in the light. Then there are other sounds. Flavia cocks her ear forward. Moans, perhaps? As LeBeau and Flavia progress deeper into the hallway, the sounds grow louder and become unmistakable. Yes. Moans – and no disputing what sorts.

Sex.

"Where are we?" Flavia asks, but she knows. Of course she does. The stories of the basement aren't apocryphal at all.

She digs her heels into floor. Her right heel squeaks. LeBeau tries to continue forward. Flavia won't have it. LeBeau spins. The portal just to the right lights half of his face. The visible eye gleams. Now uncertainty once again flickers through Flavia's mind.

LeBeau wraps her in his arms. His mouth closes on hers. Flavia squirms and thrusts her hands into his chest. He grasps her by the buttocks and lifts her, shoving her hard against one of the portals. Dim light caresses her face. LeBeau's erection prods insistently at Flavia's crotch through his pants. His chin brushes her neck as he kisses her jaw.

She blinks owlishly. Another portal shines opposite them. Flavia's eyes acclimate slowly, until she is able to distinguish that the portal isn't a light, but a portal *in* a door.

Through it, she can see people, naked but for leather face masks, forming a ring around three men suspended from the ceiling by their wrists. A woman kneels and orally gratifies the first. Another woman straps the second, her leather switch tearing angry red welts across his skin. Another woman – perhaps wearing a strap-on (it is hard to tell from this angle) – appears to be buggering the third.

LeBeau's hand slides up to Flavia's hip. Flavia can feel her panties tighten through her crotch and up the crack of her buttocks as LeBeau wraps his fist around the waistband, threatening to tear it.

Flavia looks down the hallway. How many portals are there? And what's behind each? Then she realizes that if she's pressed against a portal, there must be a door behind her. She cranes her head, but the door gives way. LeBeau carries her inside.

The room is expansive, but featureless and empty. The floors are striped, black marble. Black curtains with silver trim hang from the walls. Circling the perimeter of the room above them are three rows of black balconies – like there would be at the theatre – with gleaming charcoal balustrades. In the middle of the room is a round bed.

LeBeau drops Flavia onto the bed. She bounces, then settles, preparing herself for what's coming. The bed's surface is velvet and soft and squishy like a waterbed. The ceiling is ringed with lights that rove the chamber. Directly above is a dim circular glow – like a spotlight waiting to illuminate them. She feels now like she's part of a show. All that's needed are the cameras.

Flavia shrieks as LeBeau yanks her panties aside and burrows his face into her crotch. She arches her back and gasps, her hands clutching the bed, her thighs balancing on LeBeau's shoulders, her heels digging into his back. She closes her eyes and gasps.

LeBeau's hands slide up under her dress and dislodges her bra. He cups her breasts and squeezes her nipples. Flavia shuts her eyes and squeals. She drives her crotch down onto LeBeau and knots her hands around his head. His stubble scratches but tantalizes the inside of her thighs. It's the most wonderful sensation. Flavia whines. This is going to be quick. She can't help it. Dante has never been like this, never wanted to wrench her satisfaction from her.

Dante … poor Dante. She cocks her right leg back, pushes the sole of her right foot against LeBeau's shoulder, and prepares to push him away. His tongue delves into her. Unbidden, Dante's face appears in Flavia's mind: he mopes, the way he does, maudlin and helpless and seeking assurance. She knows he's needy and insecure and that he's always been worried he'll lose her. Now that the day has come, the sudden wellspring of guilt contends with the ecstasy she's experiencing.

Flavia opens her eyes.

And finds she's inside the Cardinal Lounge.

○ ○ ○ ○

Flavia sits up and tries to push LeBeau away. The shock of where they are shunts her pending orgasm. Thoughts of Dante evaporate.

The Cardinal Lounge is muted, the sounds of the pianist, of conversation and the general ambiance coming as if through water. Everybody also appears dimmed. It so reminds Flavia of looking through her sunglasses in a darkened room that she touches her face to make sure they're not on.

She turns onto her knees, pulling her dress down for the sake of modesty, but nobody appears the least bit interested in her.

LeBeau's arms wrap around her possessively. He tries to hike her skirt up. Flavia slaps his hands away. He is unfazed. She swivels to push him away but overbalances on the soft velvet surface, falling forward. Her hand shoots out and splays seemingly in mid-air.

"What …?" Flavia asks.

She struggles to her feet, her hands feeling the way in front of her like she was a mime. There is glass all around her. That's why sounds are muted. That's why everything seems so dim.

"Where are we?" she asks.

LeBeau gets up behind her. One arm folds across her chest, the way one might wrap their partner in an embrace. His chin presses against her neck. His lips are so close to her ear that Flavia can feel their warmth, can feel the hot air he expels tickle her skin as he speaks.

"We're inside an octagon," LeBeau says.

"What?" Flavia spins in his embrace.

"The octagons inside Prudence. We're inside the one in the Cardinal Lounge."

Flavia remembers them, mirrored and ostentatious and seemingly pointless, outside of an observation to some aesthetic conceit. She shivers. There is a thrill, standing here, as if part of the Cardinal Lounge, as if part of the crowd watching the pianist, but with all the patrons unawares of her presence. It is both wonderfully decadent and indulgent, a luxury that she guesses only somebody like LeBeau can afford.

Two couples sit at a table right in front of her, all four seeming to look directly at her. Flavia unconsciously folds her arms in front of her, but LeBeau takes her wrists and straightens her arms. He draws the shoestring straps of her dress down over her shoulders, and pushes her dress down from her torso, taking her unfastened bra with it. His hands cup her breasts and distend her nipples. Flavia gasps. The four people continue to stare, their eyes so fixed, their expressions so inscrutable, she is sure they must see her and LeBeau and be stunned at the display.

"Are you sure—?"

Spinning her, LeBeau slams her against the glass wall. It's cold against her naked back. She wants to push off it, but LeBeau is upon her. Flavia lets herself be carried away in his lust. He kneels, pulling her dress, bra and panties down her legs and letting them bundle around her ankles. He hoists her right leg over her shoulder and attacks her clit. Flavia wails. She can't help it, and has never been a wailer, but she wails.

LeBeau runs kisses back up over her pubic hair and belly, taking her right breast in his mouth, suckling at her nipple. He continues to rise, letting his blazer slip from his arms and pulling his shirt over his head. He is muscular – not sharply defined but has the build of a man who works out often. His chest hair has been trimmed into a neat V down his pectorals.

Flavia lowers herself to her knees and unzips his pants. LeBeau is not wearing underwear, and his cock, thick and hard and veined, has a slight bend to the left. Flavia kisses its head, takes it in her mouth, then runs her lips back and forth over it. LeBeau's hand knits into her hair, and he urges her to quicken. Flavia lets him fall from her mouth. He may think he's in control, but she wants him to know that's not the case. She'll control him just as she controls Dante in bed, just as she controlled her lovers before Dante.

She strokes LeBeau through the barrel of her hand, remembering what seemed so long ago to be her doubts, her second thoughts and a recommitment to Dante. How quickly that changed. She doesn't know how she got up here – perhaps some pylon that rises into the octagon – but that former vow is now nothing more than a sacrifice to a new life. She's not just going to fuck LeBeau but fuck him in this location … she's not sure how to define it. Exotic? Mysterious? Unbelievable? All of the that and more?

Then Flavia sees her: she's dressed in stilettos; torn, faded jeans, and a sheer blouse – the bimbo who had been playing pool for the benefit of Dante and the others.

Patricia.

She walks over to the bar, to a man with his back to her. Flavia recognizes him immediately. Patricia pats him on the shoulder. The man turns.

Dante.

He's taken aback at the sight of Patricia. Her sheer blouse clings to her like wax paper and shapes her curves in shades and outlines. He unsteadily lifts his Bourbon & Coke up to her, conscious that he has been drinking, and he is lost in a perilous state of hyperconsciousness, where self-image and reality don't reconcile.

"Well, well," he says. "I think my night's finally beginning to look up."

Or that's what he imagines he would say. None of it comes out. He splutters moronically, as if the power of speech has deserted him.

Patricia signals to Providence, but her eyes don't leave Dante. "Mind if I join you?" she says.

Dante pats the stool alongside him. "Be my guest," he forces out.

Patricia sits on the stool and casually rests a hand on Dante's thigh. Dante notes it with briefly raised brows but tells himself to play it cool. This could be a once-in-a-lifetime opportunity, although he knows it'll ultimately go nowhere. People like him don't benefit from such freakish occurrences; they fall maddeningly short, and forever lament what could've been. But he might as well enjoy the journey until that happens, and given his drinking, he is prepared to recklessly enjoy whatever comes.

"So," he says, "to what do I owe the honor?"

○ ○ ○ ○

If there's one universal truth, it's that revelry is disheveling.

There are the physical aspects: make-up runs, people sweat, body odor grows; then there are the emotional facets: composure's lost, judgment is impaired, and decision-making goes awry; and, finally, there's the spiritual: people face junctures that they have never anticipated.

These are not things that Constance has known in her time here. She always appears immaculate, like she spent hours preparing herself for public admiration – and consumption. And she does. The routine has become so ingrained in her that it has *become* her. Those who knew her before she came here would not be able to reconcile her with the person she is now.

She *is* composure and poise and elegance.

Now, though, a solitary bead of sweat trickles obliviously down Constance's left temple. She dabs at it, examines the moisture on her fingertips, and is aware of the stifling heat. She feels her age; the tiredness fills her body. The air is stuffy. Her breath is thick as she tries to gulp it down.

Joy leans against the desk, arms folded across her chest. "You're out, Constance."

"That's what it comes down to?"

Constance hates the tremor in her voice. She cannot recall the last time she genuinely contended with fear. The first year she was hostess here, perhaps, when she worried that people would discover she was a fraud. The Camarilla had assured her to keep playing the part. As time wore on, she learned to carry herself nobly. She became more than a woman, if not more than a person. She was a minor deity. Nothing could ever hurt her here.

Until now.

"It didn't until you mishandled me so poorly," Joy says. "That validated my judgment."

"You don't know what you're doing, what you're getting yourself in for."

"Oh, I know." Joy pushes off from the desk and approaches Constance, whispering, "I know. *Look.*" Her eyes rove down Constance's body.

Constance is not sure if she's suddenly naked, or if in her vulnerability she sees herself that way: her breasts are large and almost tremulous; her hips have small folds of skin; her thighs are thicker than she would prefer, with small ripples of cellulite just under her buttocks. Her left hand races for her crotch, her right for her breasts, to cover herself, but she stops herself. She will not grant Joy the satisfaction of embarrassment, even though Joy is young and beautiful and ageless – well, at least for now.

"I'm surprised," Joy says. "Not even a real blonde."

"Constance—?" Teo says, inching forward.

Joy turns only her head to him. Teo stops. He doesn't want to, but he can't help it. He tells himself it's for the best – he has no alternatives, after all. It's not like he can help Constance in this situation. Joy has mentioned the Camarilla – this decision is bigger than any of them. He drops his head, hating himself for the rationalization. As always, they will be monitoring what happens here. *Watching.*

"Good," Joy says.

She wheels her satchel around, opens the flap, and pulls out three pieces of clothing, their fashion a hallmark of decades long gone: a pair of sandals, the straps frayed (and one torn on the right sandal); a pair of flared, faded jeans with designer rips on the knees, and tears of wear on the right thigh, and the right buttock; and a semi-translucent white blouse with a frilly collar.

Constance feels a sudden shortness of breath – she knows these clothes, but hasn't seen them since she first arrived, and then presented herself to the Camarilla. They commanded her to strip. In the disorientation of withdrawal from her drug high, she'd done so, ready to throw herself at the mercy of anybody who would offer her salvation, or at least the appearance of salvation.

"Don't do this," she says.

"There's no choice."

"There are always choices. Walk away."

Joy snorts with incredulous laughter. *"Me?* Walk away. Not *you. Me."*

"You'll be happier. Believe me."

"I think only you'll be the one happier in that arrangement."

Constance reaches out and grabs Joy's wrist. "No, you will be. Trust me."

Joy shakes her off. "Go."

"If you're not going to listen to me, at least understand that they're doing this because I've made Prudence mine."

"We talk about the Camarilla, Constance, but we know who's truly the power."

"Naturally," Constance says. It's not a realization – it's something she has always suspected, and which now falls into the place it always belonged. "The old man," she says, more to herself than Joy.

"Then you knew this day would come."

"They'll do the same to you."

"Here, we only think we're forever."

"You don't think there'll come a time that you won't be standing here like me?"

Joy's sudden uncertainty is the first time she has been ruffled, but it's fleeting.

"You think you can make yourself irreplaceable," Constance says. "I thought that. Sarah thought that before me."

"Then I know what to look forward to."

"It doesn't scare you?"

Joy smirks. "We are vain and ephemeral. I feel the smallest flutter," she lifts her hand to her chest, "when I consider it, but for now I'll enjoy my time. Yours is over. Get dressed. You'll leave the way you came."

For a moment, Constance entertains the notion of leaving her office naked. To hell with them all. It'll be the ultimate defiance. But she probably wouldn't get down the stairwell before security seized her, pulled her into one of the change rooms, and forcibly dressed her before ejecting her – unless they ejected her naked. That's also a very real possibility. No. She must play this out.

She changes first into her jeans. They're stiff and scratchy and, given how many years have passed, tighter now, although not embarrassingly. Still, they cut into her waist and crotch, and she must inhale and battle to fasten the button and pull up the zip.

"Commando," Joy says. "The impulsiveness of another generation."

Constance refrains from responding, instead slipping her feet into her sandals, the straps also too tight. She snatches her blouse away and pulls it on over her head. It's light and filmy. Constance can't believe it was ever a staple of her wardrobe.

"I'll ask you one last time—"

"Constance, Constance, Constance …" Joy reaches out and caresses her cheek. "I have to admit an admiration for you, if not an envy. Everything about you. I'm sorry it must be this way. If there could be another course …" She heads around Constance's desk and sits in Constance's recliner. "I think perhaps it's best if you—"

But Constance is already moving. She storms past Teo – who can't meet her eye – and from the office, slamming the door behind her. She charges down the stairwell, her sandals slapping the soles of her feet, and breaks through security stationed to stop anybody from getting up into her office. They don't blink. She might've become a ghost. But it's worse than that. She's become insignificant.

The crowd in the juncture swallows her up. She must push her way through, apologizing for stepping on toes and asking to be excused when there's no room. It takes forever to get anywhere, and the juncture isn't even as crowded as everywhere else.

She arrives at the entry of the Verdant Lounge. Mr. Hermes sits in his booth. She pauses to consider her options, to measure how best to approach him. They have fenced verbally during her time as hostess, but he has never backtracked. It's unlikely he would do so now that she no longer holds the position of hostess. Whether this move is justified or has been implemented on whim, it is done. There is no room for diplomacy or negotiation. They did the same with her predecessor, Sarah. It is both pointless and hypocritical to question the same treatment now.

Constance leaves the Verdant Lounge – missing Mr. Hermes looking up at the entry, to where she had just stood – and falls into a slipstream of people flowing into the Gallery. Somebody paws at her right buttock where the jeans are torn. She spins. There are two men there, both in the twenties. Both have their eyes fixed directly ahead. Possibly, an accident, but she knows better.

Edging into the Gallery, she bustles through the crowd. Several men proposition her, as if she's just another blonde having a night out. She declines them glibly and continues moving until she reaches the South Bar, where Bodie and Ox sit. They look right past her at her first, but then their eyes widen with recognition, then incredulity.

"Constance …?" Bodie says.

"The day I feared is here," Constance says.

○ ○ ○ ○

Holly throws the balls into the rack and arranges them for what will be the final game of eight-ball. Although she wears only her bra, she nurtures not an ounce of self-consciousness. It could just be her and Marcus in here – and their wager. That's all that matters.

Marcus, now just in his leather pants, dances and gyrates for the women in the room. Cold eyes stare back at him. He yanks off his leather pants with a flourish. They detach instantaneously, courtesy of Velcro seams. Marcus swivels his hips, wearing only a G-string now. Holly must concede his butt looks good, and he's a natural showman. But the women stare back at him stonily.

Another woman comes in – Gabriella. Marcus dances up to her. She reciprocates enthusiastically initially, but the diminutive brunette grabs her wrist and – against Gabriella's protests – drags her into the throng while explaining what's going on. Marcus shakes his head. Another one bites the dust.

"To hell with you then," he says, throwing his leather pants in the corner. He spins to face Holly. "You've ruined the room."

Holly pushes the balls into position, takes the rack, and drops it onto the floor. "This is for everything," she says. "Your G-string versus my bra."

"Where do you expect to take this, Holly? You get me naked, so what? That's what I'm meant to be doing here. You think it bothers me? I get you naked, big deal. Nobody's here to see you. You're just embarrassing yourself."

Holly takes the cue ball and positions it to break. "You win, you get me any way you want me," she says.

"Any way?"

"Any way. Same applies if I win."

Marcus's eyes narrow and he tilts his head. He knows there's more to this – he hears it in her tone. This is the bait she's thrown out.

"You scared?" she asks.

"Of you?"

"Of me."

More bait. And Marcus recognizes it. The sensible thing now would be to play the game out under the original conditions, but his ego won't let him. He's not reckless and uninformed like Quinn, who bet desperately to try recoup his losses. For Marcus, every decision is calculated. He can beat her, which makes upping the ante the right thing to do.

"But we seal the deal with the truth," Holly says.

And there's her going all in. It doesn't surprise Marcus, but it does give him a moment of reflection. People value truth, but it can be a hurtful thing, an instrument of destruction. That's why it's often filtered through interpretation – interpretation can dampen it, or color it in emotion, or mitigate it through rationalization. So many mechanisms exist to make truth more palatable.

But now, though, come the end of this game, it could be borne naked.

Marcus is unsure what to say.

Holly breaks, her thrust of the cue sharp and violent. The other balls shatter, almost as if fear of her anger. The four ricochets in the corner pocket but sits there. The thirteen and eleven occupy the middle pocket. The other balls scatter into the open. But nothing goes in.

Marcus surveys the table. He could get a good run here. Now he feels protective of Holly – it's a momentary sensation that flares. She is the woman he loves. That is genuine, or as genuine as his warped understanding of love and relationships can be, and the thing is he knows his understanding is warped. It comes from upbringing, of seeing his drunken dad and overly forgiving mother, of the spurious relationships Marcus has previously cultivated where his sole interest has been sex.

"Are you sure?" Marcus says.

Holly is determined. She doesn't care that Marcus now has an advantage given the way the balls are spread across the table, ready to be pocketed. Her rage borders on righteousness. She has expected this wager to fall her way, regardless of how close the games have remained, and that they're now down to the last bet.

"Totally."

Marcus leans over the table. To the hell with it. If she wants to come at him like this, then she can have it.

"Fine." He sinks the eleven into the middle pocket. "You want to bust my balls over this?" The thirteen follows the eleven. "Don't know what your problem is. It was *your* choice. You didn't have to go with them."

"*You* set me up," Holly says.

"Nobody twisted your arm." Marcus adjusts the crotch of his G-string. Holly can see he's hardened talking about this. He sinks the fifteen into the far corner. "Well, not in any way you didn't want it twisted," he says.

"Who were they?"

"A couple of guys I met here. We got talking." Marcus lines up the nine and drives it into the far corner pocket. "One of them introduced me to Mr. Hermes."

"How'd you know I'd respond?"

"You're great to fuck, Holly, although a little safe sometimes. But I wondered … Given the opportunity, would you cut loose? I've always thought there was something wild deep down inside of you." Marcus banks the ten into the middle. "You're wicked. Personally, I think every woman has the potential to be, deep down." He leers at the other women in the room. "Yeah, you heard me right." They scowl. Some whisper to one another behind their hands. Marcus is unconcerned. He turns back to Holly. "To be honest," he goes on, "I didn't think you'd go for it. That you did was a pleasant surprise."

Holly's eyes brim. She brushes at them and tightens her jaw. She won't cry. Not in front of Marcus. But it is difficult to hold on. He is so offhand in his regard, so proud that he's manipulated and used her. If they'd talked about this, she might've considered it – a mutual decision. But now she feels *cheap*. Where would a relationship with Marcus go? Threesomes? Swingers' parties? Orgies? Gangbangs? What else? Holly sees a tawdry future where Marcus prostitutes her for his own titillation, and now reconciles what she's done as shameful.

He lines up the twelve in the far corner. "I thought if I gave you some anonymity, I could appeal to that deep-down wickedness."

Rising, he readjusts the crotch of his G-string, but this time isn't surreptitious about it. Holly can tell from the bulge that he's fully erect. She wants to kick him in it.

"Tell me," Marcus says, "when the first guy laid the money on the bar and pretended to mistake you for a hooker, was it a turn on? Did you get hot?" He approaches Holly and takes her chin between his thumb and finger. "And when the second guy joined him and they doubled down, just how hot and turned on were you getting?"

"You set up your fiancé for a threesome?" This comes from the diminutive brunette who'd initially objected to Holly's interruption. Her brows are angled sharp and there's a furrow in the bridge of her nose.

"Hey, she didn't have to take it."

"What are you? A pimp?"

"You prick." This from Gabriella.

Marcus chortles at both of them. "What wouldn't you do in the name of sexual liberation?"

"So you're just being magnanimous," Holly says.

Marcus strikes the cue ball. It collects the twelve, sending it cleanly into the pocket. "I just wanted to open you up before we got married."

"And then?"

Marcus chalks his cue. "I figured the sky would be the limit after your display."

"You saw?"

Marcus grins. "I filmed it from the closet on my phone – needed proof."

Proof? Holly almost says but, of course, Mr. Hermes would need evidence.

Marcus checks the table. He has only the fourteen left, sitting in the middle of the table. "You know, Holly," he says, as he takes up a position to have his shot, "I don't understand your indignation. You enjoyed it. Right?"

Holly's face grows hot.

"*Right?*"

Holly doesn't want to answer, although she knows her silence condemns her.

"What harm was done?" Marcus says. "If anybody should be hurt, it should be me. *You* cheated on me."

"You engineered it for … the money … hoping I'd become some whore for your entertainment?"

"*Our* entertainment, Holly."

Some of the women jeer. Marcus ignores them. Holly doesn't even know what to call him. The diminutive brunette asked him if he was a *pimp*. Gabriella has already used *prick*. But neither of those are enough. Holly doesn't know where to go from there.

"Hey, I'm not the bad guy. Quinn's got his gambling debts. He doesn't know it yet, but I did this—"

"*I did this!*" Holly says.

"—to help him pay them off."

Holly shakes her head, unable to reconcile Marcus's duplicity. "You could've told him that! He went to see that old fuck—"

"Quinn doesn't have to go through with his Temptation. He just had to sit down, hear the spiel, and introduce somebody else. I was going to tell him tonight about the money. I feel obligated – after all, I was the one who introduced him to that underground casino. Who knew he'd get so addicted? Who knew he'd be such a loser? Well, actually, that's self-evident, but I mean at gambling."

"You're one hell of a fucking guy, Marcus."

"I can't help it that people are weak. You with your threesome. Quinn with his gambling. Dante constantly tiptoeing around Flavia. Flavia wanting to be famous. Amber so meek you can't say *boo* around her. But I'm the bad guy because I know what I want and I pursue it to make it reality. I'm the bad guy because I want to live and explore life. I'm the bad guy because I take risks and have fun. *Right.*"

Marcus casually pockets the fourteen. The cue ball rolls to the center of the table, aligning directly behind the black. Holly's sigh is a long hiss. She could hit that in blindfolded. Of all the times Marcus could have a perfect game!

"What's your problem?" he asks. "Really? We're half a mil' richer, you're sexually liberated, and I'm happier. Who doesn't win?"

"I–I–if you'd put this to me … I don't know … To manipulate—"

Marcus strides up to her, pointing a finger in her face. "This was your fucking choice!" he says. "I didn't push you into it. I didn't do it then behave like nothing happened. You could've told them they were mistaken. You could've thrown your drink in their faces. You could've gotten up and left. You're not my puppet whose actions and responses I control. So, face facts, Holly. You did this! You did this and you're upset because you did it! And you fucking enjoyed it. Loved it. Fuck you. You can blame me for putting the gun in your hand, but *you* pulled the trigger! *You!*"

Holly says nothing.

He is right.

○ ○ ○ ○

Dante feels as if he's standing outside of himself, observing his drunkenly gregarious nature, frowning with disapproval, and trying to regain control, but too disconnected to do so.

Patricia doesn't seem to mind, though, sitting next to him. He wishes he could read her, but he is terrible at reading people. This is why he lives in constant fear that Flavia will one day decide she has settled, and she would be better off pursuing somebody worthy of her stature. He cannot understand how she could love him, or that sometimes two people so different can still find love for one another.

He smiles. He's sure it's a cool smile, but his eyes blatantly patrol Patricia's chest. She has breasts he'd love to shove his face into and wriggle. It's stupid, he knows, and not something he'd ever entertain with Flavia, and the longer he holds onto the thought, the more it shames him. Lacking any intellectual or emotional connection, he has lowered himself to physical attraction, and puerile fantasy.

He tries to push those thoughts out. He is here. She is here. That's the plateau they share. The only other thing he knows for certain is she's a stripper and he briefly was part of her show – well, until she decided to rewrite the narrative.

"Come to tease me some more?" he asks.

"My actions in the gaming room got me fired."

Dante lifts his Bourbon & Coke to his mouth. Some of it spills from his glass and onto his thigh. He doesn't let that interrupt him. "You deserve it," he says, taking a drink, hoping he sounds cold but measured.

"Do I?"

Her rebuke initially puzzles him – at least until he thinks about it earnestly. She was meek, playing a character for the juvenile enjoyment of a room of men. He saw only that – what others expected her to be. But she rebelled. She found something in herself, regardless of the consequences. He suddenly admires her for that – he admires her for that effusively, because everything is exaggerated now. He admires her. And envies her.

"I'm sorry," he says.

"Don't be. We all make our own choices. Mine means I'm just about out of here."

"Just about?"

"Working here requires I sign a contract. If I void the terms of that contract, I'm liable. Tonight, I voided the terms of that contract. So, I've been given a one-shot deal."

"Yeah? What's that?"

Patricia's eyes dart to Providence not too far away, ready to make Dante's next Bourbon & Coke. Providence's face is inscrutable. Patricia gets up from the stool and takes Dante's hand.

"Hey!" he says. "Where are we going?"

"Not far."

Patricia leads him to a booth in the corner, shrouded in darkness and obstructed by the octagon. She pushes him into the seat. Dante stumbles and must catch himself. Before he can protest, Patricia slides into the seat alongside him. Her hand shoots to the inside of his thigh. Dante jumps and his hands instinctively move to grab Patricia's wrist, but he stops himself.

"What're you doing?" he asks.

Patricia's unsure if she'll be able to follow through with this. The physical act itself is simple – it happened too many times during her ill-fated modeling career and is now little more than a throwaway. But grasping it beyond that is difficult. It's a test – a means of proving oneself, but in a way she believes she has stopped degrading herself.

She should leave. That would be the best thing to do. She would wake tomorrow unemployed – and, possibly, unemployable in this city (if not this country) given the Camarilla's influence – but with a clear conscience. But, as so many others find here, something draws her to push this – a means of exacting revenge on all those people who objectified her when she was an Icon.

She unzips his pants. "You don't know?" Her hand slides into his pants, shoves aside his underwear, and closes around his cock.

"We're out in the open!" Dante says.

"Not that open."

Dante's quick, nervous check mollifies his fears – the octagon obscures the rest of the Lounge from view. For people who come to watch the pianist, to enjoy one another's company, to chat and laugh, this is not where they sit.

Patricia takes his cock out of his pants. He's *not* hard – he's so self-conscious that he's blocked the automatic response, and now that he's aware of his lack of reaction, the increased pressure only exacerbates the situation.

"What's wrong?" she asks, stroking him.

"I think …" Dante's mind races through possibilities. "I'm too … I've been drinking too much."

Patricia detaches the gold locket from the chain around her neck – her grandmother gave her the chain many years ago. The locket is something cheap she bought from a pawn shop for a simple purpose: it's a container. When she pops it open, it reveals a mound of tiny triangle mauve pills.

She carefully scoops one out on the underside of her fingernail and offers it to Dante. He is stupidly wide-eyed. He knows the drug culture is heavy on the rave scene. Flavia has experimented, but he has never had the courage. He is afraid to lose control, afraid where it might lead him, afraid of whatever humiliation might await.

"Come alive," Patricia says.

"What is it?" Dante's voice is breathless.

Patricia swallows the pill. "X'cess." She plucks out another and holds it out.

Dante wants to tell himself that it's his inebriation that obliterates his inhibitions, but it's a combination of his desire for this woman, his overwhelming hopelessness, and his eagerness to impress her.

Before doubts can arise, he takes the pill and swallows it.

He does not know if he imagines it, or if his paranoia about what will happen intensifies the sensations he's already experiencing, but the first thing he feels is Patricia's hot breath on his neck – not just hot but *burning*. When she snaps closed the locket, it has the clang of somebody smashing cymbals together.

Other sounds grow jarringly sharp and pronounced throughout the Lounge – snippets that cut through him. Reflections on glasses and the bar streak brilliantly through the air, exploding into fiery conflagrations that chime with a purity he has never heard. His intoxication becomes a warmth that fills him until he is nothing but a form of heat.

The only thing that is cool is Patricia's hand, still stroking his shaft. His erection hardens magnificently until he's sure it's singing in triumph. And then, just like that, he's coming, shooting streamers of glittery white ebullience that loop through the air and land on the tabletop.

Patricia whispers in his ear, "It's okay."

She uses the hem of the tablecloth to wipe him dry, indifferently licking the ejaculate from where it glistens on her fingers.

Dante can't talk as she presses up against him and kisses him. He tastes himself on her. She is still stroking him so that he hardens again – something that has never occurred before. Usually when he is done he is done for the night.

Patricia leans over him. Her dark hair sways across his belly and lap. Her full lips close around the head of his cock.

Dante gasps as his awareness first recognizes each and every thing that has happened with clinical glee, and then that awareness spreads out to encompass the Lounge, triggering fears that somebody is watching.

But nobody is – at least not as far as he can see.

And Patricia's barely visible behind the booth's table. His hands rest on her head. She impales her mouth, then slowly draws back up.

Dante's hands clamp down on the table. He struggles to think of the most unsexual thoughts possible as a means of maintaining control. Patricia lifts her face to his. She kisses him, her tongue diving into his mouth, while her hand continues to stroke his cock.

"Well?" she asks. "Should I stop?"

Dante's world disassembles – Flavia, their future together, the engagement ring in his right pocket. Perhaps it's too late for true nobility – true nobility would've had him stop Patricia immediately – but he could still push her away and go find Flavia, still propose as he intended. He sees humor now in how this is always his intended fallback, but he never pursues it. He wants to be his own person, but never finds the strength to do so.

He closes his eyes and sees Flavia, perhaps up on the second floor with Holly and Amber, whining about what she saw in the gaming room. They'll be condemning him. He could prove them wrong. He could show them what he's made of.

His eyes open. "No," he says. "Don't stop."

○ ○ ○ ○

"That sonuvabitch!" Flavia says.

She watches Dante tilt his head back and spread his arms across the backrest of the seat, and Patricia's face disappear into his lap, her head bobbing above and below the tabletop.

When it was shameless flirting over pool that was one thing, but now he's cheating. Flavia can't believe she means so little to him. How dare he!

How. Dare. He.

"I've got a good mind—" she begins.

LeBeau spins her and slams her against the glass partition, one large hand clasping her throat, his other sliding down her hip. Flavia can feel his cock, hard and warm, pressing against her thigh. And now it's not his hunger she smells, but his disdain.

"You want to go back out, reclaim what's yours?" he says.

His fingers slide back and forth over the slit of her cunt, his middle finger finding her clit. Flavia whimpers. He hikes her left leg up, hooks it over his hip, and guides the head of his cock forward until it pushes her open.

"Well?" he asks.

Flavia slides her hands around his neck.

"Fuck me," he says.

"What?"

"Say it."

"*Say it …?*"

"Say. It."

"Fuck … me …"

"Again."

"Fuck me."

"Say it, dammit!"

"Fuck me!"

"Say *please.*"

Flavia's desperation explodes into rage that snaps into focus. "Do it," she tells him in a voice that's cold and irrefutable. "Or don't. You choose."

LeBeau drives his cock into her slowly.

Flavia emits a guttural cry. He is bigger than Dante, and his actions contain purpose. Dante moves like a kid hopping the neighbor's fence to retrieve an errant ball. Get in. Sneak around. Get out before anybody's the wiser. There. Job done.

LeBeau withdraws, Flavia clenching at him regretfully. She does not want to lose him. Then he thrusts forward so hard that her butt slaps against the glass and she grunts in his ear. So, this is the way he wants to play it. He thinks *hard* means dominance.

The hand he has around her throat lowers over her breasts and cups her buttock. She's lifted – she cannot believe how easily. She might be paper in his hands. His other hand shapes around her other buttock. She wraps her legs around his hips as he fucks her, initially with slow, long, powerful strokes, but quickening until there's only the collision of their flesh and her own uninterrupted wail filling the octagon.

She rides him with abandon, her fingernails tearing into his back, her eyes locked with his.

○ ○ ○ ○

Dante grinds his teeth. It's embarrassing, but he's going to lose it again already. Patricia pulls up, kisses his lips, his chest, and then runs her hand up and down his shaft.

In the gaming room, she saw Dante as pathetic, and now she decides he's also a fool – like pretty much everybody who ever came to watch her act. They revel in her stripping, take pride in beating her in pool – even though most would know she's throwing games – and they fantasize about her, before returning to their unsatisfying partners and unfulfilling lives. They think they have power over her, but she sees now that it's just as Constance told her – she has the power over them. She can control a room of men and reduce them to their most primal – and their most stupid and most manipulable.

That's what Dante is now: a quivering idiot who has probably conjured a narrative in his head that he is winning her, but she has as much control over him as she would a rod and arm puppet. It comes so easily that she almost feels guilty. But this is what Joy wants, and it's something that Patricia draws strength from.

"Prudence has secrets," she whispers into Dante's ear.

Dante turns to her. "Secrets?"

"Hungers.

"Hungers?"

"They feed the Camarilla."

"What're you talking about?"

"Do you want me?"

"Of course I do," Dante says.

"What would you be willing to pay?"

Dante recoils. Patricia puts an assuring hand on his.

"Not money," she says. "That's not what this is about."

"Then what?"

"What would you give to have me?"

"Anything."

"Anything?"

"Anything."

"It doesn't matter what it costs you?"

Dante shakes his head. Right now, nothing else exists for him but making love to this beautiful woman – an experience he'll not only treasure for the rest of his life but will also be a springboard for better things. His whole life can change from this moment, like sex with Patricia will empower him, transform him into the sort of man he envies, and fast-track an education that will see him overcome all those obstacles that expose his shortcomings every day.

"I can take you somewhere," Patricia says. "You can fuck me."

She almost laughs, like fucking is something one does to another person. But men enjoy that illusion. They think it gives them superiority in sex. And she *has* had partners she has yielded to, but only because they were so skilled and selfless that she could let go. Otherwise, sex is a mutual obligation, a communion – not that that's something Dante would understand. It's simpler to hook him with the bait.

"Do you want that?" she asks. "Do you want to fuck me?"

Dante nods, not trusting himself to speak. He puts his cock away and zips up his pants.

Patricia's mouth comes right up to Dante's ear. "You sure?" she says. "Nothing … is free."

Dante blanches. "You said this isn't about money."

Patricia smirks. "There are currencies other than money."

"Such as?"

"You want to find out?"

Dante's hesitation is fleeting. "Let's go."

Patricia grabs his hand and pulls him out of the booth.

○   ○   ○   ○

Flavia can't see Dante from this angle as LeBeau continues to pound her up against the wall. She throws her arms out and slaps the glass just to make sure it's there. Everybody in the Cardinal Lounge seems to be watching them. They exchange comments. Some smile. Others shift, as if the sight is arousing them. She is sure they're seeing her and reacting to her.

It's too much. The octagon spins and lights flash in her eyes. Pleasure wracks her body. LeBeau slips from her as he runs kisses up her belly and over her breasts. He bites at her right nipple; she gasps. His lips are on hers. She pants into his mouth.

"Already?" he says.

"For starters," Flavia says.

LeBeau kisses her. "It takes more than that to pass an audition."

Flavia plants her hand on LeBeau's chest. He flips onto his back; she rolls on top of him. So soon after orgasm she feels too sensitive to take him back in. She sees that the booth Dante occupied is now empty. Just as well. Her hand wraps around LeBeau's cock and tugs at it playfully.

She kisses his mouth, then runs kisses down his chest.

○   ○   ○   ○

Two members of security accost Constance at the South Bar. One grabs her by the shoulder and spins her so she almost stumbles. She feels destitute compared to the others in here, like somebody homeless who's snuck in to escape the cold.

"Begging your pardon, ma'am," one of the security members says stiffly, addressing her without recognition, "but you've failed to meet the dress standards. We're going to have you to ask you to leave."

Constance draws herself up, and even in her torn sandals, ripped jeans, and her sheer blouse, she is regal. They can take her position, they can take her authority, but they cannot take away from her who she has become. Behind her, Bodie and Ox rise, one to either side of her so that they flank her. The foolishness falls away from their faces.

They step forward, so that Constance is now protectively behind them. Security recognizes the threat. They reach for Bodie and Ox. The exchange is short, precise, and brutal. Both members of security are incapacitated and drop to the floor.

Constance steps out from between Bodie and Ox. "Let's go," she says.

VI

Maybe it's because I've never really known any different and have always simply accepted it as the human condition, but it amazes me how oblivious people can be.

For a long time, Constance was a queen in everything but name. Employees bowed before her. Patrons regarded her with awe. The Camarilla stripped her, humiliated her, rebuilt her in the image they deemed worthy, and then lifted her back up, placing her lovingly on a pedestal. They had identified the greatness in her long before she had seen it in herself, and, for a long time, she exceeded their expectations.

Now, though, as Constance leads Bodie and Ox from the South Bar, the crowd mill and threaten to crush them. Constance might as well be invisible. Ox presses ahead and flings one man from her path. His friend takes offense and swings at Ox. Ox sways from the blow, then delivers an old-fashioned roundhouse that sends the man onto his butt.

He, Bodie, and Constance continue this way, pushing, shoving, and when that fails, hurling people aside. Many recognize the threat they pose and give them a wide berth. But others showcase a foolhardy bravado, and scuffles break out, which systematically draws the attention of security.

They filter in, at first in ones and twos, but as a group they adopt a formation that Teo has taught them to suppress multiple threats. The only problem is that Teo has trained them to deal with everyday people, rather than Bodie and Ox. Constance knows security will struggle, and the potential exists that any altercation could hurt them seriously and might unwittingly hurt others.

She had made a point of getting to know each member of security, of learning about them and their families and their dreams, so that they never grew to feel like pawns who are there to be thrust into a fray and sacrificed if needed. But now when she appeals to them they either ignore her or aren't aware of her.

This is not something that concerns Bodie and Ox – they engage security with the single intent of incapacitating them as a threat. The initial fights are quick and decisive as Bodie and Ox put them down, but each fracas grows progressively nastier. Bodie and Ox could kill them, if needed, but that is not what Constance wants. The crowd rings around them, as if this is entertainment for their consumption.

I wish I could help them. There are times I believe in serendipity, but other times there's something else at work, some confluence of greater desire, perhaps the whim of the collective unconscious which abounds here every night until it schisms into its own intent, petty and nasty and capricious. Now I feel it directed against Constance.

Ox surveys the distance to the juncture. They've only made it about halfway. He is hot and exhausted already. They will make it all the way, but he is unsure how much collateral damage that will incur – and how it will tax him, and Bodie. Ox unfurls his overcoat. The handle of a sawn-off shotgun pokes from under his armpit. He reaches for it. Constance grabs his wrist.

"No!" she says. "Not yet!"

"This is taking too long," Ox says. His grip closes on the butt of the shotgun.

"You could start a panic," Constance says. "People will get hurt. We have to do it this way – for now, at least!"

"This is seriously unrelenting," Bodie says, as he spots another three members of security heading toward them.

Bodie and Ox no sooner dispatch of them than the juncture spews forth a new torrent of security. They spread to flank them, the crowd drawing back.

Another figure emerges from the juncture, standing majestically under the plaque as if it were his standard.

"How the mighty have fallen," he says.

It's Teo.

○　○　○　○

Rupe is about to surrender his vigil and take it as a sign of what's not meant to be, but then the security protecting the stairwell leave their position and bolt past him. He doesn't turn to see where they go, fearing if he knows – if he sees they've remained anywhere within proximity – it'll deter him from the course he must take.

He springs up the stairs, taking them two at a time, and reaches the door to Constance's office. For a moment he pauses, knowing he is committing himself to an action from which he can't turn back. But perhaps that's the way it should be. Perhaps there *should* be no turning back.

He tries the doorknob, but the door is locked. Of course it would be. There is a security keypad, but it does him no good. He lifts his hand to knock, but the door swings open to reveal Joy.

"I wondered if you would come," she says.

"Has it surprised you that I did?"

"Nothing surprises me about your efforts anymore."

"Can I talk to you?"

Joy is unmoving.

"Please. Just for a moment."

Joy steps aside, allows him in, and closes the door behind him. Rupe's eyes never leave her. He has been enamored with her from the first moment he saw her, but she is flawless now, glowing with a sublime beauty that makes him think that perhaps he has passed, had a heart attack or an aneurysm on the stairs, and she now stands here to guide him to what comes next.

That silly fantasy shatters when he sees what she's wearing: a black latex catsuit cut low at the back. Elaborate strapping runs from the ankles all the way up to her armpits, as well as across the bodice, exposing a considerable amount of skin. He almost laughs. Perhaps he'll be going elsewhere.

Joy guides Rupe to her desk. "Take a seat," she says. "Please."

Rupe sinks into the recliner. It's soft and molds to his buttocks and back. Joy leans against the desk but bends toward him so that they are at eye-level, the fingers of her right hand caressing his cheek.

"Rupe," Joy says. "Rupert, what have you expected?"

"What could I expect?" Rupe says. "Seriously? *What?* You're beautiful. Mesmerizing. From the first moment I saw you, you overwhelmed me. But I knew …"

"What?"

"Why would you look at me? There are more handsome men here, more capable men, more successful men, men who belong in your strata – or are at least much nearer to it than me. I guess, for an instant, I wanted to touch the dream."

"That's all I am, Rupe. You don't know anything about me. About who I am. I might be the most horrible person."

"Impossible."

Joy places one finger to his lips to silence him. "I might be cruel and barbaric. I may be pure evil. I may be everything contrary to what you imagine. You cannot hold a dream – at least not for very long."

"Of course …" Rupe says. "Since …" *My wife passed.* Again, the words choke in his throat. "I have searched … I don't know what for. Meaning. Somebody to fill the loss. I'm not sure."

"There is no meaning. *None.* And loss is not something you can fill or leave behind. It is always with you. *Always.* You may find diversion, but that diversion should not be found here. Prudence is grand and terrible and illusory, and it has a black, black soul, the sum of every decadent impulse and misbegotten desire that's ever occurred here."

I should take offense at that, because that soul is something else, a shadow that has manifested beyond my control, and pulses, seeking to grow and infect, and strengthening with every person it touches, and with every person who feeds it, until the relationship is symbiotic. While I can see things, I have no control in the way she assumes.

But Rupe deals with those words as he understands the world – through his mortal limitations and prejudices. He can only make sense of them at the most superficial level. But that is near enough, and her warning overwhelms him, that she would take this opportunity to address him as an equal. He knows that's not the case. It never was.

"Why're you telling me?"

Joy tilts her head. "Because you're—"

Rupe leaps to his feet. Joy recoils. He takes her in his arms and draws her close.

His intent is obvious, but he will not do so without her permission.

She has a moment of uncertainty.

Rupe is charming and humble and warm and compassionate and respectful and so many kind things she has never encountered in any of the relationships she has had throughout her life.

She closes her eyes and leans into him.

He kisses her.

○　○　○　○

Teo approaches, each step increasingly more difficult than the last. It's like elastic pulling him back, restraining him from getting to Constance. She is still unmoved, Bodie and Ox flanking her. Teo stops. He – literally – can't go any further. It's too difficult.

The crowd watch curiously. Others peer over the balustrade from the second floor. Their faces are listless, the same dull gleam in each of their eyes. If there is one thing that can unify groups into a single, mob mind, it is a spectacle – and this very much has become a spectacle.

"Well?" Constance says.

"You know I can't let you undertake the option you're pursuing."

Security ring around the exchange, those whom Bodie and Ox had dispatched earlier groggily hauling themselves to their feet to join the formation. They tighten their perimeter. There must be at least forty of them, although Teo knows that can't be right: he knows every member of security's schedule, and there is never more than twenty-five on duty at any time. Of course, their increased number might be due to a crossover of shifts. In any case, Teo is thankful. He needs every one of them.

His focus flits from Bodie to Ox. They show none of their regular foolishness. The effects of whatever they've drank tonight have evaporated. Ox's hand stays just inside his coat. Bodie's drawn himself up, poised, ready to strike. Teo knows what they're capable of. He helped Constance choose them, although he never thought he would be on the end of a confrontation. This could get ugly – well, *uglier* – quick.

"You knew this day would come," Teo says. "*I* knew it would come.

"Yet you helped me plan for it."

Teo lowers his head. He keeps his emotions guarded, but part of that is to hide from Constance how deeply he feels for her – their one tryst was not just a meaningless throwaway, but something more for him. He has nurtured that love and devotion all these years, respecting her authority, protecting her professionally, but hoping for something more.

"And now you ask me to accept it," Constance says. "That *we* should accept it."

"I have no choice."

"No." Constance shakes her head.

"These aren't our decisions to make."

Constance steps forward. She is no longer as glorious as she was before; no bouffant blonde hair, blinding cleavage, or provocative latex outfit. She might've just stepped out of the shower and had no time for make-up or to do her hair. In a way, she is more provocative than she has been in twenty-five years. The torn jeans that are now too tight and the filmy t-shirt should be an embarrassment, a denunciation of an older woman trying to recapture – or emulate – the material sexuality of her youth. But to Teo, right now it is why she *is* gorgeous. She beams with a vulnerability that makes her more flawed and human, and in that imperfection she is transcendent.

"Before you, there was Sarah," Teo says. "And before her, whoever. I don't know how long the line runs back – maybe not here, but somewhere. Who knows? Change is inevitable. We have to accept it.”

“Why?”

“It’s like Mr. Hermes always says …”

One corner of Constance’s mouth lifts into a smile, or perhaps it’s a sneer. Teo doesn’t know, and that surprises him. They have always enjoyed a synergy – from the moment she interviewed him, he felt at one with her: both of them damaged and seeking to remake themselves, even if only in illusion. That is why they work … *worked* so well together. But he guesses that’s just something that has either ended, or *is* ending, and he laments it.

“What’s that?” Constance says. “What is it that old fool says?”

“Flesh is weak. Temporary.” Teo seizes her by the arm. His grip tightens. She flinches. “And I guess not one of us are forever, are we?”

“Regardless of how hard we try to hold on,” Constance says.

Teo nods. “I think it’s time we showed you the door and let everybody else get on with their night.”

Again, he scans the crowd. This is just an oddity to them, just another patron evicted – it happens dozens of times a night, sometimes surreptitiously, sometimes disruptively, and sometimes (as is the case now) theatrically. But within minutes, everybody’s back to normal, as if nothing had ever occurred. They do not understand, appreciate, or even care about how momentous this actually is.

Teo gestures to security. They close on the trio. Ox’s hand sinks further under his overcoat. Constance shakes her head. Ox is unconvinced. Bodie grabs his arm, stopping him from any further action. Security now are tightly ringed around them.

“Nothing stupid, huh?” Teo says. “I want to change this, but this isn’t just about us.”

“No,” Constance says.

Teo gestures, and security usher them toward the juncture.

○ ○ ○ ○

Marcus circles the table, exaggerating his calculations to sink the black. It sits right in the middle, the cue ball not ten inches from it, and perfectly aligned with the corner pocket. It's the simplest shot. Not a person in this room doesn't believe they couldn't make this shot. Some of the women jeer his theatrics.

Holly, arms folded across her chest, sniffles, her eyes brimming. Any protectiveness Marcus might've felt earlier, any compassion, is gone now. He's enjoyed the tussle with her. More importantly, he's enjoyed beating her.

Dante diffidently told him that Flavia's fantasy was to have sex in a public place where there was a risk of being caught, as if that would add to the thrill. Marcus thinks that's just the same as having sex in private. He wants to have sex publicly where there's an audience. He sees himself fucking Holly bent over the table while everybody else watches in awe and envy – a crowning glory to his victory. He knows he won't – at least not tonight. It's just another fantasy to pursue.

He rises and leans on the table with one hand. "It was inevitable," he says. "This result, that is. You come at me with your indignation, but maybe your embarrassment is that I know you better than you know yourself – I know better what you want than you do."

"You're *so* full of shit," Gabriella says. "This way that you rationalize it."

Marcus cackles at her. "I think it just clicked in me that it's not a rationalization. You come here, you watch a guy play strip-pool – you *pay* him, so you can beat him and undress him. You leave your little lives to do this. What about you? Who've you got waiting at home? What's your prison sentence?"

"How dare you—!"

"Tubby hubby? Squalling kids?"

Marcus grins as she splutters indignantly. He's nailed it. Of course he's nailed it. The memories of his own upbringing are heavy in his mind – his father's cheating, his father's drinking, his father's abusiveness. And his mother just took it all, smiling, weak, and pathetic. He does not want to emulate his father. But that dichotomy showed him that people will go to great lengths to fool themselves into believing their lives are better than they are, that they are happy even when all the evidence screams at them that they shouldn't be.

"What about you?" Marcus points at the diminutive brunette. "Bet you've also got a family back there somewhere. Bet most of you have. What about you two?" He approaches two teenage girls who've made themselves up to look as old as possible – all of nineteen or twenty, at best. They're waifs and blush when he addresses them. "Just a night out and wanting to be naughty, huh?" He turns to the twenty-something women having the hens night. "Or, you, wanting to live it up one last night before you take the plunge? How far will you go?" He spins dramatically, his arms outstretched to encompass everybody. "How far would you take tonight – the lot of you? Wanting to pretend to be the big bad. You want to give it up. Like she did!" He thrusts his finger at Holly. "How many of you will go home tonight, fuck the old man, but think of whoever you watched play? Or just fantasize and pleasure yourselves?" He directs this at the teenagers. One bows her head guiltily, the other (on closer examination, he's sure she's seventeen, at best) covers her mouth, aghast. "Or maybe there's one last fling left!" This is cast at the hens party. Marcus laughs, lifts his hands, and gyrates his hips. "How many of you discover vicariously in this room that you want to ride a big bad that has nothing to do with your lives outside these walls? You want to be fucked senseless. To fuck senseless. To let loose and go somewhere you've never been before. You ought to be thanking me. All of you! The reality is, I'm your liberator. I am taking you somewhere you'll never get yourselves!"

"You're a bastard," the diminutive brunette says.

Marcus's grin broadens. He approaches her and juts his hips so his left buttock is pointed at her. "Touch it," he says. "Go on. You know you want to."

"You …! You …!"

Marcus thrusts his crotch at her. "Maybe you want to unwrap me – just for the hell of it," he says. "I have to admit, I'm so hard it hurts. Maybe you want me in your mouth. I'm tasty. And I bet you are, too."

"Y–y–y–ou—"

"Come on, ladies! You can't tell me not one of you isn't turned on."

"It's not enough you're a bastard," this comes from the teenager he thought was seventeen, "but that you want to humiliate your fiancé like this … I don't even know what to call you."

Marcus goes up to her and moves to put his fingers under her chin. "How about you, sweetheart'?"

She knocks away his hand as if she's swiping away a punch. "Fuck off," she tells him.

"Awww." Marcus overplays it. "So tough."

He shakes his head at her as he returns to the table. Holly's no longer brimming. Her exhalations are hisses, and her arms are down by her side, her fists clenched. Marcus must give it to her: she's *so* cute when she's angry. That is as sophisticated as his appreciation gets.

"You know what's a shame?" he asks. "Gonna be a seven-ball victory and you're," he flashes a grin at Holly as he bends over the table, "already bottomless." He finds that amusing in a puerile way, that back home a seven-ball victory means the loser runs around the table with their pants down. At least it'll be good to see her out of her last item of clothing – her lace bra. "But maybe this whole episode's just been instructive." He lines up the black and turns back to face Holly. "I think you really just need to learn your place."

Without turning from Holly, he strikes the cue ball hard. It thunders into the black. The black hits the corner pocket, jumps into the cup, but sinks the way a chipped golf ball will sink into a hole. Marcus grins at Holly. But Holly – and the eyes of the other women – are fixed on the cue ball, which cannons into the bank, bounces off the two, clips the one, then rolls toward the three.

Eyes widen. Some of the women gasp. Marcus spins, his celebration transforming into horror. In his extravagant showmanship, he's hit the cue ball too hard. It kisses the three, which sits in the mouth of the pocket. The three teeters on the brim.

Then drops in.

A loss. He sunk his opponent's ball in the same shot he pocketed the black.

Marcus rises and shrugs at Holly. "Hey, come on," he says.

Holly steps up to Marcus. The women in the room array behind her, the way a troop of soldiers might fall in behind their drill sergeant. Every one of them cross their arms over their chests. It might be a choreographed dance move. Marcus's eyes dart to the archway. It's empty. Security's gone.

"Game over, Marcus," Holly says.

○ ○ ○ ○

When Amber closes her eyes, she's sure she could drift off – not just fall asleep, but drift off into another world, although she thinks maybe she's already there. The night started so innocently – a night out with new friends as a final hurrah to their travels.

Then there was Holly's revelation and Flavia chasing Edan LeBeau. Amber still cannot reconcile the way she behaved with Savage. A simple holiday that was so innocent and fun has unraveled into something dark and perverse. She cannot fathom why.

"So who did you forget?" Savage asks.

She opens her eyes. Savage sits so close, his hand on her thigh. He's smiling and that absurd topknot ponytail flows down the back of his head. What would that look like when he's fucking somebody? Amber's cheeks grow hot at the thought, and she's surprised to find that when she pushes it out, she does so with regret.

"What?" she asks.

"I was saying that when I perform in that room, I want to make my audience forget their husbands, forget their boyfriends, forget all their problems. What did you forget, Amber? *Who* did you forget?"

"I…?" Amber sips from her Long Island Iced Tea, not because she's thirsty – she's already had more than enough – but out of nervousness. "I didn't forget anybody."

"Everybody forgets somebody."

"I have a boy—"

Amber's protests die as Savage's hand slides higher up the inside of her thigh. She catches his wrist. It's thick enough her hand can't close around it. He doesn't force it. And while she's stopped him, she doesn't want him to withdraw either.

"Who is he?" he asks.

"Who?"

"We sorta started something back there, don't you think?"

"I guess—"

Savage's mouth brushes her own and closes on her lower lip. Amber hears Gabriella screaming in her ear, *Go for it! Go for it! Go for it!* Gabriella would surrender here; Gabriella, with her tales of discontentment and lack of fulfillment that suddenly seem all too relatable and signposting a future that's all too unsatisfactory.

They kiss, their tongues fleetingly intertwining, and then as they part, Savage lightly bites her lower lip, as if reluctant to surrender contact.

Amber exhales, her arms trembling.

Savage eases back by inches. His eyes are deep and inscrutable. There's a flush of warmth between Amber's legs. Savage's hand has continued to move up, under her dress, his forefinger nestled in the cleft of her crotch.

"Can I tell you something?" he says.

Of course. She wants to say it but it doesn't come out. Nonetheless, he goes on.

"When I perform, I pick who the victor's going to be. I rig the draw. When I saw you, I knew you were going to be my conqueror."

"Why me?"

Savage brushes her cheek. She leans into the caress. He brings his mouth down her neck and traces a solitary finger down her chest and through her cleavage. "It's not just that you're beautiful," he says. "Prudence is filled with beautiful women. But they're vain. Or they're needy. You radiated with something genuine. But there's also a sadness there."

"There's no sadness …"

"Maybe I imagined it, but after being an Icon for so long, I've developed some ability to read my audience, and that's what I read in you: a sadness. Maybe it's a lack of contentment, not being where you want to be. God knows, you wouldn't be the only one. I feel it, too. But it shines out in you."

"I'm in love," Amber says.

"Is that what makes you sad?"

"Why would being in love make me sad?"

"Because some people cling to the thought of love, too afraid to admit it's really nothing but familiarity."

"No." Amber shakes her head. "I'm going to marry this man."

"Really?"

Savage's casual skepticism annoys Amber. But why wouldn't he be given their kiss, given where his hand is, given the way she feels?

"It's just a matter of time," she says, her voice a little too shrill.

"Do you know what you're getting yourself in for?"

Again, Gabriella's stories resound in Amber's mind. But surely it doesn't have to be like that. A pit opens in her midriff and her heart plummets. Maybe it *is* like that, though. It's not like her and Quinn have nurtured some great or passionate love. They just *are.* Maybe they'll become Gabriella and her husband. Maybe all marriages are like that. Maybe she's already Gabriella.

"What's to know?" Amber asks.

Savage sits back, then takes a swill from his Asahi. "I would only ever get married if I could only never live without my partner."

Amber snorts. "That's just fairy-tale love. It doesn't exist."

"Why not?"

"I don't know. It's not realistic."

"I don't have time for the cold pragmatism of life," Savage says. "I know it exists. I know there are ugly necessities that drive us all. But if I was to be with somebody, if I was to commit to them for the rest of my life, then my desire would be that my life could not exist without them. They would be the first person I would want to see in the morning, they would be on my mind until I got home, they would be the last person I want to see that night. They would nurture me through the inanities and requirements of everyday life. And they would do it not with a word or a gesture or an act, but just through existing because they are mine. They would make me soar, make me feel like I could do anything, because they saw in me the best person I could be, rather than just the person I could be for them. Maybe it is a fairy tale. If so, then love and relationships are overrated. But maybe it's true, and that's simply what too many of us *don't* have, and don't pursue: true love. Maybe we settle because we don't dare to know any better."

He speaks with honesty and sincerity – this is not something that can be faked. He believes in what he's saying, and he *does* want it. But this pursuit has only seen him find one emotionally unsatisfying tryst after another. The sex has always been great, but lust and fucking can only mitigate other relationship deficiencies so long.

"What do you have, Amber?"

Amber utters a short, desperate laugh. It's unusual that when she has become so cynical, this stripper has become the romantic. It shames her. Some people still *believe*, and she fleetingly imagines those couples as happy and fulfilled and living happily ever after.

But she doesn't want to explore that question as it applies to her own relationship. She *does* love Quinn. But, now, she doubts how genuine that love is, because here she is. Is this just a symptom of something she hasn't wanted to face? Or is she sabotaging it because the depth of her feelings frighten her? She is confused. She is inebriated. She is at a loss, and she doesn't want to be. The sadness emerges – a mourning over not knowing what her relationship is.

"I don't know," she says.

Savage leans back in toward her, his right hand resting on her hip. "Let me give you something tonight that'll make you forget everything else." He kisses her; his teeth again tug at her lower lip as he disengages. Amber leans toward him almost unconsciously. His left hand traces her cheek. Amber nestles into his caress. "You are so beautiful," he says.

Savage rises, grabs her wrist, and pulls her up to him. She catapults from the chair and spins into his embrace as if they were performing the tango. His body, hard and muscled, envelopes her own. She remembers how powerful he was before, holding her effortlessly. But all these things are physical attractions. She does not truly know this man. The irony is that while Savage yearns for that emotional connection, Amber now thinks that perhaps all that exists is physical attraction. Perhaps love is the ability to remain attracted to somebody despite their flaws, despite their actions, despite whoever they reveal themselves to be.

But, at cross purposes, they find that moment where they intersect and reside – for a little while, at least.

"Well, what do you say?" he asks.

Quinn stays on the floor, shivering. The bile is acrid in his mouth. He doesn't know how long he has sat here, or how long he'll remain. Maybe come the morning when they clean up, they'll find him still here, and sweep him out with the rest of the trash.

He hears the door open. There's a distinctly girlish giggle. Then a guy's voice, young and unsure: "Hang on. I'll check." Footsteps hurry into the bathroom. Then: "All clear!" Quinn recognizes that sharper clip of high heels across the floor. The door closes. Bodies collide. Breathlessness. The smacking of lips. Both sets of footsteps shuffling back. The door in the next cubicle thumps open so hard the walls of Quinn's cubicle shake. The toilet seat is smacked down. More kissing. An amorous sigh. The door closes. Latches.

"You sure we'll be okay in here?" the girl asks.

The voice bears no resemblance to Amber's, but in that instant Quinn's sure it's her. He springs to his feet, his right knee aching at the sudden movement. He is not breathing and there's a cramping pain in his right shoulder where his muscles have tightened.

"Don't worry," the guy says. "Everybody fucks in here."

"I don't want my boyfriend to find out!"

"I don't want my wife to find out!" the guy says.

They laugh, enjoying the humor in sharing a secret, of being illicit, of how the circumstances add excitement to their tryst. So easily are relationships and commitment navigated. These two will go home and think nothing more of what they've done – a drunken indiscretion to be locked away in some recess of the mind … until another opportunity presents itself. Then it's easy to reconcile that something done once without repercussion can be done again. I see it all the time when people come back. They might struggle to adapt to new jobs, new circumstances, to changes in their life, but they adapt to transgression, and even come to a point where they normalize it and seek it, if not seek to outdo one transgression with the next.

Quinn slumps against the cubicle wall. He closes his eyes. More kissing. The rustling of clothes. A zipper unzipping. The unmistakable slither of panties sliding down a pair of legs, followed by the clank of pants – a belt with a heavy buckle unclasping and rattling – hitting the floor.

The girl moans shrilly. They've gone straight into it. No foreplay. There's a collision of flesh and the cubicle shakes. Their rhythm is awkward, and the guy's grunting is as loud as the girl's whimpers. She tells him to fuck her harder. His efforts double. She commands him. Now there is a desperation to his ragged breath. He might've lured her in here, but she is in charge now.

Quinn pictures them as vain but confident, and although he was forming an image of what they looked like, it now metamorphoses into Savage and Amber, Amber with her legs wrapped around Savage's hips, Savage spinning her around. He would not be clumsy. Who knows how many times he's capitalized on a performance? There would certainly be no shortage of candidates. Amber will just be the latest conquest. Quinn can't believe he's given her away – that he's paid Savage to seduce her because that's the Temptation Mr. Hermes set him: *the sacrifice of love.* But what he hates most of all is how much she might enjoy it, how he will become insignificant in comparison, and how their love will be irreparably broken.

Tears brim in his eyes. He slaps the cubicle wall. The girl protests she heard something. The guy assures her it's her imagination. A guffaw escapes Quinn's lips. Now they stop to listen. Whatever else happens, Quinn cannot go through with this. It might mean his death, but better that be the case with a clear conscience. He takes a deep breath, then snarls when he exhales – just the way he used to psyche himself up before games.

"Hey!" the guy says. "Who's there?"

Quinn yanks open his cubicle door and strides from the bathroom, pausing in the juncture under the bronze plaque. He has no idea where to search and he could already be too late. It could be happening this very moment in some secluded corner. Savage might've even taken her into the parking lot.

There are so many options.

Quinn's breathing becomes sharp and that pain that was in his shoulder now jags down his chest. He needs to keep calm, to deal with what he can control. It'll do no good to bound about randomly. He has to logic this out. The gaming room where he first saw Amber and Savage! Yes, that's where this began. That's where he'll start.

The juncture is busier than ever, with lots of security whisking forward. There must be a fight somewhere. It makes moving difficult, as people have clustered to watch what's happening. Quinn excuses himself constantly and shoves his way through.

The crowds thin throughout the gaming rooms, but it turns out only because they've congregated into one. People spill from the archway. Others jump, pushing themselves off the shoulders of those in front to see what's going on. There's a chorus of cheers and encouragement.

Quinn feels the dread build in his chest. They're watching Savage fuck Amber on the pool table. He's so sure of it he can visualize it: she is bent over it, arms spread wide, body bouncing as Savage – every muscle glistening – drives himself into her. She responds with cries that are a mixture of surprise that she can feel such pleasure, and the ecstasy from the act itself. Tears blur Quinn's sight.

He has never been a violent person – has never had inclination toward violence – but now he moves with that purposefulness and intensity that drove him on the basketball court and made him such a hot prospect. He recaptures that single-mindedness and drives his way through. Bodies swallow him up. He can't breathe. The stench of sweat fills his nostrils. Screams fills his ears, as well as the smack of flesh.

Quinn burrows forward with his shoulder, although given his height it's his elbow that shears its way through. Faceless people complain. His right knee protests under his endeavors, and he stumbles, trips, and falls. There are butts all around him – women's butts. The demographic of the crowd has changed. It's made it easier for him to clear a way as he flails his arms.

He crawls into the room, finally breaking through the crowd and landing face-down on the carpet. Nobody cares. There are two women at the pool table, one to either side: one's a diminutive brunette, the other is a girl who might be only a teenager. They're each swinging something. It takes Quinn several moments to determine they're belts. He sees their own clothes are disheveled – possibly belts from their own attire.

He pushes himself to his knees and sees Marcus lying face down and naked on the pool table, his hands and ankles tied to the cups of the corner pockets with stockings – one is a fishnet, one is scarlet, one is white lace, and the other is the standard tan. His mouth is gagged with something black and silk – somebody's panties. He shrieks each time the diminutive brunette and teenager strap him. Hordes of women fill each archway, cheering them on. The brunette wipes her brow. A blonde darts forward and relieves her of the belt. The blonde begins strapping; the brunette retreats into the crowd. Somebody gives her a drink, perhaps in reward. She holds it up in toast, chuckles, then drinks.

Marcus's face contorts in pain, his jaw clenched in anticipation. His hair is soaked. But there is still some semblance of defiance in those aquamarine eyes – it is an ember that glows, however faintly, but it does glow.

Quinn rises unsteadily. He can see angry red welts across Marcus's back and hamstrings, and particularly across his buttocks. Quinn has no idea how this situation has unfolded but he needs to be out of it. It might be cowardice to leave Marcus, or disloyal, but Quinn also knows that Marcus has done something to deserve this. Something like this does not happen spontaneously, or by accident.

Staggering back into the crowd, Quinn almost knocks over Gabriella.

"Hey!" she says.

Quinn is only halfway through his apology when he places her – she was cheering Amber on. He seizes her hands. She tries to pull back, but then stops, as if recognizing him – or perhaps she recognizes his desperation.

"You were here before!" Quinn says. "Where's Amber?"

Gabriella's mouth opens but she says nothing.

"Please! Tell me!" Quinn squeezes her hands. *"Please!"*

"Who are you?"

"Her boyfriend!"

Gabriella's eyes widen.

"Please! I love her! I need to find her!"

"The restaurant," Gabriella says. "That's where I left her."

Quinn impulsively hugs her. When he breaks away, the women around Gabriella have parted to let him through.

"Thank you!" he says.

He hurries from the gaming room, the cheers receding behind him, and hopes he's not too late. Back in the juncture, people are crowded around the entry to the Gallery; some have climbed onto the shoulders of those in front of them. Absently, Quinn wonders if another strapping's occurring. It doesn't matter, though. It's not his destination.

He speeds through the juncture, past the Cardinal, Brimstone, and Verdant Lounges, before coming to the entrance of the restaurant. He skids to a halt.

Savage holds Amber in one arm as he looks down at her. She stares back up at him. They're frozen in that moment, wrapped in the insidious promise of lust and the erasure of all inhibition.

All reason evaporates. Reason won't do.

Instead, Quinn picks up a nearby chair and, roaring, charges Savage.

Holly sits on a toilet in a cubicle, arms wrapped around her shoulders and trembling. There are no tears, and she is unsure what to make of what she's feeling. The coldness she'd felt toward Marcus has evolved into something else. Loathing? Not quite. But it's not something she's felt before. Rage, perhaps? She has been angry in her life, but never in a way that she has surpassed all reason.

She sits up. This is the very cubicle she used to masturbate. That seems forever ago now. But it was such a wanton act, one almost reckless given the circumstances – just like the fornication with the two business executives. Marcus was right: he might've put the gun in her hand, but she pulled the trigger, and she did it obliviously.

Jumping to her feet, she pitches her head over the toilet bowl and is sure she's going to vomit, but nothing comes up. She wishes she could regurgitate the last week. She wishes she could undo this entire holiday, and her relationship with Marcus. But wishes are not real, and all that remains is the reality.

She wriggles her engagement ring off her finger, taking skin with it. For a moment, she holds it in her palm, reminded of when Marcus sunk onto one knee in the middle of a fancy restaurant and proffered the ring. It was such an uncharacteristic act – Marcus, who spoke so bluntly, liked to push boundaries, and grab her butt in public. This was a romantic side that had overwhelmed her.

She should return the ring to Marcus, but given the money he's made, a piddling ring will be hardly worth his while. She does not know that Marcus's mother gave him this ring, which belonged to her mother; Holly does not know that Marcus's mother felt he would never settle down, so she gave him this ring to plant the seed in his mind that one day, a relationship might be forever.

Holly throws the ring in the toilet and flushes, not waiting to see if the water takes it away, or if it just sits at the bottom of the bowl, waiting for whoever to come discover it. Now it's not only like a weight has been lifted from her, but a tether has also been severed.

She is free now.

And so is her rage.

Throwing open the cubicle door, she charges from the bathroom, down the juncture, and into the Verdant Lounge. Everybody is a blur. They might as well not be here. They don't matter. Nothing does. She's unsure whether anything will again.

She heads over to Mr. Hermes's booth, just as Nico is getting up and leaving it. Just like she knows she cannot blame Marcus, neither can she hold Mr. Hermes responsible – at least not entirely. Still, the sight of him, so prim, so composed, the corners of his mouth slightly curved, infuriate her.

"You fucking cunt!" she says.

Mr. Hermes's brows arch, as if her language both offends and pleases him. Nico stops not far from Holly. She is aware of other patrons staring at her, shocked or amused. This is more shameful than her contest against Marcus.

"Do you get a kick out of doing this?" she goes on. "Ruining people's lives?"

"I would think I enlightened you, Holly," Mr. Hermes says.

"Enlightened?"

"As they say, *love is blind.* Your fiancé has been revealed to you as unconscionable. Do you think if he hadn't pursued this Temptation, this aspect of his character wouldn't have existed? Can I be blamed because he was *capable* of this choice? All I did was show you the person he truly is. You should be thanking me—"

"Thanking—?"

"Yes, Holly."

Now, Mr. Hermes's voice is sharp, and those mismatched eyes of his narrow. While he may appear just an old man, there is something so cold about him that it is bereft of all compassion, all empathy, all humanity. Perhaps it is something that has been lost over the years he has offered these Temptations, or something that has been sacrificed from his decades of pursuing avarice. Perhaps it just never was and there is only a vacuum, one he tries to fill with the humiliation and perversion of others.

"You can bark at me all you like," he goes on. "Out of the kindness of my heart, I even set *you* a Temptation offering you the scope to mend your relationship. I offered you a million dollars to consummate your relationship. That's all you had to do – something you've done countless times before with your fiancé. Something you did for much less with two strangers. Instead, when you looked upon him, all you saw, all you felt, was your wrath."

"You …!" Holly says. "You …!"

Because how else would she react once she'd spoken to Mr. Hermes and learned that Marcus had engineered her threesome? Mr. Hermes read her perfectly. She was indignant that she had been played. The sight of Marcus had infuriated and focused her, until she became a detached inquisitor seeking only to wrest the truth from his smug, arrogant manner, as if that would force him to take responsibility.

"You *still* have a duty," Mr. Hermes goes on. "By sitting down with me, you now need to introduce somebody new to me."

"You seriously think that's going to happen?"

"It is not a request, Holly, but an obligation."

As eerily calm as Mr. Hermes is, Holly froths at the opposite end of the scale with fury that blinds all reason.

"You would not want this debt unpaid," Mr. Hermes say. "It would become a burden that you would always carry. Then again," he smiles, "perhaps you want to keep me close to you. Perhaps you feel a kinship to me."

Snatching up Nico's empty scotch glass, Holly lunges at Mr. Hermes. He doesn't flinch. Doesn't move an inch. Arms wrap around Holly's waist. She kicks and flails but is dragged away. Holly wants to scream at whoever has her, but she cannot form the words.

She's plonked unceremoniously onto a barstool. She had thought security had seized her, but it's Nico. He takes the glass from her and plants it on the bar.

"Calm down," he says. He gestures to the bartender with two fingers.

"Who're you meant to be?" Holly says.

She's still glaring at Mr. Hermes. He's still smiling at her. Holly slips from the stool, her feet planting into the floor. Nico's hand closes on her shoulder. Holly is about to tell him to let her go, but the words die when she sees he has a gun shoved down the waistline of his pants.

"Nico," he tells her. "Just take it easy, okay?"

Holly doesn't answer. The bartender puts two scotch rocks down on the bar in front of them. Holly picks up one of the glasses and downs it in a single swallow, grimacing as the scotch burns at her throat. Scotch is not her drink. Nico chuckles. She takes his drink and gulps that down, too.

"Another?" he asks.

Holly spins on the stool, plants her elbows on the bar, and runs her hands through her mess of blonde hair. She now sees the futility of it all – her relationship, Mr. Hermes's Temptation, and facing both him and Marcus down. All just games people play, just as she chose to play one with her threesome.

But now, it's all meaningless. Things she thought she understood have unraveled. She is just a stupid young woman thousands of miles from home who has lost the certainties of everything she knew. Now she struggles to reconcile what happens next.

"Why the fuck not?" she says.

Nico gestures to the bartender once more.

○ ○ ○ ○

Patricia leads Dante into the change rooms. There are others there – Icons mostly, but also staff, like bartenders, waiters, and waitresses – either getting ready for shifts or finishing for the night. Some are in a state of undress but are oblivious to Dante. He ogles them indiscriminately until Patricia pulls him into a closet in the furthest corner of the room.

She closes the door, sealing them in darkness. Dante feels like a twelve-year-old again; his first kiss was at a friend's birthday party, when he and Sophia Brambilla – the most popular girl in school – were locked in a closet as part of a game. Dante was full of bravado and had taken her in his arms, perhaps a little too tightly. She'd admonished him, then – before he could respond – had kissed him, tasting of the sickeningly sweet chocolate birthday cake that had been served earlier. Dante thought he'd done well. He'd fantasized about this moment – not necessarily Sophia, but just his first kiss. That week at school, Sophia had told everybody he didn't know how to kiss. He'd wanted to confront her, but a nobody like him didn't confront a somebody like Sophia Brambilla. He then became the butt of jokes and was mocked regularly. Although he remained stoic throughout, every night in bed he would practice kissing his pillow, imagining it was Sophia Brambilla.

"What're we doing here?" he asks.

"Not everybody knows this is here," Patricia says.

Another door opens – *slides* open. In the darkness, Dante doesn't know whether Patricia has opened it, or if it's been opened for her. She leads him onto a stairwell that twists down and opens into a black hallway with black doors. The single globes that hang from the high ceiling are unnaturally bright, if not almost blinding, although perhaps seeing them like that is a result of the pill he took.

He feels a sense of dread poking through his confused state. He struggles with change – particularly anything new and unexpected. It's hard enough keeping up with Flavia. She embraces challenges and new experiences. He likes what is comfortable. This is as unexpected as it can get for him.

Patricia leads him through one of the doors and closes it behind them. They are now on a balcony overlooking a dark room done up in black: black walls, a black ceiling – that looks soundproofed given the array of tiny sponge pyramids that Dante associates with soundproofing – and a black velvet floor. The room's size overwhelms him. Surely a place like this couldn't exist. It is like being at a football stadium.

In the center is a black metal column that rises into the ceiling. Naked people surround the column – naked except for the little leather face masks they wear, as if they're attending a masquerade ball. The bodies of some are stunning – taut, bronzed, every curve sculpted. Dante recognizes fellow gym junkies. But there are others much more ordinary – their bodies melting into flab; or flab that has amassed into pudginess. There are more people in three rows of balconies that line the room. Some are dressed similarly, while a few are dressed such as he is – as if they've just come from the Gallery or Lounges.

"Where are we?" he asks.

"Does that matter?" Patricia asks, wrapping her arms around his waist and pressing up against him.

"Why did you bring me here?"

Unbuttoning his pants, Patricia unzips them, and pulls them down to his ankles. Dante is still hard; his ability to focus on something primal without his usual self-consciousness erases his concerns. Or perhaps it's the pill he took. Perhaps that's at work.

Patricia's hands slither under his shirt. As she rises, she spreads her hands wide so the shirt's buttons unclasp. She slides his shirt, and his jacket, down his arms. They fall to the floor, leaving him naked. She runs her hands appreciatively over his torso.

"You work out why I brought you here," she says.

Dante opens his mouth, waiting for the suave response that never comes. She places a single finger over his lips.

"Sshhh," she says. "Some things aren't about talking. They're about seeing. *Feeling.*"

She takes his cock in hand. He feels pitifully small, although he is sure he is proportionate. But he wants to be bigger. He wants to overwhelm her. He wants her to be in awe of him. Whatever's happening here, he wants to be bigger than the experience. This is like the closet again. But he wants to emerge and write a new narrative for himself.

He checks the balconies to either side of him: to the left, a short, buxom brunette in a red dress is sandwiched between two burly, naked men whose builds suggest they might be Icons; on the right a thin man with glasses leans against the rear wall, his head lifted to the ceiling in ecstasy. A blonde head can be seen bobbing just above the rim of the balcony. Similar action is occurring in a few of the other balconies, while in others, people stare at the column in the middle of the room.

"What about you?"

"What about me?" Patricia asks.

Dante grabs at the buckle of her pants, expecting resistance, but Patricia throws her arms out wide, surrendering herself. Her breasts thrust out toward him, and he kisses them through her t-shirt, feeling her left nipple between his lips.

He unbuckles her pants, unzips them, and tugs them down. She is naked underneath, her hips full, her legs firm and smooth, her pubic hair just the tiniest landing strip.

Grabbing her buttocks, he buries his face into her crotch. She's wet – soaked. He doesn't know if he finds her clit, or even if he can from this position, but the way she squirms and whines is encouraging. He can't manage this anymore. Foreplay – as non-existent as it has been – is over. He has been in lust with this woman all night and cannot hold on a second longer.

But, more than that, he is in love with the moment. All the foolish bravado he has entertained the whole night, all those whimsical fantasies, and even all his insecurities coalesce and explode into a fiery need that powers him to be all the things he's always wanted, but never been confident enough to pursue.

He rises, spins Patricia around, and bends her over the balcony. Her butt protrudes toward him so round and firm he wants to bite her. She is not the waif Flavia is, or perhaps it's just that Flavia seems a waif in comparison. He cups each buttock, reveling how warm and smooth she is in his hands. This woman is his now – at least for this moment.

He takes hold of his cock and guides it toward her.

Then the grinding fills the room.

○ ○ ○ ○

Flavia runs her mouth up and down LeBeau's cock, tightening her lips until he gasps. He cups her head, and he pulls her to him until she feels his erection stab at her throat. Her eyes water, so she draws away until the tip of his cock sits between her lips. She scowls, then impales her mouth quickly – quicker than LeBeau is expecting – and is withdrawing before he can try to drag her back down. He has had his turn driving.

"You're going to be able to name your price," he says.

Flavia runs her hand up and down his glistening cock, freeing her mouth to grin at him. She relishes the control she has over him now.

"You mean that?" she asks.

"You going to stop?"

Flavia takes him back in her mouth, but she is beginning to feel ready to take him on again. It's not that he is attractive, because he has a worn, jaded look about him, but his power, his confidence, and even his arrogance are aphrodisiacs. This is a man who not only knows what he wants but takes what he wants. That is ultimately much more attractive than anything else.

Flavia clambers up and straddles him. He enters her easily. She lifts her face and hisses. He feels bigger than before. Harder. His hands cup her buttocks, slither up her hips and squeeze her breasts. She leans over him and kisses him. Her tongue fills his mouth.

She straightens slowly, throwing her head back, and loves the way he fills her. Her initial gyrations are small. This is the way she'd ride Dante. But LeBeau isn't a man to do things small. His hips piston back and forth with abandon. Flavia's cries elongate into one long wail. Vibrations course through her body.

But Flavia's rhythm slows, then stops – the Cardinal Lounge is disappearing, as if it's being pulled away. She sinks onto LeBeau, and plants her hands onto his chest. It's not the Cardinal Lounge. It's them. *They're* descending. The perimeter of the floor envelopes them. Then they're through it. Below the pylon are men and women, naked except for leather face masks, gathering and waiting. The pylon slows to a crawl. There are people in the balconies, too. Some are naked and fornicating; others are dressed and watching.

LeBeau sits up, his hands all over her – on her buttocks, up her back, squeezing her breasts, pinching her nipples, then back on her buttocks. He kisses her neck, then her lips. Flavia tries to rear back. LeBeau stands and lifts her effortlessly. Flavia locks her legs around his hips.

"These people—"

He interrupts her by thrusting into her. Flavia's words turn into a long wail. He thrusts again, harder, and harder. Flavia's entire body bounces. He kisses her once. Then his thrusts are continuous. The people are unimportant. His hands dig into her buttocks until she snarls at him. His lips twist into a sneer and he shakes his head, her grasp around his neck breaking.

She shrieks as her back arches and she hangs over the edge of the pylon, arms flailing. Below her, people reach up, almost in worship. Or perhaps they are reaching up to catch her should she fall. They can't be more than ten feet away. Some on the fringes frolic – a few kiss, some perform oral sex, others now engage in sex on the floor.

Flavia scans the balconies. They're hard to make out as LeBeau pounds away. And this room seems to have grown, as if it's expanded to accommodate their lust. She has no idea where LeBeau's brought her, or why, although she suspects this is how the wealthy and the powerful enjoy themselves – she is the sacrifice to their perversion. Perhaps that's why the basement exists. Flavia knows she should be embarrassed, but now, even with a room full of people, it is just her and LeBeau. They are the center of attention – the focus of all the energy in the room.

It's empowering.

Right now, she just wants to be the star – the envy of every woman who would wish to be here, and the desire of anybody who wants her. It is something she deals with on a superficial level in everyday life, but here it exists without boundary, and rather than recoil from it, she embraces it, and urges LeBeau to fuck harder. This is a show now – *her* show.

His body glistens in sweat, highlighting the curve of every muscle. His face is fierce, twisted into a scowl. He could be some deity, or an incubus feeding from her pleasure. Then, as the pylon continues its descent, light silhouettes him and he becomes nothing but a shadow, a wraith seeking to break her.

Flavia is unsure if she imagines it, if she lacks oxygen and is hallucinating, or if she beholds him in his true form, or if she sees him as she wants to see him: he is something greater than anybody else; something that is otherworldly and has sought her out; something that is worthy of her.

They are all stupid thoughts, gibberish mostly in throes of passion, but they also hold kernels of truth that she only entertains in her darkest desires, and in which she now finds kinship.

○ ○ ○ ○

Dante wishes he could dispute what he sees – *who* he sees. But he recognizes every facet of Flavia: her face; the fall of her lustrous hair; her tanned body; her shrill cries; the way her body bounces during sex – although he has never seen it bounce so violently; the way her breasts splay; the curve of her butt; the sounds of her cries; and the *feel* of her, this incendiary amour that is exploding before his eyes.

The man who fucks her is a giant. That is how Dante sees him, and it exaggerates how he sees himself. He is that same scrawny kid, despite all the work he has put into himself. He is that same timid man ambling through life. His cock is woefully ill-equipped

– not just in size, but in technique, and in hunger. It is small and pitiful and embarrassed in his unruly pubic hair.

He thinks of the birthday game that he plays with Flavia, the way each will grant the other's desire. Last time Flavia asked him what he wanted, he said he wanted to see her make love to another man. This was a gambit. What he wanted was for Flavia to condemn him, to tell him that he was the only one she loved and would ever make love to. He needed that assurance, that security, and as glib as Flavia has become in their relationship, that is the only way he felt he could secure it.

This is the manifestation of all his fears that she would one day decide she'd outgrown him, that she would leave him because he has neither her temerity nor her adventurous spirit – this is every fear he has ever harbored and nurtured cleaving into something that he cannot process.

But while the reality breaks him in a way that he always worried he would be broken, the sensation is something far more devastating – not that she would cheat, but that she would enjoy it in a way he can never imagine pleasing her. If that is the case, his relationship is forever a lie. He will never be enough. This proves it.

His intent for Patricia is an affectation – in truth, he would've thrust awkwardly, failing to build any rhythm that would've satisfied her; and he would've lasted no more than a minute or two before he came. He would've walked away thinking he'd done well, that he'd pleased her, that she would remember him fondly, but now in contrast to what he's seeing, he knows they're delusions of grandeur. He snorts. His erection deflates. He can't even aspire to delusions of adequacy.

Patricia spins and leans her butt against the balustrade of the balcony. Her nipples poke through the film of her t-shirt. How many men would want to be here with her? But Dante's objectification crumbles – it's *her;* whatever triggered her to rebel in the gaming room, whatever compelled her to agree with this, comes from an area of vulnerability that defines her. He does not know her story but is sure that like him she's been scarred. She's fleeing her own demons.

"Well?" she says.

Dante lowers his head as Flavia's shrieks fill his ears. It is almost as if some inevitability has been fulfilled that she is doing this. It robs him of his anger. He finds his pants and pulls them up over his deflated cock. As he zips up, he feels the ring box in his pocket.

"Why?" he says.

"What?"

"Why did you bring me here?" Dante finally lifts his face. "You could've taken me anywhere. You … wanted me to see this? *You wanted me to see this!* Why?" He grabs her shoulders. "*Why?*"

Patricia swings her arms, breaking his grip. He can't even demand the truth from her. Why would she listen? He *is* a nobody. This is why he was brought here – not because she fostered some attraction to him, but to humiliate him. It's apt. His life has been about trying to escape that childhood humiliation, only for a new experience to take its place.

She grabs him by the collar, and drags him close to her, until their faces can't be more than an inch apart. Dante can smell her – some apricot perfume she wears, as well as the musky odor of her sweat. Her big brown eyes captivate him. He sees the softness in her – the pity.

"They'll have you," she says, but her voice is so low, so rough, that Dante's unsure he's heard right. She kisses him slowly, her tongue parting his lips, her mouth closing on his lower lip. "Don't you realize?"

Dante shakes his head. "I don't know what you're talking about."

"Do you want me?"

"What?"

"Do you *still* want me?"

Dante glances at the pylon as it lowers into the people below. To his left, the thin, bespectacled man is fucking the blond against the wall, but it's not a woman as Dante anticipated, but a svelte man. The bespectacled man's rhythm is jerky, and he slips out often in his excitement. The blond has his head tilted back and is displaying all the right responses, but Dante knows they're disingenuous. To his right, he can see only the head of the buxom brunette just above the balcony's balustrade. One of her lovers is behind her and, judging by his movements, thrusting; Dante doesn't know where the other man is. The brunette's moans are hoarse, but they hold nothing but pure, undiluted joy.

"Talk to me," Patricia says.

Dante falls to one knee, his forehead pitching against Patricia's belly, his face inches from her thin strip of pubic hair. He clutches at her waist, as the shock sobers him of inebriation and the effects of the pill. Patricia rests her palms on his head. Her right hand strokes his hair. His chest heaves.

Patricia kneels by him and lifts one hand to his cheek. "I don't know if she's coming back to you," she says. "I don't mean in person. I mean …" She taps his temple.

"Why …?"

The stupid hope that surges through him is that he can win her back, that he'll do whatever it takes to both win her back and to be enough for her. He shuns the rationale that disputes the belief – neither will he *never* be enough, but Flavia will never complement him so that he can find that.

"Because we all like this, don't we?" Patricia asks.

"The misery," Dante says. It's not a question.

As Dante shakes his head, he knows he's lying – he has wallowed in insecurity and uncertainty his whole life. He has never summoned the courage to haul himself out of it, even though he has vowed to do so.

"There are things here, people here, that need it, feed on it, that take it from us," Patricia says. "We are nobody but, sometimes," she glances at Flavia, "that's not so bad, is it?"

That has never been Dante's experience, but he sees it in context now – his aspirations, his yearning, is meaningless. He thinks of the others, of how they are all chasing something in their own personalized way and reflects that's the one thing he can abandon: *the chase.*

"It doesn't matter," Patricia says. "Go."

Dante nods. That is the best advice. He never wants to return here again – he is not the first to have that epiphany, although he is one of the few to decline seduction, however belatedly, before arriving at that decision. Now, the choice is clear. He nods again.

Go, Patricia mouths the word.

Dante pushes himself up. Then stops. He doesn't understand the maneuverings, but they've gone to a lot of trouble to manipulate him here, and they've used Patricia as their pawn.

"What about you?" he asks. "Will you be okay?"

She turns away from him.

"*Will* you be okay?"

"I'll survive."

Dante wants to kiss her. She is now not the Icon who commanded the pool table; nor is she the vixen who seduced him in the Cardinal Lounge. In this very moment, they might be elsewhere – Dante stopping on the freeway to help her with a flat tire, or a friend come over to be consoled following a break-up, or two strangers bumping into another in a supermarket and discovering some inexplicable attraction.

He leans in. Kisses her on the cheek.

"Thanks," he says.

○ ○ ○ ○

Flavia's cries are monotonal in her ears, but there is only surrender at this point, surrender and the bliss. Something warm touches her outstretched arms. It's the people. The pylon has lowered her and LeBeau into their reach. Their hands are all over her, pawing at her as if association with her will grant them fortune or favor or blessing.

She wails. Orgasm engulfs her. The whole room blacks out. Her body convulses. She trembles. Her legs spasm. Then she hits the floor. Her eyes open. The room spins. Colored spots dance in front of her eyes.

LeBeau rises to tower over her, standing between her legs as he masturbates himself to completion. His first spurt sails like a shooting star and hits her on the cheek. It's hot – not just warm, but *hot*. Flavia grabs at her face. The people crowded around them cheer like LeBeau's kicked a goal in a world cup final. The second spurt hits her between the breasts, and the third and fourth land on her belly.

Hands grab her, lift her to her feet. Her legs are shaky and she has still not caught her breath. People around her cheer, their hands all over her. The cum drips from where it's fallen. She tries to wipe it clear but the crowd around her make it hard to move. They smear it over her – she is unsure if they're trying to clean her, massage it into her skin, or touch it themselves. She can feel the cocks of some of the men prod into her thighs. Breasts press into her back. They are a single mass smothering her.

She doesn't know what these people want from her and turns to complain to LeBeau. He's nowhere to be seen. She spins back and forth but he's gone. He's deserted her.

Hands pull at her wrists. Others fondle her. They've become more insistent. Through an array of feet, she sees her dress. She ducks and zigzags, fighting through an army of crotches, grabs her dress and darts for the door. Hands trail after her, falling longingly from her body, but nobody stops her.

She reaches the door, yanks it open, steps into the hallway and slams the door shut. Through the portal, she can see that there are people kissing, some fornicating on the floor. Others copulate in threesomes and foursomes, a tapestry of interweaving bodies. The lights dim and they become shadows, their features impossible to make out. She shivers, feeling as if their humanity has been lost – they have become a singular pulsating organism of carnality.

Flavia realizes she is still streaked in cum. There is nothing to clean it with, so she uses the hem of her dress, puts the dress on, and smooths it out with her hand. The wet, sticky bit of the hem clings to her thigh like an incriminating bloodstain. She rolls the hem of the dress up. It makes wearing it bearable, although now it is indecently short.

She looks back and forth, gauging which way she should be going. Originally, as LeBeau led her down here, she noticed the hallway was on a gentle decline, so the way out is clearly up.

For longer than she should contemplate it, Flavia toys with the notion of going further down the hallway. At the very least, she could peek through the portals. It's stupid, she knows. She should get out of here; she should be livid with LeBeau; but there's still a detached calmness that fosters this irresistible curiosity.

She stands there.

Undecided.

VII

Security march Constance, Bodie, and Ox from the Gallery. People have already filled the space that Bodie and Ox's fighting occupied, erasing all traces of what happened. It will become a novelty to most – a story to recount to friends. This is people: they adapt so quickly and unthinkingly as a reflex. It's only when they're tested that they so commonly find an impasse.

Constance races through ideas about how to reach Teo. He is so close she can feel the warmth of his body, yet he has never been so cold. Perhaps she is unable to find a recourse because it's been so long since she's had to struggle to reach anybody. For the last twenty-five years, the moment's she's spoken, *everybody's* listened – at least here. This is a preview of life when she is a *nobody*.

Security guide them into the juncture. Constance glances at Bodie and Ox, her contingency, although she never counted on being unable to get out of the Gallery itself. Of course, it's something she should've considered, but she had become accustomed to having her run of the place.

Frigid air hits Constance in the face. She shivers. The curtains that frame the entry from the lobby flutter. Constance can see out through the doors, like a portal into the very same night that she stumbled in here. Traffic and passersby might be snapshots into yesteryear. Constance doesn't know how she'll get home. She has no money for a taxi, and it is too far to walk. Perhaps Bodie or Ox.

"Wait," Teo says.

Security stops. The archway into the Verdant Lounge silhouettes Teo. He is a giant among men – not just in stature, but how he has supported her professionally and personally. She has always valued him, but now thinks she never truly appreciated him. They rarely speak of his past, but she has seen his scarred body. This man abided in hell, fought repeatedly for his life, and was able to haul himself out. It is why he is never truly tested here – he has seen far, far worse. This must seem so trivial to him, although she suspects that's why he enjoys it.

"Thank you," she tells him.

"For …?"

"I probably have never said it enough to you."

"There never has been a need."

"It's *my* need to say it: thank you."

Teo inclines his head. "Tell me what you would do."

"I'm sorry …?"

"If you could change what's happened tonight, what would you do? This isn't just about the old man and the Camarilla. It isn't just about Prudence, or Prudence's needs, or the old man's needs. It's just the way of things here, the way of things with the old man. You know that better than anybody else. You know what this place means to them, to *him*."

"No." The word barely leaves Constance's mouth. "*No*. The old man knows this is something greater now. This is us. *Me*." She thumps herself in the chest. "*You*." She thrusts her finger at Teo. "Bodie. Ox. Prince at the bar. Every one of us. It used to be just about him. *His* whims. His … capriciousness. And how they fed into everybody, and how everybody fed him, how they fed the Camarilla. He's a dinosaur now. That's why this has happened – he has manipulated the Camarilla in an attempt to rejuvenate his own sense of purpose."

"And your own sense of purpose?"

Constance swallows with difficulty, the question filling her with tension. This has become more than her purpose. It is her identity. What does she have without it? Is this fight nothing more than vanity?

"What do we have when we have nothing left?" she asks.

"If you fail, then?" Teo says. "You know what'll happen. To all of us."

"I can't speak to that," Constance says.

Uncertainty takes residence in Teo's face – he is usually so good at hiding what he's thinking, but now the conflict tears at him. Constance knows what she's asking goes above and beyond. If she were to succeed, as remote as that possibility is, there's no guarantee it'd be permanent. If she failed, it would cost not only her, but Bodie, Ox, and any accomplices.

She reaches out and runs her hand down Teo's cheek. He tilts his head into her caress.

"I'm sorry," she says.

Teo leans forward, his mouth closing on hers. Constance closes her eyes and remembers every day which has unfolded in the twenty-five years that have passed since they last kissed – Teo's loyalty, his unquestioning devotion, his enduring support.

This could've been *something*, if not something special. She'd never considered it, instead focusing on her self-image, but now she sees that self-image has cost her something real, if not special, and she berates herself, because it's not the first time it's happened.

The first time *should've* taught her. It didn't. She made that mistake and bandaged over it with power and opulence and, worst of all, *whimsy*. Now she is trying to hold onto that, but why? She tells herself because it's the only way to make things right. Nothing else will do.

Teo pulls back. "I'm sorry, too," he says, his voice a whisper. "Let's get moving." Then he steps from the archway, and wrenches aside the other security members who are in the way. "Go!"

Bodie and Ox are not only moving, but shotguns are coming out from their overcoats as they head through the archway. A member of security reaches for Constance. His hand snares the collar of her t-shirt. The back of it rips but she slips from his grasp, and bumps into Teo.

Constance rises on her toes, embraces Teo, and kisses him again, closing her eyes once more. He is a shield, a protector, a guardian, as he takes her in his arms and spins. Constance opens her eyes to find Teo has deposited her in the archway, then filled the breach with his massive girth. Security come at him, but in the archway, they can only come at him one at a time, and he fights like the machine of war he is. Constance doesn't know how long he'll last, though.

She steps into the Verdant Lounge.

○ ○ ○ ○

Some people don't belong in this world. Or perhaps that's not quite right. Some people don't belong in this *time*.

I don't know *how* these people come about. It's not just upbringing. Perhaps it's something spiritual, something imbued in them at birth from a previous life that continues to influence how they think in the here and now. Or maybe it's as simple as some psychological disorder – basic human decency. It could be life's cruelest irony in a world that's becomes progressively expeditious. Or maybe it just happens, and they are a statistical aberration in a population that is becoming increasingly capricious and uncaring.

When Rupe kisses Joy, he does so as a man might've kissed a woman in the 1930s; his right hand slides to the small of her back, the top of his fingertips gently sitting just above the swell of her buttock; his left hand cradles her from her right shoulder blade, supporting her as he leans toward her; his kiss is gentle, his eyes are closed.

He withdraws, easing Joy up. For a moment, she wavers, and his hands hover about her, ready to steady her if necessary.

There is silence between the two as they regard one another, Rupe hopefully, expectantly, eyes almost brimming, Joy dubiously, the smallest wry smile playing on her lips. Rupe reaches out with one hand and holds it palm-up for her to take.

"I'm—" Joy begins, perhaps about to explain, perhaps about to apologize, but she doesn't get any further. There's an explosion. The floor shakes. Then another. And another and another and another. If I could, I would grimace. These are heavy blows, the sort a boxer delivers to a doddering opponent on the verge of collapse.

Joy scowls. "No!" she says, springing away. "This won't do at all!"

Rupe grabs her wrist and jerks her back. She spins to face him.

"This is no time for games," she says.

"Don't go," Rupe says.

Joy stares at him, unbelieving.

"Let's just leave," Rupe says. "Come with me. I don't know where. Anywhere."

In that instant, and just that instant, Joy opens to me: images flash through her mind – her with Rupe at dinner at a nice restaurant, her and Rupe strolling through the park, her and Rupe as a couple in any number of situations, her and Rupe marrying, her and Rupe shopping for a house, her and Rupe getting pregnant together, Rupe holding her in his arms as she cradles a newborn baby.

She has projected an entire future in the time it takes to blink, a future that was previously closed to her – one that doesn't necessarily have to occur with Rupe, but which he now represents as a possibility. There is a whole life for her out there if she just decides to explore it, a life of love and giving rather than what she faces now. She does not know that Constance also had this insight so many years ago when the Camarilla offered her the job, and before they extolled from her the price of acceptance.

For Rupe, it's something similar: it's not just that he wants her, that she has charmed him, or that he finds her attractive, but that she represents the hope that he might love again, that there might be life after his wife with another – a prospect that once did not exist at all.

Then Joy's mind closes. I want to urge her to reconsider; I want to *will* her to change her mind; but, just as Constance was, Joy is determined. She believes she has come too far, given too much, and that there is no turning away now.

Her head bows. The smile disappears from her lips and her jaw sets. Rupe doesn't need to hear the words to know what's coming. He drops his hand.

"I'm sorry," Joy says.

She heads for the door.

Rupe hurries after her.

Bodie and Ox tornado through the Verdant Lounge.

In their right hands, they brandish automatics – a Heckler & Koch for Bodie, a Sig Sauer for Ox – which they use to threaten anybody tempted to play the hero. In their left hands, they carry shotguns, which they fire into the ceiling again and again and again.

The chandeliers are obliterated. One collapses onto a table in a conflagration of flames, igniting the tablecloth. Another explodes and ignites the curtains. It's amazing – if not unnatural – how easily the fire races through the Verdant Lounge. The fire sprinklers whiz and splutter but shoot little water. Patrons scream, instinctively flinging themselves to the floor to shield themselves from the gunmen. Among them are Nico and Holly.

Constance is terrible and imposing as she strides obliviously through the carnage. Mr. Hermes is indifferent. He is the one person in the Verdant Lounge who has remained unmoved. He has seen revolts such as this in other times and in other places and holds them in low regard.

People.

That's how simply he sums it up. People are predictable and petty and amusing, but every now and again they aspire for something greater – children wanting the box of matches they have been told are not a toy. He understands they need the grit to transform. Nothing grows in a vacuum. But he has settled into the belief that evolution will never come – at least not in the time he has allotted himself to witness it.

Constance arrives at his booth, Bodie and Ox flanking her, smoke pluming from the barrels of their shotguns.

"I take it," Mr. Hermes says loftily, "that you're upset with your replacement."

"Not with her," Constance says. "But with the decision."

"The Camarilla respects you. They still love you. But I have convinced them change is needed."

"Then you can convince them otherwise."

"They have already sanctioned Joy."

"These are all whims."

"No doubt why you think this," Mr. Hermes picks up his glass of iced water, and gestures at Bodie and Ox in turn, "can change everything."

"It's what you understand – what you have overseen yourself. Power over the weak."

"But I am not weak." Mr. Hermes takes a drink, sets his glass down, and cups his hands around it. "A fine contingency, Constance. But one without due."

"Prudence is mine. It's not too late."

"Not too late? For what?"

"Negotiation."

"*Negotiation?*"

"Yes, listen to me!"

Mr. Hermes throws his head back and laughs. "To negotiate, you must have something to offer. You, Constance, have nothing. You are past your time – a woman desperate to hold onto luster she no longer warrants."

"How dare you!"

"I dare, Constance. And more."

The heat grows stifling. I feel it everywhere. The walls have disappeared in flames. Smoke creeps across the pockmarked ceiling. Unnoticed at the archway, a bloodied Teo darts in, grabs a woman lying on the floor by the collar and escorts her out. Security charges in. Teo orders their help. Some do, falling unthinkingly under his command. Nico and Holly drag themselves up to their knees. Security try to usher them out. Nico waves them away. Other members of security – perhaps reward for initiative playing on their minds – charge for Constance with the intent of apprehending her. Bodie and Ox aim their shotguns at them. Security stop, hold their hands up to show they mean no harm, and back away.

"Prudence belongs to nobody," Mr. Hermes says. "Not least of all some petty, failed, opportunistic model, some whore who sold herself for glamour, who has nothing but gauche ego. We belong to Prudence. She is the heart of my empire. She is the soul of the Camarilla. We'd like to think we make her what she is, but she makes us what we *are*. And the reality is that she no longer needs you, Constance."

"No—"

"Constance, it seems you didn't get the point with Joy. You're dismissed."

"Dismissed?" Constance snorts with laughter.

"Yes. Nothing can change that. Not you. Not your henchmen. *Nothing*."

Ox levels his shotgun at Mr. Hermes. "We'll see about that."

○ ○ ○ ○

Holly's rage is the anchor that keeps her rooted to the floor. She *should* flee – crawl out on hands and knees, naked butt in the air, if necessary. All the other patrons have fled. That's what people do in dangerous situations: it's *fight or flight*, and the judicious have taken *flight*.

That means she wants to fight.

That possibility firms in her head, but then grows ablaze. She doesn't just want to fight. She wants to *destroy*. She wants to see Mr. Hermes razed to ashes, and here is an opportunity: two gunmen and this aging blonde. Holly *should* be frightened, but she is eerily calm, and able to survey the situation clinically.

It does not occur to her that her anger has grown irrational. Darkness has filled her – the culmination of her tryst, her confrontation with Marcus, and her interactions with Mr. Hermes. Reason no longer exists. She sits now in the cradle that Mr. Hermes occupies, but without his control.

The gunmen are focused on him. They have no interest in anybody else. Holly wants to urge them to finish what they've started, although one thing she does recognize is that there is never an ideal time to address anybody holding a gun.

The solution is much simpler: if they don't see this through, she *will*. As dangerous as the situation is, as great a risk to her well-being as it might be, as terrified as she should be, she needs to see this to completion.

She glances at the gun shoved down the front of Nico's pants. "Wait!"

Joy strides into the restaurant, Rupe bounding behind her like an adoring puppy. Flames dance around her, allowing an unencumbered path, some – Holly believing it a trick of her imagination – twisting and shaping fleetingly into towering wraiths reveling in the mayhem. She can hear their sweet pleas, enticing and mesmerizing.

"What've you done?" Joy asks, arms held wide.

I can feel the fire scorching my bricks, ravaging the stucco finish, incinerating fittings, and spreading through the walls. This isn't just fire, though. It's rage. It's lust. It's the decadence that abounds here – and has abounded here since my doors opened. But now it is unleashing, seeking its own freedom to wreak an unspeakable, irreconcilable havoc not just upon those here, but everywhere.

"This is not his concern," Constance says, pointing at Rupe.

"You've made it *everybody*'s concern!" Joy says.

"No." Constance looks at Mr. Hermes. "Just ours."

"Walk away," Joy says.

"Would you?" Constance says.

"It's my time. They chose *me*. I gave myself to them to have this. *It's my time!*"

Constance steps up to Joy. Sweat pours from her, staining her torn t-shirt and matting her hair, yet – as always – she remains unbowed.

"No, not yet," she says. "If you had a fraction of intelligence, of foresight of what lies ahead, you would turn away. Go." Then, she waves at Rupe, and almost as if scoffing, adds, "Take him! Have a life beyond these walls."

Everybody pauses. Even the flames seem to hold still.

Mr. Hermes cackles. "You," he says, "all so petty, all so greedy. For what little thing? Some small semblance of power? For some inkling of glory? It is delicious. You little fools. You're no more than pawns, hoping to make it to the other side of the board and become something greater than what you truly are: *sacrifices*. You think this is defiance? I have you all! I. *Own*. You."

And each of the people who have dealt extensively with Mr. Hermes know this is true. They have coveted what has been afforded them until they have lost sight of everything else. It has been seductive and addictive, something they have not only wanted to hold onto, but which they've hoped would elevate them.

All but Holly, who has waited quietly, who hasn't sought any form of self-aggrandizement, and has only lamented what she surrendered: *herself* to the two business executives' lust, to Marcus's largesse, and, finally, to Mr. Hermes's manipulation. She was just a plaything. Small. Unimportant. And wholly malleable.

Until now.

She grabs the pistol from Nico's waistline and, roaring, springs to her feet and charges Mr. Hermes. Rupe instinctively reaches for her. Bodie and Ox part, as if understanding her intent and allowing her the best target available. She fires one shot. The bullet *thuds* into the wall just above Mr. Hermes's shoulder. He is unmoved, unflinching, smiling at her. The gun kicks up in Holly's hand. She readjusts her aim but arms close around her, and hands clench her wrist. She is spun and disarmed. It is Nico. He restrains her, a lover's embrace.

"Sorry," he says, then hoists the gun limply into the air, to show everybody it's under control. "Sorry!"

His hand tightens around the grip of the gun, and he aims it at Constance.

"Sorry," he says again.

Constance blanches. Bodie moves to cover her, Ox to intercept Nico.

Mr. Hermes chuckles.

Nico pivots and levels the gun at him.

Mr. Hermes's eyes go wide.

Nico fires.

○ ○ ○ ○

There's nobody in the change rooms. Clothes lie strewn across the floor and on chairs, and make-up is upended on tables.

Dante heads to the doorway and stares out at the hallway. Sounds are dim here, so he pushes one ear forward, as if that'll help him determine what he's hearing. It's not the general hubbub of the crowd. There are cries. Shouts. People hollering to one another. It is the cacophony of panic.

He should leave, but what Patricia has done holds him here. She has sacrificed something in urging him to go, but at what cost? He feels it now. The heartbeat. *My* heartbeat. Thumping. Steadily. It vibrates through everybody and everything, uniting us all to the same harmony – a harmony that now shrieks into discord.

Heading back into the change room, Dante charges down the stairwell, and makes his way to the doorway that led out to his balcony. Patricia is there, zipping up her jeans. Her jaw is clenched, her lower lip thrust out petulantly. She does not notice him, instead lost in her humiliation.

It *is* her fault. Well, that's what runs through her mind. She let men and women take advantage of her during her modeling career. Becoming an Icon seemed fitting but was just another means of humiliating herself night after night. And then Joy – Joy who tasked her with seducing Dante. Patricia gave herself wholly because it *was* so easy.

She clasps the locket around her neck. Her life has deadened her. The X'cess enforced the illusion that she was alive, regardless of what she was doing. But now that truth sinks in: it *is* an illusion. She is left with nothing.

"Hey."

It's Dante, watching her with concern.

"What're you doing back here?"

"I don't know why you did what you did," Dante says. "I'm not so foolish to think it's just for me."

Patricia opens her mouth, ready to fire some assurance – an automatic response. He holds up his hand.

"It's okay." Dante thrusts his hand out. "Come on."

"Are you mad?"

Dante doesn't know why he thinks it but he's sure if he gets Patricia out of here, she'll be safe. If she remains, she'll be consigned to some unspeakable lot. Perhaps that's who the people down there are in their masks – those who embraced temptation and lost themselves to the seduction.

And the simpler truth is he knows if he leaves her, he'll always regret this decision – she could still rebuke him, but he has to know that he *tried*. He is not saving her – or not *just* trying to save her. He is trying to save himself.

"Please." Dante thrusts out his hand again.

His earnestness touches her – this is a selfless act. He expects nothing in return. He is here because she has done him a kindness.

That simplest of realizations sparks into something brilliant that shines through the torpor of her life. She does not know if this is what Constance has tried to teach her all these years – this self-worth. But Patricia feels a trueness about herself that she hasn't since she was young, an authorship of her life that she has lacked.

She snaps the locket from her neck and tosses it over the balustrade. When she turns to Dante, she sees he is frowning. He is a peculiar little man, a jumble of nervousness and uncertainty in a blender that mixes it all into a cowering diffidence, but it also offers a vulnerability that ensures he is genuine.

"Well?" he says.

Patricia takes his hand.

He clasps it and smiles. She might be this towering sultry beauty – much like Flavia, he sees now – but she's not oblivious. She is a kindred spirit, a soul that the world has battered and tormented and twisted into something she has never wanted to be, just as he has done with himself.

He drags her from the balcony, up the stairwell and back into the change rooms.

Still, they're empty.

It wouldn't matter if they weren't.

Nobody is going to get in his way now.

Quinn charges Savage, holding the chair aloft, aware of faces in the restaurant turning to him. Everything is a blur – everything but Savage. Quinn is sure he should close the distance in seconds, but Savage moves almost as if he belongs in a different timeframe.

He spins Amber away, and, in the same motion, kicks. The sole of his boot – Quinn noticing fur tassels hang from their golden buckles – thunders into Quinn's chest. The sound of the impact is an explosion. Quinn's breath belches from his mouth. He flies backward and hits the floor, the collision sounding like another explosion. The chair sails from his grip and bounces off a table. More explosions.

"Quinn!"

Amber kneels by his side, cradling his head in her lap. This is what she did in the game he injured his knee, charging down from the bleachers, pushing through players and coaches, and kneeling beside him to comfort and assure him as the doctor examined him.

She glowers at Savage. "What the fuck do you think you're doing?" she says.

"He came at me with a chair!" Savage says.

Amber caresses Quinn's cheek and kisses his forehead. Her hands are cool and Quinn smells alcohol on her – he's unsure what. His chest is locked. He tries to tell Amber he cannot breathe but the words emerge tiny and unintelligible. Some people gather around. Others hurry out. Quinn closes his eyes. He's sure the pain will pass, but the embarrassment will endure. More explosions rock through the restaurant but he identifies now they're coming from somewhere else.

"Quinn?" Amber says. "Quinn, are you okay?"

She takes what she thinks is a handkerchief from a pocket and applies it to Quinn's forehead, but to her horror it's not a handkerchief, but Savage's G-string – she must've pocketed it unthinkingly.

Quinn's eyes flutter, and Amber's sure he'll see – that he'll identify – what she's holding. In that instant, her horror and guilt coalesce. *This* is the man she loves. For each of his faults, there are multiple positives. But she let herself get carried away, and why? Because the quick gratification is easier than the toil that love demands.

She scrunches up the G-string and flicks it away.

"Quinn, tell me you're okay," she says.

He blinks repeatedly, his eyes unfocused, but in them Amber sees a plea – not just that she loves him or will be here for him (as that is too much of a simplification), but that she will rescue him just as she did when injury finished his basketball career.

This is what love is – or at least it's how Amber defines it: every moment, one partner rescues the other from disaster, from inanity, from uncertainty, from insecurity, from fear, from pain, from the next instant being lesser than the one before it.

The illusion falls away – she does not want Savage's assuredness. That is too easy a qualifier to surrender. She fell in love with Quinn because of his sensitivity and his vulnerability, and while he needs to find purpose – the sort of purpose that drove him when he played basketball – she sees the man she loves, the man she has always known she would spend her life with, and anything *and* everything else *is* an illusion.

Quinn's chest heaves as if he is sucking life from Amber's thoughts. Amber kisses him on the lips, her fingertips tracing the curve of his cheek. Savage leans forward and offers his hand to Quinn. Quinn grasps it diffidently. Savage hauls him up effortlessly and, as Quinn gasps for breath, the first thing he notices is the whiff of smoke.

"I can't talk …" Quinn says, his voice barely audible, aware that Savage is still staring – glowering – at him. "My throat …"

"I'll get you something to drink." Amber rushes to the bar.

"This your plan?" Savage asks. "To appear the hero?"

For a second, Quinn doesn't understand. But then it clicks: Savage thinks this was all a ploy so Quinn could run in, rescue his girlfriend from a predator, and appear the jealous but loving boyfriend.

Quinn doesn't know what to tell Savage. Savage is unflinching, and Quinn fears this could erupt into violence – Savage has already shown how adept he is. Quinn lowers his head, eyes bleary. And then, to his surprise, Savage claps him companionably on the shoulder.

"It's okay," Savage says. "I guess you've worked out what you want."

"Yeah," Quinn says, and then, with greater conviction: "*Yeah.*"

"This is something you'll have to carry the rest of your life," Savage says. "A *secret.*"

Quinn isn't sure if Savage is counseling him, or attempting to extort him, and is summoning the courage to ask when Amber returns with a glass of water. Quinn downs it in one gulp but feels a new nervousness. He thinks of asking Amber for another glass of water so he can confront Savage.

But smoke seeps through the walls and curls toward the ceiling. Somebody screams, "Fire!" and it becomes an alarm that is echoed. People rush from the restaurant. Quinn is caught in the exodus. He throws a hand out and catches Amber's wrist. Savage is separated behind them, but that suits Quinn fine.

"Quinn!" Amber says. "What's happening?"

Quinn shrugs as they march from the restaurant. In the juncture, flames dance from the archway, across the hallway, and to the Verdant Lounge. The opposing wall is ignited, immersing the ceiling. It is impossible how quickly the fire spreads. I feel it in my bones.

Security and staff do their best to control the situation. Some have fire extinguishers and blast them into the archway, but to little avail. Others try to marshal patrons out, but there is little order. Most bustle against one another, often stumbling, several tripping and trampled.

Quinn tries to process what he's seeing, and then work out the best course from here.

Amber eases her wrist from his hand, and then takes his hand, clenching it firmly. "Hold onto me," she says, "no matter what."

Quinn smiles. "No matter what," he says.

○ ○ ○ ○

Flavia peers through each portal as she heads down the hallway.

Sexual activity abounds in every room: one on ones, threesomes, gangbangs, orgies, bondage, and things she can't possibly reconcile – extremes that most wouldn't entertain, even as fantasies. She recoils, horrified, but cannot stop herself. It becomes an addiction to see what comes next. She wonders who all these people are. Do they all come from upstairs? Or is there another way in here? Or – and she tries to shut this thought out the moment it enters – do they abide down here, souls lost in the torment of their own desires?

The sight in the next portal surprises her most of all: a tiny blonde woman without a facemask – a woman Flavia believes is vaguely familiar – masturbates. Flavia watches her longer than she should, trying to identify her – she bears a striking similarity to a foreign popstar – and is fascinated that this room can be dedicated just to her.

But then Flavia thinks about her own exhibition. Perhaps this blonde isn't alone, and there are people on balconies watching. Flavia tries to check, but the portal doesn't offer her that vantage. One thing she is certain of, though: the depth of the room. It's *long*, and probably just as wide – like her own room was. But the portals are spaced twenty or twenty-five feet apart. The rooms seem bigger than that.

The blonde shrieks, the cry muffled as it tries to penetrate the door. Her body bucks, and then she falls limp. She lies there, still but for her heaving chest, then slowly hauls herself into a sitting position. Her face is sheepish; she looks to the left, then to the right, as if seeking approval.

Flavia is sure now there *is* an audience watching, although perhaps they're not physically there, but digitally. If that's the case, who is this performance being broadcast to? Flavia flushes. Perhaps she herself was filmed and broadcast on some private channel. Perhaps all these rooms are filmed. Perhaps it's not just the basement but *everything*.

She forces herself onwards. The portals continue endlessly. She stops and checks the way she has come and is alarmed to find there's no end to the hallway. How far has she come? The string of portals is like the illusion of looking into a reflection of a reflection in a mirror.

Everything takes on a surreal quality as she struggles to grasp the physical improbabilities of the distances involved. She must've walked thirty minutes at least. But it's only fifteen minutes back to her hotel. Can she really have walked further than that? Could the basement range that far underground? It's impossible to believe. Her gauge might be awry – perhaps it's the shock of what she's done with LeBeau.

Flavia rises onto her toes to peer into the next portal. A face shoots up – pale and gaunt, raven hair disheveled, eyes dark and sunken – and hands slap against the glass. In the instant before Flavia stumbles back and falls on her butt, she can't determine the person's gender. She looks up. There is nothing in the portal now. She pulls herself to her feet and rises warily toward the portal.

Nothing.

Nothing but a big empty room.

She sinks onto the soles of her feet. That can't be right. Of course, the owner of the face might be leaning against the door right under the portal. If so, what is this person doing? Everybody else was having sex – even the tiny blonde was gratifying herself. This person looked like they were suffering.

Flavia hears a thumping – it is her own heart. She is holding her breath, and the hairs on her arms and neck rise, slowly, as if drawn to some static electricity. Curiosity transforms into dread. She has amused herself, but this is the time to leave. But, still, there is something behind that door, something unlike any other portal she has looked through.

A creak punctures the silence. Flavia pauses. A door two portals down and to the right opens. Flavia takes a step back. A shadow is cast from the doorway. Flavia takes another step back. A short figure in a flowing robe of the darkest crimson with violet trim appears. He wears a crimson mask that has a silver lightning bolt running down from the middle of the temple, and over the right eye.

He turns toward Flavia. His robes make it impossible to gauge whether his posture is aggressive or surprised, and the mask makes it equally impossible to read any expression, but Flavia feels the sensation of cold inch from the nape of her neck across her shoulders and down her back.

It is time for a retreat. She has tempted … *well*, she decides whatever is going on down here, it has a collective whim that she has antagonized. She should have left immediately. She should *not* have come down here at all. All these regrets shoot through her mind, coalesce, then explode in fear.

She bolts back up the hallway.

The footsteps that sound behind her are steady and measured. Flavia doubles her efforts, pulling her heels off as she runs. Her breath comes in ragged gasps and burns her throat.

She has rarely run since being an adult, unless it is for a train or a bus, or to get to or from her car if it's raining, and although she does exercise, this distance exhausts her quickly. But stopping is not an option. Stopping will consign her to some ghastly fate.

Again, the distance seems askew. It's just minutes before she takes the stairs two at a time. At the top, she thrusts her hands into the doors, expecting them to swing open, but they jar against her assault. She bangs into them, startled. There are no handles on this side. She slaps at the doors and pushes them again and again until they rattle.

"Open up!" she says. "Open up now!" But her voice is barely a whisper, her breathing shallow.

Her hands fall from the doors, and she looks back down the stairs. The bottom is dimly illuminated. A shadow appears, or perhaps she imagines it. There are no footsteps. Nothing. The shadow lengthens. Darkens. No. There is something coming.

She moves to smash her hands against the doors, but they swing open. Prometheus is there, his face implacable. He tips his head to her. Smiles that big smile.

Flavia blunders down the hallway and doesn't look back.

○　○　○　○

Marcus's right cheek rests against the felt of the pool table. He wishes he could stop the tears that dribble from his clenched eyes, but whatever self-control he might've once exercised was broken long ago. His back and buttocks burn. There's a thunderous *snap*. His buttocks quiver as leather bites into his flesh. The pain is an eruption that explodes from the point of impact and mushrooms up his back and down his hamstrings. He grunts into the silk panties that gag him.

"Fire!" somebody says.

There's uncertainty. Queries are thrown back and forth. Confirmation. More confirmation. The mood shifts from vicious jubilation to panic. In his pain, Marcus can't follow it – he is just relishing the respite. People shriek. Feet stampede out and recede. Now the pandemonium sounds from elsewhere and spreads.

Marcus eases his head up. There's a tightness in his neck that is resistant to unwind. He rests his chin on the table and forces his eyes open. Whereas there had been a mob, now the room is empty. He tries to call out that he's been forgotten, but even if it weren't for the gag, there isn't the strength to speak.

Then there's the shame. How would he deal with being found in this predicament? Questions would be asked. He remembers after Constance assigned him this role, he was determined to create a legend. He has – a legend about being humiliated, no embellishment required.

A memory rears up: playing football in the eighth grade despite the desperate need to piss, being knocked over in a contest, and wetting his shorts. Everybody had laughed. He'd fled home, locked himself in his room, and cried for an hour. After dinner, his older brother had asked him what was wrong. Marcus had relayed what had happened. His brother told him he should do whatever it took to stop people laughing – to make them respect him.

The next day when Marcus had shown up for school, the football captain, Harrison Leury, had mocked him, and gotten the other kids to jeer him. Marcus had punched him in the nose. Harrison's friends had rushed him. Marcus had struck faces, punched stomachs, and kicked crotches, his ferocity more than his physicality forcing his attackers back. Teachers had intervened and he'd been suspended a fortnight.

When he got back to school, Harrison and his friends had confronted him; Marcus had fought them again, although their numbers had been too great, and they'd beaten him. Now they'd been suspended. Once they returned, Marcus sought out Harrison and beat him in the toilets, threatening to break his arm – if not now, then any other time something like this happened, or if Harrison reported him. Harrison said nothing. People stopped making fun of Marcus. Marcus learned there was power in strength.

And humiliation, pain, and fear can liberate.

"Well, well, well."

The way his head pivots to the left, it might be operating on a rusty hinge. It's Gabriella, a belt looped around her right hand. The bitch strapped him three times, her eyes smoldering gleefully. There is nothing more than that thought, though. The silence of his mind scares Marcus. Once upon a time, he would've vowed revenge. He thinks back to Harrison – a memory that usually triggers exultation, but that is gone now, too.

"You are so unimportant, so insignificant, that not one woman stopped to think they should free you," Gabriella says. "Except me."

She runs her hand down his back and onto his right buttock. Her hands are smooth and cool and, even if she is an older woman who's squeezed out a few kids, Marcus knows there was a time he would've welcomed her touch, but now it only ignites his pain.

Gabriella fishes into his mouth with one finger and pulls out the panties the way a magician might pull a string of handkerchiefs out of their pocket.

"Nothing to say?" she asks.

Marcus inhales deeply. He can still taste the silk on his tongue, and he was sure they were also wet – whether from sweat or ejaculate or something else, he doesn't know.

"What would you give me to untie you?" Gabriella says.

Marcus turns onto his left cheek. It feels so good to have his head in another position. "You wouldn't …" he says but can't get out more than that. His throat is dry.

Gabriella starts for the archway.

"Please …"

Gabriella stops.

"*Please …*"

Gabriella returns to the table and kneels before him. "Yes, I wouldn't leave you," she says, "but I want you to know that for every remaining moment of your life, you were at my mercy." She unties his left wrist, and then his left ankle. "I'm not sure somebody like you will care. I'm sure it's just a matter of time before something like this – or *worse* – happens to you again." She moves around the table and unties his right ankle. "But who knows? Miracles *have* happened." She unties his right wrist.

Marcus draws his hands up and plants them on the table. Shoulder muscles that had been locked finally relax. He propels himself up the way he would with a push up. His back burns. His crotch is sticky, and his cock is glistening and limp. There is a stain on the table. He doesn't remember ejaculating and doesn't know why he would've given the circumstances. Warmth fills his cheeks. The smell of smoke teases his nostrils.

He sits up, hoping his body will obscure the stain from Gabriella, but she is by his side, maneuvering under his arm in support. Marcus pauses to gape at her as her eyes go sidelong from his crotch to the stain on the table. Marcus looks away in embarrassment, but she says nothing, instead hoisting his arm and pushing up with her legs, giving him the leverage to clamber off the table.

"Hang on," Gabriella says.

Marcus supports himself against the table and notes that smoke trickles in and spills across the ceiling, like some living ornate web taking form. He has no idea what's gone on but knows it can't be good.

Gabriella herself shows not an iota of urgency as she fetches the leather pants he wore as an Icon and a half-filled Corona, which sits discarded on a table in the corner. She offers the Corona to Marcus – who takes it weakly – and then kneels before him and fits the pants to him, dressing him with the care and patience she exercises when she dresses her children. Given the Velcro seams, she can piece the pants together around his legs, although he trembles and gasps when she presses them to his buttocks.

"I'm sorry," she says. "But I don't think going out naked is a good idea."

Marcus lifts the Corona to his lips and takes a long drink. The beer is lukewarm, but it feels good to wet his mouth and his throat. But the relief is short-lived. He is bitter now over how the night has transpired, and while Gabriella is his savior, she is also witness to how pathetic he is.

He lifts the bottle. Tightens his hand around its neck. Sets his jaw.

"Marcus!"

○ ○ ○ ○

It's the heat that hits Dante first. It's been hot and stuffy all night, but now it's thick enough in the air that it makes it hard to breathe. He closes his hand tighter around Patricia's; it's become so sweaty that he feels it could slip right out.

"Take a look at that," he says, with a thrust of his chin.

Wisps of smoke undulate across the hallway ceiling.

"Fire?" Patricia says.

Dante shrugs, but that's the likeliest possibility.

They navigate through hallways intersecting the private rooms. The doors are flung wide open, and the rooms appear empty. Dante peeks in several as they pass: they are small, like cells, with disheveled beds – evidence of rapid departures.

The first gaming room. Empty also. The arcade dance machines blink and chirp, prompting players to be ready. There's nobody at the machines in the rooms that follow. In the first pool room they enter, cues on the floor and balls on the table suggest the game was abandoned midway.

"I don't like this," Patricia says.

Neither does Dante. He is afraid to say anything, afraid Patricia will hear the terror in his voice. People have fled en masse. *Fled.* Dante fights the urge to break into a sprint. That's the fear talking. He has to stay calm. Patricia huddles closer. He thinks she's doing it for her own assurance but sees on her face that she's read him; she's doing this to comfort him.

As they continue, voices become evident. Now Dante feels a tinge of curiosity. If there is a fire, who would remain behind? Patricia tries to burst ahead, but he clenches her wrist. She turns back to him, puzzled. Dante doesn't know what to say to her. He holds up a finger, as if to shush her, but that's not right either, so he takes the lead, almost tiptoeing.

When they reach the archway to the adjoining gaming room, they see Marcus leaning against the pool table, his bare chest glistening, a Corona in hand. Gabriella kneels before him. At first, Dante is sure she's fellating Marcus, but then it becomes clear she's fitting his leather pants to him, sealing the Velcro seams up the sides.

Marcus lifts the Corona high above Gabriella's head; Dante believes that, for whatever reason, Marcus has snapped, and he's going to bludgeon Gabriella; but Patricia remembers Marcus from earlier, remembers him as cruel and indiscreet, only she senses something is different now, something has changed, and she becomes sure that he, in a moment of self-realization and self-loathing, is going to bring the bottle down on his own head. But, then again, she knows this may just be her own wish fulfillment.

"Marcus!" Dante says.

Marcus freezes. Gabriella pivots, sees Dante and Patricia, then looks up to Marcus just as Marcus is putting the bottle on the bank of the table. She frowns. She hasn't seen enough to condemn Marcus but has seen enough to suspect something may have gone awry. Of course, she doesn't know whether Dante's cry was a warning or a greeting, and now, with the threat defused, neither Dante nor Patricia are entirely sure about what Marcus was planning to do.

Dante darts forward, dragging Patricia behind him. He's about to question Marcus over what's wrong but sees a red welt on his shoulder. Dante peers around Marcus and sees the road map of lashes, some serrated with ragged flesh standing high, while others trickle blood.

"What the …?"

Marcus shakes his head. "Just fun and games," he says.

Patricia exchanges a look with Gabriella. Neither knows the other but an understanding passes between them. Dante's seen it happen all the time between Flavia, Amber, and Holly. In situations like these, women develop telepathy. Patricia's face goes hard and her hand slides from Dante's.

"We need to go," she says.

"You okay to walk?" Gabriella asks Marcus.

"I'm king of the hill," he says.

While they know something dire is happening, they do not appreciate the true danger until they encounter a wall of flames in one of the karaoke rooms. It consumes the archway, so it is impossible to continue this way.

Marco and Dante are distraught, while Gabriella consults her memory on other ways out. Patricia does not think about taking command; it's something that occurs instinctively.

"Follow me," she says.

She retreats the way they came and then takes them on a new course. Whenever flames confront them, she detours. The others begin to think that perhaps they have been cut off from the exit entirely but, even as the fire spreads, Patricia remains cool, and is able to lead them on a roundabout passage back to the juncture – or at least what's left of it.

The walls are nothing but fire, flames crackling as they lash out. Coils of thick gray smoke march unrelentingly across the ceiling. The carpet is curling up and blackening. Fittings burn and pop. The heat is stifling, until the air feels too thin to breathe.

People stream from the funnels, jackets pulled over their heads like cowls; partners are huddled together; others scream and cry. Panic is the bigger danger now. The blaze merrily feeds from it.

Teo stands in the middle of the juncture, tall and unbowed, his skin glistening, his good eye tearing, one hand covering his mouth, spluttering as he waves people on like a traffic cop, picking them up when they fall, urging them on when they slow, and pointing them in the direction of the lobby when they're confused.

The wall above the entrance whines and spews flames. The bronze plaque shears free and crashes to the floor, covering the entrance. Fiery fragments shower people who scream and shield themselves. Flames mushroom out, driving everybody into hasty retreats.

"Back!" Teo says.

Marcus has struggled with the pain of his lashes, but now he finds a focus that drives him. His motives are difficult to discern – despite his glibness, he is struggling to reconcile what's happened to him, Gabriella's kindness, and the dread that now runs rampant. Regardless of his confusion, though, he *is* calm.

While others are despairing, he scans the plaque. He thought it was a solid piece, but it looks more like a shell that's hollow on the inside, which suggests it's not as heavy as he first thought. But it's glowing hot. He shrugs off Gabriella and Dante, then rolls his shoulders.

"Marcus, what're you doing?" Dante asks.

Marcus charges, lifts his shoulder, and bullocks into the plaque. Its heat scorches his skin, but the force drives the plaque into the blackened doorway, shattering it. Marcus's momentum carries him into the lobby and onto the floor. People cheer him as he hauls himself up. He is grim and sullen, whereas he should be jubilant; he should be flattered but instead, he is lost in something he has never known in his life – connectivity.

He and everybody else are in this together. He doesn't have to be the iconoclast; nor does he have to move through life in disdain. Previously, these attitudes have been part of a regimented programming, but now there's a glitch – an instant of self-awareness. Tainting it is the resentment – he finds difficulty in trying to integrate himself into the whole, and he spurns that closeness because it scares him just as much as it calls to him.

Before I can read which way he falls, he heads out, running less from the fire and more from the insight he has gained about himself.

Dante, Gabriella, and Patricia are speechless.

The wall to the right of them collapses. Teo pushes them clear, but debris strikes him in the back and knocks him to one knee. Two other men are pounded to the floor, their jackets on fire. Teo covers one, smothering the flames with his body. Dante falls on the other. He, Patricia, and Gabriella help the men to their feet. They spill into the torrent of people.

Dante's instinct is to follow but wiping the cuff of his sleeve across his eyes, he surveys Teo, who is still on hands and knees on the floor, his back bucking as he coughs, spittle dribbling from his mouth. Dante wonders how long he's stood here shepherding others out. But the answer is simple. *Too long.*

Kneeling, Dante folds his hands around one of Teo's giant biceps. "Come on!"

Teo pushes himself to his feet. Patricia is under his other arm, supporting him. He coughs, the sound so dry and rough Dante's sure his throat must be shredded. Dante gestures for Gabriella to take his position, and she slips under Teo's other arm.

"What're you doing?" Patricia says.

"Go!" Dante says. "Go!"

"What?" Patricia says.

Dante bundles her, Gabriella, and Teo toward the lobby. "Now!" he says. "Get him outside!"

They stagger out, Teo's tremendous girth weighing down upon Gabriella and Patricia until their backs bend. At one point, Teo falls to one knee. Patricia and Gabriella hoist him back up. They scramble into the lobby, leaving Dante to look around frantically. Others stumble past blindly. He urges them on.

"This way!" he says. "This way!"

Patrons flock to his voice, loud and unusually commanding over the fire. Burning beams fall around him. Sparks sizzle through the air. Yet he stands resolute, continuing to cry out.

"This way! This way!"

He herds people into the lobby. Cold, night air swamps them. Sirens wail in the distance – too late probably, as I feel the fire ravage me.

o o o o

Quinn almost trips as people burst from the restaurant and into the juncture. Amber stumbles, rights herself, but her sweaty hand slips from his own. He grabs her by the wrist and hoists her up. They embrace.

"Don't let go," he says.

"I won't."

Savage passes them, waving everybody forward. "Come on!" he says. His bronzed skin shines and his topknot flows behind him.

They charge down the juncture, doubled over and coughing. The smoke is everywhere. A figure is silhouetted in the exit of the lobby, calmly directing the patrons. Quinn envies him – the danger brings out the best in some people, such as this person and Savage.

Wood shears. A beam falls from the ceiling. Amber should not be able to move somebody as tall and heavy as Quinn, but she instinctively jerks him clear. The beam strikes Savage in the back, knocks him to the floor and pins him there. Quinn and Amber kneel by him. His face is dazed. He paws at them helplessly.

Quinn grips the beam. It is charred black and the top end is still on fire. The wood burns his palms. He tries to lift it, but the beam is too heavy. Savage wheezes, blinks, and stares at Amber, touching her face with one hand.

"Go!" Savage says.

"But—" Amber says.

"Now!" Savage says.

"Quinn—?"

But Savage is right. The situation is hopeless, and they're only risking their own lives by remaining.

Quinn shoves Amber into a crowd of people as they storm for the exit. She tries to fight their momentum. The silhouetted figure at the end of the juncture urges them on. Quinn takes one step to follow her. Then another. There is nothing he can do for Savage. And perhaps it is just as well given everything that has happened. But Quinn grows convinced that is his guilt forcing an ugly rationalization. If the positions were reversed, Savage would not abandon him. Savage has already shown a begrudging nobility.

Grabbing the beam by the corner again, Quinn tries to lift. His muscles strain and his chest – particularly where Savage kicked him – cramps up. The beam elevates no more than an inch, but he does not relent.

"Go!" Savage says. "Save yourself!"

"Shut up," Quinn says.

His palms blister and sparks pockmark his pants and shirt. Muscles he hasn't used since his basketball career ripple throughout his body. Then Dante is at his side.

"What're you doing here?" Quinn says.

"Amber sent me!" Dante says.

He grabs the same end of the beam. Together, they are able to hoist it up, inch it from Savage's body, and throw it to the floor.

Savage wheezes, his eyes rolling up into his head.

They take his hands and haul him to his feet. He totters, barely conscious. He could be injured fatally, although a petty part of Quinn's mind suggests Savage's physique cushioned the blow. Quinn and Dante flank him, and stagger to the juncture.

"Take him!" Dante says.

As soon as Dante steps away, Savage falls to his hands and knees. Quinn moves without thinking. He grabs Savage's arm, throws it over his neck, thrusts his shoulder into Savage's midriff and lifts him into a fireman's carry.

He lurches into the lobby, expecting Dante to be right behind him, but there is nobody. Quinn spins on his heel, Savage's weight threatening to topple him. Dante stays in the juncture, surveying the flames and the stragglers who are still filtering out. Smoke engulfs him, as if he were an illusionist about to pull off some trick – he is the composed marshal in the midst of the pandemonium.

"Go!" Dante says, waving Quinn onwards.

Quinn's strength is deserting him. Sweat pours down his face and his hands seethe with pain. The only thing that does not hurt right now is his knee.

He turns back, and blunders into the night.

○   ○   ○   ○

Flavia is lost, although she knows that is stupid – or at least it should be. She recalls when LeBeau brought her here thinking they'd slipped into some other place. Now, all she sees are towering hallways and marble walls. Her breathing is uneven and her vision blurs. Perhaps it is a panic attack, although she's never had one before.

Another possibility occurs to her: the drug that LeBeau gave her. That must be the cause of all this – to the loss of inhibition, to the loss of perception and spatial awareness, and to these physical symptoms. Relief overwhelms her. She is not safe, but at least she has an answer – and a big answer at that, too – for everything else that has gone on.

"Hello!" she says.

Her voice bounces through the hallways until she's sure it echoes back to greet her. She can imagine another version of herself – perhaps the idealistic version who only wanted to meet LeBeau – emerging to bid her farewell. But that is stupid, too – the drug again. She never should've taken it.

Plunging onwards, she remembers somebody once telling her that if you kept your hand on the right wall in a labyrinth, eventually you would find your way out. Who knew how many dead ends that involved, though? She just wants to be out of the darkness.

She stops. Holds her breath. Were those footsteps? She listens but cannot hear anything. The drug has made her paranoid – as much as it has become a panacea to address the series of bizarre events, it is now the culprit.

Hallways twist and weave, and several times, Flavia thinks she has somehow circled back to an area she has already passed through. She's sure that's not the way it was before. LeBeau's path *seemed* direct. But maybe she got it wrong, following LeBeau blindly. LeBeau. When she finds him, she'll lambast him, job be damned.

Footsteps. She spins. But there's nobody. She thinks of the robed figure. It's not that he was frightening, but it was just so damned unusual. She shivers. She cannot help it. The shiver runs from her shoulders down to her thighs where the hem of her dress still sticks to her.

Light ahead. Flavia is sure of it. She hurries. Yes. The walls become red-bricked. Then, there are the archways of the gaming rooms. Smoke is thick in the air. She doesn't know what that is about.

Checking back over her shoulder, she smiles triumphantly. Whatever – *whoever* – was following her, she is clear now. Perhaps it was LeBeau playing one final game. It doesn't matter. She is done with him, but she knows that's an empty declaration.

Spinning, she runs right into somebody. It's the crimson robe from the basement. He grabs her wrist – only, it's not a *he*. The robes might hide her figure, but up close Flavia can see the person is her height, and that the build is slight. Her fingers are slender but strong – a woman's hand.

Flavia flails, but the woman's grip is unbreakable. The mask seems to twist into a leer. The gray eyes are cold and ageless and knowing. Again, Flavia imagines she's found herself; there is a doppelgänger under these robes, only it is not the idealistic version of herself, but one at the opposite extreme – a version of herself that has shed all earthly ties and filters, until only this tormented, joyless, lost soul remains.

"Let me go!"

The robed figure shakes Flavia once, by the wrists, but hard enough that her resistance ceases. She leans in as one would to a partner to give them a tender kiss.

"I'm sure we'll be seeing you again," she says, then releases her grip.

Flavia sprints through the gaming rooms. Smoke embraces her, and filters into her mouth and down her throat. Such is her terror, she does not question it. Or the absence of people. The fear has brought focus, and within minutes, she has shot out into the juncture.

She raises one arm to shield her eyes. People are everywhere, stumbling, lurching, and pushing onwards. She has no idea what has happened, but it's not difficult to recognize the danger. Standing central to it all is Dante, ushering people out; he is calm and commanding and purposeful – something he has never been before in all the time Flavia has known him.

She cries out to him, although her voice trembles: "Dante!"

When he turns to her, what strikes her is the change in his face – the loss of the diffidence, and a newfound bleakness that has little to do with the fire. He is *changed*. Just as dealing with LeBeau has changed her, something has changed Dante.

He pulls his shirt up over his face and approaches. A beam falls from the ceiling right before him and crashes into the floor between them. A wall of fire erupts. He gestures for Flavia with a grandiose wave.

"Come!" he says.

"I can't!"

"Now!"

Flavia looks at the sheet of flames before her. She should be afraid. But given everything that's happened tonight, this presents the least trepidation. She closes her eyes and jumps. The heat scalds her and singes her hair. Her dress burns and pockets of it melt. Hands close around her, strong and unyielding. She's sure it's the crimson-robed figure. She has jumped to her.

When Flavia opens her eyes, they're so bleary she's sure she sees that face mask. Her vision clears slowly, reluctantly. It's Dante – the man she fell in love with, the man she had planned to spend the rest of her life with, and the man she cheated on. The shame lashes at her. He is too sweet and good-natured for her.

"Let's go!" he says.

He drags her to the lobby as a troop of firefighters charge in, hoses blazing. The air sizzles and steams around them.

Dante totters onwards blindly, carrying Flavia into the coolness of the night.

O   O   O   O

Holly has never seen anybody shot before, other than on TV shows and in films, and she has often wondered how realistic those depictions are.

In the instant between Nico pulling the trigger of his gun and the bullet hitting Mr. Hermes, she expects him to be punctured, the way a balloon might, and for there to be a splash of blood.

But there is none of that.

Nico's gunshot thuds into Mr. Hermes's shoulder as if it is hitting mud, disappearing with an understated, if not undignified *plop*.

Holly is sure that cannot be right, that the bullet must be a dud, or that Mr. Hermes must be wearing a vest that protects him – surely a man with his past, a man who does what he does, would take precautions. But even if that is the case, the impact drives him into the wall. He flops back into his chair, and clutches at the wound.

There is still no blood – well, at least none that Holly can see. "Nico …?" Mr. Hermes says.

Nico continues holding the gun aimed at Mr. Hermes, hand trembling. Whatever impulse brought him this far has already been spent. Now the doubt floods in. But all Holly feels is detached glee. She has no sympathy for Mr. Hermes as he sits there with that mildly astonished look on his face, but she understands now that taking a life is a lot more than she would've been able to accept.

"I'm sorry," Nico says. He releases the gun, and lets it fall from his grip like its touch repulses him.

Mr. Hermes lifts his head and bellows with laughter. The astonishment falls away. His mismatched eyes seem to be burning with different emotions – the gray, the flash of a knife's blade before it plunges, stern and terrible; the blue, the sparkling of an emerald as it catches the light, cold and amused. Whatever humanity he has shown this night, whatever seeming interest in the people for whom he sets Temptations, it is gone now, and whatever remains is not only unbound, but fearless, and feeds from the anarchy.

Holly takes a step back as her rage transforms to terror. What had she attempted? What is she doing here? Common sense reasserts itself as she appreciates, truly appreciates, that Mr. Hermes is privy to wickedness and fury and capriciousness that they cannot even dare to grasp – or should dare to grasp. Some truths are better left in the shadows.

This is truly his playground now.

"The boy finally stands up for himself and he apologizes," Mr. Hermes says. "Have I ever apologized for your father's death?

Never. You're too pure for this business. You best flee now. Before it's too late. Like your father. Hide yourself away. And when the world becomes too painful, when the price for success too high, then hopefully you have a friend, a confidante, a partner, who can hand you a gun so you can end it all and be done with it. As for you," he turns to Constance, "this cheap physical victory – do you really think it will be enough?"

"It's a start," Constance says.

"But not the one you expect!"

Mr. Hermes shoots back to his feet, although he still clutches his wound. Flames leap up around him, almost as if they have lifted him and support him and drive him, fueling him with an incendiary wrath that transcends mortality, and is almost divine in its scope and ferocity.

Holly is transfixed, again sure she sees figures in the flames – imps and demons and other things that don't have names. They are his allies, his servants, his propagators. The ceiling collapses behind her. Embers and sparks spray her and Rupe. She shields her face as the fire roars and the smoke thickens. Her clothes cling to the sweat on her body.

"You stupid woman!" Mr. Hermes says. "I give *you* Prudence. *Handed* it to you."

Holly points meekly at herself, sure that he is addressing her. She wants to be gone now; it was arrogance to think she could challenge this man. Her legs are leaden, and her mind opens to the possibility that she would do anything to escape him, regardless of what it means for herself.

"You promised things to me, promised an end to the indulgence and largesse and *graciousness* that have become staples under Constance. But look at you."

It is when Mr. Hermes exaggerates a shake of his head that Holly understands he is not addressing her but Joy. She has been luminescent this entire night – until now. Now she is a sad dim shade eclipsed in the conflagration. She lowers her face, like a child being admonished by a parent.

"You've already proven soft. Weak."

"No," Joy says. "Not weak—"

"Yes! Weak! You had the power to oust her! Did it not occur to you she might have some contingency?"

Joy looks at Bodie and Ox; she had danced with them both but had been indifferent about who they might be. *Dismissive.* But she sees Constance's genius in choosing them: being *who* they are disguised their motivations, and encouraged her to not study them further, to not ascertain that they were more – *much* more – than they appear.

It is a drastic error in judgment. Constance's ploy is the sort of thing the Camarilla would laud. They would appreciate her planning. But not Mr. Hermes. Mr. Hermes wanted Constance out. *He* should've seen this. But then Joy wonders if he did see it, and instead used this knowledge as a test of her abilities.

She puts a hand on her hip, determined not to admit failure. "Didn't it occur to you?" she asks, jauntily defiant.

"Why would I care?" Mr. Hermes asks. "This," he throws his arms out, the roaring flames growing, "is my contingency!"

Rupe steps up behind her. "I don't think you should be angering him," he whispers into her ear.

"You insolent fool," Mr. Hermes says to her. "She was your first test, and already you fell complacent, certain once you had displaced her, she would just walk out into the night, just as alone and powerless as the night she arrived. You, you gave yourself to the Camarilla and thought that would be enough."

He thrusts one hand at her. The palm and fingers are bloodied and his exposed wound festers, although that should be impossible given it is fresh. On closer inspection – in the instant Holly has –

she sees that the shredded flesh around the puncture writhes. She thinks of maggots and becomes sure they nest there. At first she believes they are feasting on his flesh, but then she becomes sure they *constitute* his flesh.

A tremendous splintering fills the Lounge as one end of a beam, blackened and alight, shears from the ceiling and collapses toward Joy. She stares, frozen and wide-eyed. Rupe leaps in front of her and shoves her aside. The beam strikes him flush in the face, breaking his nose and fracturing his skull. He is knocked to the floor, the end of the charred beam pinning his chest.

Joy kneels by him, cradles his head on her lap, and strokes his face with her hand. "Rupe?" she says. "*Rupert?*"

Rupe weakly lifts a hand, as if to caress her cheek. He smiles, just a small smile, but it makes him young and unconcerned – a man from a lifetime ago. But then he looks past her, and his eyes alight. I do not know what he sees, but it's something that brings him both comfort and peace. And love. He is immersed in love until that's all he becomes. He lets go of everything from this night – the one individual in this troupe who *can*. Then his hand falls limply by his side, and his head lolls.

"Rupert!" Joy says, streams of mascara running down her cheeks as she cries.

"Such weakness," Mr. Hermes says.

Nico tries to grab the beam, although flames run across its surface and the cracks of it glow orange. Bodie and Ox gape at one another, then at Constance. Her face is distant, her eyes brimming, as if she is recalling her own sadness. Bodie and Ox holster their guns and grab the beam. Together, the three men try to hoist it, but it is heavy, and Holly can hear it splintering from where it remains attached to the ceiling.

"Much like you, Constance," Mr. Hermes says. "Do you remember when you first came here?"

"Don't," Constance says.

Mr. Hermes snorts as pockets of the walls explode. Holly thinks it is because gas mains have ruptured, but I know better. I feel the entire Lounge trembling, like a heart that spasms out of rhythm before it fails. As it dies, the organs that rely on it shut down.

"Stoned on heroin, your lover – your fiancé – retreated to your car out in the lot," Mr. Hermes continues. "He called you. Begged for your help. Begged you to come to him. He knew there was something wrong. And what did you do?"

"Stop it!"

Mr. Hermes grins. "You were given the test of ejecting Sarah, just as Joy was given the task of ejecting you," he says. "You – personally – took her by the scruff of the neck, marched her to the front door, ignoring her pleas, ignoring her cries, ignoring her pathetic groveling, and threw her naked out onto the street. There, your legend was forged before a crowd of worshippers. Then you assumed her office. All while your poor lover expired in your car."

Tears stream from Constance's eyes but evaporate on her cheeks in the heat. "You bastard."

"No, not me. You paid that price. Happily. Lustfully. Greedily. Just as *you,*" Hermes directs his ire at Joy, "now have. But *behold* her." He thrusts a finger at Constance. "Is she happy? What has this brought her? She is a cautionary tale, but you gladly and willingly rush to that fate for just a moment of power."

Fire blusters across the Lounge, shooting from the walls and the floor and the ceiling. The other end of the beam which pins Rupe crashes down. Roused, Joy stumbles back, arms held wide, and she shepherds Nico, Bodie, and Ox to safety. The entire Lounge shakes and sparks fill the air like buzzing fireflies.

Joy steps through it all, and it is only here in her loss, that she finds that tragic regality, that unattainable beauty, that so marks Constance.

Kneeling by Rupe's side, Joy places a palm on his cheek.

Holly runs her hand over her eyes. Sweat pours from her. Tongues of flame lash her body, just as they – those sepulchral figures appearing fleetingly – dance around Mr. Hermes, almost as if in accompaniment with his amusement.

"All of you!" He laughs again. "Such foolish weakness. And you," he looks back at Constance, "who would remain queen! Don't you know where you are? What you're doing? What *it* takes?"

"Enough is enough!" Constance says.

"No, Constance. It is never enough. *Never.* You have forgotten your place. You have forgotten how truly ephemeral you are."

Constance shakes her head. "No."

"You, who would take this action. Prudence is about me. Prudence *needs me.* Not you. Not the Camarilla. *Me.* It's like I always say, the body is weak, flesh is temporary, but some things, some things are eternal – such as the repercussions for what you've done here. You will know them. Now. And forever."

"We'll see about that," Ox says.

He draws his shotgun and pistol and fires at Mr. Hermes. Bodie flanks him and draws and fires his weapons. For as much as they have been the jokers over the years, they are now ruthless. This is *why* they are here and *what* they have waited for. They have no personal stake in this outside of being in Constance's employ and cannot be tarnished by Mr. Hermes's manipulations in the same way that the others can.

He is pinned against the wall as bullets tear through his body. His arms flail, and perhaps it is just a twitch of nerves, but his lips curl into the smallest smile.

The gunfire ceases.

Mr. Hermes falls back into his chair and teeters there. The bullets have shredded his clothes and his torso, but there is remarkably little blood – only the smallest rings of red around the wounds. He sits there, oblivious to the fire as it burns, melting his suit, singeing his hair, and blistering his skin.

"At least I am part of one last great show," he says.

He reaches for his glass. The ice has melted, and the water has overflowed. He picks it up just as the ceiling collapses. The table disappears under the weight of flaming debris and a fireball that explodes across the Lounge.

Holly acts instinctively, grabbing Nico's arm and dragging him to the floor. Around her, Bodie and Ox shield Constance, and dive on top of her as Joy covers Rupe as best as she can. Holly feels the hairs on her neck incinerated as fire races over her and a stifling roar fills the Lounge.

She *feels* Mr. Hermes on top of her, *feels* his hands caress her body, *feels* him slip insidiously inside her. She has unwanted images she cannot push from her mind of deep-throating Mr. Hermes, of Mr. Hermes fucking her, sodomizing her, demeaning her, but it is not Mr. Hermes – or perhaps it is him when he was young: he is tall and powerful, a build labor has hardened, that the elements have tempered into something bronzed and leathery, and that time has deprived of any feeling. He has made love to countless women and men – has indulged in their bodies, has used them in ways that have left them full of self-loathing, and then discarded them in ways that have humiliated them so he can feed from their shame. And others have watched. Others have revered him. Others have enjoyed his depredations, and fed from the corruption of lust, the rape of innocence, and the surrender to perversion.

That is the show he speaks of, the show that his Temptations attempt to manufacture, and on which the Camarilla dine.

He has done this because he *can* do it, and in a world without boundaries, without rules, without morality, there is no greater sustenance than twisting others to the same whims and needs.

It is a world that exists just under the periphery of everyday people, a world that many would deny exists, for to accept its existence would to be confront the simplest yet most profound truth: nobody really has any control of their life.

Not really.

Holly knows now what a mistake it was to come here. She is sure the tendrils entwined her friends, subverted them for the amusement of others, and that it was folly to confront Mr. Hermes and give him one last chance to ensnare her.

His voice fills Holly's ear whispering inexorably, and although Holly cannot understand what it is he is saying, his words demean her and fill her with a cold dread, yet still she is lured, still she feels an attraction to the unknown and what treasures it might yield.

It is what powered her into her tryst, drove her to her confrontation with Marcus, and fueled her attempted murder of Mr. Hermes – a need so primal it eclipsed all good reason, and intoxicated her with its allure of recklessness and bliss and desire. It is a part of herself she fights to deny, but it teases at the periphery of her consciousness and acknowledgment, an enemy that unrelentingly examines and probes her defenses, trying to find a way back in.

Gritting her teeth, she pushes at it, tries to shunt it into some corner of her mind, tries to expunge it, but all she can do is bat it away, hopefully forever, but likelier temporarily, conceding that deflection is no genuine substitute for excision.

The roar abates and only the fire remains, crackling around them. Holly lifts her head. A giant bonfire rages, the tips of the flames sporadically blue. She shivers, clutches her arms around herself, and drags herself into a kneeling position. There's nothing but a wall of flame in front of her. The thickening black smoke rolls across the Lounge.

Shadows appear, amorphous but darkening. They are the wraiths, come to claim them at Mr. Hermes's beckoning. Holly recoils, then falls onto her butt. Joy sits up to nestle Rupe's head in her lap. Bodie and Ox rise, supporting Constance, although she is the least fazed of everybody.

"What've you done?" Joy asks.

"What you thought couldn't be done," Constance says.

"At what cost?" Joy strokes Rupe's hair from his face.

"There's always a cost."

The shadows darken. Something sizzles. The smoke thickens. One of the shadows solidifies as it bursts forward. Holly scampers back.

"Watch out!" Nico says.

Holly spins her head and sees she has almost backed directly into fire. She freezes as more figures appear, but they are not wraiths, but firefighters in their gear, hoses aimed at the blaze.

She closes her eyes.

They are safe.

Then she hears Mr. Hermes's voice, or perhaps imagines it, in her mind.

For now.

VIII

Sirens chop the night into disorienting flashes. Police have used their cars to block off the street, as well as cordon off the onlookers who have gathered in the cold, their breath misting, their hands stuffed in their pockets. Ambulances are parked haphazardly, paramedics scurrying frantically as they tend to the injured. Four fire trucks are parked end to end as firefighters direct an army of hoses at the blaze.

They are too late, though.

I feel my flesh incinerate, pluming into thick black smoke that darkens an already-cloudy sky. My bones scorch and groan and crack. Floors collapse in surrender. Electrical equipment explodes like an array of fireworks. These are just *things*. They can be rebuilt or replaced. It's the incineration of the greater sum of who I am that pains me.

I have accumulated the thoughts and feelings and whims of countless individuals, as well as their collective attitudes. Despite the years, despite the way people and groups change, those attitudes are primal, if not selfish and self-destructive. It's rare that they will surprise you, as did Dante when he risked himself to help save others; and rarer still for any adult to show the charm, naiveté, and hopefulness of a child, as did poor Rupe.

But now Rupe lies dead on my floor, burning, the decency of rescuing his corpse for burial sacrificed as firefighters navigate the danger to safety; and Dante paces on the street, his racing heart only settling now, his hands screaming with pain, as he tries to assimilate the shock of everything that has happened.

Crowded together, shoulder to shoulder, everybody else watches, some joking at the misfortune of it all, some reveling in the fact that they now have a story to tell – about how they escaped the fire – which'll exalt them, and a few stare mutely at the destruction, considering how lucky they are to escape.

How many of them will take the events of this night and use them as catalyst for change?

And how many will remain the same?

The fire consumes me as the second floor crumbles, and Constance's – or perhaps it should be *Joy's* – office tumbles and smashes the juncture just as the last of the patrons ride a torrent of flames and smoke into the night.

It is, for now, my last hurrah.

o   o   o   o

Amber and Quinn sit on the curb, side by side. Both are quiet. A cool breeze brushes past them, although it is thick with the smell of burning. Amber huddles closer to Quinn, wanting him to put his arm around her as he usually would. But he sits still. She has never seen him like this before. Even when the knee injury ended his career, he was neither this solemn, nor this quiet.

"Well," Amber says.

Paramedics and police scurry around them. Smoke fills the air and billows in thick black coils into the sky. A fitful drizzle spatters haphazard drops, but not enough to help the cause. The lights of various sirens flash, a multicolor panorama that is more so distracting than an indicator of the gravity of the situation – at least for Quinn. Now that he's out here, all he can think about is his relationship, and how something that seemed so *sure* just hours ago now hangs so precariously.

"What happened tonight?" Amber asks.

Quinn's face is so callow. Amber can see he is hurt – he is so obvious, although that is something she's always loved about him: that he is without guile. So few people have that forthrightness and honesty.

"I saw you," he says.

Amber's mind flits through the night. Surely nothing extraordinary occurred – well, nothing that she recalls. But, of course, there's a fog, courtesy of a succession of Long Island Ice Teas. As Amber slowly recomposes herself, she discovers not just a surprise, but a series of surprises that began in the gaming room and culminated with Quinn swinging a chair at Savage.

Quinn's eyes search the hubbub around them. He notes Savage, arms held up, the V of his torso pronounced as a paramedic wraps bandages around him. Savage catches his scrutiny, then nods once, in acknowledgment and gratitude. That is something. Whatever happens tonight, Quinn is proud he did the right thing. But Amber mistakes his denouement; the sight of Savage pains Quinn because Quinn *must've* seen something incriminating. Why else would he be this way? Amber doesn't know how to broach it without surrendering herself.

She reaches across to Quinn, takes his hands, and shakes them. "Talk to me," she says.

"I came into the gaming room where you were," Quinn says.

Amber has an urge to blurt out the truth, to acknowledge it before it is used to condemn her. Confessing the truth *would* be the right thing to do.

"And?" she asks.

"He was holding you," Quinn says. "Swinging you around."

"That's it?"

Amber's question carries a mixture of relief and delight – if Quinn had seen the kiss, then she knows this situation would be irredeemable.

"Isn't that enough?" Quinn says.

Amber throws her arms around him. "Maybe I shouldn't have done that," she says, and then – when Quinn tenses – amends, "I *shouldn't* have; no, I shouldn't have. I just got caught up in what was happening."

Quinn says nothing. He can't even look at her.

"He picked me up, spun me around."

Quinn still won't meet her eye.

"If you saw that, you would've seen we were surrounded by other women," Amber says, the words tumbling out of her mouth before she's sure she's formed them properly. "It's just … the show."

"Just the show?"

"Nothing was going to happen. It's no different to dancing with somebody."

"Except he was naked."

"I wasn't."

"So that makes it okay?"

Amber puts her arm around Quinn's back. "It was stupid fun," she says. "Like if you'd gone to strippers with Marcus and Dante and one of the strippers paid you attention. You're not cheating. It just is what it is. In that moment."

She can almost hear Quinn trying to frame it in a way that's palatable. Given the opportunity, Marcus would take advantage of it. Amber sees that in him. He would relish it – indeed, he'd probably instigate it. Dante would be shy but entertain it because it would speak to his lack of self-esteem. He'd be flattered and crave the attention. But Quinn's different. Quinn would be chaste in every way because that's who *he* is.

"I'm sorry," she says. "But nothing *did* happen. That was it."

"Nothing?"

Amber shakes her head.

"What about in the restaurant? He had you in his arms."

"He came to talk to me."

"That's it?"

Amber considers how much Quinn knows, and how much he's guessed. Savage kissed her. Twice. But as much as Quinn *suspects*, he doesn't know – not for sure.

"He *was* flirting with me," she says.

"Flirting?"

"You know."

"No, I don't."

"He tried to pick me up, okay?"

"Looks like he succeeded."

"No. *No.* He grabbed me by my hand and pulled me to my feet. That's when you came in. But I had told him to go."

"You'd told him?"

"Yes."

"Really?"

"If you don't believe me, ask him."

Amber's indignation steels her resolve.

"So that's it?" Quinn asks. "Nothing else happened?"

"No."

"No?"

Amber's attention fixes on Savage. While he has been bandaged up, he shows no other sign of distress, and now moves freely among the patrons who've spilled onto the road, talking to them, joking with them, checking to see they're okay. He could be a sovereign checking on his troops after a prolonged battle. Sometimes, he'll signal to paramedics; other times, he'll put a reassuring hand on somebody's back, smile, and say something. The other party nods and laughs. They are enamored with him. Or in awe. Or a combination. Amber doesn't blame them.

"Hey?" Quinn asks.

Amber recalls feeling Savage's erection pressed against her crotch, separated only by her underwear; she recalls kneeling before Savage, that gargantuan cock lowered before her. She had kissed it. Perhaps impulsively. Perhaps alcohol had fueled her. Perhaps a lot of reasons. But she had done it. And in doing it, Amber was sure she'd had the wherewithal, the awareness, to understand what she was doing. She could rationalize it. Say it was done with the knowledge that it would go no further. But it had been done, nonetheless.

Savage had sought her out, had attempted to seduce her – she'd let that go too far, allowing him to touch her, to kiss her. She does not know if she would've put a stop to it had Quinn not intervened but vows now if she can just get through the night, everything will be different – she will honor her love for Quinn just as she expects him to honor his love to her.

Quinn is unsure how to distinguish between how much he *wants* to know, and how much he *needs* to know. He solicited Savage to seduce Amber. Quinn does not know how close Savage got to succeeding. *Very*, it would seem. But Quinn also thinks about how Amber responded when Savage kicked him. She was protective of him. Surely, that came out of love. And he discovered he cannot be without her.

The whole matter is a quagmire from which the truth can never, and *should* never, be extracted. For as much as the two have diverged throughout the night, now they converge, coming to the same unspoken conclusion: some things are better left buried.

"Nothing happened," Amber says.

Quinn puts an arm around her, pulls her close, and kisses her forehead.

O   O   O   O

Holly stumbles out into the night, shielded by firefighters. Paramedics rush her, one attempting to escort her to the back of a waiting ambulance while another shoves an oxygen mask onto her face. She pushes them away and doubles over, coughing until her chest wracks with pain. Spittle runs from her lips, and she's sure she'll vomit. Her eyes sting and the stench of smoke is ingrained in her skin. Somebody thrusts a plastic bottle of water at her. She takes it, uncaps it, and straightens as she lifts it to her lips.

Then stops.

It's Marcus who has handed her the bottle of water. He is dressed in his leather pants and has a blanket folded around him.

Holly lowers the bottle, then casually flicks it at him. He catches it against his naked chest, grimacing – Holly thinks it's from the rebuke, unaware it's from the way the blanket grates across the lashes on his back.

"Come on, Holly," he says. "It's a bottle of water."

"I don't want anything from you," Holly says, voice a rasp.

"How about we take what happened in there," Marcus says, "and just leave it in there? It's gone. Burned away, with the rest of the place. We can start over."

"I don't want to see you again, Marcus. *Ever.*"

"I'm sorry."

"I'm not. Enjoy your riches. I hope it was worth it."

Marcus reaches for her hand. Holly snatches it away. Nico takes a step forward. Marcus's hands come up to his hips.

"Can I help you?" he says.

"I don't know," Nico says. "Can you?"

Marcus snorts at Holly. "Really didn't take you long to move on," he says. "Should've known. All things considered."

"Is that it?" Holly asks.

"What?"

"If that's your parting shot, fine. If it's not, get out whatever else you've got, then go."

Marcus opens his mouth as if to rebuke her.

Holly is unblinking, her eyes teary – although that is as much from the fire as it is from her being upset. But she has never been more resolute about anything in her life.

Marcus takes a step forward – Nico matches him – and leans into Holly, gently placing the bottle of water against her chest. She takes it and holds it there as Marcus glowers at her.

"One day, you're gonna realize what you lost," he says.

"Can hardly wait."

Marcus pivots so quickly that the blanket swirls dramatically, but Holly can also see the pain in his face and the grief in his eyes – it's about the most human expression she's ever seen on him, and fleetingly makes her doubt herself.

Fleetingly.

"You okay?" Nico asks.

Holly focuses on the blaze, which continues unabated. "I'll live," she says.

Dante sits in the middle of the road, knees folded up to his chest. His hands – red and blistered, burns scarred into the flesh – shake. Police have already spoken to him and commended him, as have firefighters.

He is a hero.

But when he closes his eyes, he thinks not of the fire, nor of how he could've died, or of the lives he helped saved, but of Flavia.

She sits at the back of an ambulance, a blanket draped around her shoulders as a paramedic examines her. She is not hurt. Dante knows that. At worst, she is miffed. That is a good word for Flavia; life *miffs* her. Her unflappability is her strength, as is her ability to cannibalize any situation for her own ends. She will use this to further her celebrity. It'll be the story where she regales friends and acquaintances, or even strangers, because it'll make her the center of attention – that's what she's always desired.

She nods once to the paramedic who asks her something, and comes over to Dante, kneeling by him. Dante notes that the hem of her dress is folded, and it clings to her without a single ripple – she is not wearing her panties. Of course not. They're still lying on the floor in the basement somewhere.

"You were very brave," she says.

"I don't know what got into me," he says.

Flavia takes his hands and turns them over. "Do they hurt?"

He nods.

"Who's she?"

Her voice is so sharp and the question so unexpected that Dante flinches. Flavia gazes over his shoulder, her face hardening, her jaw tensing. Dante doesn't have to look to know Patricia's there, getting checked out by another paramedic.

The nerve of Flavia to show jealously, given the circumstances. He pushes himself to his feet and clenches his fists despite the pain that burns in his palms. Relaxing his hands, he shoves them into his pockets; his right palm closes on something soft – the engagement ring box. The box's velvet finish feels like sandpaper.

Flavia rises before him, the folded hem of her dress hiking up almost indecently. She pushes it back down, then folds her arms across her chest, the way she does whenever she wants an explanation from him. It's astonishing how quickly this relationship dynamic has reasserted itself.

"She's an Icon," Dante says.

"An Icon?"

"They play pool and strip with each loss." Dante would usually couch such a truth in diplomacy or hide it altogether. But how dare she confront him.

"She's dressed."

"What?"

"Is that how she was dressed when she played pool?"

"She'd finished her round. I'd met her in one of the Lounges."

"Met her?"

Her question is a challenge – her whole manner is a challenge. Dante tenses. She knows! That's the only explanation for Flavia pushing it. Dante helped numerous people out of the fire – Patricia could've been somebody entirely random. But Flavia *knows* that's not the case.

Explanations race through Dante's head. Did Flavia see them somehow? Impossible, given what Flavia was doing. Unless she saw something prior – perhaps through surveillance in the Lounge, like they had in Constance's office. Is that what prompted her sleazy little tryst?

Dante stops himself. He doesn't have to justify himself given what she's done.

And he doesn't have to make excuses for her.

"Where were you?" he asks.

"What?"

"*You.* Where were you?"

"Me?"

"I tried calling you."

Flavia reaches into the little purse she keeps strapped to her left wrist and pulls out her phone. It doesn't alight when she tries to activate it. She twirls the phone around. Her fingers go to the on/off switch. But then she twirls it again.

"Battery must've died," she says.

Dante wants to snatch the phone out of her hand. He's sure her actions suggested her phone is off and she was about to switch it on, but she realized how incriminating that would be. He should check for himself. But he doesn't. It's just another lie to add to the rest. She puts the phone back in her purse.

"Well, where were you anyway?" he asks.

"Having drinks."

"With?"

Flavia pauses longer than she should. She has no idea what Dante knows. He might've been with Holly and Amber. He, Holly, and Amber might've been throwing back shots with Marcus and Quinn. The wrong lie here could condemn her. Dante can almost see her mind ticking over, considering her alternatives.

"Meet somebody, did you?" Dante can't stop himself.

Flavia's teeters just for an instant, before steadying herself. Just as she knew something happened between him and Patricia, Dante is certain she's detected that he *knows* what she got up to.

"No," Flavia says. "Just some ... other women."

Dante could challenge her, but he knows where it'll lead — accusations, recriminations, shocking truths. Then, it's all over. And just several hours earlier he was contemplating life with her. How quickly it has changed. Worse, how *easily* it has changed — not just with her, but himself.

He *should* walk away. *She* should walk away. That's what sane people would do but love and relationships have little to do with sanity. The night is an aberration. She has wronged him, but sanctimony is hypocritical given he has also wronged her. Now it's move on or ride the bump.

"Let's just forget it, okay?" he says.

Flavia's face softens. "Sure."

Dante pulls the engagement box out of his pocket and thrusts it at her. Her reaction genuinely touches him: her eyes go wide, her mouth drops open, then she bounces up and down on the spot and waves her hands in front of her face.

"Oh my God!" she says.

Dante opens the box. His hands and fingers hurt too much to pluck out the ring, so she does it herself, sliding it onto her finger. She holds up her hand, the fire reflecting on the single diamond so that it flickers like a flame puffing to life. Then she throws her arms around him. He embraces her. She *does* feel good against him. He kisses her. All is forgiven – well, that is the affectation.

They part, Dante's hands linking around the small of her back, Flavia's around his neck. She smiles that big smile that transforms her into the celestial, sultry beauty that he has always deigned to orbit.

"Let's do it as quick as possible, hey?" he says.

"Really?"

"Really. I don't want to wait."

"Okay!"

Flavia tightens her grip on him and kisses him again, this time passionately. Dante's hands move down to her buttocks. He wants her – as soon as possible. He wants to take her until she's quivering and whimpering in his arms and wailing in paralyzing orgasm – not something he's accomplished previously, but he's going to try, dammit.

"Hey."

It's Edan LeBeau, stepping from the blaze of flashing sirens as if he's emerging from the fire itself.

Flavia flushes guiltily – Dante can almost feel the heat of her embarrassment, and it takes him several seconds to identify this is the man she was fucking.

Dante's arms tighten around Flavia. She squirms around so that she is facing LeBeau. Dante sees a series of small, circular bruises run down the back of her bare legs. He watched her dress this evening before they left their hotel – those bruises were not there then.

LeBeau shows no interest in Dante, and his gray eyes are slates of granite. There's not a hint of lust or warmth, but ownership. He looks at Flavia like somebody who has gone to claim luggage at an airport carousel after a long flight.

"We have a couple of projects coming up you might be good for," he says, holding out a business card. "Give me a call during the week."

Flavia takes the card.

The corner of LeBeau's mouth twists into a grin. "You could be a star," he says.

He takes the gold case that contains his triangle pills from his pocket, pops it open, and extracts a pill. He tosses the pill into his mouth, and then is halfway through snapping his case closed before courtesy changes his mind. Reopening the case, he thrusts it forward toward Flavia and Dante.

"Mint?" he says.

Flavia is horrified. There is no way they can be mints. That would mean that she has to take responsibility for her own actions. She dismisses LeBeau's claim; he is toying with her – that's what he does. Just like he dares to approach her now when she's with somebody else. She knows what she felt after taking one of those pills.

Dante immediately identifies that the pills look identical to the ones Patricia was carrying – except for the color. Patricia's were mauve. He would not normally question this, especially against somebody as intimidating as LeBeau, but curiosity wins out.

"They look like X'cess," Dante says.

Flavia nods feverishly.

"I tell people that sometimes," LeBeau says, flashing a smile at Flavia. "Helps them loosen up."

"Are you for real?" she says, her voice shrill.

"What do you think?"

LeBeau winks, then thrusts the case at them again.

Dante waves his refusal; he wants nothing from LeBeau – well, other than for LeBeau to leave, and never be seen again. But Dante doubts that will be the case. He sees this for what it is: Flavia fucked LeBeau for career advancement. This is just the newest ugliest truth in Dante's life.

LeBeau closes the case and puts it in his pocket. "Call," he tells Flavia.

His eyes catch Dante's, but there is nothing there: no form of acknowledgment or guilt or condescension – or even fear. LeBeau has come face-to-face with the partner of the woman he fucked – he should have the decency to show even the littlest bit of trepidation or embarrassment. But Dante simply doesn't exist.

LeBeau pushes his way through the crowd, then walks off into the night.

"How do you know about X'cess?" Flavia asks.

Her tone is sharp; she is on the offensive, wanting to divine how he could possibly know anything that hasn't been filtered through her. Dante's initial response is to fumble for an answer, but then decides he doesn't have to. Not anymore.

"I learned some things tonight," he said. "What about you?"

"Same."

"Who was that?" Dante asks.

"Producer I met."

They stare at one another, the silence between them laden with the threat of truth. But they have plotted a course now, and one where truth does not fit and lies are the new meridian. They will try to make this work, they will try to ignore the uneasiness that the other will betray them again, and they will try to love one another – rather than see their behavior tonight as symptomatic of what this relationship has been become: self-destructive. Like so many other couples, they embrace the dream, because in that embrace the dream promises a *happy ever after.*

Reality is a different matter altogether, and rarely do stories end so sweetly.

Flavia tucks the card into the cleavage of her dress, examines her ring, then kisses Dante soundly.

Dante is unresponsive momentarily.

Then his arms fold around her and he kisses her back.

○   ○   ○   ○

Constance wraps her arms around herself and shivers. She cannot remember the last time she has been this cold. This is about more than the night, but the feeling of loss and desolation that leaves her empty and unsure.

A paramedic approaches her, but she shoos him away, and threads a passage through the survivors who litter the street. She recognizes employees, and even many of the patrons. Some look as if they're preparing to kick-on through the night. Others have blackened faces. Some are burned.

Emergency services hustle tirelessly around her. Police contain gawkers and take statements. Paramedics treat the injured. Firefighters fight the blaze, which Constance keeps behind her, thinking their battle is useless. This isn't a fire that will be beaten. It'll have to burn out. That means time.

Her focus shifts to the cabin of an ambulance in which Teo lays wearing an oxygen mask – smoke inhalation, apparently. Bodie and Ox sit with their backs against a fire truck. Somehow, they've found Prince. Constance almost expects he will have a beer for the two. Ox looks up at her, still wearing his stupid sunglasses. Flames reflect in their lenses. He rises, comes over, and drapes his overcoat around her. Constance nods a thank you. She wants to continue, but a voice pulls her back.

"Was it worth it?"

Constance doesn't have to turn to identify Joy but does so anyway.

Joy's still in her latex suit, but the majesty is gone. Her eyes are rimmed red – she might be a child who has thrown a tantrum and refuses appeasement. Constance is unsure what to say to her. There is plenty that *can* be said, but not much of it is appropriate right now – if it ever will be. Years ago, Constance would've welcomed the confrontation. Now it seems meaningless.

She starts away.

"Don't you turn your back on me!"

Constance pauses a moment but reminds herself it would be unproductive to argue – at least not here and now, given what's happened. She continues. But Joy's stilettoed feet patter behind her and, in no time, she's in front of Constance, barring her escape.

"Well?"

Constance doesn't push it, but Joy offers no recourse.

"*Well?*" she says again.

"You think this is my fault?"

"Isn't it? *Isn't* it?" Joy's voice grows indignant. "Who refused to go quietly? Who had gunmen there as a contingency? Who shot up the Lounge?"

"Just goes to prove you *didn't* know everything. Nor do you still. You really are insignificant in the grand scheme of things."

Joy swings her hand to slap Constance. Constance catches her by the wrist, Joy's palm just inches from her face. Joy tries to shake her hand loose, but Constance holds it firm.

"I was insignificant in the scheme of things," she says. "That's why the Camarilla chose me. They wanted me out because I became *significant*, although obviously the old man was behind that – he didn't want anybody on par with him. I'm sure that's why he convinced the Camarilla to appoint you. But don't think you've filled my shoes just yet." She releases Joy's hand. "You remind me of myself. Young, headstrong, and sure you know it all."

"Except I'm not a junkie."

Constance doesn't flinch. "You don't know the person I was when I came here. You don't know what I've seen since I've been here. You don't know *who* I've become. Nor what I've done – usually unthinkingly. I'll tell you a truth: my biggest regret in life is taking this job. I should've packed up and went home. Things could've been different. *Everything* could've been different. Life might've been mundane, at least by the standards I know now, but maybe that might've been more than enough. Do you understand that?"

The hardness in Joy's face dissolves and she totters back on one heel. Her eyes brim. She has recognized a reality that it took Constance over twenty-five years to reconcile: that there *are* other choices. For Constance, it had been too late – or at least that was what she told herself.

"I don't know what it is," she says, "but leave Prudence. Take that other road."

Joy brushes her eyes with one wrist, and then she is back – sultry and unassailable. Hands on her hips, she shakes her head once, as if to shake off whatever sentiment had been about to grab hold of her.

"I saw that opportunity you're talking about," she says. "I even projected where it would lead. Maybe I should've taken it. But it's too late now."

"Nothing's too late."

"Tell Rupe that."

"Was he your lover?"

"He was just a man I met."

"There are other men."

"And … what? Go on dates? Dinners? That whole rigmarole before you find somebody worthwhile? I turned my back on Rupe because I thought he was a silly man. And probably he was. I doubt anything permanent would've happened."

"You doubt? Or is that something you tell yourself? I used to tell myself the same things."

"I don't know. But whatever he represented, I think it's harder to get there," Joy's eyes dart toward the fire, "than here."

"I'm sorry," Constance says. "Truly. Ultimately, this became everything for me. *My* everything. Maybe that's why they chose me originally because they knew it would consume me that way. Maybe that's why they chose you because they knew you would be the same. If you understand that, then you should understand why I didn't just turn and walk out. I tried to make something of it – possibly, to compensate."

"So you sacrificed it all," Joy says. "Even Prudence herself."

Constance finally flips a gaze back over her shoulder at the fire.

"Prudence will be back," she says. "Just try and stop her."

IX

When Holly walks in, she is amazed how I seem *truer* than I was before – the fire has eviscerated the façade, and what remains is the character. Others *don't* feel it. But she *does*, although she is not sure what to make of it. A flood of emotions overwhelm her – memories of that fateful night, what happened to her, and what she *tried* to do.

It has been exactly twelve months – twelve months in which many deliberated what should be done with *me*. Some argued I should be knocked down. Others insisted I was an institution, and such treatment was sacrilegious. The debate raged back and forth, but the point was ultimately moot.

Edan LeBeau used every single one of his media forums to speak persuasively, becoming the public face that drove the restoration. Few knew that he'd finally gained a place at the table of the Camarilla, and that he voiced their desires – not that he needed much prompting, though.

The Camarilla dipped into their depthless coffers; other wealthy sectors contributed. They were all criticized for their largesse – money that could've gone to charitable causes or humanitarian needs. But some things are more powerful than altruism. Some needs are greater.

Such as vanity.

The restoration was attacked with unrelenting vigor. Now the paneling is gone, revealing the original red bricking, although there is evidence of scorching – the charred blasts stand out like the blood splatter of victims at crime scenes. The marble floors that were discovered underneath the carpeting and floorboards have been scrubbed until they are unsullied (or as good as). It's hard to believe that a fire almost destroyed me, although when Holly pauses in the lobby and takes a deep breath, she is sure she can still smell the smoke.

Something catches her attention – the bronze plaque, which has been re-mounted above the entrance. Despite the attention that it was given in the refurbishment, ugly black smears remain evident upon its face, scars of a night that will be immortalized.

Standing under it, dressed in a skimpy yellow cocktail dress, is Flavia; her camera crew film her as she glibly reports on the grand reopening, idiots crowding behind her to get on TV, gesticulating, as if that'll endear them to audiences. Dante's a little bit further down, leaning against one wall, a whimsical expression on his face as he feverishly spins the wedding band on his finger. Holly cannot tell if he's proud or bemused or sullen.

Heading up the stairs onto the second floor, Holly finds the table she had occupied with Flavia and Amber – well, she thinks it's the same one, although the truth is that table was destroyed in the fire, and this is a duplicate.

Still, duplicate or not, she's surprised it's vacant given how increasingly busy it's becoming. The table might've been waiting for her, a companion to welcome her back into the fold. She feels foreboding now, like this has been orchestrated to ensare her.

She approaches warily, then sits, and looks over the balustrade. Bodie and Ox are seated at the bar. The refurbishing might've occurred around them, leaving them untouched. Holly wonders if they're still armed. Do they remain contingencies? If so, against whom?

That was something else that night: the power struggle between Mr. Hermes, Constance, and whoever else was involved. And for what? Holly has thought about it often during many sleepless nights. These are people operating in a different strata, and so divorced from everyday life, from real people, that whim becomes currency, and humiliation entertainment.

Her phone vibrates. She pulls it out of her pocket – Amber.

Holly answers, pressing the phone to one ear, and her hand to the other to block out the music. One year ago, they sat here together. She had shared the secret of her threesome. Now they couldn't be further apart.

"Hey!" she says. "Where are you?"

"Quinn and I aren't going to make it," Amber says. "It's …"

Amber doesn't finish, but Holly shivers, and can imagine what Amber was about to say: *It's that place.* Every patron from that night was invited to the reopening. Expenses – such as flights and hotel accommodation – were taken care of. Amber and Quinn were reluctant suitors. Holly had to talk them into it – just as a reunion. Well, they made it as far as the hotel.

"Maybe we can do lunch tomorrow?" Amber says.

"That'll be great," Holly says. "I don't know if Flavia's free, though."

"If she's not, she's not."

Amber is uncharacteristically dismissive. While she and Holly have kept in touch regularly, Flavia has been busy nurturing her burgeoning career, hosting an entertainment show, covering social events, and even releasing a memoir (although it should really be classified as *fiction*) about surviving the fire. Both Holly and Amber are happy for her, but know that while they'll keep their own friendship, Flavia will become little more than a footnote in their lives – somebody they once knew.

"I'll buzz you tomorrow morning," Amber says. "Have a good night."

"Thanks."

Have a good night. As if that's possible. More and more, Holly is regretting returning. Amber and Quinn must've reconciled that truth. They didn't need to come to experience it. They're safe and comfortable in each other's company. Holly envies that.

A hubbub cuts through the music. She sees the crowd part as Teo escorts Joy to the bar. Joy is dressed in a smart charcoal business suit, the lapels black but glittery. Every set of eyes fixes on her. She exchanges effusive greetings with Bodie and Ox; they part so that she can sit between them. Prince serves Bodie and Ox another Gallia, Joy a Vermouth, and Teo a Pisco.

Holly rises and weaves through thickening clusters of people to reach the stairwell. She makes her way down and sees Flavia once more. She has a champagne flute now. A waiter with a muscled bronze physique and wearing a little leather g-string – LeBeau's one aesthetic contribution has been to dress the wait-staff so provocatively that it borders on indecent – pours her champagne. Flavia takes a drink and declares the reopening official.

Her crew disperses. Edan LeBeau is immediately by her side – Holly does not know where he was lurking. He pats Flavia on the shoulder, commends her, then kisses her on the cheek. His right hand roves down to her hip, their manner suggesting the familiarity of lovers. But then Holly decides that's a misnomer – *lovers* would suggest *love*. This is something primal – a combative lust. I see the truth of that – glimpses into degenerate trysts that Flavia and LeBeau perpetrate in his office. Dante scowls and pushes off from the wall, hurrying down the juncture.

Holly continues her tour, and soon finds herself in the gaming rooms. Around her, Icons captivate patrons, just as they always have. Holly stops under the archway of one entrance. The Icon she sees is familiar: Marcus – he has taken part-time employ here, although he spends his afternoons on street corners, sketching, while his family back home wonder what's become of him. But Holly is glad for him. He is talented, and hopes this frivolous job is just a pitstop for him on his way to something far more meaningful, like Savage, who left to complete his nursing studies. With Marcus, though? Holly is doubtful.

This version of him – dancing up to the crowd, exciting them by gyrating and thrusting his hips – is the incarnation of everything that's wrong with him, and it dominates his choices. She wishes he would turn his back on it but knows everybody must contend with their own duality.

Among Marcus's admirers is Gabriella. He sidles up to her, pivots on his heel and presses his back against her. Her hands run down his chest and glistening abs. Holly must admit his physique is spectacular. It was always good, but now it's lean and chiseled. He has also shaved his goatee, which was always just an ugly, depreciating smear on his face. But, most of all, he has magnetism. That's *why* she was first attracted to him. But magnets can repel, too.

He sees Holly and his smile flickers, although only for an instant. Then his face grows steely. He hugs Gabriella to him, his hand clutching her buttock. She is surprised, but then laughs, shapes her hands around his butt, and squeezes.

Holly remembers sharing the same juvenile exchange with Marcus when they first became openly affectionate and is sure this is not just physical banter between him and Gabriella.

Something is going on, although Holly now often suspects that – since that night, she has gained an insight into relationships and interactions that often leave her uncomfortable.

She has seen enough – not because she is jealous (although she is surprised there *is* a spark of jealousy), but because of the sense of inevitability. Everybody at some point in their life must face *who* they are, although most spend their lives running from that encounter – at least until they can run no more. Holly worries that despite the facelift that's been applied to me, everything else is *too* samey, and if she stays too long she will lose her newfound self-awareness.

She quits the gaming rooms and makes for the Verdant Lounge – the heart of what happened. As she reaches the entrance, her breath is short, and she feels stifled around her collar. Her first instinct is to leave. Her second instinct isn't just to leave, but to flee – to scurry for the exit. But this is the reason she came.

To face this down.

She enters.

The Verdant Lounge exhibits no evidence of the fire, which is astonishing given this was the fire's origin. But nothing: the décor has been replaced, although now the style is Victorian, offering a sense of formality that has little to do with me – at least as far as today goes. The chairs are mahogany, with intricate floral designs carved into their backs, and the crystal light fixtures are resplendent.

Dante is seated at the bar, drinking one of his Bourbon & Cokes as he chats with the barmaid, Patricia, although her name-tag now identifies her as "Pristine". They joke and laugh, despite an obvious caginess that Dante exhibits. Patricia's expression is soft and sympathetic.

Again, Holly sees much *more* here, her perspective broadened by her own experiences. Dante and Patricia share some bond, a trueness to their connection that Dante does not enjoy with Flavia. Yet Dante and Flavia persevere with the fiction of their relationship because they're indebted to a past that owns them, and don't want to uncover what they've done to one another, and the ugly truths that will manifest. Holly is unsure just how long such a disingenuous reality can last.

The insights jangle in her mind, so incisive they cut the little composure she does maintain. She stops and tells herself to calm down, although she thinks the problem is this Lounge. Mr. Hermes might still be here, scarred into the room and permeating the very air she is struggling to breathe. She closes her eyes, expecting the fear to stab at her the way a traumatic memory would. But there is nothing but quiet and that is worse, because it is laden with the dread of expectation.

She opens her eyes. Mr. Hermes's booth is directly opposite her. Seated in it is Constance. Her blonde hair is as bouffant as ever, but whereas once she would've adorned some provocative dress, now she wears a double-breasted cream suit and a simple white blouse. Mr. Hermes was such a vacuum of darkness, but Constance is bright and lively.

She *is* beautiful – *unnaturally,* some might (still) say. It has little to do with her physical appearance, but with how she carries herself. Holly feels she can trust her. This is a woman she can speak to, can confide in, and can take counsel from. The impression arises inexplicably – it was not there *that* night – but it *feels* right to Holly *now,* and she is more and more learning to rely on her instincts.

Constance gestures for Holly to take a seat opposite her – that wave of her hand streaks a contrail of glimmering crimson through the air. Holly thinks Constance must be bleeding. That deep red could be a savage cut. But then Holly sees that Constance wears a ruby ring on the third finger of her left hand; the ruby contrasts against the pallor of Constance's skin, jars against the green decor of the Verdant Lounge, and sparkles like a siren to warn of danger.

Holly can only think it's an unusual choice for a wedding ring, if that's what it is – and indeed it is. Unbeknown to her, Constance and Teo married in the Gallery one afternoon a month before the reopening. Each have found a contentment that has previously eluded them. That contentment complements Constance so she is comfortable, *truly* comfortable, in herself, rather than needing the marquee she previously coveted.

"Sit, please," she says.

Holly sits as a waiter, dressed in his little leather g-string, arrives with two cocktails – a Manhattan for Constance, a Tequila Sunrise for Holly. Holly has not ordered a drink and can't imagine *how* they know the Tequila Sunrise is her cocktail of choice, or that she would end her tour here.

"I really shouldn't," she says.

"One won't hurt," Constance says.

Holly stirs the drink with its straw until the sunrise has become pink. She sips from it.

"I didn't think you'd come," Constance says.

"I … just had to see it," Holly says.

"Why?"

"I don't know what happened that night," Holly says. "Just everything unraveled. I mean, even before the fire and everything with … with … Mr. Hermes." She shakes. "I needed to come back."

"And now that you have?"

"I've been anxious about this, wondering how I'd face it. Now that I have, I understand some things are better left in the past. I'm just trying to understand *what* exactly. Something *did* happen, didn't it? Beyond the fire, I mean."

"We all face choices in life," Constance says. "Especially here, where people let go, and emotion often overrules reason. That night, you were going to commit a terrible act – admittedly, it would've served my needs. But it would have been at a terrible cost to yourself."

"You don't know *why*, though."

"It doesn't matter. You're fortunate. You're aware you can just walk away."

"I don't know what that means for me."

"But you'll search inside yourself. Most never do that. Most ..." Constance tapers away, as if only now reading something that was not immediately evident. "You've realized that, I take it."

"What if I don't like what I find?"

"That's something you have to answer for yourself."

"And what about you – are you sitting here offering the same Temptations?"

"My outlook is a little more altruistic," Constance says. "It's an indulgence that's been afforded me. For now, at least."

Holly wonders if it's genuinely an indulgence, or if it's just a part of the reopening. Mr. Hermes was manipulative and sordid. Maybe what Constance is doing amounts to good public relations. Or perhaps this is the way Mr. Hermes started, although Holly is sure Constance is not of his ilk.

"Why?" Holly asks. "Why any of this?"

Constance leans forward like she wants to share a secret between conspirators. Her hand comes up to shield her mouth as she brings it close to Holly's ear. But then, perhaps fearing being overheard, or being seen by some unknown arbiter, Constance pulls back, and her expression grows enigmatic.

"Maybe it's something to think about," she says.

Nico approaches them, dressed in a leather jacket and jeans. "Hey," he says.

"You're looking well," Constance says.

"Thanks, Constance."

Nico has found himself. His dreams were always *huge* – befitting his family. That night has taught him that is the last thing he wants – or *needs*. He is studying writing and bartends at a modest bar to make ends meet. If his life stays small and unobtrusive, he will be just fine with that – or at least that's what he tells himself, despite the glimmer of doubt.

He holds his hand out to Holly. She takes it and slides out of the booth.

"What're you two up to tonight?" Constance asks.

"Dinner," Holly says.

"So, you're leaving already?"

Holly takes one last look around the Verdant Lounge, then nods. "I'm glad this worked out for you."

"Thanks. I imagine we won't be seeing you again."

"No. I don't think so."

"Have a good life."

"You, too."

Constance leans back in the booth. "I'll try."

Nico puts an arm around Holly's back and begins to guide her away.

Now it *does* come.

Mr. Hermes is all around her, clawing at her, not wanting to let her go. She's sure if she turns back to the booth, he'll be seated there. But then another image arises: it won't be him. *She'll* be seated there – the murderous version of herself frozen in that instant of hate and rage. Holly wants to check, just to be sure, but also doesn't want to see herself that way.

She hurries on, catching a glimpse of Dante still at the bar laughing with Patricia; and when Holly's out in the juncture, it's Flavia chatting with LeBeau. Flavia sees her and perfunctorily lifts a hand in acknowledgment. Holly nods back, briefly considers stopping to talk, but then she feels the cool night air filtering in through the lobby, and decides she just wants out.

People bump against her, slowing her progress. Others block her course. She grows impatient. This is like when she and Amber were trying to find Flavia. The funny thing about that night is they never did. They each found something else entirely.

Holly tries to shove her way through just as a part in the crowd forms. Stumbling, she almost slips and, in righting herself, she looks up and sees the scorched plaque again, but now her attention fixes on the words under the emblem:

Veritas Vos Liberabit

She saw these words that night when they entered and dismissed them as ornamental, something chosen to generate mystique. But now they are striking. She does not know what they mean, but she feels, she *senses*, that this is a message she must understand.

"Do you know what that says?" she asks, pointing.

"'The truth will set you free'," Nico tells her.

It's a strange aphorism, so obvious, if not cliché in today's world. She *does* want to dismiss it, but the more she thinks about it, the more confronting it becomes. This is not something that was chosen at random. It may be a warning. She faced many truths that night.

And she wonders now if any of them set her free.

Like the plaque, Holly knows she is marked, and, in an instant that overrides everything else, she feels a synergy with me. I don't want to let anybody go. At least that's what *she's* thinking. In here, people are corruptible. This is the boon that Mr. Hermes laid on her because she never introduced anybody else to him.

Part of Holly wants to stay, to surrender to unknowns that are dark and seductive and pleasurable. She did it once before, she enjoyed it (despite the retrospective remorse), so perhaps that is the course to take, regardless of what it will cost her and who she'll become.

This is her truth, surely.

Her wrist is grabbed – it's Mr. Hermes. She can feel the boniness in his fingers. He has come to claim her. Some debts are never repaid. Some experiences are never truly left behind. And some mistakes will never stop claiming a reckoning.

He had a hand in her threesome. She does not know why that thought springs to mind, but somehow in interacting with Marcus, Mr. Hermes perverted her, and wants to continue to do so – to bend her and subject her to unimaginable carnal desires. He will break her, no matter what. And while she might initially fight it, inevitably, she will lose herself and enjoy it, until she becomes a slave to her amour and knows nothing else.

When she turns, she sees Mr. Hermes smiling coldly, his face knowing. She recoils, trying to pull away. His grip tightens. The sharp pain around her wrist rouses her. She blinks, and then he's gone. It's not Mr. Hermes who holds her, but Nico, obviously concerned – so obviously concerned. Definitely not Mr. Hermes.

"You okay?" Nico asks.

Is she?

She thinks about her relationship with Marcus, how they began as casual lovers, then elevated into a steady commitment, and finally they became engaged. Everything had seemed so right. But that's a conceit that so many couples endure.

Love takes many courses – some love unconditionally, finding the best in one another, and, through that, try to create a future together; others build relationships on secrets or misgivings and hope they'll navigate their way to something worthwhile;

some are mismatched in their commitment, and war endlessly, martyring themselves to some hopeless ideal; others love to hurt and spite one another, whirlpooling self-destructively into mutual oblivion; and a few are just content to try to figure it out as they go.

She is free of Marcus, free of a doomed relationship, and now she needs to free herself of blaming him. That will just continue to give Marcus – even in absentia – a power over her he has no right to enjoy. There is no Mr. Hermes either. He is done. Dead. Burned away. All these justifications have been nothing more than excuses, rationalizations and evasions, ways to abrogate herself of responsibility. It's just *her*. Her, her choices, their repercussions and how she decides to deal with them.

Holly knows she's made mistakes, and that she'll make them again, but all she can do is the best she can.

This is her actual truth, and she's fine with that.

"Holly?" Nico says again.

Holly nods. The crowd around them thins. The doors are unimpeded. She casts one final dismissive glance at the plaque.

"Let's go, huh?" she says.

Nico nods and escorts her out into the night.

Acknowledgments

Writing's a lonely pursuit. You sit there at the computer, typing away, trying to find the right words to form the right sentences to build the right paragraphs to construct the right chapters that assemble the right story.

You rely on a tribe of like-minded people, writer friends who get you and your frustrations. So a thank you to my tribe of Blaise van Hecke, Ryan O'Neill, Laurie Steed, Bel Woods, Kim Locke, A.S. Patrić, and Angus Watson (among others), with whom I often talk writing.

I originally wrote *Prudence* as a screenplay way back in November of 2000, unsure what I was dealing with, but didn't novelize it until 2014, right after I finished the first round of revisions on *Just Another Week in Suburbia*.

The *Prudence* adaptation wasn't easy given the ensemble cast of characters and multiple viewpoints. Inevitably, I came up with the solution that is now in the final book – an omniscient viewpoint offered by the club itself.

The story evolved over the years, going through multiple drafts, incorporating numerous changes (only a handful of characters retained their original names and backgrounds), and becoming what you've finally read today.

A big thank you to my best friend, Blaise van Hecke, who for years tried to convince me to go indie. And here I am. I just wish you could've been around to see it, Blaise.

She's always championed my writing, was always my alpha reader, and somebody I would sit down and talk about my books over a cup of tea at a local café. Blaise, I'm going to miss your input, our talks, and, most of all, your company.

Thanks also to Kim Lock, a good friend whose feedback is always incisive and invaluable, to my editor Laura McCluskey, and a young, talented upcoming editor in Sophie Breeze. *Prudence* would be less without your contributions.

Thanks to Rosie Giuliano for the image of Prudentia.

And a thank you to my readers.

About the Author

Les Zig has always believed in the magic of storytelling – in finding a book where you lose yourself in the story, and lament when you realize only a handful of pages remain.

He's had two other published novels, *August Falling* (Pantera Press 2018), and *Just Another Week in Suburbia* (Pantera Press 2017) and, under his Young Adult moniker of Lazaros Zigomanis, *This* (MidnightSun Publishing 2023), *Song of the Curlew* (ECG Press 2022), the tweener version, *Pride* (Busybird Publishing 2017), and the novella *The Shadow in the Wind* (ECG Press 2022).

His stories focus on characters trying to find their place in the world while dealing with adversity.

Book Club Questions

1. Holly is propositioned by a strange man in a bar who mistakes her for an escort. What would you do in such a situation?

2. Marcus, Dante, and Amber all enjoy some risqué entertainment. Is such behavior innocent fun or something more insidious?

3. Quinn is offered an incredible sum of money if he can carry out the Temptation that Mr. Hermes sets him. What would you do if you were offered such a Temptation?

4. What do you think of Flavia giving herself to Edan LeBeau to further her own career?

5. Until their roles were revealed, what did you think Bodie and Ox were doing in Prudence?

6. Both Patricia and Savage have come to be icons from different places in their lives – Patricia a failed model who struggled to find employment elsewhere, while Savage gave up studying nursing. Do you think there's a commonality behind why two such different people would come to the same vocation?

7. Edan LeBeau and Nico are brothers, but they are diametrically opposed as people. Why do you think they are so different?

8. Why do you think Mr. Hermes was intent on deposing Constance? Why do you think she wanted to stay on?

9. Joy is overconfident and cocky. What do you think her background is? And what do you imagine she thought she'd get out of being Prudence's hostess?

10. Who – or what – do you think Mr. Hermes is? What are the purposes of his Temptations?

11. Prudence is full of capricious, licentious patrons, but Rupe would seem to be an outlier. He is the only character who pays the ultimate price in the events that transpire. Do you think there's a reason for his death?

12. One of the big themes throughout the story is fidelity. Various characters have their fidelity tested or betray their fidelity. How true are these relationships given the acts these characters commit?

13. Amber and Quinn stay together but do so by keeping secret their indiscretions. Do you feel relationships can survive when partners keep secrets? Are there minor and major indiscretions? Or are they all equal in a relationship? What are the boundaries? What is acceptable and what isn't?

14. What do you think will become of the people who visit Prudence – Holly and Marcus, Amber and Quinn, and Flavia and Dante?

15. Who do you think the people in the basement are? Also, do you think that the basement is still a part of Prudence?

16. Who do you think the robed person that Flavia encounters is?

17. Often, characters reference the "Camarilla", a wealthy consortium that owns Prudence. What do you think their role is as far as Prudence is concerned?

18. What do you think the purpose of the club Prudence is? Is it just a club? Or is it a playground for the privileged and decadent? Or something else? Something more?

19. Would you ever visit a club like Prudence?

20. Who is your favorite character? And why?

Other novels by Les Zig …

Pantera Press
August Falling
Just Another Week in Suburbia

As Lazaros Zigomanis …

MidnightSun Publishing
This

ECG Press
Any More Complicated Than That
Song of the Curlew
The Shadow in the Wind

Busybird Publishing
Pride